"The mind and body of a triathlete is a compelling proving ground in Mason Boyle's *Bark On*. With vividness and clarity, the novel shows terrain that can be both exhilarating and challenging. The relationships and rivalries have the same complexities. Boyles connects the trail runs and swims with the journeys of the mind to create an engaging read."

—Ravi Howard, author of *Like Trees, Walking*

"Reading this novel is like traveling in an old truck at a 100 miles an hour. How Mason does this is a rare act of talent and vision and originality. You're simply flying down the road in great literary style. You'll want to hold on to your hat to keep it from flying off. You don't want to stop reading once you start. It has a great plot, totally memorable characters, and a captivating Southern landscape. What a book!"

—Lawrence Naumoff, author of *Silk Hope, N.C.*

D0172106

PRAISE FOR
BARK ON

"*Bark On* is one of the strongest debut novels I've read in years. There's nothing weak about it, in fact: from the sentences to the story to the beating heart of it all, this book has an extraordinary musculature. I really enjoyed this novel."

—Daniel Wallace, author of *Big Fish*

"Every sentence, every paragraph, is dense with inventive language. [...] Driven by uncanny energy and imagination, *Bark On* is a gripping and insightful novel..."

—Kristen Rabe, *Foreword Reviews*

"*Bark On* is a novel squarely and worthily in the tradition of such high-style masters of Southern vernacular as Barry Hannah and Cormac McCarthy. It immerses you in the coastal-Carolina low country, where the streets are 'named for the nearest water threatening to sink them,' where 'thunderheads anvil down' and the language is a flood of startling invention that somehow feels both ancient and inevitable. It takes you both inside the world of elite triathlon training and to the extreme edge of that already-extreme sport, exposing the 'meticulously random' cycle-of-abuse training methods of a charismatic, celebrated coach and two young, uncelebrated prospects he's grinding down and grooming. This is an outstanding and even breathtaking debut by Mason Boyles—a novelist who's here for the long haul."

—Mark Winegardner, author of *The Godfather's Return*

"Boyle's novel is an intense, hectic work with a terrific premise and lifelike, earthy characters that all easily express what drives them. The narrative shows a fervor for language and boundless energy..."

—*Kirkus Reviews*

"Mason Boyles writes incandescent prose, searing, exacting, utterly shocking, and all in service to a story of vicious determination, desperation, and a very true and perverted love. *Bark On* is a brilliant debut."

—Michelle Latiolais, author of *She*

"Mason Boyles is an electrifying writer, pushing language to its limits in this propulsive novel, as remarkable and uncompromising as the ultra-endurance athletes he conjures here indelibly. Sentences crackle with vitality and surprise. Characters brim with fierce convictions. Every detail of this world—the coastal South, the Ironman subculture—proves impossible to forget. This book marks the introduction of a new and important American voice."

—Sarah Shun-lien Bynum, author of *Madeleine is Sleeping*

"A mesmerizing tale of death-defying acts and the highwire magic of hurling your body toward an impossible edge. With its phantom pains, mind tricks, and prose as spiky as it is tender, *Bark On* by Mason Boyles is not to be missed."

—Karen Tucker, author of *Bewilderness*

BARK ON

MASON BOYLES

DRIFTWOOD PRESS

Independently published by *Driftwood Press*
in the United States of America.

Managing Fiction Editor: James McNulty
Cover Image: Jessica Seamans
Cover Design: Sally Franckowiak
Interior Design & Copyeditor: James McNulty
Copyeditor: Jessica Maple Holbert
Interior Image Design: Jerrod Schwarz
Fonts: Bembo MT Pro, Sitka, & Trajan Sans Pro

First published on February 28th, 2023
ISBN-13: 978-1-949065-19-0

Please visit our website at www.driftwoodpress.com
or email us at editor@driftwoodpress.net.

BARK ON

Ezra

Benji ties them to the truck. Runs ropes from the hitch to their waists and starts driving. Casper and Ezra chase it up Bromine Avenue, a leash each, the pickup iced to cruise control at twelve miles per hour. They turn north toward the main drag of Kure. Sunrise congeals the boardwalk, clotting around storm-shuttered condos and the dormant Tilt-a-Whirl and the rickety Ferris wheel like amber preserving the bones of a beached sea beast. Late July and the island's already fossilized. Benji beams the truck along Ocean Street. Woody Hewett Bridge vaults over the inlet. Ezra starts to fall back as they climb. He gives it his finishing kick, but his rope tightens. His torso goes acute with the grade.

Casper's talking, a sure sign he's hurting. His head tips toward his left shoulder. "Giddy up, Robo...Cop. Let's...stroll."

Ezra's already sprinting. Traffic snorts past in the left lane. Casper swings wide amid brakes and honks and accelerates. How floral the kid looks in the truck's sideview, stem-thin through the torso, his buzzed head branched with veins. Ezra's a crumbling boulder behind him. Striations fissure his thighs with each footstrike. Training and hunger have weathered the muscle from his broader bones. Doesn't bedrock break down into soil? Casper's growing ahead of him, Ezra thinks, his lead nourished as Ezra erodes.

Casper catches up to the driver's side, the wind smearing his scream. "Where's the beef?"

Benji taps his sideview, where Ezra sees himself reflected. He keeps his face plastic, breaths rounding out from his cheekbones like beads off an abacus; somewhere inside him a score's shifting.

One more for Casper's bank. The kid's been beating him for so long that it actually calms him when the kid does the inevitable and pulls away.

Ezra's rope jerks taut and he sprawls, bellyflopping on the blacktop. He sleds along on his stomach. The pickup brakes.

Benji oozes out of the driver's side like he's melting. The seeping scent of him—that stale, manufactured smell, like turning meat and cheap sunscreen. His legs spill onto the asphalt. He's wearing Ezra's flip-flops; his heels squelch off the insoles as he approaches. That ankleless gait, like his Achilles tendons are the only solid part of him. The lenses of his Oakleys mirror them in chrome-tinted miniature: Ezra aching to his feet, Casper jogging in place. It's as if Benji isn't just looking at them, but rather staring them into existence. Ezra almost says something—*sorry?*—but Benji speaks first. "Get him next time."

Next time could be anytime. Benji never warns them; wants them guts-first, he says. Leave your brain in your helmet. Ezra and Casper eat when they're told. They sprint when instructed. They sleep on command, ontologically, on the boat cabin's sport carpet or the track or even between laps in the pool, chins fishhooked over lane lines. They doze until Benji shakes them out of it. He feels braille from their pulses, reads fatigue at a touch and plots workouts from there. It all hinges on his What the Hell Principle: Benji pushes them until Ezra pauses, asks, "what the hell?"

When Casper first got here, he'd ask that, too. But lately the kid only laughs. His taunts tow Ezra forward. That's the real rope.

They fumigate in the truck bed on the drive back to Kure. Casper's dozing, head pillowed on the tire well. Ezra picks gravel from his ripening knees. He bruises easier lately, like the hours of panting have hollowed him from within. It's all lung in there. He needs as much space for oxygen as he can get.

The truck hooks onto Bromine Avenue. Every block inland's another dropped tax bracket. Duplexes surrender to bungalows, trailers. Asphalt digresses to gravel. The road stubs into an ashtray of a cul-de-sac. The bones of the Dow chemical plant a click to its southwest, through a waft of pines thin as smoke. The woods are crosshatched with trenches and parched vats that sieved bromine from seawater. That alchemy spoiled the water table a decade ago, then the real estate market. A popup camper and trailered sport boat are on the only lot no longer vacant on that cul-de-sac, sitting south pole to the turnout. Both belong to Ezra's Ma, who's riding her bike the longest way across Canada. His rent is monthly sponge downs of the *Not That Fogerty*. His new roommates aren't on the lease. Benji's an honored guest, but Ma'd left before Casper showed, the Canada crossing the last death-defying item on her kick-the-bucket list. She was going to ride out and back, sleep in the van, then drive up to her turn-around point the next morning. A yearlong trip she'd been putting off for a decade. As soon as Ezra'd left for college. As soon as he got his pro card. But this had been the year she was really doing it. Ezra was twenty-five. He could fend.

When Benji'd claimed Ezra needed to cocoon in the training last Thanksgiving she'd already been packing. She'd left the same evening, burping stuffing; Casper'd shown up the first day of December. She doesn't know about her latest tenant. She doesn't know Benji's got all three of them sleeping in the boat. They pee right off of the deck, trying to ripple the ditch with their streams. Benji calls that casting a line. They don't have to live like this—Ezra doesn't—but it's all Benji's call, the boat, everything. He claims that they need to exist egregiously. One more task Casper's beating Ezra in.

The kid naps in the back of the truck, his square head bouncing off the wheel bed with every pothole they bounce over. Benji seems to be swerving to catch them. Casper won't stir until the man says—not even for his own screams.

Benji spills out of the truck now, preambling. "Overload, tootsies. Got to shut off your off-buttons."

The Piston. Ezra punches his quivering legs.

A medieval torture system of a thing. Benji's dungeon-mastered it together by welding a brakeless bike to a wind trainer. The ergometer's mounted backwards, chocked in front of the back wheel so it spins in reverse. Since the bike's rigged fixie, the pedals spin backwards with it. You have to produce an equal-and-opposite force to keep your legs from following. It's been a fallow threat for two weeks now, corroding outside—accumulating rust for extra resistance, maybe.

Benji drags an extension cord out the backdoor of the camper, still talking. "Goal's desensitizing." Meaning neurons: how they short-circuit contractions when muscle tension's too high. He plugs in the wind trainer and gives the saddle a coital slap. "It's this or a knife to your Golgi tendons."

This is Ezra's Next Time. But Casper's bounding forward, already mounting the bike.

The shoes are clipped to the pedals. Benji seals them with duct-tape when Casper slides his feet in. Benji toes the wind trainer's switch and the flywheel starts up with a soldering hum. Casper huffs out of the saddle to pedal against it.

"Sit," Benji says.

Casper settles. He props his elbows on the handlebars, panting, obedient.

There's no timer—with Benji, there's never one—but Ezra counts. Thirty seconds. A minute. Benji moves in front of the Piston. The way Casper watches him—a stare like a sponge. The kid's grinding his teeth again. The ergometer parrots him, serrating its pitch. Two minutes.

Casper's head goes diagonal. His inhales make sine curves from his ribs.

"Slow," Benji says, slicking his palms over the kid's scalp. "Water," Benji says, and Ezra understands this is directed at him. He grabs a gallon jug from the boat, peels the cap, sneaks a swig. The water's melty with plastic. He brings it to Benji, who spits his bitten cuticle into it. He adds a pinch of the humus he keeps buried in his pocket—a proprietary crumble of bark and leaves—and swills it, lifting the jug to Casper's lips. Casper slurps until he pulls it away.

The flywheel's hum frays an octave. Benji swats at the noise, chewing a wisp of his mullet like a bit. Sparks shrapnel off the ergometer. Then the hum shatters; the flywheel whirs silent, and Casper's cadence speeds, his legs blurring as he pedals.

Benji turns to Ezra, distancing his eyebrows from the tops of his Oakleys. "Mama's missing an off-button. That's how Robo-Cops should be."

Should it irk Ezra that this doesn't irk him? He's just glad the Piston busted before he had to climb on and slog. He starts clapping.

Benji cuts the cord and ravels it back into the camper. When he's gone, Casper coasts to a stop. Ezra peels the duct tape off Casper's left shoe and sees blood smutching the back of it. The kid's heel is gushing.

Casper bares his flat molars at Ezra. "Want a lick?"

"Goggles!" Benji hollers, banging back out of the camper.

The kid rushes into a crouch as he reemerges. Hiding the heel.

"You hurt him," Ezra says, more for the sake of his own pain—goggles means they're going to swim.

Casper crab-walks away when Benji grunts down beside him.

"Lemme see," Benji says. Instead sniffs.

Casper sags still, obedient. Benji slides his hands around the heel in a probing way that makes Ezra think the guy's eyes are shut behind his sunglasses. Ezra pictures him blind. Pictures empty sockets. Casper shudders. Benji lowers his ear to the ground beside the kid's foot. He presses his mouth to the wound and hums into it. Ezra thinks he hears words in the tune, but the din of the flies saws off whatever syllables Benji might be singing. Benji's lips twitch. Then he takes a wet suck. Casper's eyes suction shut.

"You're shitting," Ezra says.

Casper grins. "You can't hurt like me."

Casper

What RoboCop don't get is how hurt makes you heaten. Moving hurts because it heatens you, and heat's just the littlest of you moving. Atoms squirming loose. What's he think is sweat? It's the you melting out of you. You pool down to wet, even spread out sky-wide as steam. That's what RoboCop's afraid of, spilling out to dampen some ditch the varms drink from. Reckons hurt's a thing you got to go hollow to hold. That's why he strives so thermos. Plays cool like he's metal. Plays sealed to keep from sweating. Tries to harden to contain the hurt, but Benji's the one holding us. Digging a ditch for us with instructions. RoboCop's got this hunch I empty when I run, but I just let myself liquid and flow whereverso Benji points me. Hurt's heat, and heat's moving. Put a cube of ice up against a puddle. Put a puddle up against steam. RoboCop must've missed that day of science class. Gander him stomping my heel so the hurt-heat thermometers up my leg, heaping his glare onto me. That's why Robo-Cop stays behind: he don't see how hurt-heat turns to speed.

See him irking at me jumping standing. Hear him groan when Benji goes-gets our swim goggles. RoboCop gaums my arm and I swat it. Because plus and minus can't touch. Robo-Cop's plus and I'm minus and both-us are held together by the nuclear of Benji. Like the littlest bits of one atom. Saw about them on a poster once. The poster was done up on that kind of plastic that glows so white with light it shines over its own image. Stuck on the wall of this man who picked me up hitching away from a rainstorm south of Gastonia. I said *toward the dry* to his ask of *where to*. And we drove some keeping quiet, just clucking his blinker and squawking the wipers. Had them going before the monsoon even caught up, like they might clear his own thinking. Then the thunderhead anviled down and he said he couldn't conscience me out on the roadside with this weather and did I want a bed for the night or at least till this drench blew over, only he'd already clucked his blinker about eight miles back and turned off the highway and the whole full of that silence since it had already been decided and I'd sat in it and knew. Only question was which end he wanted. Said the son was off at college; said his wife was visiting kin down-way of Knoxville, but from his front door down the hall I didn't see one picture. Plain wall until the atom poster in the bedroom he took me to. Like he'd had a thought to keep letting on, then reckoned if he got someone this far they were both past the fib. And you do wonder what starts and quits a man. This one said reckon you'll catch cold if you don't get out them clothes. And I stepped out my shorts without waiting for him to step out because ever since he'd clucked that blinker we'd been past that.

"Ain't stupid," I said.

His sitting squealed the mattress behind me. "So come here. Teach you something."

I backed up and kept my eyes on that wall-atom, wondering what kind of microscope and where was it pointing when whoever discovered that. The whole meantime he was tugging my worm I stared all my hurt at it. Him saying *I'll show you* like I hadn't been busting in trucks and tents and toilets and dumpsters ever since Ms. Ida rubbed that first hurt-heat out of me. Bet RoboCop busts to bikes. *I'll show you,* the Atom Man said, only he wasn't saying that to pretend to me. That was his own act because his other hand was working his own worm the whole going. Going till the hot melted down and founted and some more me had leaked out of me. It pooled in my lap while his other hand was on himself still a-pumping. My gunk stuck his palm to the back of my hand when he grabbed it. Pulled the chap off my knuckles; had the eczema real bad around then from dry winter and chlorine. The rain he'd picked me up from was the first good soak of that year and it was nigh on to February. Dumb to remember them things. Funny what-all the brain snags on when it's trying to divert from worse—which I'm fixing to get to. But first the Atom Man put my hand on his own little worm and I looked up at that poster and read the word I'd been staring at: *atom*. A tom, like one cat. I'd always reckoned it was Adam like the first person, the most basic unit. And I snorted in the middle of tugging him and he said, *don't you laugh at it. Show you something funny.* And he did. And I melted more with the heat.

One more funny thing is this varm-trap of an island. One good rinse shy of a sandbar. The beach access juts out them dunes and midairs like a toothpick, the sand gulped out from under it. Shorebreak backwashing right through the fenceposts clenching dunes. RoboCop stubs up behind me. I jump off into the sand and my heel mouths open, yapping. I don't fall; just sit down real fast.

"You got shots?" RoboCop asks.

"Fuck a vodka."

"No. Vaccines. Like for tetanus."

The soft in his voice turns me. There he perches, curling his toes over the edge like a diving block. Looking at me like I'm the pool he's fixing to dive into. Like he thinks I'll hold the hurt he's fixing to go through.

Then Benji presses up behind him. "Pier and back, Tootsies."

Both-us gleamed off his sunglasses: RoboCop plussing up on fleeing me. I hop into the water and swim out of the feel of his plus-shove and don't look back because Benji taught me. Because before that. Ever time I turn full-around I see all them years before Benji like the bad half of a glass. One lifelong of empty.

The day I took the Atom Man's truck he was still going on about his wife and son, both-us sprawled on the bed and long-busted. I just stared up at that atom poster. The June sun scrubbed the picture off it with like a paintbrush white-washing graffiti. Atom Man talked himself to sleep. I reached his wallet from where his piled pants and left him no more than a smear of his own burst gauming the billfolds together, which was the undoing of how he'd done me in February. I walked up the hall chewing on what he'd gave me to laugh about that first evening. Filled my head up that way to keep from noticing all his frank-kindness. Like him tying his shoes real slow in front of me to teach me the knot without ever saying he was teaching me. Like the hotdogs cut up and lumped in with the macaroni. Like a pool out the back and his own treadmill and anything. The Atom Man's name was Adam. That was what he gave me to laugh at; he'd meant that statement plain instead of threatening.

What RoboCop wouldn't understand was how Adam making me laugh was worse than the hurting I'd been expecting. Because that—the not hurting, but his plain-meaning—was why I stayed those four months. And Adam said it then because he knew it would be. So I lathered up a wrath over that as I was leaving, scrubbing even his frank-kindnesses until they shined like what they all were: the same trap. Because I could've gone soft eating them hotdogs. Could've tied my shoelaces to run on the treadmill when it was airish out or raining. Could've bumped down the speed if I was sore, and next thing I'd be staying in bed the damn livelong, and then four months would bloat up like my belly and I'd no-count in Gastonia never moving or hurtening or amounting to anything. That's what Adam wanted. Thinking that wrathed me right on around and I went back to his pile of pants for his truck keys. I stood up and he'd stirred, maybe from their jangling.

"Fixing to run," I told him. Standing full-facing him with his wallet and keys.

But he hadn't seen what I was up to, or the footboard was blocking his view, and anyhow he was still thick with half-sleep. Could've used them windshield wipers about then on his thinkings. A nod's all he gave. Antsy, he called me.

And I came over and planted one on him, which I'd never

done. Because it wasn't never like that—never lips but hands only. That kiss went about like an atom's pluses and minuses touching, that brushing adding all the more force to our aparting. Me planting one should've tipped him. Maybe he knew I was for-good leaving already. Maybe "antsy" was him good as telling me *take the pickup*. Frank-kindness can be hard to plainsay. Well, I ran from Gastonia how I told him, driving off in his truck, and it was easy as sitting up on the hoods and masting your back to a tailwind. Just had to get going. I'd lived as his alleged insect for whole seasons, playing his little Antsy from February until June.

Adam the Atom Man. The world sometimes is the strangest stuff. And I know he weren't lying about his name because I had his license with me.

A sob and some siphoned gas after that I took a 2.4-mile dip in a lake and dried off with a bike ride and topped it with a little marathon at the Chapel Hill Ironman. Well also some naps in the truck. Also parking out back of hotels and hopping the pool fence to swim. You try getting up a good hurt with ten yards of open water between flip-turns. Enough to make a man's head go like that branch RoboCop's rotating. Sometimes I wobbled inside saying I forgot a towel. Puddling heelprints right up to the front desk in that icebox seem-like that's common to all hotel lobbies: as if the A.C.'s coming up through the tile, the same freeze cramping up through your fascia cooling up through the air to where you're just waiting to see your breath steam. Sometimes did. Swear. Sometimes asked the desk person for one-them complimentary chocolates. Took the elevator up and grubbed off left-out trays of room service, even. You wouldn't believe some-them bounties. They got this enchilada I guess no one likes at the Hyatt. You can count on folks taking a bite or two before quitting. Sometimes seemed I was eating better than hotdogs and macaroni in that period. But I biked all the lard off. I went longer than live-long, pedaling on through the night. Times I was so crapped I propped the bike way-off at the far side of a rest stop and left it out there when I stiff-legged into the bathroom, hoping I'd come out and find it gone and the ride would end preemptory. Because the ride wouldn't end otherwise. But I always came out and there it was by the sign where I'd propped it. That brought the sobs. Climbing back on the bike, wiper-eyed and lungs rattling. Keeping on even past dozing off, waking up to honks and red lights. So all that. Maybe it was all part of the same shoving-off I got after planting one on Adam. No tell how long I'd've gone on if I hadn't snagged Benji's eyes after the Chapel Hill Ironman. I was taking a lap of the parking lot to jog the steam off, savoring the just-doneness when he bulged up on me. Swelled out the medical tent gnashing on his hair's long part. Wasn't even looking my way, but I sweat-felt his waiting. That belly-his convexing him, like a nuclear the above and under of him was circling. Biting on them split ends. That haircut's got a name, I was thinking. He just stood there gnawing it till I ran even with him. Then he hummed. That tune kudzu'd right on up my legs and tangled me.

"You run like you hump." First thing he told me.

I let him have that one. Hunch on him like he knew both halves of it, how a glass does: holding all my full and my empty. He stuck a receipt to the sweat on my chest. A phone number was scrawled on the side facing up. He told me to call after Thanksgiving. Promised then that he'd've found a home for me. Adam gave me home like a bed, but Benji was going to give me a fence. I could see it in the see-through of his looking. Them big sunglasses gleaminger than that atom poster, reflecting instead of whitening—showing me to me. More than that, showing him: Benj was looking through me. Then he told his secret name. And then-on ever day I was counting days.

Thanksgiving come and gone and I called the first second of midnight. He picked up before the first ring. Both-us had been sitting up, and that knowing right away petted me. All he said was an address. Said it twice, sticking his words to me like that receipt. Then he hung up and I drove to this flooded varm-bed of marsh they talk up like it's a beach. And that's the windup to how I am, swimming after his tug with my heel yapping. That hurt's heat, and heat's speed. Only thing to it is to how I always done and keep moving.

Ezra

After the swim Benji feeds them canned corn and tuna. They eat on the deck of the *Not that Fogerty*. There's no talking, just squelching metabolism. Their tongues and knuckles stay cut from the rims. They eat with their fingers, with Benji just watching them. Ezra's never seen him put anything in his mouth but the ends of his own mullet. Wonders sometimes if the guy even eats. Pictures him binging on a stash of freezer-burnt PowerBars hidden wherever he's keeping Ezra's phone and laptop. Pictures him eating the phone and laptop. Pictures him eating Ma, wolfing her down and strutting around in her clothing.

"Go on," Benji says, his sunglasses reflecting Ezra's stare.

Ezra drops his eyes to Casper's heel. The salt's scrubbed the grit to reveal the gash: a vulval slit brindled with brown. Something's lodged in there. Shrapnel from the flywheel. Casper tweezes up a rusty speck of debris.

"Flesh wound," Benji says.

Casper flicks the shard at Ezra. Ezra ducks it and the kid double-legs him, playfulness bursting from him like a sneeze. He pins Ezra, pulling his bloodless penis out of his shorts.

"Wormhole!" he shouts, cackling.

"Settle," Benji says.

Like that, Casper rolls off. This is what gets Ezra: not Casper one-upping him, but his easy obedience. He goes right back to sipping corn from that can.

Ezra scratches Casper's head. "Benji's got you kenneled."

Benji's hair slides out of his lips. Nerve struck. Ezra tilts his head back and barks.

This is the seventh dog-year since Benji began training him.

Ezra'd been twenty-five in human time, trying to win the Chapel Hill Ironman. He'd placed tenth the previous season, nine minutes and inches shy of the winner George Wispler—self-referentially, 'Wispy'—an ex-FSU swimmer who'd moved to Wilmington last year and displaced Ezra as top local. Wispler earned his pro card and a Laguna Resorts sponsorship; Ezra got a t-shirt that said 'Finisher.' In an eight-hour event, the difference between them could be whittled down with equipment—disc wheels, saddle angles, Wispy's minimalist Hokas to Ezra's clunky Asics. Ezra'd tossed for too many nights calculating the cost of four extra ounces of shoe weight per stride multiplied by a marathon; the next year he rejected all tech and went primal.

He thrashed out of the Morgan Creek Reservoir slapping the swim leader's feet. In the rush of transition the energy gels fell out of his tri-suit and he followed inertia, tossing the rest and tearing off his bike's power meter. Fuck pacing. Fuck nutrition. A mile later he was drafting off the lead vehicle. Photographers tore past on scooters, lenses chomping. He hammered up Frat Row, past the blue blurt of body-painted co-eds as dressed and loud as if they'd turned out for Tar Heel basketball. The same jerseys and screams tailwinded him along Franklin Street on course record pace. Then the tunneled trees of Jones Ferry Road shaded him. His brain couldn't grasp the split times the volunteers were giving him—were those hours or minutes?—but knew he was slowing because the lead vehicle's brake lights kept blinking. Rounding 15-501 black spots spored his eyes. Then the asphalt bucked like a bullwhip on the long climb up Raleigh Street. He slowed to his teeter, thrashing his bike up the grade. Then the Bianchi suctioned by. The bike moved so fast Ezra mistook it for another press moped. He looked again and regretted it.

The kid was wearing a Speedo. His race number flagged off the back of his seatpost—three digits, code for an age-grouper. Ezra downshifted, but his femurs were anvils. The bike shrank up the road.

He'd been dropped by an amateur on a ten speed.

Was it the sun-struck asphalt or Ezra's vision rippling? He watched the kid waft into the skyline with the ease and speed of steam. His own body was wobbling. His legs rippled out from under him, nerves evaporating. He tipped over and struck curb and laid fallow.

He came to in the medical tent, humming flooding his senses. The sound clogged his eardrums, then his sinuses—someone's breathing. Rotting meat and swallowed sunscreen. His tastebuds felt raked by fingernails. Something coiled on his tongue. He swallowed. The hum stopped. Sitting up felt like a sucker punch. *Was* a sucker punch: a damp fist rapped his chest, pressing him back to the cot. Ezra with the delirious sense that this fist was knocking. Wanting him to open the double-doors of his ribcage. Instead it opened to offer him a phone.

Ezra watched himself crumple on-screen. He'd been running on the bike course, apparently, leaving his ride bent on the curb where he'd crashed. Coming up Franklin Street his legs had just Slinky-ed. Blacked out. DNF.

"You run like you're pulling out," the fist said. Ezra traced the arm up to its face and his brain hopped a chainring.

Benji Newton, the Mullet of West Memphis, cheesed down at him.

Ezra's first words were the ones Benji's been coaxing out of him ever since. "What the hell?"

…was Benji doing here? At his bedside, in this medical tent—at an Ironman, of all races. Shorter events were his stomping ground. The peloton and sprint finishes. He'd coached four athletes into the top ten at the Olympics, yet here he was critiquing Ezra's stride. "Hips should be forward. Think fertile."

"My last load dried up in T2."

Benji's laugh was singular, like a sneeze. "All the great ones are neutered."

That was it. Benji walked off, leaving Ezra to wallow. He was just starting to doze when the emcee's alto burled the PA, barding the first of the age-groupers down the finishing chute.

That waif on the Bianchi. Ezra yanked out his I.V. and wobbled to the line.

The kid ran like he was sleeping—dozing forward, reflexive, involuntary. All his effort above-the-neck. His lips cricked; his square head sagged sideways. His name scrolled over the Jumbotron's leaderboard. *Casper Swayze.* He crossed the line in 8:20—a course record. Ten minutes under Ezra's personal best for the distance.

The kid was eighteen.

Ezra trailed him to the parking lot after the awards ceremony. The pock-marked pickup Casper stopped at was stickerless. No M-dot, no swim-cycle-run phylogeny. Shattered Christmas lights dangled from the sideviews, dull as rosaries.

"Where'd you come from?" Ezra asked.

Casper smirked up at him. He was five feet, tops, with a millstone mouth—canines ground flat. "In here."

He popped the camper shell, revealing an air mattress.

Ezra spent the next week deloading. Mostly deloading meant spending shifts bunkered in Ma's office at WheelsDeals, dodging the condolences of age-groupers and probing Google for the kid. Ma said, *no sweat.*

Ezra said, *Casper Swayze.*

A fitting name—as far as he could tell the kid was pure ectoplasm. The only trace Ezra found of him was that year's Chapel Hill finish, an effort that had catapulted him to fifty-seventh in the world Ironman rankings. Ezra had yet to crack the top hundred; still, a relief to find Casper's name absent from other races. Triathlon was a sport, after all, of seconds and split-times. No room for a wildcard among quantifiables. That objectivity was the very insulation Ezra savored, what he was still putting off college to incubate himself in. He loved the womb of fatigue that came with hard training, gestating in the constant low-level throb of it. Sometimes suspected he craved that more than racing. What did Casper crave? Ezra was haunting that name into Facebook's search bar again when a message from Benji Newton pinged into his chat-box.

Ten-mile run. No watch.

Ezra hadn't so much as limped since the race. He stared at Benji's profile picture a long second, a shimmering sheet of blue. What was that? A bird's eye view of a lake? Ma craned over his shoulder. "Holy split. Is that—"

"Yeah." Ezra hadn't told Ma about Benji visiting him in the medical tent; when he'd come to below those Oakleys and mullet, she'd still been slogging through the run. She'd crossed the line in a personal best, meting her excitement at the news of Ezra's spectacular withering. In the precarious balancing of their divergent aftermaths he'd chosen not to mention it. Chalked it up to a dream. Yet here was Benji messaging him, his strange profile photo dripping more ellipses.

Bust a nut, he added.

Ma squeezed Ezra's shoulders. "I'd go."

Jogging out of the camper, his hips were grating in their sockets. He thrust his pelvis forward and thought fertile. His strides yawned. Halfway up Bromine Avenue they were gaping. He didn't have a watch on. Unnumbered minutes later he rounded the camper and flattened down on the boat deck, blinking up at an animal sky. He'd sweated out chromosomes. He was down to pant and rasp, coldblooded under slithering sunbeams. Couldn't catch his brain. Once he mustered enough warmth to think he realized why: he was laughing. This was the thoughtless fatigue he'd been chasing ever since he'd left tag to run laps around the recess field in fifth grade. He'd forgotten what it felt like to run himself stupid without thought of split times or rankings.

He stumbled inside to another green dot on Messenger.

All I ask, Benji wrote, *is to leave your brain out of your helmet.*

All month the workouts came staccato. Some days Ezra gnawed around until 3 p.m. awaiting instructions. Time smoothed over, assuming a leisurely quality. Ma was giddily cowed, taking every workout Benji sent as confirmation of Ezra's potential—a quantity in which she maintained an indulgent, enabling belief. The guys at WheelsDeals were less sold. Told Ezra this was some troll, he should sweat it, he needed God and coffee. Ezra found a darker alternative trickling through the triathlon forums. Rumors that Benji's West Memphis training compound had imploded. Internal scandal. Blackballed by the U.S. Olympic Committee. The chair issued a vague but firm condemnation for Benji's "orchestration" of the same events that the committee seemed bent on covering. No one quite knew what he'd done, but everyone was certain it had been unforgivable. Ezra was too tired to know which way he leaned. Between workouts he smeared through his days, dozing over the portions of orzo that Ma made and weighed for him, stirring when Benji's texted demands quivered his phone. And somewhere—over or underwater, or sunken in the deep end of his sleep—coyotes screeching.

Then, in October, Benji asked for Ezra's address. Wanted to send him a package. Two days later the man showed up at the camper with a poster. Ezra stepped outside to find Benji unfurling him: an image of Ezra crumpled on the curb at Chapel Hill. Benji dangled it like a muleta, adopting the packed crouch of a matador.

"I'm getting hands-on," he said. "I've decided."

Ezra told him shucks.

Benji stepped inside and looked back at him. "Come on in."

Ezra rolled out the white flag; Ma, the red carpet. Benji's been landlording it over them ever since. Took one snort at Ezra's prep for a long ride—the carbohydrate gels, the espresso, the electrolyte drink mix suspended over his bottles like tallow particulate; and Ezra himself, pinup-posed atop a foam roller with his heart rate monitor hitched like a bra—and cried RoboCop. Ezra's brain was in these instruments instead of his helmet. He cut holes in Ezra's compression socks and took a hammer to the wattage meter on his handlebars and spat in every batch of whey isolate that Ma offered, a violent Luddite. A sadist, maybe. But never impolite: a slow workout was the only rudeness known to

Benji.

He and Ma were eye-to-eye that way. She left Benji to direct Ezra, departing on eight-hour bike rides with her stomach as empty as the pockets of her cycling jersey. Ezra'd wake to her rolling in after Benji'd bossed him to sleep, wobbling across the camper with her helmet-mounted headlight winking.

The family-sized packs of Nature's Path granola rattled like tambourines in her shaking hands. She'd pour the milk right into the plastic bag and wince with each spoonful that she crunched, like she thought that—her chewing instead of the din of her entry—might wake him.

Not being a nerd about the fueling made sense, but riding that far fasted? Ma cited Dan Plews, claimed she was getting fat-adapted. It seemed like an excuse, but for what? Ezra was too tired to suffer the discomfort at the end of that line of thinking.

It wasn't like she was dropping weight. In fact, she was maintaining it—replenishing exactly what she'd depleted. She left her caloric calculations on the fridge's magnetic whiteboard like for proof. She'd always been skinny. Productively skinny. So had he. A certain level of thinness was productive for the sport; underweight in the scheme of the general population, maybe. But they were athletes. What seemed more troublesome was Ma's preoccupation: the extra hour she spent at that fridge, converting the wattage from her bike's power meter into caloric expenditure as if she weren't riding the same route at the same speed every day. A family pack of Nature's Path was 24.7 ounces—3,120 calories. 1,350 more in the half-gallon of milk that she topped it with, plus 480 for the four level scoops of whey protein. The food and her TDE balanced like a chemistry equation. Ezra felt compelled and afraid to say something. Be less precise. Try a diet with more variety. But how was her focus any better or worse than her other obsessions? She could've been graffiti-ing the fridge with the wind tunnel data comparing deep-dish wheels to discs, or the induction stovetops that came standard on the Winnebago Ekko's latest model, or—worse—Ezra's projected Ironman splits.

The closest Ezra came to broaching the subject was offering Ma some frozen blueberries to top her granola with. Ma went full physiologist on him, citing the compromised aerobic adaptations exhibited in populations who consumed post-workout antioxidants. She told him to do him—which really meant to do what Benji told him.

If she had so much faith in Benji's tactics, why wasn't she taking notes? Her dawn-to-dusk rides were too far and frequent to be completed at any productive intensity. Ezra had a feeling she was chasing something besides training. But didn't doubt that Benji's approach was the syntax of victory. Ezra's legs were the subject; the Chapel Hill Ironman, the object. They all wanted him to win. Didn't they? The verb, thus, was whatever Benji told Ezra to do, which turned out to be cocoon. When Benji brought that up—over Thanksgiving dinner—Ezra was so exhausted he couldn't tell if he was nodding off or nodding along.

They needed to narrow Ezra's life, Benji said. Hermit down. Get egregious. Why didn't Ma get a head start on the Canada crossing? She'd kept on carving their trashcan-fried turkey through all of this. Was she looking at Ezra? Waiting for some reaction? Ezra's head had too much inertia. He drooped over a plate of mashed something, anhedonic off exhaustion.

"Canada it is." She set down the knife, slid her chair back, and finished packing.

Ezra lagged out to help. They had a routine of silence on the mornings of races, when the tension of anticipation burdened every word. They crammed the last of her gear into the van that same way. In an hour she was leaning out of the driver's side, swapping cheek-kisses with Ezra. His left a lipstick-stain of gravy. Ma wiped it off like her skin might absorb the calories.

"Champ," she said, doffing her bike cap.

Ezra brushed the back of his knuckles over the side of his face, his head grumbling like the ignition. "Got something." The most thought he could manage.

"Don't get histrionic," she said. That was it. The last thing.

Not that they hadn't rehearsed this. She'd left him to fend for plenty of stretches, steering the Sprinter van to ultra-endurance events that kept her moving for weeks. An Appalachian Trail run. A bike ride across the contiguous United States. Her Kick-The-Bucket list. The passenger's seat was always open for Ezra, but such excessive feats would've disrupted Ironman training. Ma the more recklessly robust of them, in it more for the endorphins than results. She'd been leaving Ezra with a pantry wall-to-ceil-inged with canned goods, a ten-gallon barrel of trail mix, and a cap doff every summer since he was fifteen, but the Canada trip would take seasons. And having the place to himself was different than having his head and home hogged by Benji.

He watched the van rumble up Bromine Avenue, spraying gravel and dust. Ma's best Ironman time on the vanity plate. The bumper sticker matching the cursive tattooed across her left clav-icle: *what doesn't kill me bores me.* Her arm waving through the window. Their old habit: he'd watch and she'd wave until they fell out of eyeshot. But Ezra's vision was already steaming. He turned around before she flashed her blinker. In the camper he found Benji unplugging his laptop.

"Cocoon, RoboCop." Benji dripped out one hand. "Gonna need your phone, too."

Ezra only paused to thumb a text to Ma: *Going AWOL. No tech in the cocoon.* When he looked up again Benji was holding out Ezra's running shoes.

"Swap," he said, and they did.

Benji was pacing Ezra through a tempo run when a pick-up fishtailed onto Bromine Avenue. Christmas lights windblown back from the truck's sideviews.

Benji honked his moped as it passed. "Your carrot's arrived!"

Casper. Ezra stopped running. So much for cocooning.

He's been chasing the kid's tipping head ever since. Watching him erode. Casper's talk grinding down between his flattened teeth, his mind smoothing the way Benji sees as necessity. Disci-pline, Benji claims, is an act of subtraction. Cull your thoughts—

your decisions—and there's nothing but your body stopping you. Fitting that Casper's silence breaks with his stride. The taunts spill as soon as his head tips toward his shoulder. RoboCop. Plus-er. Shadefoot. Ezra doesn't understand half of these; doesn't think Casper cares, either. The kid's only talking to defy gasping. He's insulting Ezra as much as his own exertion, his effort's approaching edge—the existence of that edge. Denying the same point Benji's pushing them toward.

Ezra's been lucky to have Casper ahead. The real drop-off, he knows, happens as soon as you step into the lead. Then you're left with nothing to fall through but the pound and pulse you can dredge from your own pelagic body. That's the kind of plunging effort Benji wants. So in some quiet way Ezra's the defiant one. He kept his brain in his helmet all winter the way Benji'd insisted: not a glance at social media or the race rosters or even a call snuck to Ma on a payphone, all doubt and longing muffled with fatigue. But not once since Casper showed up had he passed the kid.

Maybe that was what drove Benji to tighten the cocoon. He'd pried himself off the sofa that March and announced that the camper was too comfy. Egregious existence. Had to isolate variables. Cocoon, then enclose. Inside in his sunglasses, sucking his mullet. They were moving out to the boat. Ma's boat. The *Not That Fogerty* beached in their backyard behind the trailer.

That was what it took to ruin Ezra's fugue. Not Benji shooing Ma or taking his technology; not even that Benji'd invaded his home, but that the guy was displacing him. A sore pattern around Kure. Ezra'd seen the bromine plants brown the grass into dirt up the road and take away all his neighbors. The north end of the island sandbarred by erosion. Hurricanes chasing folks off the beach. He propped himself to an elbow and asked the question he'd spent six months not thinking. "Why me?"

Benji had Olympians on his résumé. He had national champions, world medalists, hall-of-famers. He had Casper. What was he proving with Ezra?

Benji pulled his mullet out of his mouth, and it looked like those spreading strands were cracks opening across his cheeks; for a frantic second Ezra thought he'd shattered the man. Then Benji spidered his fingers over their heads, miming magic or puppeteering. "Wanna see what you'll do."

Which sent Ezra's brain back to those rumors from the triathlon forums. True that Benji's stables had high turnover. He'd made his name as a name-maker, plucking talent from mid-pack, or prompting it. Conjuring, maybe: he'd contracted hick magic from the Arkansas slump-country he'd crawled out of. Banksia nectar instead of Gatorade. Athletes racing with blood-stuck buzzard feathers for shoes. A hillbilly crone channeled death through a pointed bone. Benji channeled victory through a pointed finger. When he was promoted to the U.S. Olympic coaching staff he'd lost the litter he was picking from, inheriting folks at the top of the heap. Less moldable, maybe. Maybe he'd broken them. Is breaking what Benji wants from Casper and Ezra? His instruction seems meticulously random. Ezra gets the sense that Benji's shuffling productive and purposeless workouts, disguising his system from them as if their fitness is a magic trick: it would be spoiled if they knew how he was doing it.

Whether by mind or magic, the guy does know something. Benji'd been coaching before he could drive, inheriting an entire swim squad at thirteen. He'd coached athletes twice his age to national championships. Not just people. He'd honed his eye for movement with horses and greyhounds, learned how the dip of a leg or dropped head was its own kind of confession. When to push harder. When to ease off. Benji listens to bodies. What he hears from Ezra's isn't quite clear. A plea for instruction? An openness to feedback?

Or maybe, Ezra's been thinking—ever since Benji confiscated their phones and laptops—a roof. His career may well have been damned by whatever stories are breaking. He's ducking it all out here in Kure. Say this is less about coaching than a place to lay low, this half-evacuated beach town a storm surge shy of seafloor. He'll surface as soon as the hurricane blows over. Will Ezra float with him or drown? A worst-case he's too wiped lately to entertain.

Benji's keeping them stoned off of exhaustion. Two weeks before race day he's still increasing their mileage when the rest of the RoboCops are knee-deep in compression gear, feet up and tapering. Benji sends Ezra and Casper snailing and sprinting and sloshing forward, their order intact: Casper, then Ezra. Casper, then Ezra, Casper leading, Ezra wondering what leap it might take to shuffle them.

Casper's told them about the roulette of fosters. The ex-marine who made him do pushups for dinner, the tweaker plumber whose liquor cabinet he raided; how, when he'd puked a flask's worth of Jim Beam on the tile, she'd made him lick it up as punishment. Juvie was his summer camp. Freight-hopping, Greyhounds, hitchhiking rest stops, the creep who'd pressed Casper's head into his lap as soon as they got on the highway. Hence Benji's moniker for him: Mama, the one thing Casper can't run to. Benji wants Ezra just as desperate. But Ezra has a home to fall back on, arms to sag into; he has Ma. He doesn't need to win to eat. Is that what keeps him trailing?

Sobbing frays Ezra's sleep. He peels off the carpet in crane of Casper, but it's not him. The kid snores beside Benji, their sleeping bags bundled synaptically—like thoughts are passing between them. Ezra has the sick sense that they're dreaming the same thing. He gulps a sob of his own. The thought of Casper weeping was a truce, or a prompt, opening some hurt he's kept closed; but the sound's coming from outside. Ezra ducks out of the cabin with a flashlight and pins a jagged flank to the backdoor of a camper. A coyote. It opens its mouth as if to swallow the beam. Its jaw spills like a waterfall, a gush of fangs snarling.

Ezra hops off the boat deck by some below-the-neck instinct. When his brain catches up to the reflex he's already landing. For a slow second, both are frozen: him and the coyote, tethered by the beam. Then it darts off from the door, yanking Ezra into stride, beating him across the yard and sieving back through the pines. The sobbing gargles to a whine. Ezra slashes the shade with his flashlight. Ember eyes. Dozens of pupils kindled in the beam. They multiply as he halts, leaping like sparks, dousing themselves just as quickly—a pack of them rippling in and out of sight. Only then does Ezra's spine splint with panic: how easily they evaporate, vanishing like steam. The whining stops. The night a drained basin of quiet. Then Casper's squeal spurts out of the cabin. The air floods with Benji's hum.

Ezra stiffens up the boat ladder feeling like he's submerging. Benji's humming fills his sinuses. Casper lies openmouthed and shut-eyed, face looking like a cage his voice is crawling out of. Benji leaning prayerfully over him, mullet brushing his lips like a rosary. Both seem to be confessing. Benji hums into his ear, and the kid's sobbing quiets as if flushed by that melody. Casper quiets without waking. Benji rises gently, pulling strands of his mullet out of Casper's mouth, and Ezra hangs on the cabin door with the air feeling closed, watching. Benji takes such wincing care that it seems that each hair is a splinter he's extracting. Maybe Benji's coaching is like that, Ezra thinks—a delicate operation he can't understand.

"Shadefoot." Benji says the word like a sentence.

Ezra backs up as he crawls out of the cabin. Benji looms to the prow, his paunch a round figurehead. "Shadefoot. Ever hear of it?"

Ezra has, but can't place it. Doesn't want to.

"Old hillbilly haint," Benji says, talking without turning. "Someone's shadow tears off and makes whoopie with a coyote. Shadefoot's their spawn, and it lives in folks' footprints. It'll lick your neck and howl and every fucking et cetera trying to get you to turn around. That's how it gets into you—through the pupils. It's your body it's after. Doesn't have one of its own, owing to its shadow half. But it can't leave your tracks unless you look at it. So long as you keep facing straight, you're dandy."

"So what?"

Benji casts a line of piss off the prow. "Don't look back."

Ezra lies down in the cabin. Benji rattles down the ladder. A dream later, Ezra wakes again to him paunching onboard, dragging a mammal stench. He mouth-breathes for a toss, then sits up. Benji's cross-legged on the boat deck, crushing herbs. He mashes them to a hepatic clot in the knifed-off bottom of a water jug. The stuff smells like enzymes. Magnetizes flies. He crushes the bugs into the mixture, humming.

Ezra leans out of the cabin. If Benji looks up, his glance stays dammed behind his Oakleys. The lenses greased with the buttery moon melting below the tree-line. He sets the paste aside and smears his fingers on the deck carpet. Leaves and seeds sorted around him in piles, plucked from the cursive of flowers he's scribbled across Ma's planter boxers—a sentence seems spelled in those stems' winding ligatures. An incantation like his hum: something Ezra recognizes the logic of without translating. Before Benji took his phone, he'd looked up the species. Spurges. Nightshades. Angel's trumpets. Neurotoxins and cure-alls. The same plant can be both, dose-dependent. A single tooth of stinging nettle leaf prevents clotting. A full leaf takes the breath out of your blood. You cramp, then you gag, oxygen siphoned from your lungs before it reaches your veins. A valve cut; slow drain. Benji adds a pinch to the mixture and his hum skips a pitch, steadying like instructions. He knuckles and crinkles it into the paste and stands with the scalped jug. At some point Ezra's opened his sinuses. He breathes deeper.

Benji smears past Ezra without a word. He unzips Casper's sleeping bag without stirring him, flapping the fabric off of his feet. The cut has budded like another of Benji's flowers, sprouting florets of pus. Ezra gets the sick and sudden sense that it's something Benji's cultivating. Benji rubs the paste into it, releasing a stale-sweet scent like cum. Ezra wants to stop him, but the cabin air feels shut. He hinges his fingers on the doorframe.

"What're you doing to him?"

His words pick whatever bolt's locked between them. Benji quits humming and Casper scrunches awake, jerking the sleeping bag over his foot. Which one of us is he hiding his hurt from, Ezra wonders.

Benji pats Casper's heel through the sleeping bag. "Gonna duck out for a jiffy."

Casper cranes up.

"Stay." Benji halts him with a palm, then flattens it. "Keys."

He ducks back out of the cabin, hopping down from the boat deck. The hull lilts with his lost weight. Casper's pickup rumbles off and the kid's still propped up, this gape stranded on his face.

A vague urge twitches Ezra's arms. He can't tell if he wants to hug the kid or hit him; instead he pats Casper's head. "Conk out."

Ezra seeps down on the carpet but can't sleep. The cabin's stuffier with just the two of them, absent the hepa-filter hum of Benji's sleep-breathing.

"You got the hair," Casper says.

Ezra sits up. "The what?"

"The hair. He won't feed me none." The kid's got his hand to his mouth, brushing his lips.

"What hair?" Ezra slides up beside him. "When he hummed. He was telling you something."

"Naw."

"There were words."

Casper tilts his head sideways like he's trying to drain a thought from his eardrum. Is that what he's doing when he runs—spilling the hurt and the quit? "Don't let them varms fake you."

"Fake—what?"

"Varms learn to whine like your hurt version. Wail up a nursery, carrying on like a boobooed bunch of babies."

"The coyotes."

"Varms. You run out to help and there's the pack waiting to morsel you."

"That's what he told you?"

Casper pats his own head. "Better conk."

He squelches back into his sleeping bag. The herbs' organ odor. The flies sawing past. Ezra can't shut the door. He stares at the empty between the pines.

The kid's whisper sounds stranded. "He was just humming me dreams."

It's light by the time the truck clambers back. Benji slams out of it, shouting, "Saddle the steeds!"

Ezra aches up. Casper doesn't stir. Ezra dangles in the doorway, looking out at anemic dawn. Clouds sap the sky. The truck's parked at the edge of the yard, its bed crammed with spring traps. The drained light dulls their steel as slick-pale as sardines. Benji wrenches one open with a sound like snapped marrow, a belched threat of its function.

"What's your grudge?" Ezra calls.

A sleeping bag's zipper squawks. Ezra turns and catches Casper rushing a sock over his heel. "You should scrub that."

"Scrub your butt."

For the first morning all summer Ezra's first out of the cabin.

Benji crouches in the pines, gaping traps. Feeding them something. Ezra walks up to him, into an internal smell. Benji's mashing nightshade into wads of ground beef. The strands of the beef spurt through his squeezing fingers like worms. The combination reeks beyond the sum of its parts, sulfuring into something half-digested. He puts the clumps in the jaws of the traps.

"You're shitting," Ezra says.

"Get your helmet."

"This is excessive."

"You're shitting." Benji echoes Ezra's baritone so precisely that Ezra pinches his mouth shut. He sucks at a strand of mullet like a cigarillo, exhaling. "You heard them last night. They were baiting you."

Ezra's mouth fishes open. He feels like he's waking up back in that medical tent: Benji handing him that phone with the video of his collapse, showing Ezra to himself again. But this time Benji isn't smirking. He takes Ezra's hand, welting it with the paste. "And you bit."

Ezra wraths back toward the camper, groping for the root of his anger. That Benji's superstitions are their own kind of RoboCop; that Ezra himself is sweating them. That Benji's concern is pointing in so wrong a way, setting spring traps instead of taking Casper to a doctor. He glares past the kid, who's already straddling his Bianchi, and ducks into the camper for his own petrified Trek. The steeds. It's Benji's call to train on these fossils. Carbon frames are RoboCop. Ezra creaks outside, knees and bike harmonizing.

Benji smears around front with their running shoes pinched by the tongues. "You'll need these."

That means a brick workout. They'll ride, then they'll run, the blood in their legs mortaring. Ezra's pulse jacks at the prospect; he's anaerobic already. Benji struts to the moped and straddles it. He stows their shoes in the crate at the nape of its seat. He cranes his head as he does this, keeping Ezra pinned in his Oakleys. Waiting for him to ask what the hell. Wanting that. He tips the moped like the pendulum of a clock, shifting between his splayed feet.

"Got a suggestion?" Ezra asks.

"Get your bark on," Benji says.

Ezra scrapes his bike forward. Casper stays put. He's perched sideways on the top tube.

"You good?" Ezra asks, and gets the same stranded gape as last night. The kid's not all there. Rather, he's all *there,* somewhere separate from his own body. Zenning, Benji calls it. Ezra calls it concerning.

Benji snorts the engine. "Don't mind me!"

"Mama's comatose."

"He's sportsmanlike. Take the handicap, RoboCop. Let's choo-choo."

Benji spurts the moped into Drive. Casper leans into the handlebars as they walk their bikes across the lot. He's winced up on the tiptoes on his left foot, keeping to the ball. Limping. Lagging so Benji won't see.

They clip in at the top of the cul-de-sac. That's their starting line, where the dirt gets gulped by asphalt. The finish is Benji's call. He hasn't told them how far they'll go; the moped's back wheel is their only prerogative. It's already a block up Bromine Avenue. They crank into chase, gnashing chainrings with cogs. Upshifting to bridge distance. Benji winks the turn signal. They catch the moped as he corners, tethering to his slipstream umbilically.

They aim north toward the main drag of Kure. Boarded hotels. Boarded boardwalk. Charter boats' barren catch boards. Skirting the marina they get hooked by a crosswind and Benji swerves onto Canal like he's following it. Casper skids wide to corner. They've been riding parallel, but Ezra slices the tangent, gains half a bike-length. This nudge is enough. Casper spurts ahead and budges in on his line. Ezra drops back, tucking into the vacuum—another body now knifing the wind for him.

"Quit off, Shadefoot!" Casper hollers.

Ezra only places the word now that it's returned to its origin: one of the kid's insults, that incomprehensible litany. Benji's voice had disguised it last night. Before Ezra can shout back— what? why?—that wet drawl comes backwashed on the breeze.

"Big chainring! We're grinding."

They make a long lap of the island. Canal onto Ocean, Ocean onto River Road, streets named for the nearest water threatening to sink them. Way the hell south to the rolling end of the island, where a Civil War battery looms between dunes— jerky rises, like the one where Casper'd passed Ezra in Chapel Hill. Casper springs out of his saddle to climb. Ezra stays on the drops. His fatigue feels severed, unzipping, an asymptote. He could hold this speed forever.

Benji turns around at the last beach access. They orbit the island again more as the sun noons. Sweat and urine bake to crystals in their bike shorts. The third time they reach that beach access, Benji pulls over. He twists back to quarry their running shoes.

"To the toothpicks," he says, pointing north, toward Kure Pier's pilings. They'll run on the sand. Four miles each way.

They brisé off the bikes and Benji tosses them shoes. Casper yanks one on his sore foot, shifts his weight and tips. Ezra watches him fumbling. He's already stomped into his.

"This look like a rest stop?" Benji asks him.

Ezra slumps into stride. He's too used to their order—Casper a step or a stroke or a second in front, always leashing him. He lags down the access, waiting for Casper to rattle onto the planks. At last the kid bangs up behind him. Ezra slows, but Casper won't pass. The boardwalk's too narrow. He only pulls level when they barge onto the beach. His head tips as soon as they strike sand; he's been putting off breaking until Benji can't see.

So Ezra opens up. The kid clings behind, teeth grinding audibly. The air tastes like December. The dunes are bolstered with recycled Christmas trees, a tactic to beat back erosion. Delay's best-case—one good storm-surge will glaze them. A clump of teens ornaments the boughs, cheering taunts. It gives Ezra a toes-on-the-ledge feeling to realize his personal record means nothing to them. When he gets angsty, or sore, or shown up by Casper—when he starts thinking *what the hell?*—he pictures waking up to a day undivided by training. Without the burden of the next effort, he'd never get up; it would be crippling, the freedom to do whatever. Better to cocoon in exertion, exhaustion, routine.

Casper's breath dulls. The gap between them is widening. Ezra feels it like a thread's flex, but he doesn't look back. You surge and you hold until the hope's torn from them. He's grizzly now, ruthless with exertion. The pier looms. Something's snarling.

A coyote coils in the shorebreak. Its front paw is stuck in a crab trap, the crab trap wired to a piling. It bites at its leg. Ezra stops running and the coyote lifts its head; in the place where it was chewing, he sees tallow bone.

Casper limps up beside him. They stand there a long time, the two of them, staring. The coyote gnaws its leg with sickened calm. The serenity of certainty, Ezra's thinking. A feral thing does what it has to. Swallows pain for necessity.

Casper laughs. "Keep your bark on," he says. Then he's sprinting.

Ezra chases, but the hurt's catching up. Syrup heat. No lung to his breaths. Casper's rusting, too. His exhales seem a thing chipping off of him. With every left footfall his whole body cricks. It's down to who will slow less. Ezra passes through pain into something denser. A cauterized stiffness. As numbly stubborn behind Casper as a shadow. Shadefoot, Casper'd called him; the kid glances back and Ezra snatches that thread. He's reeling Casper in all the way up the beach access. Casper spears his elbows, smacking Ezra's sternum. They pound off of the planks and Ezra swings wide to pass. But a part of him's lagging. He doesn't quite sprint.

Casper trips past Benji an instant ahead, sprawling prone on the pavement. He crumples like he's losing his spine—a spent windup toy, the zip cord of his vertebrae yanked out of him. Ezra coasts to a jog. When he circles back, Benji's Oakleys are framing him.

"Some kick," Benji says.

"Your dog needs a vet."

Casper tucks his leg, but can't hide it. The whole heel's spongey with blood.

Benji stoops over him. "Let me see."

Casper's flat teeth grab the air, snatching breaths. His chest throbs like he's sobbing.

Here's the thing: to dodge liability, Ironman requires medical screenings. Standards are stringent, pushing paranoid—Ezra's heard of athletes DQ'd for sprains, sinuses, viral bouts stymied weeks before race day. If Casper gets so much as a prescription he risks being flagged. Casper knows this; when he hid the heel from Benji, he knew. But the fix he gets from training is immediate, the warm fugue of fatigue. Exhaustion blurs any thought toward the future. Benji's eyebrows are scrolling above his Oakleys. Even in dumb exhaustion, Ezra susses the stakes. First, Benji's bush medicine hasn't worked. Second, Casper's hidden that fact from him, showing his own will in doing it. Third—worst—there's the risk of failed screening. Does Casper have insurance? Ezra's seeing Benji slashing his own heel, getting a prescription for himself to feed Casper off the books. Or Ezra's. Anything to get Casper racing. That's what Benji wants, isn't it? To see what they can do?

He's sniffing the kid now as he crouches, fisting up crushes of herbs from his pockets.

Ezra presses a hand to Casper's forehead, but his own run-hot blood keeps him from finding the fever. "He needs medicine."

"Benji's giving it."

Benji puts his mouth to Casper's heel and hums. Cheek flat against the asphalt as if conducting some chthonic instruction. Casper's eyes shut. Benji's voice serrates like the Piston's flywheel whining before bursting. Varms fake hurt sounds to bait you. Is that what Benji's doing now, mimicking the breaking machine to lure metal out of Casper's cut? Ezra swears he feels Casper's forehead cooling. Conducting his palm's heat like the ground.

"You don't believe this." Ezra says it to all of them.

Benji swallows his hum. His mouth seems to've become the cut. His chapped lips look scabbed. Stray flecks of leaves rust his tongue. He presses his thumb into Casper's knee like he's testing a patched tire. He shrugs off all ceremony as fast as he stands. "Meet me at the pool, Tootsies."

"You're shitting."

Benji's already straddling the moped.

Casper swats Ezra's hand. "Quit off."

"You need rest."

"He needs rinsing!" Benji hollers. The moped snorts off, leaving the two of them throbbing.

"Ride home," Ezra says.

Casper's head tips like he's considering it, but only for the slit of an instant. He swallows his breath, spits. "Gotta beat me the hard way."

But Ezra hadn't even been thinking that kind of selfishly. He'd wanted to skip the swim with Casper. Solidarity. But if the kid's going to the pool, so is he. Shadefoot. A varm fakes a baby to lure you; but Ezra'd mistaken the coyotes for Casper. He moans over, hands-to-knees.

Casper giggles. "RoboCop's got an 'off.'"

His cut sneers up at Ezra, drooling Benji's spit. Ezra steps on it. He sinks his weight slow, mechanically, and Casper's smirk inflates.

"Not me."

Casper

RoboCop lets me up and the two-us perch our bikes. I grate my pedals over. My heel yaps with each downstroke. RoboCop's chainring mutters behind. I stomp harder and the muttering slurs. Picture him franticing faster, them twig-legs wind-sped into tumbleweeds. About right. This main drag's a high noon shy of buzzards. Soulless as a shootout. Ever square-inch storm-shuttered. And it's hard not to shiver as we pass them tombstony hotels, ever shade-patch they cast a grave we're riding over. Hold my breath to keep from breathing the ghosts thrusting in. Ever trucker and foster and friend I ever brushed moaning my skull into an auditorium. I tip my head but the Everywhen's already welling up.

The Everywhen. Shivers. That's how time brackishes when you're sleep. Ever person who's gone into you crams back in one sudden, ancestors bundle-stuck in a cocoon of now-through-history. Benji hummed it to me meaning comfort. But I'd never known kin. I had to make myself, taking in others' bursting. Because bursting's how your ancestors make you. So instead of getting soul-stuffed with my own folks, Benji's hum flooded up everyone who'd ever burst in me. Benji only meant to soothe. But his hurting made room for more soothing. When my dreams crowd, he slurps the ghosts out my ear. Then he hums in his own kin, whispering his living air into me.

But Benji's up-offed ahead now, and my heel-hurt's boiling up, and the Everywhen's cramming in. Shadefoot, too. Hear RoboCop gasping back there. I stomp-stand the pedals and sprint, rushing my breaths enough to tamp down any squealing. Past beach stores. Through the glints of mailboxes rinsing me with sun-warm. Out of the feel of the plus-shove of RoboCop, but I don't look back; not again. He nearly caught up after I snuck just a glance.

Bad enough what's in front of me. The gate to the pool neighborhood's shut. And grumbling out front is the Benjiless moped. Fear slithers my guts.

"Benji?" My voice sharps out screamy.

I thump the number box some but the gate won't open. RoboCop never told me the code; maybe did, but I can't conjure it for my heel and ghosts yapping. I squirm there long-waiting for RoboCop to show up, sickening more with every next-second I'm alone. The Atom Man and Ms. Ida and the Galardes climb my spine like the hurt-heat from my heel, heartbeatening and heaving full of fever. I hip-hump my bike over the gate and pry myself up and only when I perch atop it do I see Benji.

He's crammed between the bushes and the wall upside the gate. Like my ears were waiting up for my eyes, only then do I hear him humming. Same tune he first stuck me with a near-year ago at the Chapel Hill Ironman. Closed around me like his lips close around that sidelong hair-his. Only this time his hum ain't for me. A varm's bellied down in them bushes. Got its forepaws tucked upside its snout, head longways'd atop them like deep-sleeping. Benji's getting kissy with its perked ear. The varm's ear veins ripple under its skin like they're getting ribbon-blown by his breathing. I slide off the wall and crush down through the bushes beside them. My heel yaps, but what yaps louder is the quiet I'd heard: never before have I missed Benji's voice, not even sleeping. I thrash down to a crouch in urge of his nuclear tug.

"Benj?" Benji's secret name sneaks up my throat with the scald-speed of steam. He said to call him that in my brain only. Don't ever say; around RoboCop, don't even think. "Ee!" I rush-say, but too late.

Benji's ears twitch like hands raising with answers. He gulps his hum and I know I've made a nail hole: same leaking feeling

I got before running off from ever other place, from that bed-bugged museum of a children's home to Ms. Ida's three squares and snacks to the Atom Man all the way to today. Benj's secret name was the nail: he hammered it in me to seal me. Leave it to me to pry it out. Sluicing shame. Spilling me.

But Benji just presses my hand to the side of the sleep-seeming varm. His own other hand sinks my buzzcut. Shivers trickle down me from his touch.

"If you hide your hurt, I can't hold it."

He pets all the way down to my heel, leaving my skeleton earthquaking.

"It don't yap much." But it docs, and I *was* hiding; Ms. Ida used to say if you don't like it, don't look at it.

"How're the ghosts?" Benji asks.

"Yapping."

"Same."

"Unc?"

The varm's squeal bucks my hand, and I know Benji hummed it Unc. My fear-slithered guts get joined by envy-slithered ones, caduceusing up my spine with the hissing rise of steam-plus-snakes. A nuclear can only have one minus and plus. I don't remember much, but I took a brain-picture of that atom poster. "You feed it hair, too?"

Benji pinches my heel like one-them beads they gave us at the children's home to rub for praying. Some dunces sported them like necklaces. Some chewed them like Benji's hair. But I rubbed them to keep from scratching at bedbugs. All the nightlongs I pressed them beads, jointsore from docenting folks through the plantation. My shivering becomes them bedbugs.

Benji's voice deeps and rounds like I'm hearing it from pool-bottom. "Remember what I promised."

Choking seconds before my voice bobs. "A home."

Then we're up-out the bushes and solid. Benji punches the number box and the gate scrapes open. He rumbles the moped ahead.

"What about RoboCop?"

"He'll come."

"Because you fed him the hair."

Benji never fed me the hair. Says he's afraid how far I'd go if I had some. Asks do I want to be like RoboCop? Nuts to that. But still. Just that RoboCop got something I don't. Envy slithers above fear on my guts' spine-climbing caduceus.

"Because you looked back," Benji says.

Wet gulp. "What'll happen?"

Benji just jerks the moped ahead, leaving me to minus. Part of me hates how he knows I'll still follow.

I spit, but there's just air in my mouth. Squeals seeping through the varm's snoring. And no nuclear tug or plus-shove. I stand crane-waiting to feel them, my fear-slithered guts overtaking my envy-slithered ones. The Everywhen drowning both of them. Add RoboCop and Benji to those ghosts wailing. Benji promised me a home, but I looked back like I wasn't supposed to. What if the three-us un-atom because of me?

Benji

The kid's hurt is beyond all your armfuls. Haven't held this much since leaving Unc's farm last spring. Slick your hand from his nape to his heel, the shrapnel-seeded root of his fever. If you could just pluck the leaves. If the kid'll just get through this swim. Unc had never known the spell to be broken, but Unc had never wanted to break it. Said some folks were just born into the wrong reflexes: couldn't quit them any more than you could quit a rutting ram from curling its lip.

You'd never meant to feed your hair to Ezra. He'd snored it in while you hummed to him last year in the medical tent. When you tried to pluck it off his tongue, he'd nearly swallowed your fingers. Skittish. You'd wanted to pry his ribs open and reel the hair out of him, but the spell was done. Hair of the dog cures the human. Hair of the human makes the dog make a cure out of you. Once one swallows your hair it'll need you like medicine, walk off its own paws finding its way back to you. And Ezra's as mutt as they come. A whelp's guts. How he'd run himself broken-legged in Chapel Hill, brainless; his head had bounced off the curb and you'd thought *that one*. But you'd sworn off the hair both times you left Unc. Should've brushed your hair back when you hummed. Should've cut it. But reflexes.

Chewing your hair ever since Unc taught the spell. Can't cure yourself, Unc said, but you still couldn't quit. You woke up to the buzz of the shears and spent the rest of that summer with sweat pooling in the ditches the clippers had left on your scalp. But the stubble that grew back did feel good to rub. It did pearl some, studding with sweat. You did wonder if this had been more prevention than punishment: whether Unc had gotten sick of the porch sagging with strays baying for you. This one sheppie followed you to the truck every morning. You'd shut the door on it and it'd try to jump into the bed. The smack of it falling short shook the cab. It bit the back wheel on one desperate morning and Unc kept his foot on the gas. You kept count of seconds, sitting clenched in the passenger's. The dog held on. Those wet thumps of it spinning. Your wrong reflexes: tallying how long the dog would hold on for you. By the time you reached for the wheel, Unc was already waving his hand at the mammal clot shrinking in the rearview. "See what you can do?"

You'd sworn you'd quit the spell then, but it tickled your throat like the first simmering promise of sickness back when you were still swimming. Like every sore throat you'd ever tasted coming on before big meets, you savored it. Never because you'd wanted to get out of racing; it had been the excuse for losing.

Hadn't kept Unc from pulling you out of the water. You'd quit liking sore throats when he started training you to be a coach instead of an athlete, but the spell kept on teasing you. Twenty-seven years biting yourself with your hair, biting back the urge to use it.

Then your whole squad flushed their seasons last spring. Shit results. Threats of getting wiped off the national coaching staff. Smears from triathlon forums. Tootsies were making an asshole out of you. And you as exposed as an orifice, clenching your jaw like a sphincter.

Grizzled March. Along the Cross-City Trail, transplanted palms frowned their fronds, their shaggy trunks bearding. Needing shears. Tootsies needing banding. Wrench had left his brain between Old Lady's legs. (Wrench for his stiff-armed, jerking swim stroke; Old Lady for how she hunched over her strides when she was hurting.) Hood Ornament's brain was in Ducky's head (her compulsive front-running; his webbed toes, he thought, but actually the shady bust that his silhouette cut when he pulled his ball-cap beak-low on his chinless head.) Ducky's brain was on his nickname, on Hood Ornament dusting him every group ride—surging past your moped, setting her own pace. Wrench and Old Lady riding side-by-side. All of them losing races.

Ducky'd apparently left his legs behind when he aged out of Juniors. Hood Ornament kept blowing up on failed breakaways. Old Lady on a DNF streak. Wrench walked barefoot across the finish line of the Cancun World Cup two minutes outside of the podium and threw his shoes at you. He'd found the feather you'd slipped into his insoles. Had suggestions for what else you should charm, other places to put your hoodoo. Filed a not-so-anonymous complaint with the U.S. Olympic Committee. The suits started trying to flick their sweat off on you. Athlete stipends were performance-based, coaching appointments subject to change. The Chairman's voicemails reiterated that they weren't funding a religious organization.

One 5 a.m., Hood Ornament rode her bike into a couple stumbling out from under a blush of azaleas. The kids seemed sunburnt together, peeling apart with apparent pain. Hood Ornament brushed the strand of bone straying from her forearm like she was trying to tuck a stray hair behind her ear. Ducky looked from that bone to the bulge below kid's waistband, snorted. *They both popped a fat.*

The whole squad was rutting. Needed castrating. Could've used the closed focus that came from a long dunk in Unc's cocoon.

Twenty-seven years he'd been begging you back, claiming he had something to show you. Meaning he wanted to atone. He'd come back from Dasharath with a cure, but for who? He wasn't calling you home because he wanted to help you; he wanted to absolve himself of you. But Unc himself said that some folks were just born wrong. You'd coax him back to his old reflexes, the humming ones that you wanted to subject Tootsies to.

So you drove them back to his property. That swaybacked clapboard. The scalped grass grafted with hay. You could see the whole property from a mile out, the road smirking down the scooped hills to that last ragged pasture of sheep. It was wind instead of wool to keep warm these days. Before fleeing to Nepal to try and shut his third eye, Unc had contracted half his acreage to the TVA. Turbines sliced the sky. Their blades churn wasn't much louder than the van's air conditioner. Seemed wrong for something so huge to be so silent. Wrench told you to stop casting spells; you hadn't even noticed that you'd been humming. Old Lady snorted. Wrench put a dire hand around the sliding door, threatening to jump out if you didn't quit.

You braked up to the clapboard scattering strays and loose sheep. Those bucktoothed porchboards. The propped front door inhaling. You went around back. That water trough still ladened the yard, the sheet metal lid like a scab sealing it. All the times you'd waited while Unc laid in it.

The lid was as heavy to lift as you remembered. The hinges crackled rust. There bobbed Unc, right where you'd last left him.

"How'd you get in here?" you asked. "Who shut this?"

By the raw look of him, you could nearly believe he'd been in there for twenty-seven years. His glare wooly with cataracts. His legs bent with the promise of a limp.

"Still got this shit," he said, pulling your hair. "You stop at Citgo? What'd you bring me?"

You gave him the nod and the gnaw of it. Tootsies' brains out of their helmets. You sweating it. Unc holding you by your mullet through it all, rubbing it under his fingernail, humming. He plucked out a strand. "Tried using this?"

The idea, really, his. You'd learned from him to train people like whelps, but you'd never thought to charm them the same way; or you had, but had wanted to wait for someone else to do it. But Unc was you. His fingers pinching yours every time you pinched herbs, his hands the units of measure: a thumbnail of stinging nettle eased headaches, but a pinky's length poisoned. Tinctures you still used to nourish Tootsies.

That night you added your hair, a strand for each portion whirlpooling green in the blender. Wrench dumped his glass on your lap and stomped into his running shoes. Old Lady slid her chair back, but made a marathon out of standing. That end-of-run hunch that you'd named her for. She watched Wrench even as she stooped over you, mopping the drink off your legs with her napkin. Wrench looking seasick, folding over in the doorway.

"Fuck a potion."

Unc winked.

Wrench left, but the rest stuck to you, putting in declarable work all the way through to Easter. Ducky's nut-busting runs under the turbines. Old Lady swimming laps in the pond, un-zipping the algae jacketing the surface. Hood Ornament sweat-ing her cast loose on the windtrainer. The time you caught her smacking her arm on the handlebars to try and crack the plaster, as if healing were a matter of getting it off. You and Unc pass-ing binoculars on the porch to watch Tootsies running. Craning their necks as they surged, squinting back at the house to be sure you were seeing them. Your sunglasses clicked against the eye-pieces. Glimpses of fur. Hackles surmounting the tall grass like beads of dew.

"This shit," Unc said. "What'd you bring me?"

Coyotes.

That night they trickled into the pasture. You stumbled out-side with the sheep roiling, a turbid blur of wool and blood and streaked shit. The coyotes' squeals severing their weak bleats. Tootsies' shouts as they bulged out the front door behind you. But above those sounds—and under, around, containing them—was Unc's hum.

His voice made a jar around the pasture. The panicked and wounded sheep settled as one snore. Their backs crested and fell. The hipbones of coyotes surfaced like dorsal fins between them. The coyotes' vacuuming, exhaleless snores. Sheep intestines ed-dying. And Unc wading out from among them, humming them all into dream.

He limped around back and you followed him.

"About this," he said, slapping his crooked femurs. "Since

you asked, something landed on top of me."

You wanted to laugh but were afraid to. Tootsies spilled outside and aligned behind you. The blood and shit that he tracked warmed your bare heels. Someone's flashlight blurted its beam. Straining the lid off the trough, Unc appeared key-lit. Age had sunken his strength instead of sapping it—his scrunching arm muscles furrowed with sinew. The lid apexed and he released it to gravity. Its rebar ribs struck the trough's flank with a wind-knocking clatter. Your own breath felt taken. Unc swallowed his hum. You stood shade-close behind him. Your toenails scraped his heels and he didn't turn.

Tootsies waited breathless behind you. Unc was waiting, too. The rending feeling of stepping around him. The biting heat of the water-trough, as if the tin had been daylong in the sun. The wailing dark you lowered yourself into. The water inside was as warm as your skin, so precisely similar that you felt no wetness slipping into it. No surface. You'd been in there once, and that once had stretched for so seemingly long that it had gone beyond the specific—a part of you was still submerged in it. The water's warmth and buoyancy skinned you: you became what you were held within.

"Shadefoot forms from footprints," Unc said.

You spat in the water. "I'm done with cocoons."

And stormed inside before he could finish, but your head echoed the rest of the truth. Shadefoot forms from footprints. It comes from what's ahead, so its ancestors are whatever it follows: its Everywhen is loud with its future.

That night Unc hummed you awake. Tootsies snoring at the foot of your bed.

"Don't make them how I made you," he said.

"You didn't break me. I was born wrong."

"Who told you that?" Unc had. The outfall of his sob spread across his darkened face like a rash. That was the second time you'd ever seen him shivering. You'd brought him to that.

"You said to feed them the hair."

"I only asked if you had. We're all of two minds, at least. I've got plenty more than that inside me. You only took one." Unc pressed an ID into your hand. Eva Fogerty, a brown-blonde girl with sawed-off looking cheeks. Home address in Kure, NC. The license had expired in 2000. "I made more than you," he said. Told you that he and her had a son; that one had been born right, he said. All you had to do was push him to the edge.

"Then what?"

"He's going to break your reflexes." Unc smeared his palm down from your scalp to the nape of your neck. "You need someone who won't believe you."

You asked him if this was his idea of atonement. He told you not to mention him again—not to Eva, not to her son, not to anyone. Thoughts fed the Tulpa.

"The what?"

Unc grabbed your mullet. Pried your head back. He'd grabbed you just like this the day he decided that you weren't meant for swimming. "Be different than me," he said. "Please."

You tore out of his grip. Ran downstairs, swearing your own clicking ankles were his teeth chattering.

The trough was too heavy to tip. Slosh and clank of the too much of what was in it. You dropped your shoulder and rammed yourself into it.

"Take a dip." Unc slouched in the doorway. His shadow trembled. "Look back."

You ran a long lap around what was left of Unc's property. The sheep and coyotes still charmed to sleep. Turbines sliced the breeze. Your feet disappeared out from under you, plunging into dark.

The cocoon was where Unc drowned in his Everywhen. The lid's top side—the outside—was overlaid with a maze of rebar. The iron writhed like the scars on Unc's chest, and with the same purpose: to keep what was inside from escaping. The trough sloshed with the voices of his ancestors when he climbed in. The lid took someone standing outside it to open it. All the nights you'd nodded off waiting for him to knock, lying in the yard beside it. Summers the tin stayed sun-hot after dark; winters the lid froze the skin off your fingers when you lifted it. The metal exaggerated whatever weather—as if the Arkansas seasons weren't egregious enough on their own, the temperature as rolling as the topography. Unc's knuckles splashing inside the lid, the contact hardening into thumps. Like his own fist was freezing. You'd always wait until the sound was solid, afraid he'd evaporate if you let him out early. But he was more him every time you strained the lid off the trough, blind and tall-bald and naked. His cataracts leaking brightness like they'd absorbed the sunshine that had caused them. His alfalfa eyebrows thickening as if photosynthesizing. Unc joked his whole head used to sprout hair the same shade until the sheep ate it off; the risks of hay-blondeness. He'd step out and leave the lid gaping.

"Still here," he'd say. "*More* here."

An invitation you'd only ever once taken. That had been the same spring that you'd left, the one when you saw Unc's larger system. Now he was telling you to swerve from the way that it had shaped you. Yet there it sat. Twenty-seven years later he was still insisting you into it.

You ran back down the driveway and got charged by Tootsies.

They were panting like you'd fed them too much nightshade. You slammed into the van with Ducky yanking the door handle, Old Lady throwing herself against the passenger's window, Hood Ornament standing around front, and you couldn't quit thinking of that sheppie biting the tire. You shifted into reverse, scythed around back of the clapboard.

The trough's lid was thrown open. By the time you saw that, you were already backing into it.

It sloshed as it toppled. It scraped as the van's bumper shoved it and it was just like that sheppie: you counting instead of smashing the brake. The van bucked; another, wetter thump. The trough cracked like knuckles as the tires surmounted it.

The lid bent open. Water gushed. A wet lump rolled out with it.

You braked to a stop with the chassis rattling.

Tootsies rode around the clapboard on their hikes. You stomped into drive. The tires cleared the trough again. The rust cracked, or someone was cackling.

The tendon-rending tension of braking. You climbed out and limped back. Unc laid in the water spilled from the trough, the breath crushed from his body. Heartbeatless. His voice had been shoved out from his lungs. It swelled through the air, surrounding you with his cackling. The way moonlight seeps, like the spread of that sound. Every spirit of his had leaked out with the water. The Everywhen had spilled free. Tootsies huddled around, lapping at the puddle. The cackling gave to a hum.

Had to contain Unc to keep him from spreading. You scooped him up and carried him to the water tower. Threw a rope over the ladder's top rung, tied him to one end, and hoisted the other until his body leveled with the landing. Tootsies still huddled around the trough, drinking the water you'd dissolved in. You tied your end of the rope around the ladder's bottom rung and climbed up to Unc, cut him loose from the binding. The cataracts had broken up in his eyes, lumps of white in the blue irises like tiny, sandy islands. You propped Unc by the door to the tower, grabbed the sewing kit, and stitched his eyelids shut. The hum fell out of the air.

Tootsies wailed up from where they crouched and sprinted for the tower. You shoved Unc through the door. He belly-flopped into the water and floated. You threw the rope in on top of him, and it coiled across his back like the lines he'd scribbled across all those portraits. Tootsies fought up the ladder, shoving each other off the rungs, but you stood there until Unc's body sank. Slammed the door shut. Left him to dissolve. Slid down the ladder into Tootsies' arms.

"Run until you can't." That's what you told them.

And Googled Eva Fogerty while they bounded off. A decade's worth of race results. Pictures of her with her son, Ezra. The kid's blogspot. His mediocre WTO Pro Ranking. His name on the Ironman Chapel Hill start list.

You floored the van through the near pastures with Tootsies chasing. You felt a tug as each of them dropped out of the van's slipstream, your scalp straining like a hair pinched and plucked. The highbeams flashing off of coyote eyes. You cut the headlights. You drove without looking back, trying to misremember that laughter into rust—needing not to think of Unc crushed in that trough, broken-bodied but still cackling. Wishing your mind's eye would develop a cataract.

A part of you must've known that Unc had climbed in. You'd seen the lid open. You had braked; you did brake. Just too late. You were just born with slow reflexes.

All the way out to the turbines' wrong quiet. Their motionless propellers seemed snagged on humidity. Yet a hum still fell from them like a string, as if stillness had unspooled rather than stopped their hum. You stopped the van tangled into the sound. You'd fed Tootsies the hair and the coyotes had come. Your kin. The only way to save them was to leave them.

The cocoon of those next months. A scatter plot of rest stops along I-40, tugging hair, strawing gas, parked between semis until the coyotes caught up. Paw prints puddling behind the van. Claw parks streaking the bumper like dew, or runes. There were sentences hidden in those scratches. The van was marked. You sold it in Nashville and hitched. East and east with someone else's voice welling up until Ezra collapsed at the Chapel Hill Ironman. His gasp like hearing your own thinking outside you. You'd hummed over his cot, your hair dangling low. Could've brushed it back. Didn't want to. And he'd swallowed. And you'd followed him to this sandbar of an island hoping you'd lost the coyotes.

Braking up to the pool with their squeals spilling. Their kin-need for you. Ezra needs you, but wants to kin with kid. The kid just wants a home. Hear him riding up as you park the moped. Smell him passing, glanding a ripe ribbon of sweat and adrenaline. Darling. He rides right onto the pool deck, props the bike on a diving block, and shivers in. You haven't even tossed him his goggles. Before you can kickstand the moped he's swimming.

The same *go* you'd first seen in him the eve of the Chapel Hill Ironman. Riding past all stomp and gasp on the Bianchi. Cadence rattling the drivetrain like a tambourine. Square head wedged sideways on his shoulder. Shoulder stamped with his race number; the night before the Ironman and he was hammering the big chainring. The next day you'd watched him cross the finish line and keep running and you'd known: you only kept going like that if you didn't have a place to go back to. Kid might've carried right on to Canada if you hadn't hummed him over. Same tune Unc had used to still the lambs before banding. Your voice wrapped the kid as tightly as the elastrator. He fell in front of you how the lambs' bloodless testicles sloughed off—something drained. You were already bulging with the prospect of how far he might go for you, hating your craving. A near-year later you aren't sated. Now he swims with slapping strokes, blood unspooling from his heel, and the pleasure of his effort's leg-buckling. Without even swallowing your hair. What he'll do.

Ezra's phone throbs in your pocket. That cracked screen. The chewed case. Drizzle your thumbs over the keypad, filling in the passcode. They spill into each digit like rain ponds in a ditch, finding the shape of what's holding it. Check his Facebook. Scroll through the messages his ma's been sending. The latest: a living moose snorts flues of breath behind a MOOSE CROSSING sign. *Like my painting?* she'd written. Thinking it's Ezra seeing this, sneaking peeks. All the ellipses you've dripped in that chatbox. The words brimming. The urge to become into his footprints. The longer rain gathers in one place, the taller it grows. Throw the phone. Pick it up again. You can't quit a reflex, but you can cut a tendon. If you can just make Ezra crack. Slide through that hairline before he shatters. It has to end with you alone, feather-blown, leading off the coyotes. You've just got to get him and the kid to quit following.

Ezra

The island's only lap pool is locked in Sloop Point. Ezra
got the gate code from the HOA president, who sucks wind in
the last pack of WheelsDeals group rides. He can hear Casper's
smacking strokes as he thumbs in the code. They're already going.
He sulks his bike through the flexal streets. The development was
built by his own great-auntie Opal, demolitioned by hurricanes.
The north end of the neighborhood's already been sandbarred.
Brimming ditches. A FOR SALE per mailbox. The pool's empty
aside from Casper and Benji. No sunbathers, no lifeguards—no
witnesses. Just Benji wadded in a chair and Casper punching the
water. If you didn't see the speed at which the kid was crossing
the pool, his frantic strokes would look like drowning. Hard not
to wonder if that's how the kid had learned to swim—someone
throwing or pushing him in. Holding him under. The kid swims
with his fists. Flails like he's life-fighting, getting a move on in
spite of it—or because of it, desperation trumping technique.
Ezra props his bike beside Casper's.

Benji's mullet sticks to the chair he peels up from, stretching
like spat gum. "Hop in. Water's broth."

Ezra crams his hair into a swim cap. Since Ma left, he's been
letting it grow. The brown blondes where it frays down around
his shoulders, greening some from chlorine. Nearly as long as
Benji's. Ezra idles on the coping, triple-knotting his speedo.

Benji reaches around and yanks the strings. "Put your head
in, Peter. It's the Atlantic, not Galilee."

Ezra eases into the lane beside Casper's. Benji presses a heel
to his head and dunks him.

Ezra ducks out and splutters up, shivering. "What the—"

"I want you splitting." Benji means the lane. Ezra waits for Casper to flip-turn, then ducks the rope between them. The kid casts his fever like a shadow as he passes; a displacement in the shape of him. A silhouette of sick heat.

"Go on."

"How far?"

Benji nods after Casper.

Ezra slaps up behind him, his own strokes warped by the wake of the kid's flailing. He's wondering about that phrase Benji goaded them with before the brick. *Bark on.* Like a dog without bite? Like a tree? He cannot synonym. Cannot math the laps, even. He stops swimming when Casper stops. Benji tosses them paddles and pull buoys.

"Ten 400s pull. That's no legs, RoboCop."

"What's the interval?" Ezra asks: how long to gasp between repetitions? Benji's tilted the pace clock away from them.

"Go on me."

They squirm into the gear. Casper bunches high on the wall, like they're racing.

"Markssss," Benji drawls—also like they're racing. "Go!"

Casper humps a long streamline off the wall. Heaving off the far side he sneaks kicks.

"*Pull,*" Ezra spits when they finish the first repeat.

Benji's already waving them off. Two, three, four 400's. They're missing the interval. Soon as they touch Benji launches them again. Casper starts blatantly kicking. He scissors ahead and Ezra tastes iron—the kid's heel is unspooling blood. They gasp to the wall.

"Go!" Benji hollers.

Ezra stays barnacled to the coping. Here's the thing: Benji's sitting on the dive block. The pace clock's behind him. There *is* no interval.

"I quit," Ezra says.

Benji nods.

Ezra lets the buoy float up from his thighs but doesn't climb out. He says it again. "I quit."

Benji's nod lengthens. "Doesn't look like it."

Casper flip-turns at the far wall, stroking back toward the two of them.

"What do you want? A hand up?"

Just instruction. Benji's left Ezra like kudzu, needing another structure to cling to.

Casper whips into the wall and flip-turns, raising hackles of splash. The water's surface gems over with blood. Does Benji see this? Does he care? He folds over on the dive block, belly squelching.

"You're scared of how fit you are. I saw on the brick. You were zenning, but you dogged it. You're afraid to see what you can do." He flicks his shoe across Ezra's forehead. "You've got an off-button, RoboCop."

"Fuck off."

Benji chuckles, but lowly; all goading's gone from that laugh.

Ezra slugs onto the pool deck and leans into his breath. That lathered, raw odor as sweat-thick as humidity. He hates himself for inhaling.

Benji funnels his voice through cupped hands. "Go on me."

Ezra spins toward home feeling short a few organs. A whomping rises behind him; a disc wheel's urgent churn.

"On your left!" someone hollers.

A giant on a Trek Equinox sucks up alongside him. The bike's top tube is level with Ezra's chin—a size 56 frame and a chainring with just as many teeth. "There he is."

Wispy. He shoves up from the aerobars and plants his hands on the hoods, the tapered end of his aero-helmet pointing back like a duck shoulder-checking.

"Long time," Ezra says.

"That's on you. We've been missing you at morning Master's."

"I've got a pool over here."

"I dig it. The Dave Scott strategy."

"A cocoon." The word falls from Ezra's mouth like a reflex, stale as Benji's breath.

"Cuck who?" Wispy says.

"Cute kit," Ezra says.

"New, too." Wispy scrapes his fingers up the logo on the side of his tri suit. 'LAGUNA RESORTS' is capitalized from the thigh to the armpit in a single racing stripe of bold print.

"Where your guileless dreams come true."

Ezra rubs his eyes, feeling more nightmare-like. "You're in hospitality."

"I'm receiving it. They're flying me over to that Phuket race and giving me the full Macca treatment. Flight, buffet, lodging all included. Google the Nirvana Suite. Sauna in the bathroom. The freaking tile's heated."

"Seems like the atmosphere would just do that."

"Marble doesn't absorb sunlight. I'm going to ruin my racing legs standing on that shit. Going to be the Styx to this freaking fasciitis. I call the front desk and they'll bring me a live koala."

"Like, to eat?"

"For whatever. To pet. I don't know the animal laws."

"A koala."

"These people are laying palm fronds where I'm running."

Ezra coasts so slow that his bike grows unsteady.

Wispy brakes and torques the handlebars back and forth, wobbling.

"You cooling down or what?"

"Just moving."

"Good on you. I bet my plantar would patch right up if I had enough discipline for an offseason."

"I'm not taking one." Ezra's turn to flaunt. "I've been working with Benji Newton."

"Like, *the?*" Wispy cranes around like the guy might be on his wheel; the own back of Ezra's neck gets a firecrackered feeling.

"I heard some dark shit went on in West Memphis," Wispy

says. "Blood magic. Bloodletting? Some medieval shit."

"He's just training me."

"But you've been to that compound."

"He came to me."

"Shit, man. Have him burn some sage for my sake. Second thought, don't mention me. I'd rather have neutral juju."

"Break a leg in Phuket."

Ezra puts his foot down. Wispy stops, too.

"Don't let me hold you up."

"I'm doing VO2 intervals," Wispy says. "That's a 2:1 work-to-rest. I've got forty seconds."

Ezra counts them.

"A koala," Wispy says. "The species isn't even endemic."

"I don't think that's the word you're looking for."

Wispy's watch beeps. He clips his left bike shoe back into the pedal.

Ezra points up the beach access. "Thailand's about fifteen Ironmans that way.

Benji

Ezra leaves you and the littlest Tootsie in obedient peace. Casper's swimming in a zig-zag, clipping either lane line with his fingers. Has the kind of fighting stroke Unc would've blamed for his cataracts, but you coach better than to talk an athlete out of shit technique. The worst thing you can do is say something that gets a machine like the kid thinking. Thinking's what got RoboCop talking himself into running off. So you don't risk mentioning higher elbows to Casper, or reaching from the hips. Better in the water than in your head—that is, his.

Tootsie lifts his head to sight off of you as he approaches. On the laps where he swims out, he keeps rolling over into a backstroke and tucking his chin. His stare feels like a grip, checking to confirm your presence with the repetitive desperation of a compulsion. He overshoots his stroke at the far wall and smacks his forearm on the coping. Lean over the diving block. Hum him a kiss.

An empty ache trembles your achilles tendons. The haunt of an old pain. You slide off the diving block for a pace. You walk the deck next to lane one and Casper ducks into it. His strokes start to splash faster. He stabs his arms into the water at an even steeper angle instead of stretching and anchoring to accelerate. He keeps pace with your progress, breathes to the side facing you. You'd like to sketch him. You'd stare yourself blind to do it.

A yip yanks your gaze to the pool's gate. Two coyotes lurk behind it, forepaws bent through the chain links. And does one have the stiff-limbed stance of Wrench, and does the other have Old Lady's scoliotic hunch? Have they come back to fill up Ezra's absence? No. This isn't Unc's trough. Fish a poisoned wad of beef from your pocket. Hang your arm over the fence. They eat as gently as horses, lick the tainted meat off of your palm. Good Tootsies. Swallow your hum. They stay where they are, staring. A wrong quiet falls.

The pool behind you is silent, and has been, and by the time you turn to see the kid blurred to a blot at the pool's bottom you're already sure he's been down there for too long.

You dive into the shallow end with your clothes on, streamline open-eyed underwater. Bubbles torrent from the kid's face. Blood slithers up from his heel like an animal crawling out of him. Swam himself unconscious on your command. You hate the prickling satisfaction this gives you, despise how you squat at the pool's bottom for a precious second to savor it.

He's tragically easy to lift, no heavier on your arms than the sleeves of your soaking shirt are. You drag him to the surface and beach him on the deck of the shallow end and stand knee-deep in it, pressing both palms into his ribs. Your hands sop up the chesty heat of his fever. Every sixth pump, hum breath into his chapped lips. You sicko. You psycho. You self-loathing, power-tripping, manslaughtering fucker. Some folks were just born wrong, and you're one of them. His throat ruptures. What he coughs up is yellow Gatorade-colored. Roll him onto his side. His heaves shrink to gasps, which blur into chants of *sorry*.

Back at the fence, the coyotes are watching.

"I'm getting back in." Casper crawls toward the lane.

And a wrong part of you would love to let him. Just to see. You grab him by the armpits before he can slide in.

Casper nocks his head under your chin. The plush stubble of it. "He ain't forever gone."

"Who?"

"RoboCop. Don't mountain his molehill."

The kid shrugs out of your arms and slants into the pool.

"You shouldn't," you say. "How're you feeling?"

"Plum peachy."

The length of that lie. You've had runners wear compression

socks to disguise the bruises from stress-fractured shins, kids who snuck out of exams and funerals and their own birthday parties to keep from missing practices. When Ducky broke her ulnar, she'd sat on the pool deck during squad practices, joking that she'd get vicarious fitness. She'd stuck around after the rest left. You'd gone back in and caught her swimming the workout one-armed, her cast propped on a kickboard. You'd sighed at the time, but now you know how that ended.

The kid sculls with his head out of the water, staring at you like he's waiting.

"The swim never won Kona for anyone," you tell him. "Enough water for today."

Casper can't pull himself onto the pool deck. He presses his palms into the coping and hops. His elbows buckle under his scant weight. You reach down to drag him, but he wades out through the shallow end. His gashed heel mutters blood. You bend down and swab it. The wound's inside is tie-dyed with all kinds of wrong colors. Casper lists toward his bike.

"Nope. You're with me."

"But my bike."

"You'll run back for it later."

Casper grins. "Trot and a rinse." He jolts toward the gate, where the coyotes stay waiting.

You rush ahead of him. The coyotes part for you, stepping off the sidewalk.

Casper nods to them. "Varms," he says neutrally. His head tips.

He sits on the moped like he's been sutured to it. Like how a whippet's panting lips don't gather foam until the race is over, Casper's illness only shows when he quits moving. You mount the moped behind him and slide your arms under his.

You tip from one foot to the other. Casper's scant but slack weight thwarts your grope for balance. "Sit up."

The kid straightens. His back muscles shiver against your stomach like a squatter's under a heavy barbell.

You wobble into the bike lane.

The nearest Urgent Care is five miles north, on the mainland. Casper braces his palms on the handlebars. Your forearms ache from fighting to keep them straight. The moped jerks and stutters. The speedometer's needle leans left of 20. It sinks below 10 as you climb Woody Hewett Bridge. Casper presses back against you like the wind's pushing him. Blood strands back from his heel in the breeze.

You lean around him, put your chin on his shoulder to see. His ear brushes your cheek.

"Tell me," he begs.

Your mouth runs from the night you first crawled to Unc all the way up to the one when you'd run over him. The words need to work on Casper's brain like your breaths had on his lungs. Forget thoughtlessness; you've got to think for him. Explain who Unc made you into. Give him your other, secret name. Warn him never to whisper it, even as your brain begs him to. The kid stays silent. Good egg. Just don't crack yet.

Urgent Care is the second right after Monkey Junction, behind a parking lot shared by an above-ground pool outlet and a Golden Corral. You swerve up the handicapped ramp onto the sidewalk. Ride right through the sliding doors to a front desk covered with gallon-sized bottles of hand sanitizer. The receptionist thumbing a Nintendo DS behind it looks suspended in the bottles' contents, a manchild preserved in formaldehyde.

"Y'all got an appointment?" he says.

You're all out of voice by then.

Casper twitches his head. "Benj." His mouth cups the name like a gem: who you are with yourself taken out of you, the 'I' fallen off the end. You weren't the only one who'd driven the kid this way; he'd gotten up every day, muted his aches, and gone along with the training.

You both brought each other to this.

A nurse hunches into the lobby with a wheelchair. The kid kicks it into her shins. You hum to him, pat the seat. His eyes get that look like a sheep when it surrenders to shearing. You push the kid back into an exam room and mouth mindless answers while the nurse frisks a desktop's keyboard. She ducks out without looking at Casper. The kid does leg extensions with the air in front of him, straining like he's locking out the full stack on a Cybex machine. Rumble from the back of his throat like he's gargling.

Ezra's phone pulses in your pocket. A URL texted from a guy goes by Wispy. A picture of Ducky frontrunning at the Mazatlan World Cup is the thumbnail. A followup message underlines it. *Praying for you, bruh-bruh.*

The link opens to a headline from Slowtwitch. "Meltdown in West Memphis." Every breathing and beating part of you plummets. You scroll between rectangles of text without reading. The photos alone are plenty. Far-off shots of Unc's farm, the clapboard barred behind turbines. The south pastures clotted with what was left of the sheep. The water trough that you'd run over embedded in the mud. The ground rough with paw prints and tire tracks. A photo of you and Unc from the summer he'd pulled you onto the deck. His elbow propped on your head. The stopwatches weighing your neck. One for every swimmer. Their names duct-taped on the backs of them. You can remember that day down to the test set: 10x100 best average on a sendoff ten seconds above each swimmer's goal split. Your thumbs had grown so sore from clicking the watches to get their splits that you'd quit timing them, just told each of them they were slow by tenths of seconds. That had gotten Unc's nods. You'd never timed anyone since. Took Ezra some time to catch onto that, but he'd waxed as defiant as Unc had promised when he did. Unc had said that Ezra was born right, that coaching him would rid you of your wrong reflexes, but Ezra had stormed off and you'd still stood on the deck and watched the kid drowning.

A sob burbles up through the kid's gargling.

"Doctor's coming, darling."

"Shucks a nerd." He rubs his throat. "Show me how to hum

Robo back. Need him see I can hurt more than him."

But it's too late for that. You delete Wispy's text, but someone will get word to Ezra. You've lost him, and losing him might well mean you've lost the kid. You don't trust Casper to choose you over him. If you could just fade out the way Unc had promised. If you could just go back—but can't. You'd tried that at Unc's farm, and look at what had happened. Only safe way is to leave them.

Ezra

A coyote corpse mars the camper's front porch. Worms of ground beef burrowed in its fangs. Benji's poison. The breeze lifts that half-digested reek from the coyote's slack jaw like it's still breathing. Toothmarks stipple its snout and flanks; it's been dragged. Paw prints pock the cul-de-sac. The air's pungent with sun-hot clots of beef. Through the pines, sunlight shrapnels off of spring traps. Sights and scents like pinched nerves. Ezra's all starve and parch. He goes in around back, feeling squinted at and squinting back through the trees—but not turning. Trying not to leave tracks. He swallows trail mix like pills, gulping a long-turned Yoohoo from the back of the fridge until corn syrup sticks to his teeth. Still not looking behind him. He spits back outside to the planter box and uproots Benji's herbs. They prickle out of the dirt like words gulped back from the cusp of speech.

A low whine wafts out of the woods. It rises to a squeal, more thickening than multiplying. Ezra slams inside and it clings to him, smoke-like. He beams the shower until it quiets. First rinse in a month. Dirt and grit hurt like scabs peeling off. His hair's uncombable, dreadlocked, reeky from chlorine. He gawks the futon and sprawls on it without drying. Milk-sick stomach. Calling his own bluff. He'd won his first youth triathlon at twelve, and he's quit every few seasons since. In smaller ways, it happens daily—hurt-deep in a tempo run or long bike ride, sitting up to coast while his thighs whiplash with lactate. Stepping off the track. If you don't want to stop, Benji says, you aren't going hard enough. But what's worse than any workout is the clarity that comes without training, how his brain chafes with days when it's not dulled by fatigue. Ezra's too used to that ambient ache. Too dependent on the way that it muffles things.

Ezra peels up from the sheets. A spin into town, he's thinking. That ambition's nixed as soon as he hurts standing. Like coal-walking, only the coal's inside his feet. A low burn marrows his bones. He hobbles around in weak search of his laptop and phone, though he suspects Benji threw both in the ocean. Dark clots in the camper and he doesn't turn on the light, letting his hands vague in front of him. By the time the moped chuffs into earshot he feels ghostlike. He steps out front through a screen door of flies, the burrowing reek of the beef and the dead coyote.

Benji parks, slits the engine, and sits. He's wrapped around Casper. Their bodies one weft silhouette. Ezra has to stare hard to unthread them: Casper's folded in Benji's lap, snoring tectonically. His hips are so narrow that he's sliding between Benji's thighs; Benji's feet still fit on the platform as he straddles him.

"He passed out in the pool. I had to dive in."

Casper's left foot is noosed in bandages.

"The heel?" Ezra asks—wants Benji to confess it.

Benji drips off the back of the moped with Casper distending his stomach: Benji's arms wrapped around Casper's tucked knees, fingers laced as if over his own gut. A wrongly jolly arrangement. He totes the kid around the side of the camper, humming. Ezra follows him back. Benji lays Casper down by the tipped planter boxes. He gathers the uprooted herbs, nodding as if greeting each of them. Ezra stomps on his fingers. Benji keeps humming, reaching for plants with his other hand.

"Drop the hick shit. Get him medicine."

"Did." Benji gnaws a sopping strand of hair. "It's MRSA. The doc up at Urgent Care cut out the infection. Prescribed Cleocin. That trap caulks your lungs, not that it licks a difference. They said he can't sweat on it."

"How long?"

Benji shoves up his Oakleys. The un-sunned skin around his eyes is as pale as gull shit. Ezra stares at that, afraid to look into them. Benji shuts his eyes as if sensing this. "Past Chapel Hill.

Three weeks."

Ezra's voice rashes up his throat like bile—that hot, and that urgently. He pukes the word. "Leave."

"If you let me."

Ezra stares at his foot. Was it the Piston; the brick? Was it the first time Casper passed him, or before Casper even arrived—was it something entirely inside Ezra that made Benji pull out all hope for him? He grinds his heel down on Benji's hand before lifting it.

Benji crawls toward Casper. Ezra stomps between his shoulder blades, flattening him.

He steps over Benji's back and racks Casper's knees on one arm, stringing his other behind Casper's shoulders. An outfit to lift. No more weight to the kid than wet clothes. Ezra carries him to the backdoor of the camper. He hears Benji standing behind him. Popping joints. Sand snorting under footsteps. Ezra pauses with the camper's door propped on his knee, feeling the stirred air of his approach.

"Ever walk into a greyhound shelter?" Benji asks. "One of these dish-licker shitholes. Sounds like construction. That's their teeth chattering. When whelps don't run, they get tremors. Get to shaking to where they can't eat. That's what I like about greyhounds: all nerve and no brain." Benji's breath scrapes his neck, voice snagging like a razor. "No such thing as skittish."

Ezra narrows through the door. He leans the kid's feet to the carpet, fumbling for the latch. The lock clucks. Casper's torso drifts down his legs.

A damp silence; then, through the door, humming. Benji's voice stretches as he rounds the camper, as if echoing in the very space that he's vacating. Ezra lunges for the front door, but he does the wrong thing: instead of locking it, he opens it. Screen of flies. Night browning the sky like turning meat. Casper's pickup slithers out of the cul-de-sac, shedding a snakeskin of gravel from its tires, and Ezra stares it all the way up Bromine Avenue without blinking. Benji swerves onto Ocean Street, and they're marooned.

Ezra slouches over to Casper. The kid's fever strobes. His body flickers with chills, a scant candle of heat. Ezra nerves a thumb to Casper's heel.

"Quit off," the kid whispers—talking past him. "I'm sleep."

A face-full of wind wakes him. Ezra cranes up, sluicing sleep. The door's open. Ezra trips out through the mesh of flies, the cloud-cut night behind as slick-pale as raw poultry. Casper stands in the middle of the cul-de-sac, swiveling.

"He'll be back."

Casper lifts his bandaged foot. "For what?"

Meaning *who*. Even Casper knows that Benji's only really been training him. How'd it take Ezra eight months to reckon it?

Ezra's pushes the words out like he's purging them. "He moved here for me. You're the carrot."

Casper fixes on Ezra a moment, then continues compassing. A skewed needle. His bandage unravels as he spins.

Ezra grudges over to him. "What're you doing?"

"Hearing for him."

A gathering hum. The sound wells and thickens like humidity. It clings to him, drawing sweat up from his skin. A soiled warmth microwaves his insides—the same sting he gets at the starting line.

"He's off with them varms. Hear him back in them trees." Casper stops and squints past Ezra. "Got show him. "

"You can."

"Open your own self. I'm too fast to be full-up of beans."

Ezra steps back, fumbling to translate that. *Open up..can of..* "

"I'm fixing prove it to him," Casper says. "Need him see I'm still moving."

"When he gets back."

"He's not backing. I got to go to him."

Ezra grabs Casper's arm. Casper stops spinning. In that exact second, Ezra has the sick sense that his grip has had the exact opposite effect of his intention, like how pumping the brakes on a bike to try to stop a collision causes the wheels to lock and the bike to slip into a skid. He lets go.

"Stop," Ezra says.

Casper shakes his head. "If he's gone, who's going to move me?"

The kid lunges into stride. Ezra stomps on his bandage on some dumb stubbing instinct and time totems; every motion stacks into one vertical instant.

Casper swings at Ezra as he trips, windmilling his fist into Ezra's chin. Ezra drops to the ground as fast and true as a plumb line. Casper runs off through the trees, the gauze unraveling like a fuse.

Ezra wobbles up with his vision sloshing but finds enough brain to think *flashlight*. Slumps back to the camper for it. Catches a toe on the coyote corpse and flies rise from it like shrapnel. Long grope for the flashlight. Then he's out the backdoor and urging through the parched pines, exhaling Casper's name— wanting the kid to hear him, but wincing at his own voice's volume, afraid of being heard by other things. Around spring traps washed by his flashlight. Through a humming that has a weight like laden air on his skin, as thick as humidity. Squelching over wads of Benji's poisoned ground beef. Dodging the sharp glint of spring traps. Ezra pictures Benji licking the traps' steel teeth and gaping them. He can't decide which idea makes him more queasy: Benji sleeping beside them, or leaving them alone to set traps for coyotes. Both are better than humming into Casper's dreams.

Ezra narrows his mind into each stride, but even his effort is spoiled by Benji's coaching. *Hips up. Fertile.* Benji's cues.

Ezra follows an old holding trench toward the Dow Plant. The humming divides into whines, distinct voices forming from the uniform noise like drops of dew.

The scrub baldens. The Dow Plant's tanks appear as Rorschach blots of dark. Ezra aims his flashlight to the ground. The beam spills into paw prints.

"Casper!" he shouts, then pinches his throat shut to mute his own breathing. "Mama," he tries—but quietly.

The kid's gasp is worse than that humming; worse, even, than the kid's midnight squealing. It's all inhale, like the inverse of a hiccup. The sound drags Ezra ahead like Casper glancing back at him. After the brick, the kid had been breathing just like this, laying his effort like an offering at Benji's feet.

The pines part around a clearing the size of a pool's deep-end. Splits ends of sumac sprout from the sand. The weeds are tangled around snapped branches and busted pinecones. More than that. Ezra's flashlight splashes off steel: a spring trap.

Instead of a coyote, it's gnashed around Casper's shin.

Casper. Mama. The kid. A fallow heat haloes him, and Ezra thinks of that warmth like the overflow of signals from Casper's nerves—as if the pain is too big for the kid's body. As if he's sweated it out, maybe.

Casper reaches up with both arms and pulls his torso over the sumac, dragging his leg and the trap behind him. No agony betrayed from his movement. Just intention. Exertion. *Bark on,* Benji'd said. Maybe he'd meant bark like a tree, Ezra's thinking: holding feeling inert in your roots. Outward, inward, same difference between effort and suffering, him and Casper.

The kid crawls toward the pines. Ezra thinks of the way that animals seek cover to die, wishes that he hadn't. He squats next to Casper. The kid growls at him.

The hum surrounding them simmers down. Nowhere—everywhere—straining breathing.

"We've got to move," Ezra says.

"Am."

True that Ezra's the one crouching. He breathes a mammal, carnal, backwashed burger kind of scent.

Snouts saw through the shadows between the trees. Ezra's flashlight glances off of yellow eyes between the trees: six, ten, a sudden dozen, eighteen. He cuts the flashlight beam to cut himself off from counting. The coyotes are circling, choking in on the clearing.

Casper tells Ezra, "Leave."

For a shard of a second, Ezra considers it. The idea passes through him like poison. He spits.

Casper's still crawling, dragging the spring trap. Pleading. "Leave."

Ezra gropes up the pine branch and slashes it in a circle. The coyotes snarl back. They form a crescent on the side of the clearing opposite Casper, and Ezra understands that he can hold them back just like that. Fend them off for as long as he swings. The same trick Benji thought Ezra couldn't learn: to bark brainlessly on, hold the pain and keep moving.

M a

The call comes nine minutes into Food And Feelings group. Cathy's in the middle of a sob about her fat-phobic stepmother's conflation of a healthy diet with morality. Picture Stevie Van Zandt cosplaying that Pokémon trainer lady you used to have a crush on. Bingo: Cathy. Sidebraid, clinic-disapproved crop-top—she even clutches the Body Neutrality Teddy to her stomach like that animé trainer held her Pokémon, shielding the rest of group from her flaunted abdominals. It's all I can do not to shout *thank you!* when my phone rings.

"Excuse me?" says Cathy.

Doro lunges out of his chair and opens the door for me.

Airplane mode is facility policy, but the hope for your texts has been the only thing keeping me still in these sessions—not so much those texts' content as the thought of you sneaking out of Benji's cocoon to message me, that we might transgress as a team. I've been waiting for you to call ever since leaving, darling; for two months I've been grating my teeth. And now here I am squealing at your name on my screen. I jog into the hall, all *sorry* and *emergency*.

And get an earful of humming.

"Ez?" I say.

But know who that voice belongs to with the same reluctant certainty I'd had when I first felt you kicking me. Your dead father is calling.

The hum broadens and reaches. It has tendrils in it—a texture and a grip. And a past. Twenty-seven years back, it had wrapped around me in Dasharath and tugged me under the grandstand of an abandoned soccer stadium. Twenty-seven years

I've been waiting for my thoughts of him to become him, some-times wanting it. He'd taught me that mental energy could take a thoughtform, growing into a being of sheer feeling. He'd made me promise never to follow, bring up, or think of him, but here he is—summoned. All these Food and Feelings sessions must have drawn him from the thoughtless parts of my mind despite my efforts to visualize otherwise during guided meditation. "Hello, Tulpa," I say.

The hum ends.

"No. Ezra."

The voice is too croupy to come from your lungs. It's got the sludgy pitch of a surrendering appliance, like when the com-pressor broke on the Sprinter van's fridge. It would be one thing if your father's reincarnation were calling—another if you'd in-herited that hum, or were channeling him, even. But it's not. "You're just Benji."

"I'm the curse," Benji says. "It's like the ocean pushes back the island. How it should. I have to push Tootsies ahead so I can flood into their footprints. But I'll drown them if they stop moving."

"Who taught you to hum?"

"I welled up in Ezra. I had to crack him."

"Let me talk to him."

"I am."

I pace the stuccoed hall, bright with a sloppy mural of fruit-ing trees. Each one's got a kid's Sharpied signature under it. I look at every fruit depicted and see its macro and micronutrient contents—the freaking Rain Woman of calories.

"He's zenning," Benji's saying. "Record shape. You should see."

"Give him the phone."

The brushed noise of the phone cupped and passed. The scrape of it pressed to a stubbled cheek. "Ma?"

The voice is too yours to be—not even warped by the con-nection's distortion, as if you'd pressed your lips to my ear to whisper. And the breath is too wet. I picture you swallowed by Benji, his jaw hinging open to spit your voice like a Pez dispenser. His stomach distended with your shape. Better him than me. "You're sick," I say.

"Why I left. What I'm saying." He swallows. The Pez shuts in my head. "I'm saving them."

Then the pleated beep of him hanging up on me.

I bore my forehead into a blotchily painted blueberry bush (per five ounces: 84 calories, 4 grams of fiber, 25% of the RDA for manganese). Cathy's describing her stepmother's evangelistic Atkins kick loudly enough for me to hear clearly. All these sessions give you narratives to retrofit to your experiences: anorexia as a grope for control, a way of numbing feelings. Most of these people are here to come up with a reason that they're a victim.

A plaque bolted below the bush says, *Courtesy FRIENDS School of Tetlin 5th Graders, Class of '01*. You'd've been in their year, running laps around whatever patch of permafrost they got released on to shiver through recess. But that's not the swerve my life took. If it's up to me, you'll never even know I set foot here. We each have our cocoons.

When Benji'd said I should leave, I'd been proud that you hadn't protested. Took you long enough to wear out my company. Don't hear me wrong, darling: I'd be stoked to keep you on as a permanent roommate, but selfishly. You deserve bigger and brighter things. So I'd left you to do you, went to give a shot at getting back to doing me.

I scroll through our Messenger thread, re-reading the updates I've been sending. All those photos I'd taken on my discretionary bike rides are blued by the underlying checkmarks of your 'read' receipts. Has Benji had your phone this whole time? Has he been the one seeing me?

I thumb over to your profile page. George Wispler's shared a *Slowtwitch* article, tagged you in the link. "Meltdown in West Memphis." I open the page. An ITU-looking type hoists a finishing tape over his head in the photo at the top of the article.

Garth Yelton achieved a World #1 ranking under the tutelage of coach Benji Newton, the caption reads. *Two weeks after Yelton quit Newton's squad, three of his teammates were declared missing.* The tagline blurts below: "One of the sport's most prominent—and controversial—figures has paved over disaster on his path to fame." Strange that Benji isn't pictured. I scroll farther down, skimming. A training camp on an Arkansas farm, Benji's childhood home. Partial quotes from Yelton about potions and spells, bent into the syntax of the author: "Yelton claims that the entire squad had made light of Benji's superstitions until they arrived in West Memphis, where "everything escalated...[Newton] had them dancing to his literal music." My heartbeat fills my stomach. My gut feels as packed as the fourth box of granola.

Two springs ago, authorities had responded to a 'distressing' 911 call from a West Memphis farm owned by Benji's uncle. The responding deputy had found the last three of Benji's athletes racing around the perimeter of the property, blind to his signals and deaf to his questioning. Violent upon the deputy's attempts to restrain. All had run the soles off of their sneakers. Heat strokes. Severe dehydration. Incoherent upon stabilization. Psychotic breaks. Benji and his uncle nowhere to be found. Rumors that the uncle had bugged out to Nepal. Benji still AWOL.

I scroll farther. Pictures of a clapboard house valleyed between rolling pastures. Wind turbines. A crushed water trough tipped on its side. A photo of a young Benji on the pool deck, his neck laden with stopwatches. A man props his elbow on Benji's head. I know those long cheekbones, those pale eyes. My thumb rests on the man's head. I press into the screen like I might smudge it, but I swear I can feel his face's contours under my fingers. All the times I'd traced those features in Dasharath nearly three decades back, magnetized by his humming.

That's your father standing next to Benji.

"Was that him?" Doro leans out of the meeting room. His shawl is bunched around his shins like pant-legs, the hem tucked into his steel-toed work boots.

"Not the him who you're thinking."

I've done my best to shut up about you since checking in, passing the Sharing Spoon every time Doro pushes the subject toward family in Group Therapy. He brought me here as a 'Participatory Speaker,' waiving the admission fee and providing a private room. Most of my speaking looks like abstractly answering his questions about you. I don't like the claim behind his inquiries. The way that he asks, you'd think that you two were related; sometimes I think that he thinks that's true. Your lifetime is long enough for someone's fears to become wants, for wants to get daydreamed into truths.

"It wasn't anything," I tell him.

"Great." Doro props the annex door. I get the gist: either I get back to nodding and snapping for Cathy, or share with him. So I fill him in. Sorry; 'fill' is a trigger word at this clinic (his). Let's say that I bring him up to speed about Benji and the cocoon that he's spinning.

Doro gives me a look like I just hot-potatoed the Sharing Spoon. "So this was your getaway."

"I didn't say that." But feel the truth retroactively, the way your tendons only ache the day after strength training. "I've got to go back."

"Is that a need, or a feeling?" This is one of Dr. Reyes's DBT refrains. Doro's voice drops and rasps when he resorts to that rhetoric, like he's smoked four decades' worth of cigarettes in one second.

"Benji must've taken Ez's phone," I say. "He's had it the whole time, maybe."

"You're telling me that you're worried because your son's adhering to the terms you, him, and his coach agreed to?"

"It's not just that."

Doro lets the door slacken shut, waits for me to explain.

Twenty-seven years ago, your father had begged me to forget him; before I could make that promise, he was gone. I've done all I could to follow through, but fallen short of that mark. His bones lurk in your face, Love. I thought that some time away from you might help me shut him out of my brain, but it only shifted his state: ever since I arrived in Tetlin, I've heard his humming in everything from the tardy water spurting toward the shower head to the whir of my Cervelo's churning chainring.

During our two seasons in Dasharath, he'd taught me that a Tulpa only gestates in its maker's concentration; once it's been in these dimensions long enough, the umbilical that tethers it to its creator breaks. It starts to fend for its own food, forcing itself in front of people to feed off the belief that each encounter creates. Your father had told me to forget him so that he'd disappear and spare me the grief, but some more rudimentary part of him has been fighting for nourishment ever since the stadium collapsed on top of him. What sentient being doesn't run into rifts between desires and instincts? Benji can't know about that summer in Nepal, the nearly blind man who helped make you with me. Whatever I'd heard him hum had gotten bent into your father's voice by my own memory. I have to believe that. I can't risk explaining.

Doro leans in and nods like I'm already talking. I can't let the Tulpa have his belief to feed off of; I could tell the man I was the corporeal avatar of Pachamama and he'd start heaping offerings at my feet.

I brush past him. "I've just got to go back."

"Why don't we take a walk about it?"

Like that I'm eighteen and pretending not to be pregnant, Doro bare-chested and handstanding on the Malecón. Walks have been our default for drawing out whatever isn't happening between us ever since that day I dropped my whole wallet into the sawed-off gallon jug he was busking with. "If you use your feet," I say.

The sliding back doors are rimmed with spritzers triggered to douse us in eucalyptus and lemon oil—nature's DEET. Alaska in August is all bald eagles, dead salmon, and mosquitoes big enough to blood-suck a moose woozy.

We take a long lap of the facility. The main building's façade is cement sculpted like logs, complete with a solid decorative chimney. It's the kind of synthetic cabin that might house a restaurant at Magic Kingdom. (Remember how we'd run between rides; how you'd dip your turkey leg in your Dippin' Dots, which summed out to 632 calories?) The Theodore L. Rankin III Memorial Wellness House is Doro's vision, bankrolled by his family's goldmining money. A tax writeoff for his father; for him, a chance to recover evangelistically. Doro'd emailed me invitations for sixteen years—offering discounts, then free enrollment, then room and board and a salary.

He'd said I could come here and start a new life. I felt like he'd meant more than the kind that recovered Anees, Orthees, and Buleemies describe—one where every waking second isn't hogged by thoughts of food. I've been getting the hunch that he's picturing me staying in Tetlin, following through on the life we'd brushed up against twenty-seven years ago in Peru.

"You need to consider this," Doro's saying. "You're making real strides in your relationship."

"With who?"

"Food."

This from the man who'd taught me how starvation could soothe.

We veer off the gravel path that perimeters the property, through the hemlocks flanking its four acres. Soggy singletrack striates the trees. Roots and soft patches of mud make the going ankle-breaking. Good luck running fast enough to get out of Zone One without tripping. The terrain seems designed with this in mind: walking is the most strenuous of the Wellness House's Approved Activities. Doro and I had done more than our share of that between Herradura and Pachacamac. He'd covered the path on his hands, looking like he was floating, but these days his physique's more Emeril than emaciated; during Group Movement, he wears a powerlifter's wrist wraps to demonstrate handstands.

"I think it could be productive to share about this in DBT," he says. "Try and get down to the emotion behind the motive."

"What's that mean?"

"That's up to you." Doro says this with a speed that suggests he's got his own thesis.

"Go on."

"I guess what I'm wondering is, do you want to go home because Ezra needs you, or because you want him to need you?"

We round the southwest edge of the property. The statue of Theodore Rankin Jr. towers a half-mile up Main Street, glowering at us through the trees. The air is stippled with lemon-drunk, cockroach-sized mosquitoes.

Tetlin is the remnants of a boom town gone tie-dye, founded by Doro's great-great-grandfather. The original Theodore Rankin had panhandled gold out of a stream and bought up the whole slope that it ran down. He'd treated his miners so well that folks stuck around even after the gold was tapped out. Their descendants tended toward that trope common to inheritors of prosperity, pursuing obscure mediums of the arts. Lots of elaborately furred mailboxes and lawns brooded over by sculptures made from torn-off action figure arms. Theodore 'Ted' Jr. had opened an art gallery. Doro's grandfather Trey, the third of the Theodores, sculpted the bronze statue of Ted that's staring us down. Doro's father, Theodore 'Just Theodore' Rankin IV, is at work on a sculpture of Trey to hunker heavyhandedly in its shade. Two generations of Rankins will soon glower down at art shoppers. Doro insists that he's the fifth and final of his name.

When I told you I was riding through the Yukon, that wasn't all-the-way true. I drove up to Tetlin to heal my relationship with food. My peers are mostly heirs and heiresses with partially-completed liberal arts degrees. Their monthly allowances likely exceed the property value of our dirt patch in Kure. Many have been here more than once. Girls like Cathy tally up past admissions like tours of duty. Some so skinny that their legs look like they have extra joints in them from the jut of their hipbones.

Others with cut knuckles and dozen-pack-a-day gum habits and yellow teeth. They call Doro Adoro, or Dory; they might want to drain him of the active ingredient for a sixth Theodore Rankin. Doro says he hates it, and I believe him. Softy never had a horny bone in his body. The same singlemindedness that had landed him that pommelhorse scholarship to UA-Fairbanks keeps him focused on the rhetoric of recovery.

The other patients talk about wanting to starve themselves small, to fast until they feel clean. That's no longer my problem. I need to feel exact: to know that I've replenished every calorie, electrolyte, and vitamin that I've spent. Doro was the one who'd made me believe I belonged. He'd told me that a disorder was anything that got in the way of your daily functioning.

Darling, you've seen how I am with food, making an optimization problem out of every plate. It got worse after you swooned at Chapel Hill. I was testing your perspiration for sodium, asking you to step on the scale before and after workouts to reckon your sweat rate. I had to keep you from bonking again, balance output and expenditure like a chemistry equation.

Sometime around the time Benji arrived, I realized I was putting more effort into calculating calories than goal times. At some point I quit optimizing and started maximizing, taking daily long rides and replenishing with entire boxes of granola. You thought I was preparing my legs for the Yukon cycling; really I was trying to open up enough space to take in as much food as possible without slipping above racing weight. No room for speed work or recovery days. It was more about movement than optimal race preparation.

That was enough to convince me I needed a change. When I'd been planning that cycling trip to the Yukon, this was what I'd always intended—but I'd kept putting it off, telling myself that you needed me. That was just my excuse.

For the past eight months, my waking hours have been just as crammed as my summer of dawn-to-dusk cycling. Mornings start with process group, which leads into interpersonal effectiveness before proceeding to Food and Feelings, followed by body image group, culinary group, mindfulness group, and an unofficial, optional secretive vape group on the back patio during nap or rest hour. Then come the afternoon therapies: art, nutrition, dialectical behavior. Three meals and three snacks to fuel us through this. All food is prepared and portioned by staff, without a single scale or nutritional label. The kitchen is stocked on a meal-by-meal basis. When we eat, we're required to keep touch with all five of our senses. No one leaves the table until everyone's cleaned their respective plate.

In Process Group, Marjorie has us log the extraneous elements of *Where's Waldo?* illustrations. (The idea is to appreciate the entirety of the composition, resisting the tendency toward detail-oriented thinking.) In Art Therapy, we fondle Play-Doh as a tactile mindfulness exercise. In DBT, Dr. Reyes teaches us to inhabit self-wisdom by paying nonjudgmental attention to our feelings; we have to allow our rational mind to recognize our emotional mind's needs. Every 3:45 Alaska time you'll find me listening to her run a striker around the inside of a penny-filled meditation bowl while I visualize my safe place. Dr. Reyes asks us to remember a bad time, then restore our mental image of that safe place. *Bad time, safe place,* she'll say, prompting us to shift states. The picture books, the Play-Doh, Dr. Reyes's "Red Light, Green Light" style games—there's a definite preschool vibe, but also the exhaustingly holistic approach that belongs at an Interfaith Convention. I've navigated every exercise like a grudging atheist, praying to no one that something will change my mind. Doro's strategy seems to be to expose us to every coping strategy and see where we stick. I fall back on old tactics.

As soon as Cathy struggles down her last bite of dinner, we're released for free time. I spend all of mine on the bike.

Every evening I ride for as long as the generous daylight permits. Cycling is not an Approved Activity. Approved Activities include and are limited to 'naps or rest time, meditation, supervised walking, and staff discretion.' Doro had had the discretion to let me bring my bike, honoring the sole term I'd insisted on before accepting his offer to serve as a Participatory Speaker. Every night he sits up for me in his office. There's an aerial photo of Herradura behind his desk, the southern arm of its bay marred by the abandoned planetarium where he and I starved the summer before you came wailing. Doro glanced from it to me every time I wheeled my bike by. After a month of my silence, he'd told me that was where he went when Dr. Reyes played her meditation bowl. I'd hoped he'd picked that place because of the way that he'd felt at the time—the dumb calm that comes from chronic hunger, a slow slide down Maslow's Hierarchy—not because of who he'd thought I could be. I'd just nodded. He'd been slow to cut the porch light and lock the door, moving with the deliberateness of someone waiting to hear something. But I'll never tell him my safe space. It belongs to you and me. Every night, Doro asks with his lagging. I answer with a goodnight high-five. I wheel my bike to my bedroom. More pictures of Lima on the wall. The Bajada de los Baños. The Domingo Orué Metro station. I can't decide whether Doro redecorated for my arrival, or originally furnished the clinic this way—surrounding himself with pictures of the place where I'd mistaken him for your father, the man he never quite tried to be. Has he been trying fool to trick himself, or fool me?

My headboard is engraved with the Eating Disorder Victim Acceptance Speech, a spiel invented (if not etched) by Doro: *My relationship with food inhibits my daily functioning. I will repair that relationship until order is restored.* It took that phone call from Benji to fully believe that this statement applied to me.

How had I not seen whatever this was coming?

These months in Tetlin have helped me dredge up feelings that all those years of starvations and stuffings had been smothering. When Dr. Reyes whispers, *bad place*, I've been coming across pangs more like nausea than starvation—not the lack of something so much as the presence of a mistake. I was being poisoned by something. First I thought it was what Doro'd talked me out of doing in Lima, but maybe it was what I'd left Benji to do to you.

"I have to drive back," I tell Doro.

"Look," he says. "Listen. If you really think it's this urgent, why don't you fly? Check on him. Leave the van. You can pick up with us next week. I'll send you the worksheets."

"Can't miss the worksheets."

"Continuity is important for habit reformation." Doro takes my arm. His palms are as hard they were twenty-seven years back—more like heels than hands, with callouses as bulging as blisters. "This has been a long time coming. You've done so much work just to admit that there's work you should be doing. Don't walk away from that."

"I'll be driving."

"I'll book you a round-trip ticket. I'll get Ez one, too. Bring him back with you. Intake's low. He can have his own room. You know I've been meaning to meet him." As if the thing keeping you and Doro apart has been his own schedule instead of me. "Eva," he says, "Please."

He uses my name with the weight of a word he's been speaking for decades—like he's been chanting it in my absence, invoking me. I never should've told him about Tulpas. But it's the way that your name came out of his mouth that sickens me. He said it like he's the one who picked it. For a second, I let myself pretend that he did.

Picture what your childhood would've been if I'd accepted his first invite: nighttime bike rides and slow jogs over the ankle-spraining singletrack and your college paid for by a man who wears fair-trade alpaca-wool shawls and believes that our planet is a sentient woman starved into a coma by humanity.

Would you have called him all but Dad? Would you have hung so hard on Benji's every word if you had? I'm all for dismantling the patriarchal familial model, but I still can't help feeling that my single-parenting deprived you of something.

I bet you'd want to come back with me. I think I want that, too, and that's why I know that I have to leave. Just as clearly as the past that you didn't have, I can see our alternate future: if I fly home and return with you, there won't be any more Ironmans. You'll practice handstands forget about your VO2 max and never toe the line to find out how far your body can take you. I can't deprive you of that opportunity. I'd rather spend the rest of my life nodding off counting calories instead of sheep.

"I'll go ahead and book your ticket," Doro's saying. "I can drive you to Fairbanks in the morning."

"But you'll miss out on your worksheets."

He tilts his head back and spits. The saliva spreads as it falls, like a cast-net expanding. I'd seen him do the same at the offerings the rich laid before a saint. I have a feeling he and I would place him on opposite sides of that analogy.

"Why don't you want Ezra to know about this place?" he asks. "Is it me?"

The same reason I can't tell you all the way about your father: the part of me that needs treatment would only be nourished by your belief. You see me as all empirical, a walking scientific case study, but I only cling so firmly to the double-blind-proven concrete because that's what I wish everything in the world would be.

Behind Doro, a dog trots out of the trees. I'd know that black-and-gold brindle and thick coat on any continent: a Tibetan mastiff. The same sheepdogs I'd once watched your father fill a soccer stadium with and hum into a sleep so deep that they starved. It drops its jaw without barking, and I swear I can hear the hum brimming in its throat like a pipe channeling distant water.

Doro follows my stare over his shoulder. "Shit."

"Don't look at it."

I run back toward the main building. Through the front window, the Food and Feelings group crane out of their chairs, watching. I can picture what this must look like to someone crushing on Doro. I slow to a walk, hoping to save as much of his face as I can.

"Kermit!" someone shouts. "Jesus!"

I turn slow. Doro's holding the mastiff by its leash, walking it toward the road. A lady dressed in a tourist's excessive Gore-Tex jogs toward them. She takes the leash and blows Doro a chapsticked kiss. The dog follows her down the street, but gapes back at me.

Doro sidesteps me.

"Thanks," I say. "For this. Everything."

He yanks the Wellness House's door so open that it lays flat against the false logs. "Don't come back until you want to be here."

Ezra

He unspools himself swinging circles with that pine branch. Pictures his DNA unwound and rearranged, reconfiguring him into a plant. Rooted by his rotation's momentum. A soiled heat sprouts in his hands. It vines up his biceps, his shoulders, blooming. Cramps thorn his ribs. His lungs shrink from the prick of them. The hurt blurs: he's slashing laps of a pool, orbiting a track, grinding into the big chainring, draining his lungs screaming. The coyotes lurk just out of the branch's reach, lingering.

Every infinite instant. Ezra falls into the awful extension of an Ironman marathon's middle miles. The repetition of his task obscures time, the over and over and over of the circles he swings with that branch as taxing and simple as willing race-laden legs through identical strides.

Then they're gone. It's less leaving than drying up; Ezra detects their absence by moonlight's entry, the silvering of spaces before shaded by solid bodies.

Casper's passed out in the sumac. A rug of blood coats the ground. Ezra can't stop himself swinging. As soon as he goes still, he'll crumple beside the kid. A grating fills the air, as of cramping machinery; Ezra's mind flies to the Piston, then swings back toward Casper and sees.

Of course. The kid's teeth are chattering.

Ezra spins and spins. Has the dizzy idea that his rotations are keeping everything suspended, like current stirring sediment; as soon as he stops, the consequences will settle. Kid's heel jerking up like a beckoning finger from leaves jeweled with blood. Sun gleaming off those ringed grabs of sumac. The sky tallows with sunrise, waxy light dripping between the leaves. Ezra spinning.

Casper facedown, flicking his un-trapped leg up behind him like the back half of a stride.

"Woah, there!"

Ezra spins into sound. A guy leaps back toward the home-facing side of the clearing. He shields himself with one hand, fumbling with his other to hitch up his jeans. Ezra keeps spinning. He takes in the intruder in glimpses with each revolution, like a zoetrope going too slowly to suggest the illusion of motion. Guy shirtless under his leather jacket. Seamless crease from that rawhide to his salt-hard chest. Slickly thin: his waist narrow but toneless. Sharp precipice of pelvis. Jeans slanting off of his left hip. Wading into the sumac, leaping back. "Lord."

As if his eyes are nerved to this guy's, Ezra stops spinning. His vision settles on Casper. No vertigo. No twisting intestines. Just the nauseous smear of the kid's leg.

"I was putting out traps."

Guy says it like Ezra'd asked. Only he isn't holding anything but his phone and his pants. He taps the home button twice, then jerks his thumb up the screen to whisk off whatever app he'd been on—appearing for a moment to be hitchhiking, the thumb stalling at the apex of its sweep; and he is, really, hopping onto Ezra and Casper's emergency. Where'd he been going before that? Not church. No wholesome reason for some rando to wander out here. Ezra gets the queasy feeling that this has to have been caused by Benji.

The guy's dialing with the phone close to his face. Three beeps, then he switches it to speaker. He hangs up on the second ring.

"You do that?"

"What?"

Guy glances from Ezra to Casper. Casper's still swinging his free leg toward his butt as if running. Ezra wants to stomp on it. That incessant motion somehow makes the kid seem less alive.

Guy's holding the phone half-mast to his jacket. Scraping his tongue off his teeth like hair's stuck on it. "Did you do that to him?"

The woods are suddenly very empty yet full of them. Silence but for the skid and squish of the kid's free leg as he swings it. The guy's finger twitches on the phone; with a click like a ruptured tendon, the camera's flash winks. Ezra knows that Benji's seeing this with the sub-logic certainty of a dream.

"What shit did he feed you?"

"Who?"

Ezra grabs the guy's phone-holding wrist with both hands and bends it back. The guy drops it. The phone lands face-up, the Emergency Call display blanching its lock screen.

Ezra dives to it and dials.

"911. What's the location of the emergency?"

Ezra muffs his ear with the phone. The screen's an ice cube thawing against his lobe; he only senses his own sunburn by that contact, the phone's flat-wet coolness. The guy backs away with both hands up, like Ezra's still swinging that branch.

"Sir?" the operator asks.

"Yes?"

"Are you in danger?"

The guy whirls and sprints. One arm pumping, other pinning his jeans. Stiff as those first steps off the bike in an Ironman.

"Him," Ezra says, and throws the phone after him. His nerves feel to roll down his legs as he stands. He tips over, falls flat beside Casper.

The kid's teeth are still chattering.

Casper

Dag-nab, is this fever welling. Melting up to my head like a too-hot GU gel taped upside a Felt DA's top tube, pinched between some Robocopping age-grouper's teeth. And varms licking their snarls like they've bonked and I'm the very sweet sauce that might restock their glycogen. No can, varms; y'all're just arched off Benji's poison. I can't cure what ails me.

Their panting reeking as rich-sweet as the gel-breath of them age-groupers. It'd smell swell if you didn't see the snarls it was coming from. Heard once dirt's only dirty when it's out the ground. But what's the ground in? What if the GU gel's packet is gel? Picture the kind of world that would be. 'What is Pre-Creation?' To give y'all the *Jeopardy!* Sky and sea and ground would un-sort and we'd all swill down to Firmament. Not that I wouldn't used-to. I can get settled just about anyhow. One trick I got going for me. Been times I was so neck-deep in hurting I'd conk out on the bike and keep pedaling. Waking up red-eyed as the light I was running, trucks swerving and honking and my numb legs still chugging the biggest chainring. Benj calls that Zenning. Says it feels like he's petting me. Yessir, I can used-to about anyhow, long's I stick one way long enough the squirm ebbs. Long's I don't try to hold myself and instead let the place hold and decide my shape. I can't let myself get stuck the way I was rut-bound with Adam the Atom Man. Whittled full seasons away staying stagnant, feasting fat.

RoboCop had that branch a-slice and a-whomp. The thirstiest varms still slurping their snarls, or the least horny. And that yap came back up my ankle like my own nerves were the bitch squeaking her heat to where even the Everywhen started seeming cozy. So I done what I always do. Oozing down. Getting used.

Ezra

New Hanover Regional Medical Center looms more college than hospital, a sleek conglomerate of beiged cement, stainless steel, and gently bulging glass walls that look like they belong from one to a whole cluster of buildings depending on where you're standing. Ezra chases the ambulance around back on the moped. The EMTs wheel Casper's gurney through a set of double-doors. A security grunt-points, then escorts Ezra around to the public entrance. Ezra wants her to carry him, feels in egregious need of his own gurney.

The atrium is crowded with inexplicably angled ladders. They flank the pleather chairs in the waiting area and loom over the opposite wall's plastic foliage, their tops falling full basketball goals short of the ceiling. A toolbox and a cell phone are marooned on the platform topping the one beside the front desk.

Shania Twain trickles out of invisible speakers. The receptionist mutter-hums along to it. Her desktop's screen is reflected off a mirrored magnetic board mounted on the wall behind her: Basspro.com. Camping supplies.

Ezra leans both-handedly on the counter. "Mama."

"Oh, darling." The receptionist sucks in her cheeks until the suction makes a wet sound. "I'll need her name."

"His. The kid with the leg. The spring trap. He just came in the ambulance."

The receptionist's cheeks recede deeper. "Name?"

"Ezra Fogerty."

"And you are?"

"Next of kin."

"Darling." The receptionist sets an inch-thick stack of forms beside his face. "These will just take a minute."

Ezra shuffles through the papers. Intake form. Insurance waiver. Dozens of pages asking to check off any and all that apply to the patient's family history: cancer, heart failure, schizophrenia, toe fungus.

The receptionist says, "Just the tics."

"Come again?"

"Your signature." She taps an 'x'-marked line beside 'signature of representative' on the first page. "Just sign by the 'x's. Tic-tac-toe. Get it?"

He writes *Casper Swayze*. He puts his own name down under 'patient'. Ma's BlueCross policy for insurance. He forges through his forgery with his hand cramping. Eight hours swinging that branch. Translate that effort to an Ironman: 50-minute swim, 4:25 bike, 2:40 marathon.

The sliding doors roll open with the exact sound of the receptionist sucking her cheeks. It matches something else he's heard before, some regular effect from a program on the SyFy channel. Spaceship doors?

A guy in a construction vest slouches toward the ladder.

"You're back soon," the receptionist says to him.

He sings Blake Shelton loud enough to drown out Shania Twain.

The receptionist mouths a word that looks like *tenure* at Ezra.

He slides the form to her.

She drops it beside her keyboard; Ezra watches her add a tent to her shopping cart in the magnetic board's reflection. She points toward the chairs. "He's not ready to be seen."

As if the kid's backstage donning an Othello costume. Ezra's stuck deciding between the sock and buskin; isn't sure whether he's on the edge of grinning or crying. The kid won't be toeing the line. Wispy unpacking his bike box at the Laguna Resort for an all-expenses-paid starter's fee and suite. Forget a course record; Ezra could tempo to the finish line. Nothing between him and the win but him. Not even Benji.

Ezra snack-dispenses a Snickers and takes a germ-upholstered seat. Sun seeps through floor-to-ceiling windows, its brightness petrified into the congealed shine off the tiles. It lathers a nauseous ficus's plastic leaves. Ezra shuts his eyes, listening to the guy on the ladder and the receptionist humming separate tunes. The hums fuse into Benji's. Behind Ezra's heavy eyes, coyotes leap over spring traps.

A nudge spares him from dozing. A nurse stands over him. "Dr. Walsh is ready to see you."

"Not me."

"You're the brother, right?"

"Whose?"

"Ezra's."

"Casper?"

"You're built just like him." She takes him back to a closet-sized room walled with x-ray lights.

A lady holding a leg shoves through the door on its far side. She swings the foot at Ezra. He leaps back.

The lady tucks the leg under her armpit and offers her hand. "Kidding. Sorry. I'm Dr. Walsh."

Ezra stares at that leg. Only plastic. A prosthetic. He'd nightmared it into Casper's actual limb.

Even the lucid truth of it's gruesome. MRSA had spread to the kid's blood, Dr. Walsh says, then his bones. *Necrotizing.* The trap hadn't even been the deciding factor. No choice but disarticulation of the lower limb.

Casper

Coming to in full bleach. Bright like a soap bar and the blow off an air conditioner scrubbing me. Feeling like a mouth's inside getting rinsed out, with a hunch I was the cuss getting cleaned. One second my leg's the GU gel packet that trap bit into, squeezing all the sweet energy out of me; then this gleam and noise biting into me, coffined in an ambulance at the back-end of one blink.

Our rush roadkilling varms. Another under every bump that we're taking. Way they get my trapped leg to yapping has me swearing I'm standing, scrunching it between the jumping floor and gravity. I try-tip up, but RoboCop's leashed me down. Wish it were Benji, but I don't crane around—glancing trickles back hope to who's chasing you like the red out a melting GU gel. RoboCop on my ass slurping the very glycogen out of me. If I could just stock Benji's muscles like glycogen, but he might as well be on some Dave Scott keto bullshit. I don't give a hoot if they feed me jizz or nothing or tuna. Don't need no fuel for my move but the fear of Shadefoot sneaking up to me.

I look stiff ahead with my eyes tunneling, but the walls instead of the end are the light, and that trap gnashed on my leg's the farthest I can see. Cracks spread up them walls as I reach. Then I see wider: them cracks are my veins sprouting out my elbows. They run up to racks where my organs are hanging and my blood's gone clear inside—paled with my own scaredness. Past that a screen's winking. And ever wink has a beep. And them winks and beeps match each out-punch of my heart and I'm as coward as I'd ever been, seeing my *in* taken out of me. Swapping it with RoboCop's engine oil filling. My very glycogen. But I'd rather be nothing than him. I won't be done into no machine.

Yet here I beep, strapped down with my out-tugged tendons tying me. Getting field-dressed. One foster I run from sent me to stir the ducks when her pointer pulled up with gout. Once it's hit, a duck's eyes roll down. The growing ground's their last sight. And I'll be damned if ducks' eyes don't stay that way when you gut them, like they're looking at their insides coming out. Them morsels typically went to the pointer, but that time I fetched them the foster said I should eat them. After four forties her saying turned to making. She pushed those guts to me with the muzzle of the Remington and held the organs out. I'd put worse in my mouth. When I finished she said I should lick her fingers.

"Dog's work, son," she said.

I ran that very gloaming. Left her conked by the muttering fire. I poked an ember with a twig and burn grew up it and set the twig at her hair's edge and left her, the burn growing as she snored. I ran on account of the guts, but I put the flame in her hair for what she said: son's one thing I won't abide no one calling me.

There I go sinking into Everywhen. Bringing that past up to get some shade on this shiny place. So much for facing your reckoning. I face my face to that trap. Only there's no trap, and no bumps, just one-them skinny TVs with a grease-painted burger lipsticked in ketchup, slow-spinning. The sound's killed, and the food looks like sheer sex without the distraction of the commercial man's yapping: that as bun slick as if someone's busted on it, squeaky-shiny as the varm bitch crying her heat. I'll take duck guts over Hardee's ten times. Infinity. Goes to show what kind of country. Benj telling me how to move feels just as sex-sweet. Ever time I run how he wants, this warm wells up my legs like the sticky of that GU gel I was mentioning.

Like a worm pre-to bursting. And I don't never want to burst with Benj or vice-versa, but when I do how he tells, I just know that we both get that same busting feeling. But where in him does it well? Them long hairs he chews, maybe. Maybe that does boil down to sex—a thinner version, but still sex's essence: like how water stays water through thin and thickening, heatening from ice into wet into steam. Busting's the vaporous striving brought on by that heat. It's instructing ever atom's nuclear from here to Creation's hem. The sky reared up and sea sifted down to denominate and land fractioned a hairline between but they all blend to one blue in the distance and that's because they emerged as one substance split into separate heat-speeds. I'm saying sex is that substance. And my skull's like to bust. Cannot brain all I'm thinking. Too much glucose. Where's Robocop to slurp the GU out of me.

I swing off the cot to quit that TV. Sure, swinging smarts some, but welcome to my every-daily. I reach a foot down. My veins rear from my arms. They tear off with the clear in them spurting. The yap of my machined heartbeats seals into one wail. I lurch a next step with the bit leg and that foot don't come under me. The floor leaps up and I take it like a duck, falling and staring down into a set of shoes I too-know the stink of. Here stoops RoboCop. Cheeks slick-shined as the tile I'd slid out on, sending my stare sledding. What he mouths I can't ear, but his voice roughs my face and I know from the shoved air he's shouting. I nose his breath staled with panic. Then some clogs fart through the door and I'm getting armpitted up and slabbed back-flat on the cot, a nurse with a mouth like a purse poking veins into my elbows. She puts her lips to a bug on her collar, voice jangling like coins dumping out.

"Dr. Walsh to Floor 4." Then she dumps some on me. "Keep these put. This one's fluids. This one's morphine. Dispense it with this button, but we'll hold off for now. Dr. Walsh is coming." Saving her eyes from mine. "She'll fill you in on the disarticulation."

"Disarticulation." RoboCop says it different, like a roach his voice is stomping.

"The amputation."

"You lopped it."

Nurse shuts her eyes. "Dr. Walsh can address—"

"We want lawyers."

A Tall Drink pours herself through the door.

"Here she is," Nurse says.

"Thanks, Marcy. I'll take it."

Nurse dodges out with her heels farting off her clogs, and I can see where her socks are dark with scared sweating.

"Sir?" Doctor nods her eyes down to RoboCop, who's got a look like he's been caught with his fly gawked.

He stares down at hisself with the rest of us, spectating.

Doctor raises her eyebrows ahead of her stare. "Casper." Calling RoboCop me.

Then I remember I'm RoboCop, too, the glycogen outboarded out of me. Someone sobs.

"Oh, hon," Doctor says, now to me. "The first waking's disorienting. We have you on PCA. Self-administration. Here's the button." She puts a bug in my palm. "Would you like me to give you two a moment?"

RoboCop sobs, but his cheeks are parched clean. My face feels mopped.

"I'll just step out," Doctor says. "Call me in when you're ready."

And she offs. RoboCop come-clicks the bug's shell and one-them organs hanging from the rack clucks like a rewinding tape. Then the clear bulges through them veins and warms into me. My voice underwaters. "What-all'd they lop off?"

RoboCop just bends my thumb to the bug. "That's morphine."

My senses bunching like the end of a 100-yard sprint no-breather. "Lopped your worm."

"You shit." But Robocop's voice is tuned to *phew*—glad to hear that there remains some me in me.

Only I need one-them bags like the clear's in, a packet to hold the GU gel in me. That packet used to be Benji. Warm wells up my nape like my brainstem's aimed for bursting. My balls are in the knee of my trapped leg, all the burst throbbing up from it. But that ankle's stopped yapping. I look down and don't see.

RoboCop shakes like a dog shagging off wet as he's leaving. The bright in that room leaves no room for his shadow. What side's it fall at when light's all around? Ever air atom its own bulb a-glowing. Don't know. Sex is Benj telling and the clear them veins are pumping into me. My brain bucks and bursts. And that damn burger's back, hogging the TV.

Benji

Nadir of the night that you leave them. Driving off of Kure for a sob and a drink. Plowing the kid's truck one last time down this fallow drag, asphalt furrowing the tilth dark in the rearview. All the times you'd grinned back at Tootsies wilting in that mirror, quenched by lengths and speeds they were willing to reach for you. If they'll just grow where you planted them. If the home you've seeded will just bloom. If you could just cut off your reflexes like a tendon—but can't. The coyotes always snap back.

Carrying the kid around the camper, you could hear their canine panic, the clinging need. Craving a shape to bite down on and dew to. Hating your own equal need. How the kid sank in the pool. How he'd looked like he was solidifying under the stilling surface, as if the rippling had been an aspect less of the substance surrounding him than his skin. Hard not to picture him taking your shape in Unc's cocoon. Harder not to let him.

You'd stood on the coping for a full minute before diving in.

Sometimes you do think of this island: how the same waves that gulp the beach chew inlets that drag the sand back, depositing it on the island's sheltered side. The island staying above sea level like that, spat back as the ocean advances. Maybe it's the same with the kid: a cohesive cycle. He has to get hurt to be soothed.

Smashing his chest, heaving your breath into his mouth on the pool deck, you'd filled him with confessions. Truths you can't remember. Had he swallowed them? Will he tell Ezra? Should've left him on the steps. When Ezra'd come out you shouldn't've said anything. If he'd've just shut the door on you. But it was just like leaning over him in that medical tent, letting your hair fall into his mouth—you'd lifted your sunglasses and let him let you in. Now you're in his chest. Nightshade uses a coyote's living to kill it, spreading through its bloodstream by its heartbeats. His fitness from your training. Your craving to take his shape. Every time Ezra's pulse rises he's spreading you.

Brooding north to the mainland, the past eructing up on you. Burped stomach acid as sour-sweet as the table sugar and herbs Unc brewed for the swimmers. Alkalize the blood. Replenish glycogen, Tootsies. The pickup feels like Unc's cocoon, full of you. No border to define yourself against. Pick up Ezra's phone. Scrape down its bitten edges. How he used to gnaw the case waiting to hear the next workout. Put your teeth to it. Your molars and incisors fit those chewed grooves as snugly as water fills a low place. The cab cups a squeal, as of wind. Seal the windows and it amplifies. A chorus of drenched squeals and voices. Shut your mouth, trap them to one hum. Bite down on the phone and your teeth slip. Disperse like a shadow lost in the dark, bleeding off to the Everywhen.

This was your start as Unc oathed it, his sworn version of how you'd first come crawling to him:

Coyotes in the pasture. Panicking sheep. Unc had hummed them to sleep and slit the walking tendons in the hind-limbs of the coyotes. Loaded the coyotes in the bed of his pickup and drove them to a grassless patch of pasture. They dragged themselves by their forelimbs in thirst of water. Unc watched through binoculars. Slugtrails of blood stretching. After a week he'd drive out with water and meat. If a coyote growled, he'd stop feeding them. They'd all be lapping water from his cupped hands after another week. Unc's need to hurt so he could help. His need for them to need him.

An aberration in this pack. A coyote that wouldn't take anything, just kept moving. Its smearing progress paled through Unc's cataracts. The blood path lengthened and neared. The morning the front porch filled with squealing, Unc took the machete and marveled out to you: a lump at the base of the porch steps, socked with blood. Coyote become human: wounded you.

Unc stepped right over you. Meemaw'd taught him not to touch until he knew a thing's come-from. Not a hand or footprint in the yard; just that line of blood stretching behind you umbilically. He'd traced the trail all the way to where he'd dumped the coyote and walked back and plucked six hairs from your head, wrapped those hairs around a coyote's bleached paw bones—how Meemaw'd taught him to reckon kin. He'd tossed the bones on the porch and read your past in their scatter: you'd followed the coyote, or become from it. Your feet flopped wrongly when Unc bundled you up. Gashes above your heels. Both Achilles tendons cut.

Thus was the history you limped into. The story landed as laden on your ears as a curse every time Unc recited it: over dinner, between sets at swim practice—bending over the diving block and spooking the other athletes to duck out of your lane.

Shadefoot left no footprints. Shadefoot flew into victims through their pupils and stole their bodies by their hearts, spreading through their bloodstreams. Shadefoot became out of their senses: it grew feet when they heard its footfalls, stole its breath from their noses when they inhaled its scent. Its fingernails grew at the same rate that they felt them rake their nape. It took the eyes of whatever looked back at it, so that the last thing that thing saw was itself flooding in.

The other swimmers never looked all the way at you. Unc said he'd been spared by his cataracts; that day he'd looked down he'd let in no more than a ventricle of you. He'd scarred mazes over his heart with shears to prevent you from spreading beyond it—patterns to trap you before you could infect the rest of him.

Shadefoot formed in footprints, so it came from what was ahead: its ancestors were the shadows thrown back by whoever it followed. How you hear your next athlete rattle their bike past or bounce their helmet off the curb and know like a knee-jerk. Those sounds already flood your Everywhen.

The Everywhen. That tenseless, Bends-bringing dream.

Ear-bursting pressure of future and past meeting. Your hum stings your mouth like a fishhook. Let it reel you up. Surface in the kid's truck feeling spat, sliding along the tongue of US-17. Roadside pines dense as baleen, the wet night roofed like a mouth. Your windshield fogged as if breathed on.

"Ez?" someone says.

Only feel the cold of the phone's screen on your chin as the voice quivers out of it. Pry it off. Ezra's, set to speaker. The call timer ticks past a minute. MA capitalized in the contacts slot above.

"Hello, Tulpa," she says.

Her voice works like that first slit of light when Unc opened the cocoon, defining the difference between self and surface as the lid lifted. A relief at first; then a blinding sting, the too-much-ness of everything pouring into your senses. Shadefoot, Unc, the hair spell—all of it welling up. A whole too huge and hurtful to hold in. Unc had told you not to tell anyone about him. He'd said that Ezra was the Tulpa, the obedient one who could cancel out the defiance and fear that you'd formed from. "No. Ezra."

"You're just Benji."

"I'm the curse. It's like the ocean pushes back the island. How it should. I have to push Tootsies ahead so I can flood into their footprints. But I'll drown them if they stop moving."

"Who taught you to hum?"

"I welled up in Ezra. Had to crack him to run free."

"Let me talk to him."

"I am." A gulped thickness to the silence. Dulling wind-speed; your foot's slid off the gas. The truck's speedometer grows acute, the needle slumping as it coasts. You trickle to a halt in the right lane and you sit. "He's Zenning. Record shape. You should see."

"Give him the phone."

Ghost your fingers over the screen. Everything preserved how Ezra'd had it. Every page and application left open. All those evenings he'd scrolled through the Chapel Hill Ironman roster way after the race closed for entry, refreshing last year's results like the outcome might change. Hunching over forums and group-chats and pro updates, bobbing for apples in the peanut gallery. Windsucker. Age-grouper. Couldn't run out of sight on a dark night before you'd gotten to him. Now he was Zenning and he'd told you to leave. His voice fizzing as he'd said it, though. It still carbonates your eardrums, a soda-sweet sting crackling. You can't help it. Let his voice spill from your sinuses. "Ma?"

A stiff clunk on her end, then a transmission grumbling. "You're sick."

"Why I left. What I'm saying." A wet stretch, just the phone-muffled burble of her accelerating. How can't she see the larger system? You tell her, "I'm saving them."

And hang up with the seatbelt clenched in your lap. Back in the awful solipsis of the truck, a void as empty yet full of you as Unc's cocoon. You've gotten too used to the sardine-ness of the boat cabin: restless Ezra, squealing Casper, surfaces to bump into. Distinctions. When Ezra rolled or rose, you'd rub your head on the silhouette of sweat that he'd left, mopping it up with your mullet. By sucking your hair, you could taste his fatigue. Another trick of Unc's: lick them. If their sweat tastes like bleach it means they need to take it easy, the broken-down muscle staling their perspiration with ammonia. Casper's sweat had been Clorox all along. But Ezra's had sweetened over the course of this summer, as if his fitness were outpacing the training. The way he'd jogged around after that brick today, mouthing off; no wince or gasp to him, not even hard-breathing. You'd fine-tuned him. There's more he can do. You can't go back, but you're greedy to see. US-17 stretches ahead as empty as a race course in front of the leader. Plead your foot back to the gas. Pull off at the next exit.

The road punctures an inlet. It fishhooks around a marina. Stop at the bar glowing at its north end, the dark barbed by its neon gleam. Shrimpers and night-shifters drink breakfast, blam-ing the scent they dragged in on the breeze lifting off the water. A splinter of a place. Fishnets for porch screens. Preview of the

Alabama Stakes on the corner TV. You walk to the bar doubled over, and before you've even wormed onto a stool the bartender sits one down in front of you.

"That bad?" the guy to your left says. "Been off the sauce long?"

Guy's look about like something the shrimpers would haul in. Skin leathery as his bike jacket, sunburnt smooth. You need ears, not a drink, and he'll do. You slide the tumbler to him.

He throws it back without taking his eyes off of the horses. "You're welcome. Cheers to your sobriety."

The TV winks as it cuts between jockeys. You nod the bartender back to refill him and your friend pries his eyes off the screen.

"I'm taken, rockstar." Guy tells you. He nibbles the ear of the bartender, who's pouring her cleavage for him just as much as a drink.

"Rockstar," she echoes, whistling a strand of something.

"Corey Hart." The guy pokes your Oakleys, drawls, "*He wears his sunglasses...*"

Just nod to the filly on TV. "Put your money on Point of Pride."

And tell them both she'd have it by the five-eighths pole. And tell and tell until closing time. Turns out these two like to take paychecks to the greyhound track in Topsail. The guy has a napkin out to jot down your suggestions on how to spot a winning whippet in the stall. You have your own glass. The bartender pours them as straight and tall as you like them, and your buzz is less from the whisky than the blunt force of them listening. And you pulling at your hair, already greedy again. Sit on your hands. Try not to think of all you could already get them to do for you. Nor the cocoon of the truck cab, the waiting Everywhen. But reflexes are stronger than shame; and maybe, too, every time you use the spell there's a growing momentum to it. As the bartender slides down the counter and the guy hunches over his notes you pluck out a hair, drop it in his drink.

Sit there after closing. Just you three and the fillies galloping on TV. The bartender's counting bills out of the register. The guy leaning into you like it's your ear he'd rather be nibbling.

"A favor," you say, and his hand darts to your lap—but not that. (Never that, though sex is always their first reflex: those strays you'd charmed on Unc's farm backing against you, dragging their haunches over your legs in damp heat.) Write Ezra's address on a napkin. "There's this kid. My kid. Check in on him for me. I'd go, but it's better—I can't."

Guy nods. "I get it." But still pets your lap. His hand slides across you as thoughtlessly as you'd dialed Ezra's Ma—as urgently as you punching in Ezra's passcode—and you know he can't stop any more than you can stop that. You slip Ezra's phone out of your pocket. "Give this to him."

The guy stands when you slide your stool back. "Where you going?"

You aim for the front door and he follows you, asking if you're good to drive and do you need a place to crash. Your hand stops on the knob. If you just hadn't fed him the hair; if he just wouldn't look back. But your reflexes are wrong.

"My kid. Just give him that."

"Should I say something? Like, to him?"

"It's unlocked, Rockstar!" the bartender calls.

Your hand still on that knob. The guy reaches for your thigh and you catch his arm, lifting it to a handshake. "Send me a picture."

Push out the door with him reaching for you. Back the truck out of the lot with the brake lights sloshing over yellow eyes: hackling by the dumpster, already, a coyote.

A drowning drive. The lane ripples in front of you. The night floods with squealing. Slump the tires off the road's shoulder into mud—that damp thud, the chassis crackling like old hinges—and Unc's shutting you back into the water trough, cocooning you in the Everywhen.

Your Achilles tendons had healed stiff. They'd raveled up as if in permanent cringe from the cuts that had slit them. Going to your tiptoes cemented both calves with cramps. Your feet dragged rudders at swim practice. Biggest kid in the slow lane. Smacking your forehead on the diving block between laps, six-year-old girls fluttering past. Some folks were just born wrong, Unc said, dropping paddles and a pool buoy on the coping beyond your reach.

His vision was already wooly when you were that age. He'd spent too many morning swim practices squinting into sunrise; blamed West Memphis Parks and Rec for building a pool that faced east. Blamed his swimmers' sloppy strokes. Claimed he had to watch their every lap to correct their sloppy technique. He'd perch on the diving blocks with his training binder awninged over his eyes for entire practices, unfazed by the splashes of flip-turning swimmers. He'd stick his tongue out to catch the flying flecks of water. *Protect your eyes, Tootsie.* Even after his sight lost him his license, Unc insisted on taking his own truck to practice. Older swimmers took turns driving him, parking their cars by the barn and praying his '81 Nissan to life. By that time, you'd always ride in the back.

All those prickling dawns. The chatter of epsom salt in the water trough was your alarm. The salt crunched as Unc stiffened down into it. Maybe that crunch was his bones. You hoped so. The stovetop stayed crowded with pots lozenged by thermometers. You pulled them off when the temperature settled to 98.6. Then you'd brim the trough with that water, your own eyes fuzzy with 3 a.m.-ness—wondering whether this was what the world looked like to Unc.

He'd sigh flat in the trough. The lid took both hands for you to close over him. You'd lie down in the dirt and doze until his knocking woke you. Whichever swimmer was giving you and Unc a ride would be coming, their car chattering over the gravel drive.

Never a towel for Unc. He always stepped wetly into his

khakis, climbed dripping into the Nissan's driver's side. He insisted on putting the keys into the ignition himself. The swimmer would help him around to the passenger's side, then sit in the soak that he'd left on the seat.

The comas of those commutes. Your sinuses chlorine-cured to the fissured texture of jerky, throat ripe from draining nosebleeds. You stared at the swimmers' feet pressing down on the gas. Tried stretching your ankles with your hands. Even banded them with the Elastrators, thinking how those rams' testicles withered and slid limp—if you could just get your feet to hang from your ankles that way. That had lasted a day. Unc asked why your steps sounded so stiff. He felt his way from the couch to your feet and cut both Elastrators off with his pocketknife.

"What the shit were you after?" he'd asked. "Did I bring you to this?"

He'd only led you. You'd been the one desperate enough to band your feet to keep up to speed.

"I just rough you up to make callouses," Unc had said. That was the one time you'd ever seen him shivering.

The next practice it was your neck that he reached into the pool and grabbed. You pried yourself out of the pool to find him patting the diving block with his binder. You sat. He dropped the book in your lap.

"Some folks're just born wrong," he said.

From then on, he trained you to coach.

Unc liked to say he came from a bottom-up school of swimming: a kid would find the fastest way to the surface if you let them sink. Extremis forced efficiency. He wanted swimmers thrashing the water, life-fighting it. A hundred 100s was his idea of a drill set. Make the pace for enough of them and by the end your arms would wither down to your best technique. He'd pull swimmers out of the water if it looked like they were thinking: reach down from the deck and catch them by their napes while they flip-turned, accusing them of looking pretty. It's not ballet. Brain in the deep end, Tootsie. Unc known to do this in the middle of races that his swimmers were winning. Every one of them stopped to listen. If he weren't bald you'd've suspected he'd fed his hair to them, but Unc had other ways.

You put dirt in a swim cap. You held the dried hind-leg of a toad under your tongue. The important part was that the swimmers saw you do that; the important part was that you never gave them explanations. There was a speechlessness around Unc's kind of magic. If you saw the larger system it would collapse. Unc claimed charms had an etiquette: by behaving certain ways—biting the right fingernails, arranging rocks like silverware around a plate— your position, world-wise, would be elevated. And like etiquette, the charms failed if they had to be explained. You had to know without saying.

You followed Unc down the pool deck with leaves and Ziplocks of ram shit in your pockets, anointing the diving blocks with them. Your neck laden with stopwatches. One for every swimmer. Your thumb sore from punching the buttons as they stabbed into the wall, juggling them to record splits. Unc never looked at the times after practice; he sopped the sheets in sugar water, wadded them up, and ate them. His binder held drawings instead of workouts. Swirling sketches of swimmers: torsos writhing with patterns like intestines, limbs tangling mazes. When one was falling behind he'd fill in the patterns with charcoal, and you didn't ask—etiquette—but you understood he was trapping the swimmer's pain in that paper, containing it like the scars kept Unc's heart in his chest. You longed for Unc to sketch you. Watched and copied and rolled your ankles. That was the summer after he'd shaved your head; your hair was growing long enough to suck, growing in staggered, scab-colored hunks as if preserving the ruts his razor had cut into your scalp. Maybe those cuts had been your sketch. A maze he'd etched to keep your own pain from escaping you.

Your hurt was skullbound, unlimbed, and unstomached. Exhaustion withdrawal. There was a presence, a firmness in soreness—a confirmation. Every muscle fiber and nerve were accounted for when they throbbed. You'd gone from thirty hours a week of swimming to sitting numbly on diving blocks, squinting into migraine dawn. You pointed your toes until your calves seized before standing to be sure that your legs hadn't evaporated. Your body felt gone. Couldn't eat. Couldn't sleep. Wafting out of bed as soon as Unc's snores rattled the floorboards to run through the dark, chasing fatigue. Your ankles kept you from reaching it. Their stiffness shackled your strides—too tight to reach a pace that strained your legs or breathing. Long stumbles through fields scattering bursts of sheep. Only in the dark, never out-and-back; afraid to see that you weren't leaving tracks. Unc bobbing in the trough by the time you lurched home, saying look what the cat dragged. Calling you roadkill. Warning you not to attract scavengers.

But the coyotes were already lurking back. Their squeals spilling down from far pastures. Not long before you got up to run and found Unc humming in the sheep pen. The sheep slumped asleep. The yard rugged with snoring coyotes. Their flews rippled with their breaths, shuffling their lips' dank serrations. You followed Unc to the nearest one. He rolled it off his haunches, ran a thumb down its hock, and handed you the machete.

You set the blade against the curve of the hind leg, cupped a hand around its stifle, and sawed. A limp pop. The coyote's paw drooped. You saw the tendon through its fur like a snake slithering under a rug, a long bulge shrinking up its fibula. The coyote didn't stir. Still sunken in Unc's hum. You cut all their hind legs and loaded them in the pickup and the swimmer who picked you up knew better than to ask when you pointed them to the brown pasture. Magic had an etiquette. It didn't work if you saw the larger structure. But Unc had told you all your life how you'd crawled to him; you laid the coyotes out in the pasture how he had, and Unc gulped his hum. His pale-blind eyes belched your reflection in their cataracts, as if he were looking out from you.

"See what they'll do for you."

He sat back while you led morning practice, brushing his hand down the pages of a paperback copy of *The Tibetan Book of the Dead,* claiming that his third eye was the one that needed the cataract. You ran the water and beef out to the coyotes that afternoon. Their hind-legs trickled out from their rumps, stretching like they were melting. That morning it had felt like you were hearing Unc tell the story of cutting their tendons instead of doing it. Now you stood alone with the whimpering consequence. You waited for your stomach to fist. Longed for it. To respond the right way. You wanted a visceral shame, a nauseous, dyspeptic sensation. But you had the wrong reflexes. You'd already fallen into Unc's footprints. Your urge was his urge, and it jerked you as inevitably as those cut tendons. You coiled your hair into the beef and fed it to the coyotes. They gnashed the meat, their teeth chattering. You turned home and didn't look back. But the wrong sound of them dragging themselves after you—like splashing. The wetness of it made you seasick. You sprinted the noise faint.

Next morning you lagged back from your run with four of them dragging after you.

Unc bobbed in the trough. "Brought some shadows."

The coyotes nuzzled your heels. Their blood streaked your path like the charcoal in Unc's drawings, covering the ground you so feared that your feet hadn't printed. Only a body cast a shadow. Being followed stiffened your shape even more than soreness, keeping you in your anatomy.

Unc clicked his teeth. "Now you're solid."

Humming smears the dream. Rattling.

Reach for the kid and smack your hand on the window and moan—the truck cab, not the cabin. The phone vibrates in the cupholder. Put your teeth to the case—so used to those chewed edges of Ezra's—but it's yours. The messages are from Ezra, heaping up the screen. With each new notification the phone looks like it's shivering. Press it to your chest and conduct it. The guy you'd fed your hair to; send a picture, you'd told him. Joking.

But here it is. They are. As you'd asked. Notification banners barring the screen. Brush your finger across one like a strand of hair to unlock the phone, the slickness as rich on your thumb as the flavor of Ezra's sweat in your mullet—savoring his obedience.

The same picture sent over and over. The kid pooled in the sumac, his left leg an ooze: the limb itself bent like the blood it's leaking. A spring trap cups his calf. The trap could be nursing the wound instead of inflicting it, its gnash and pinch hidden by the image's stillness. The jaws press gently into the kid's skin. Your teeth against his ear humming into him. Ezra watching from the cabin's doorway. His head hangs above this message thread the same way: his contact photo surmounting the pictures of Casper, a looming moon. Seems to lift the kid's liquid image more than your scrolling. The tidal two of them. You swear the pictures would keep rising if you took your thumb off the screen. Your eyes shut around the image of the kid's leg like the trap, streaking the insides of your lids as if smashed. Loosen them. Bleed your stare past the screen.

The truck's parked in a patch of marsh grass. Above the grass a flat bright, a pleated sunrise hemming east. Withers cross-stitch the reeds. Coyotes sit and stand and lie whimpering. A needy pack. Their claws rasp off the doors. The phone's stagnant in your hand, but the cab's still rattling. They're leaping into the truck's flanks, trying to jump into the bed.

Slash the shifter into Reverse. Churn the ignition. Swerve back toward the highway with them squealing after you and twisting the rearview with both hands, wrenching until it snaps off its plastic. The sound's dry: a single click of Unc's teeth.

Stomp the brake at the turnoff for US-17. If you could just go back to Kure. If you could just hum into the kid's injury. Just explain the larger system—but can't. They'll hate you, they'll blame you, and they'll grow together in your absence. A poison can be watered down to a cure. A wrong reflex can do good if it's aimed the right way. A storm surge cuts an inlet through an island, and that gash keeps the ocean from drowning the sand,

and the water bleeds through and spills back to churn, forever cresting and breaking. Shadefoot flows through footprints, then the pupils of those who look back. Then their veins. But his flowing poisons the pulse that propels him The heart stops or the door shuts; whether the person looks back or not, Shadefoot can't ever settle into a home. He always drifts.

Plunge the window. Throw out the rearview mirror, then the phone. Squeals well behind you. More coming. Ducky and Hood Ornament and Old Lady and the barfly from last night and Unc and dragging packs of coyotes and strays. But not Ezra. If the trap will just snap the spell, too. Let him fall out of the thrall that he'd swallowed with your hair. Leave him hating you.

South is Kure. If you stay on 140 you'll hit 74, which will dip down to 20 and take you to West Memphis. Just to check in the water tower. Just to be sure Unc dissolved; your kind lose their bodies if no one looks at them for long enough.

Slump the truck straight. Your calf cramps as you accelerate. The road pulls you home with a muscular stiffness. One last trip ought to cut that tendon.

Ezra

They're keeping Casper in-patient, calling him Ezra. Keeping Ezra, too. Six days cooped up in the perpetual noon of that room, the gleaming tile and the blue-lit TV and the florescent bulbs leaking through his eyelids even when he masks them under the nightly complimentary blankets, a brightness of bleach's precise hue and sting. An ambient panic of machines chirp and bleat steal his sleep.

The kid nods off and on, calling Ezra RoboCop, asking what-all they lopped off, blinking at his bandaged knee like a stray eyelash he's ridding from his pupil. *Disarticulation.* Clenching that PCA button, which he keeps calling the bug. Sometimes—or the same time in this sustained noon, petrified in the florescent lights' coagulated gleam—Casper moans, *Benj,* like he's wishing.

"It's just me," Ezra says and keeps saying, wishing for his own IV.

This is rapid-titration morphine. Walsh said the button delivers a 4 mg bolus, a unit meaningless to Ezra. He'd've grasped better if it were translated to terms of a workout's exhaustion. Is a mg equal to a long run in its resulting depth of sleep? Casper's sleeping like the night after an ultramarathon, but his heartbeats throb through his stump more like he's running 400-meter repeats. A blanched ache forks out from Ezra's own leg, like Casper's phantom limb is his real one. Pictures Walsh's stump stitched to his own knee. He stares harder at the throbbing stump, trying to bloodstream up some drugged coziness. Swearing he can feel or picture it. Every time he starts to nod off, Dr. Walsh opens the door as she's knocking, barging in. Long-gone are her covers of follow-ups or explanation. She's here to interrogate him. What's he think about those tieless shoelaces, about aero-bars and mass swim starts, and should she be practicing peeling out of her wetsuit? Wants to know all about fructose versus glucose.

She's training for her first sprint-distance, her novice enthusiasm as shiny as the just-bought Trek Equinox she commutes on, flying-dismounting it in front of the double-doored employee entrance performatively. Transition practice. Her pants are rolled up to show her 2XU compression socks. She likely goes to sleep wearing her workout gear for the next a.m. Goggles for an eye mask. Ezra explains about FTP tests and upstrokes and how the easiest way to slide into your wetsuit is to put grocery bags over your feet.

Races used to keep him sleepless for excitement instead of the urge to get it over with; him and Ma on the state triathlon circuit, crosshatching the Carolinas to reservoirs and lakesides and beaches to camp out in race sites. Staking out packet pickup from afar to spot rivals. Pre-race pizzas delivered to the back of the Sprinter van. Ma pulling him from school early on Fridays, careening the van around the tobacco-stained spirit rock stuck like a hocked dipwad on the carpool island. Spring-warm sun chafing with winter gusts. Goosebumps deliberating like so many groundhogs along his arms, peeking up and ducking back, uncertain of season. His body hairless from his head to his blood-blistered toes. Razor-burnt, aero, chapped from chlorine. Shaved and tapered, they called it. Called a full lap of the race course a warmup. Ezra'd been called The Kid then. He raced Open category with local pros: ex-college swimmers and runners his double in age and quadricep circumference. The still photos of such moments front-paged on Triathlon Carolina's website every spring season. Ezra had the look of a fetal bird in those picture—all rib and elbow and bones hatching from skin. About as big at twelve as Casper is now.

The kid lifts his thighs off the cot like to finish the half-stride he'd been haunting through when the EMTs reached him in that sumac. Running a leg down, in spite of the morphine.

"Remarkable," Walsh keeps saying. "6:30 a mile. For a marathon. Off the bike."

"The course is a couple tenths short," Ezra says.

Casper stirs. "Naw. Was me."

In Ezra's humble opinion, they're stretching the definition of stabilizing treatment. Ezra—Casper—is in his last year of family coverage. A lost limb. Surely Blue Cross would call her? Then she'd call him. Maybe has been. His phone's still AWOL, lost or lake-bottomed. Ringing with the fishes. Or worse, getting answered by Benji. Ezra doesn't want to picture that conversation any more than the one that she'd have with him. Doesn't even want to picture the one happening now: Walsh eyebrowing Casper's groans about burgers at the TV.

He bites down on the dispenser's button. "Squish, bug." Tries pinching fluid down the IV tube with his fingers.

"Nope," Walsh says, slapping his hands back into his lap.

The kid goes as clear and stagnant as the morphine. Maybe the bug he's talking about isn't the button, but the IV bags that only seem to grow, bloating like ticks. Ezra's effort in the woods had sapped him the same way. You could only go hold so much exertion. Push past a point—grow too hot, dart too fast—and you'd crack. All that work you were doing and had done would leak out. He pictures hairlines in his nerves; those rhizomes of soreness wedging into them, absorbing months of welled effort. Tapping into his veins. Six sedentary days later his heart's still at race-pace. His blood storms up his brainstem, dizzying him. His senses streak when he stands. A task to so much as prop his way to the toilet.

"Squish," Casper moans, biting the bug again. "Squish. Burger quit. Benj."

That—his chanting need for the man, those incomplete invocations—seems the most urgent thing for Ezra to be watching.

Because when they leave the hospital; when—Lord forbid—they *get back* to that coyote-ridden, poison-soaked sand trap of an island, what'll Casper have? No cash. No truck. No insurance. No left leg to stand on, let alone train with; no Chapel Hill Ironman. And no Benji to kennel him.

"They'd have begun immediately in ideal conditions," Dr. Walsh is saying, on the back-half of some explanation. "But given the infection, I've recommended holding off till his fever's dropped."

"Ideal?"

"Stable. I've recommended that we transition him to orals. Percocet. We're keeping Cleocin for the infection. I wanted to gauge your thoughts."

"Looks effective," Ezra says.

Dr. Walsh shuts her eyes as if trying to empathize with his sleeplessness. "I'm talking his preparedness. Do you feel that he's ready to start physical therapy?"

"Ah." Hard nod. Shake it off.

"I'm recommending it. You'll like Shiela. She prefers working with athletes. Expect her to come by after lunch." Walsh stands up. "You do know we have a cafeteria. It's downstairs."

"Ate."

"When was that?"

Ezra punches his stomach.

Walsh swings the door open, then hangs on it. "Casper."

Ezra looks at the kid before remembering who's who to her. "Yeah?"

"At least sleep."

Casper

Then the Percs start to hit. More like droops, ha—scarce perk to them. My brain follows them pills down my throat, sliding down the *in* of me hooting *whee*. Down on to the root. The nod them Percs give is good as bonking.

Next I nod on, I'm getting handshook by a lady named Shiela Petey. Her saying a cute phase has three goals: manage pain, reincorporate, set up expectations.

"Ain't school."

Petey clears something fake out her throat. "What's that?"

"Quit learning me."

RoboCop swallows a sob. Baby. Climb on into this cot and go sleep.

I haul my legs off to sit up and Shiela *woah*'s, spidering her fingers over my shoulders to settle me. My trapped leg explodes: my knee-caught heart's throbbing back up toward where it fell from and ever nerve gets to yapping with its beat.

"We don't want to let the limb hang. That slows healing."

Shiela Petey scuttles her fingers down my trapped leg. "How's your sensation?"

Ever one of her knuckles like spider's eyes, plus them webs of hand-bones behind; I'm picturing them reeling up to her shoulders, sucking her arms like a spider shrinks its web up its butt. Must've been her ate my bug. But something's missing past that, besides Benj. My trapped leg's sucked up like that spider. The air under my left knee's pure-tee empty. Shiela Petey's kneading its end like she's trying to pack it up tighter.

"Any sensation?"

I fess that it's been yapping.

Shiela Petey nods like she just asked the right *Jeopardy!* "Your brain has a map of your body in its neurons. The parts that mark your leg—the neurons—are still there, even after amputation. It's not uncommon to continue experiencing sensations in the limb. You might perceive changes in pressure and temperature, even fatigue."

"Not me."

This lady sure loves telling. Creeping them fingers down where my skin's puckered, that zag matching the trap's chomped-shut teeth. "I'm going to examine the suture line, and I'd like for you to move your hands along with me. Touching will help reincorporate the residual limb. Our first step is to establish it as a part of you."

I buck my leg. She jerks back. "If you don't feel comfortable yet..."

Her voice fishhooks up with hoping, curling like she's baiting me. I ain't biting. You done dug your grave, Shiela Petey. I swat her scuttling fingers, smearing spider blood down my knee.

"Okay. Good. Yes." Her spider-hands writhing under mine.

"Triathlons," says RoboCop.

Shiela turns to him like he was just humming the tune for ice cream. Folks sure are sore from the sight of me. Must be some kind of haint, the way I'm spooking off gazes.

"Put down triathlons. Ironman."

"Ironman." Shiela's spider hands writhe together like they're breeding. "That's the longest one. He finished that?"

"Finish? He *races* them. 8:20. Write that. You asked his athletic history." Sends himself right back to baby by saying so, just shy of crying.

Meantime I'm fail-fending some squirms. I throw a kick trying shake it and get bee-stung where my leg quits past the knee. Little stump of shin under it. Little worm smirking up, that pink slit of sewn skin like lips pursing. Stitches zag like the trap's teeth, like my leg's still puckered from kissing what bit it. Ain't blaming; I'm still spitting bursts I gulped years ago. I do know how a bad taste can stick.

Shiela Petey's yapping at RoboCop again. "The Amputee Mobility Predictor's a functional outcome test. The goal's to establish Ezra's K-level, which will determine what kind of prosthesis he's eligible to receive through insurance."

Woman loves her some goals. We're eye-line on that, at least. And she's finally figured RoboCop's the one needing treating.

He un-slumps from his chair like string coming out her spider fingers. "How much?"

"That's going to vary depending on the type of prothesis and his coverage."

"But the insurance covers it."

"The assessment determines—"

"The test's free?"

"That's a question for his insurers. There could be a copay."

"Can I—Ezra—can he ask first?"

Shiela glances back at me. "If he wants."

And if my heart's fallen down to that stump, and that stump's a worm, and the bee sting on its lips is a bite from Shiela's spider fingers, then I got honest venom seeping through me. Enough to squash the bug. But the spider ate the bug, and now it's just Percs. I crane to the table to reach me one and no bottle. I try-perch on the leg I do full-got. All the blood smacks the roof of my skull like I'm headstanding. I put my foot in warm-wet and slip on back to bed, the piss-pan skidding out from under me.

"Woah," Shiela presses me sitting. "Nothing to prove. Hon, would you grab an orderly?"

Robocop's already ajar-ed the door.

Shiela turns back and says, "Oh," then the room's full-up of the alone of us.

Funny how alone grows even bigger when you share it with someone. "Try athlon." Hear the space she adds in it. "I'm impressed. Nothing to prove, hon."

RoboCop totes a wet mess of paper towels, wadding them into one clot. The tile's glossed with their drip. He kneels and smears that clot on my heel, low-eyed like he's ashamed or wor-shippy. Maybe those is two angles of the same thing.

Shiela Petey turns toward him like she's fighting a crick. "No need, hon. I'll go grab that orderly"

"Don't," RoboCop says.

Shiela raises her eyebrows, then stands like she's trying to catch the rest of herself up to them "Tell you what. We've cov-ered good ground—no pun. Let's hold off on the assessment."

RoboCop rubs my foot like his worm, feeling sex from it.

"I'll just come back tomorrow." Shiela hopscotches around the puddle sloshed from my piss-pan. Her voice shuts with the door. "I left you with some pamphlets."

I'm shut of being flopped. I droop because I'm thinking up an even fuller, worser empty than this: what the boat will be like with no Benj to break the just of us, RoboCop and me. Rob-oCop's fixing to break down without him. And I'll leak. And both-us will puddle brackish for varms to slurp because without Benj telling us into shape we'll be no one, neither him nor me.

"Hell's my Percs?"

"You just took one."

"You done."

RoboCop won't meet my glare. He just rubs. I try and kick him, but the kick quits in my nerves. Getting drowned out by a burst. His rubbing's turned my foot into my worm, sure enough. But not just the rubbing: there's a needing how he does it, the heartbeating pressure he presses into my foot. Petting me like he's breathing. That worsens my squirms even as the burst floods up like the breath when you run past a Port-a-John in a race but need air enough to where you just suck in that stinking. And you're gasping even as atoms of shit taint your tongue. And it's also like Adam the Atom Man: wanting it to end but needing it, the needing fighting the wanting because his rubbing's the only thing holding you in you. His touch good as Adam Man's. And you can't leave any more than you can tell him to because when he quits you'll be nothing but oozing move. So I didn't and don't kick.

My foot dries. The towels crinkle. RoboCop keeps right on rubbing. Then a thought catches up to my senses, lagging behind what I done-been seeing: he's making my shape! He's keeping me in me! He's that plastic packet around my GU! And I epiphany that RoboCop can be my new Benji.

Benji

One long sob from Topsail to West Memphis, the kid's leg in your head and the truck rumbling along the turnoff like Unc's guffaw. Stop off at the Citgo to gas up. A sheppie tied to the bike rack strains at its leash. Spot the attendant inside, a guy with the hem of his hoisted tank-top clenched in his teeth. His hunch that hyperbolizes his paunch. Raised scars cross his chest like the rebar that had weighted the lid of Unc's cocoon, like the scribbles Unc had trapped his drawings of swimmers behind. The attendant squirts lotion on his finger and traces those scars.

You crouch behind the pump. You know the guy, Briggs. An old shearer and swimmer of Unc's, a guy who'd let Unc knife designs into his chest to keep you from getting into his heart, but looked you dead in the eye as soon as Unc left the room. Briggs didn't buy those Shadefoot stories; just wanted to fuck with you. The simp. Unc had put the two of you in the same lane before you'd stopped swimming. Had you leave the wall five seconds behind Briggs—swimming freestyle on the same sendoff that he was breaststroking, haunting his widened wake. Unc's idea was to scare him into Olympic Trials shape. Briggs's best 200 breast was a second shy of the mark. Once you took over coaching, you switched his stroke. Had him swimming nothing but butterfly—30,000 yards of it per week. Just to see if he'd do it. He'd blown out both rotator cuffs, but gotten his O.T.

You ease the nozzle back into the holder on the pump. Climb into the truck and ease the door shut, guide the pickup's shifter into drive. Briggs glances out the front window and locks eyes with you in the rearview. He jerks off his stool. Floor it toward the turbines. Park in front of Unc's farm with the fuel gauge drooping back to "E".

Walk around to the water tower, just to see. Unc should've dissolved after this long without anyone looking or listening. The rope's still tied to the ladder's bottom rung. Climb up and open the door to the tank and choke into a stench like the corpse of a poisoned coyote decomposing.

The water as dark and solid as a mushroom. The tank's insides watermarked with rust. Tug the door shut. Feel your way to the stairs at the edge of the landing. Ten steps bring you down to the belly of the basin.

The water reaches your chest, but the air and dark are so thick that you might as well be submerged in Unc's cocoon. Shuffle ahead. Don't swim breaststroke. Your left flip-flop stubs on a shape like a curled rake. Slide your foot to those prongs' sharpened ends. A matching set mirrors them.

Ribs.

You crouch in that water and wait to leave your own skeleton. Your sense of self has to dissipate, disappearing into the chorus of the Everywhen. Coyotes' howls. Tootsies' whimpers. Unc's instructions. What decays slower: a spirit or a body? Yours are still linked. Nerves too tightly tied to the parts of you squandering energy pulsing and beating. Hunger rumples your stomach. Parch thickens your tongue. Slurp the fetid water. Swallow Unc. Nausea burns over your hunger. Nothing like that time you'd lost all sense of passing seconds in the surfacelessness of Unc's cocoon. Every next second etches a new notch in your esophagus.

A vehicle crackles down the drive. The creak of that ladder. A knock on the tank.

The door scrapes open. Briggs stands caramelized in a trickle of sunlight, a grocery bag dangling off his wrist. "Almighty Mark Spitz." He lifts his tank top over his nose. "Smells like something got field-dressed."

You only feel the parts of yourself he can see. Below the water's surface, your nerves stop. You crouch lower, hoping yourself into head and neck only.

"I followed your tracks to the ladder. Hard to hide anything in this mud."

"Wasn't trying."

"I'm James Briggs. Used to swim for you. With you. My folks run the Citgo."

"I know."

"You getting in some laps?"

"You can."

Briggs sets the bag on the landing. Gatorade. Twinkies. For a sweaty second, you think he really might get in. He takes a step back. "Thought you might want some rations."

Never let Tootsies see you eat. They have to think you're more than, you don't need it. "Don't need them."

"Right." Briggs steps back again. He stands on the threshold of the door. "You laying low or what?"

If only. You clench yourself small, but your nerves are sprouting beyond you, growing to fit that tank's shape the way Shadefoot expands into footprints.

"Saw those kids of yours running after you left," Briggs says. "What the hell did you feed them?"

"Same recipe."

"Well, you've been getting an audience. Bunch of front-crawling tri-geeks. They keep pulling over at my place to ask what you did."

Your brain blanches. "What're you saying?"

"Your uncle went to Nepal."

"He did."

"Is that where he is?"

"Part of him."

Briggs shoves his hand through the arm-hole of his tank top, spanning his fingers like he's trying to palm the scars.

"What do you say about me?"

"Why I stopped by." He takes a step back, but crouches. "Give me your side of the story."

Looking for you to tell him how to be. What to say. If you told him to dive in one more time, he just might. He'd slurp up all this tainted water and lick the drops off of Unc's sunken skeleton if you commanded him.

"Well I'm out," says Briggs. "Smells like someone died. Naw, like someone who ate someone dead died. Could be some rats drowned. They'll gnaw right through your shit. Leave a sheet of tin like Swiss cheese." He ditches the bag. "Can't quite say nice to see you."

His tires crackle out of earshot up the gravel drive. Tear into a Twinkie. Your nerves follow that first gulp down your windpipe. They spread out from your stomach, retracing your torso. Solidify with every gasping bite. You're back in your body within seconds after trying to dissolve for days. Your constant state: fighting to be one way, getting beaten back by your nature.

You were born wrong. Unc was right.

An hour north of West Memphis, I spot the turbines. AR-77 junctions with I-55 and then those pale blades are slicing the west side of the skyline. I take the first turnoff to my right, down a cracked asphalt road. The *Slowtwitch* article didn't list an address. The asphalt gives to a gravel path of its exact shade, as if I'm driving over an eroded section of road. The pastures I'm passing look the same way—like the weeds are frayed blades of grass. The turbines churn ahead of me, large in the scaleless way of the ocean: they look about a mile up the road, but I still haven't reached them after twenty.

I brake up to a crabgrassed-over Citgo. Swim caps are taped inside the top half of its front window. Each one's Sharpied over with what look to be autographs. An Australian shepherd curls around the bike rack by the door, sleeping with its leash in its teeth. The guy at the register has scars so thick and dark on his chest that I can see them through the strained fabric of his size-too-small undershirt. They wind like the lines Unc had drawn through the picture he'd made of me in the Dasharath dirt. The attendant follows my stare to his chest, then hoists his shirt high enough to expose the scars to me.

He points down the road before I apologize, or ask anything. "Keep going how you're going."

I drop a twenty on the counter, grab a whole box of king-sized Reese's, and go.

The pastures roll. The road remains low, a flat slash between them. The turbines are aligned north-to-south on either side of the road. On my thirtieth Reese's Cup, I pass through first row. There's one every quarter mile or so, stretching on farther than my sight goes. The road plunges down to a clapboard house. A barn rots about an acre to the southeast. A water tower rusts on the lot's northwest corner, the tin kind about two stories high with a conical roof like a rice hat.

I park in the yard. The ground's scored with shoes and paw prints. I climb the porch and knock. Nothing. The door's locked. The windows are plastered over with fine-printed pages. Each has a single jagged edge, as if torn from a book. I peer at the text. My Nepali never got me much farther than entrees and street signs, but I can still recognize the flatheaded characters of its alphabet. Hard not to picture the first story flooded, your father bobbing in the water and dark. He ought to be crippled. He might've dissolved. The *Slowtwitch* article said that he'd left for Nepal, but that order was backwards, if not wrong: Nepal was where your father had left me. Must've left his nephew before that. The whole drive down here, I've been trying to wrap my mind around that added branch to the family tree: if that had really been your father in those old swimming photos, it meant that your cousin was Benji.

I follow the paw prints around the house. They flood in the backyard. Lying on its side, gagged with mud, is the water trough where he must've tried to dissolve. The moment I'd seen that photo of it on *Slowtwitch*, my mind had gone to the rain-filled garbage bin that your father had passed every night that I'd known him in.

The trough's crumpled mostly shut, the space between its caved flanks packed with mud. I grab the snow shovel from the van and dig out what I can, coasting off the sugar rush from the Reese's. Superb core work, to the point where I'm sweating how the soreness might affect my next swim—one more wrong thing for me to be thinking, among many. I'd driven right past the route home in pursuit of a ghost. For all I know, Benji could be talking you into his own trough. He did say that you had to cocoon. He'd siphon your father's hum through his lungs; maybe he's used that hum on you. You'll understand why I had to take this detour if he did.

I couldn't help coming to West Memphis any more than I could resist your father's hum the first time that I'd heard it. He'd given me the vector I'd left home in hope of—not just a direction, but also a sense of that direction's consequence.

Those aren't the only urges I've caved to. Doro'd sent me off from Tetlin with enough orzo to feed the entire facility, claiming that a meal out would help everyone practice nutritional flexibility. I'd knocked out two Tupperwares' worth by the time I hit AK 2. After less than a southbound hour, the insides of my legs had started itching. I'd sworn I could feel each grain of orzo burrowing through my bloodstream like worms. Cycling until my quads burned seemed the only solution; your father was the first one who'd gotten me still, and the only way to undo his influence seemed to move.

So I slept for eight hours, trained for eight hours, and drove and ate for the remainder of each day. Runs over fir-blanketed dirt. Rides up the foothills of the Northern Rockies. Wetsuit swims in salmon-thick lakes. I let the orzo sit in the fridge, supplemented with full packs of moose jerky and trail mix bought from hiking outlets in Koidern and Quill Creek and Destruction Bay. All these long bike rides have skewed my appetite beyond the scope of any restorative mantra or therapy. Regardless of whether or not I exercise, my stomach's not satisfied with anything less than 5,000 calories. My only answer remains the same: I've got to keep moving.

The AK-2 broadened into the 97 through Canada. I meandered off to whichever lakes and state parks looked worth moving through. Like I said, there were detours. The TTT 38 dropped me into North Dakota. Cornless fields flanked the 52. The 94 blitzed me east through Minneapolis to Chicago. From there, 40 would've gotten me home, but I dropped down the 57 South. If I saw the land that your father had left me for, maybe I could get his spirit to leave me.

I'd felt his presence hitched to my back ever since that stadium collapsed. He'd been alive after that, if *Slowtwitch* was to be believed, but you don't have to be dead to be haunting. All those pit stops I'd taken to train had been about burning off more than calories; I'd been trying to evaporate him with my body heat. That hadn't worked. Pouring him back into this trough is the last solution I can think of.

I excavate one final lump of mud. My intercostals are so fatigued that my ribs feel barbed when I'm breathing. I squat and shove up on the inside of the trough's rim. It won't budge. I run my hand down the lip of the side that the trough's lying on and feel half-buried hinges. Of course. Your father had always insisted that I shut the garbage bin's lid.

I scuff the dirt that I'm standing on until my toe stubs on rebar. Clear a patch with the shovel and unearth more of the stuff, all welded to a sheet of corrugated tin. I lever the sheet up with the shovel, then work the shovel under the trough. Not even that fulcrum will budge it. I get down on all fours. The trough is too crushed to fit all the way into, but I do what I can, what I have to: I stick my head in.

And dream back to that abandoned Dasharath stadium, the creation story that I still owe you. I might've made you and your father. But before I can get to that, I have to explain what brought me it.

My Auntie Opal swooned fatally off her veranda the Tuesday before I turned eighteen. An aneurism was what got her: stagnant blood. Heritable predisposition. Ever since hearing that, I've been antsy to keep moving. I put her estate on the market the same dreary day that we put her in the damp ground of Kure Beach Cemetery. The house got full asking price, funds enough to supply a galactic walkabout. I opened her world atlas and dropped a dreidel to pick my destination.

A week later I was renting an unfurnished apartment in east Tel Aviv. The Hasid landlord stood with his back against the wall, swearing the only trouble in these parts came from the journalists and the junkies. I asked about a month-to-month lease. He whisked me to his office. Only when I came back did I see the dime-sized hole in the wall where he'd been standing. It opened on a bus station outside. The Ashkenazi I snuck home from the disco the next night would tell me that hole was bored for or by a sniper. I stuck to a sleeping bag rather than seeking out a mattress. In three weeks I'd walked down every alley of that city. I opened the Atlas, dropped the dreidel, and flew to Nairobi.

And on and on like that. Chang Mai. Bombai. I walked out of airports and kept moving until I found something interesting. In Calcutta I hiked between all 120 city police stations, filling a manila envelope with the signatures of every chief—all that paperwork just to rent a brick walkup. At city hall the official flicked through the thumb-thick stack to the four hundred ruples I'd tucked into it, plucked them out, and tossed everything else into the trash. At a Burger King in Antananarivo, I got stuck in line behind a tour group and watched a Malagasi cashier take orders in ten separate languages. In Selfoss, I handed a seven-foot-tall pickpocket a spare wallet stuffed with my high school ID, an arcade bar punch card, and a hundred krónur bundled around two boardgames' worth of Monopoly money. Then let fall's first rainy gust blow me to the next country. Rented by the month. Used weather to overcome inertia—only stayed in one place long enough to see the season change. Novelty and that dreidel were my only two compasses.

Nepal was the first place I got used to. Walking myself lost in Dasharath, a stampede of dogs and sheep swamped me. They swarmed out of muddy alleys and converged on the harder dirt road I was following, brushing past nervelessly. Not a dog snapped at a sheep. Not a sheep flinched from a dog. I wish I could tell you that was the strangest thing I'd ever seen, but Love, that was just the beginning, and just the first sense that went skew for me. I stumbled along on the momentum of all those moving bodies and got wrapped up in a hum.

Yes, this sounds crazy, but you of all people ought to be

lenient: the sound had a texture and a pressure, like lassoes tightened around me. I rushed toward it with the dogs and the sheep, feeling tugged.

I reached an overgrown soccer stadium. The field was crowded with sleeping dogs and sheep. More poured in and laid down among them. My own eyes and legs ladened. I was ready to lay down among them when the noise quit.

A sunburnt man crouched out from under the grandstand with a bottle of Chardonnet. held under his lips, whistling his voice over it. "What'd you bring me?"

"Nothing," I said. "It's just me."

"Let me see." Something was wrong with his eyes: the faded blue of those irises and the drooping lids made them look like they'd been over-microwaved. He looked just to my left.

I stepped into his line of sight. "Were you making that noise?" I asked. "Where's your instrument?"

He took my hand, cupped it on his throat, and hummed. My hand felt magnetized to his windpipe. I gripped it with my other palm. Never felt anything like it. His voice caressed like an internal touch. It started working on parts of me you'd rather not hear about. He pulled my wallet out of my pocket and I just watched, helpless and wantless to stop him. He took out my license, slid the wallet back into my pocket, and rubbed it on his open left eye. "I was worried I'd made you."

He was old enough to have; had the easy width and smoothed age of Sean Connery—the kind of face that looks like it took growing into. You'll fit yours one day.

"Were you looking for someone?" I asked.

"Trying to get away." His baritone twanged. "Out of sight, out of mind. Out of mind, out of being."

"Right," I said. "What's that mean?"

"Ever heard of a Tulpa?"

I hadn't. He explained that it was like an emotion's corporeal manifestation. When a feeling got too big to hold, it became something like a soul; that soul blistered off of your own and belonged into a new body. Sounded like one of Auntie Opal's Dybbuk stories to me.

He pocketed my license, plucked a hair from his head, and dropped it in the Chardonnet. He tipped the bottle my way.

He didn't have to hum; I was that stupid, that addicted to interesting. I tipped back the bottle and drank. The hair snagged in my throat. I chugged what was left of the wine; it stayed stuck.

"Would you listen to me?" he asked like I hadn't been.

It was the best offer I'd gotten in days. I followed him off the field. "Walk beside me," he said. "Not behind me."

We went under the grandstand. The shade was crowded with overturned goals and garbage cans. Behind us, the sheep and coyotes were still sleeping.

"You're some kind of singer," I said. "Or a priest."

"Just a coach. Not even. Used to be." He shook his head. "You put all of yourself into someone and they take everything from you. I guess I set myself up for that, maybe."

I told him I was sorry. He said I had no idea what he meant, but that if I wanted—if I needed to—he could make me feel it. He flung the lid off a garbage can brimmed with muddy water and hummed, nodding down at it. I swore I could hear more voices in his—bleating sheep, and dogs barking, and the soft splashes of fast swimming. I climbed in.

"Go all the way under," he said. "Hold your breath."

I did, then I did. He closed the lid.

I held my breath until my lungs wilted. Pinched my nose. The hair singed my throat. I waited and waited and waited. The water roared to a wailing pitch. I imagined that I was trapped in this man's throat, that this stadium had been full of fans who he'd swallowed by talking them into this garbage can and swallowing them. I shoved off the lid.

He was squatting ten feet away, dragging his finger through the dirt. Drawing a life-sized woman. Held my license cupped in his hand.

"You almost drowned me," I said.

"I didn't do anything."

"I was waiting for you," I said, but to what? Assuming something would happen. Something had.

Your father lifted my license up to his face and squinted. He haired and eyed the woman in his drawing. "Don't ever wait up for me."

I nodded down at his picture. "That's me."

He dragged both pointer fingers through the dirt, wound a maze of lines over the drawing.

I tipped back and forth hard enough to overturn the bin. I slammed down on my elbows. The water rushed through the trenched dirt where he'd dragged his finger. I crawled out onto the drawing.

"Did you feel it?" he said.

"Nothing."

"Exactly. You were expecting me to make you feel something. That's what they all wanted. Well, I gave it to them." He righted the garbage can and wheeled it out from under the grandstand. "It's going to take months for this to fill back up."

He awninged his left eye with my license and stared up at the sky. You've never seen a horizon like this, Love; in Nepal, the clouds stack as solid and tall as the Himalayans. Sometimes it looks like you could climb right off of the mountains in the distance and keep summiting through the sky.

"I'll wait," I said. It wasn't so much that I was curious, or even that I was smitten; I had this feeling like it would hurt to get too far away from him. Even with twenty feet between us, there was this pressure in my temples like sinking too quickly when you're diving.

"You can stay," he said. "But just here. No more talk about before. I'm trying to stop looking back. And you've got to promise not to follow me when I leave."

That was your father, my crackpot vagabond. That term for him was my own and only: he told me that sharing his true name would dilute his soul. Said most called him Unc, like a UNC fan misreading their own t-shirt. That was a dig at Auntie Opal's alma mater. I'd left Kure thinking that I needed to move, but what I really wanted was to find something compelling enough to stop me. He was the first one to do it. He claimed that he'd wished me into being. I was tethered to him, and I'd evaporate if I left.

He'd come to Nepal to find better things to believe. According to *The Tibetan Book of the Dead*—to his reading—a large burst of emotion could coalesce into a conscious being. That thoughtform fed off of whatever feeling had created it. Fear. Longing. Giddiness. Grief. Sounded right out of Auntie Opal's Halloweenified take on Kabbalah. I told him I'd never liked Tim Curry as Pennywise, that he was ripping off a shitty adaptation of Stephen King. He said King's third eye worked like a tube that had siphoned off of the collective unconscious, that his own had proved a practical canal for (his term) entities of psychic energy. He was trying to find a way to dam that incoming current, fighting upstream.

When I asked him to prove it—to prove anything—he just hummed me silent. Felt like he was siphoning the air from my lungs, that I was hearing my own voice inside of his. I've since spent plenty of YouTube searches trying to convince myself that he was using the same technique as Nepalese throat singers. That double-hum has been used to debunk the demon-speak of allegedly possessed people, but it doesn't explain how the sound literally, physically moved me. This was some Pied Piper type shit, Love. Maybe his humming *was* the proof I'd requested. There've been plenty of Ironman marathons since when I could've used him. But back then I was still trying to fake skepticism. I told myself I was only listening because he was interesting.

And looking at him was easy. He wooed me with those long bones he passed down to you; you've seen them. That photo didn't just fall out of my racing suit. Consider the picture passed down to you as much as the widthy skeleton of the man standing in it. Those tall cheeks. The wide shoulders. You're his dead ringer, darling.

That night he dragged a stack of rocks and hubcaps around the garbage can and climbed in. Told me to put all that crap on the lid. I shut him in, piled the stuff on the lid, and swore I heard him say, "Snug."

I laid down on the still-drying dirt where he'd drawn me. I had this urge to get raw, to feel the soil boring into my skin. The hair was still stuck in my throat, keeping me sleepless. If I'd had tweezers handy, I'd've stuck them down my windpipe to pluck it. Instead I crammed my fingers down my mouth and gagged. I puked a green puddle. A hair swirled in my vomit. I plucked it up, dug a hole, and buried it.

For a winter and spring we squatted under the grandstand of that half-abandoned soccer stadium. Every day he flung back the lid of the garbage can and hummed at the sky. It rained hard once or twice, but never reliably. At night he climbed into the can and squatted in water that reached his knees. I wanted to climb in with him, but who would pile on the debris? I shut the lid on him and heaped it with the rocks and hubcaps. I was starting to get the feeling he only breathed when I looked at him.

One morning I bored a hole in the side of the garbage bin with a broken piece of glass; that night I closed the lid on him, counted to four thousand, and peered in. I couldn't see his silhouette. I shoved off the rocks and yanked open the lid and of course it was only a trick of the dark, but I swore for a second that his body was swelling from the water's surface like a time-lapse video of a blood blister.

"Don't do that again," he said. "I was almost where I wanted to be."

The dogs and sheep slept in that field for weeks, shrinking with starvation. In March they got chased off by protestors who'd been beaten out of the city square by the State Police. The animals wobbled off on atrophied limbs. The protestors lit tires on fire and rioted ambiently. I sneezed black from the rubber smoke.

The day that the Communists won the electorate, the grandstand collapsed from the sheer force of protesting feet. Your father and I were being crushed in a mosh of raging zealots before the steps even started coming down. Rusty bolts rained around us. While I thrashed against the crowd, he took my head in his hands and pressed his temple to my stomach. That was when I decided that he was my Tulpa, a mystery formed from my urge for wandering. I wanted to force him back inside me, shelter him with my skeleton. Sections of step to our right and left were slanting down like depressed keyboard keys. The folks who'd been standing on top of them jumped and fell on the fleeing rioters in wailing heaps. It looked like they were crowd surfing.

Your father begged me to leave him behind. Said I had to promise not to follow him. I told him that this wasn't the time, that we had to keep moving, and even as I said it I saw the step over his head bending. He told me he was snug. He put my license under his tongue and hummed, only the sound was bigger than he was; I swore I felt his voice climbing my own throat, heard it spilling from the mouths of the rioters around us. My legs felt yanked out from under me. Took all my muscles clenched to stay standing. Your father climbed into his garbage can. I urged toward him, but each step was like fighting a cramp. Someone bumped the can over. That's the last thing I remember seeing.

I woke in a Nepalese hospital with a doctor fanning an ultrasound at me, chanting the word 'blessing' through chipped teeth. That image was my first look at you. I swatted it away and yanked the IVs out of my arms and limped down the hall. Bandages unspooled from my bruised legs and arms. I looked through every room in that hospital, asking every nurse and doctor who worried up to me whether they'd seen a man who looked blind, if they'd heard anyone humming. No one had. As far as I knew, you were half-orphaned before I even had a clue you were coming. I cupped my stomach where your father had bored his forehead. He must have had a hunch about you.

I come to with a damp stamp on my chest. Come back ahead of that past, I mean; I come to. I pull my head out of the trough, into gloaming. An Australian shepherd's nuzzling me. I shoo it back and ache to my feet. The dog's wet nose and the rusty tag on its collar leave welts of cold where they touched. Pooch gapes over my shoulder and whimpers neutrally.

"Former swimmer?" The Citgo attendant hunches on the clapboard's back steps, sucking a Twinkie.

"Still am."

"But did you swim for him, I'm asking." He holds his right thumb and forefinger up like he's about to pinch the view he has of me. "200 fly. I was a better breaststroker, but butterfly's the event that Unc put me in." The guy snaps. The sheepdog sprints to him and sits.

"I never swam for him."

"But whatever he told you to do, I bet you listened."

I'd done my best to, keeping him a secret from you. He'd told me that attention gives a Tulpa physical strength, but he's taken up more of my head every day that I haven't mentioned him. Maybe it's less a matter of growth, then, than redistribution: the less here he is corporeally, the bigger he looms psychologically.

"You aren't the first tourist," the attendant says. "But you're the first broad I've seen dumb enough to touch something. Are you terminal?"

"What?"

"Is it chemo?" The attendant rubs his head.

"Buzzcuts reduce drag."

"Did he tell you to do that?"

I find my shovel, use it to prop myself standing.

"Got to eek out every second," the guy says. "He used to tell us to grow out our fingernails so we'd hit the wall faster."

"You swam for him."

"I lived for him. You know how it is." Guy rubs his thumb across his scarred chest. The sheepdog leans in and licks it. "Sheared his sheep. Drove him into town when he lost his license."

"Did he ever hum to you?"

The guy snorts again. Something snagging in the sound. I picture Unc forcing his voice up the man's throat like a fist shoved into an undersized hand-puppet. Every windpipe a finger hole. No one esophagus large enough for the noise of it.

"What about Benji?"

"Swam for him, too. Wouldn't believe the shit he talked me into."

My stomach fists with the thought of all that you might be up to, the length of those eight hundred miles I've got before I can get to you. Hard not to stare at the guy's scars. "Did he hurt you?"

"Bastard blew out both my rotators. Hardest training I've ever been through. It was all hard yards. Zero drills. Guy didn't believe in technique. You can't swim good times for a long time, is what he told me. But I got my O.T." The guy slaps his shoulders, stands slow. "I'd try and forget him if I were you."

"Is that what you did?"

The guy points to the water tower. The dog wedges between his legs, whining. "Go that way when you leave."

Three coyotes pace around the tower's posts, snouts tilted up toward the tank. They hold their heads up as stiffly as if an invisible muzzle yanks them.

"Shit."

"They won't see you," the guy says. "Just treat them the same."

I make a hunched approach. The coyotes swerve around me, keep circling. A ladder leads up to the tower. A rope's tied to its bottom rung, the other cut end of it hanging over the top one. I climb up to the rickety iron landing at the top of it. A door shorter than I am is cut into the side. It doesn't budge with my shove. I brace my back against it and dig my heels into the tops of the ladder's straights. The door inches in, releasing a contagious stench. Smells like the time a squirrel gnawed its way into the

Sprinter van's black water holding tank. I pull my shirt over my nose and peer inside.

The door opens onto a concrete landing. Stairs descend into murk on its far side. The water's surface is striped like sunlight striking a puddle of gasoline. Empty Gatorade bottles and Twinkie wrappers pitch across its surface. I hold my breath, step closer, and squint.

The water's rippling.

A head juts up from the far side of the tank. Sunglasses. Hair plastering both cheeks.

"You brought me back," Benji says. "I was almost there."

"Almost where?"

"Out of this." He slides his hand up his stomach. "In the air." And stoops into the water tower like he might pull something up.

I remember how your father had seemed to solidify under my gaze the night that I'd opened the garbage bin's lid on him. Benji had risen from the water that way—more like he was forming from it than standing. Wish I'd brought up that shovel. "I knew your uncle," I say.

Benji straightens. "We weren't blood. We were neuron. He just thought me up."

"He told me that kind of shit. Said I was his Tulpa. Talked about how the third eye's a pipeline for inter-dimensional beings."

Benji rubs the lenses of his sunglasses. "Not just the third eye."

"You still believe him?"

"I'm what made him believe." Benji wades across the tank and climbs the steps to the landing. Flip-flopped and flat-footed. His pale, pruny paunch looks drained of shade. How can someone so sloppily made know so well what it takes to make others' bodies fine-tuned? He sidesteps me, exits the tank.

I stare at the water. He'd stooped like he was going to pick something up. He'd been shut inside of this reeking thing, somehow breathing. "What were you doing in here?"

"Told you. Dissolving." His breath heats my shoulder, like he's leaning in behind me. I whip around with my elbow out and strike air; he's already lowering himself down the ladder.

"Show you something." He grins up at me.

"Is it him?"

"Do you want it to be?"

I suddenly, desperately know that I don't. I'd driven down to look for your father, hoping I wouldn't find him—the way you used to check the Sprinter van's Stowaway every October to confirm that we didn't have any monsters hitchhiking. I follow him down.

Benji glints like he's dripping, but the ladder's rungs are bone-dry.

He takes me to the barn. The building's house-facing wall is fitted with a sliding door. Benji jerks it open. I picture what's left of your father behind it, but there's only a pickup parked inside. String lights dangle from the sideview mirrors. Animal pelts are nailed to the walls and ceiling. The furs look canine, or feline—bigger than a house cat, but finer than the coats of most dogs. All are variations of red, brown, and grey, the colors of a rust-brindled sink.

"I thought he farmed sheep," I said.

Benji slams into the driver's side. The hides blanch under the truck's highbeams. I try the passenger's door, but it's locked.

Benji rolls down the window. "Shut the door for me."

He backs out of the barn. I slide the door shut and he pulls away, rumbling through the pasture parallel to the road. He dangles his arm out the window, pinching his Oakleys in his fingers. The rearview reflects his blue-white eyes. He drives slow.

His hum grows above the truck's engine. The sound ladens the air like humidity. Only then do I let my brain think what my eardrums heard the moment I picked up his call: your father's spirit's stuck to Benji, not me. I can't blame Unc for what I almost did in Peru—what Doro stopped me from doing. (I'll get to that, Love. Just let me work up my gumption.)

I run up to the driver's side, parallel with the window.

Benji's weeping. He bites off the hum. "Unc told me to find Ezra."

"What'd you do to him?"

"Just left him. Just trained him. He's zenning. I told you."

The truck eases ahead. I speed up to keep even. Benji's irises seem like they're paling, the blue drawn off through the veins splintering across the whites of his eyes. He slides on his sunglasses, accelerating. "What did Unc do to you?"

I get this itch at the back of my throat. Feels like I might gag if I speak.

Benji punches the odometer's dial, then cruise control. The speedometer's needle freezes a hash-mark above ten. I narrow into my stride, the sweet insides of those Reese's coming back up on me. He nods along to the rhythm of my foot strikes. Each tilt of his head feels like its tilting the road farther downhill, easing my effort. Is this what your past eight months have been like? Benji's pulling me ahead like your father's hum, tugging against my tightening hamstrings.

The gravel conglomerates into fissured asphalt. We pass the first row of turbines, move through swatches of night undivided by skyscraper-sized poles. Benji cuts the headlights. He punches the odometer's dial. "17 flat. You just ran that for 5k."

The pickup brakes to a stop. I jog on.

"How much of a P.R. is that?" he calls.

It's my best time by thirty seconds, but he doesn't deserve the satisfaction of knowing. I double back. Benji swings his door open and steps out behind it, holding it like a shield between us.

You know how it burns after spending so long at your VO2 max—all the blood that's been pumping through your extremities rushes back into your torso, and the only way to keep from getting queasy is to ease off the pace gradually. I brace my hands on the pickup's window, refluxing Reese's. A brown-green stream of me lands on Benji's flip-flops.

"Good," he says. "Empty out the calories."

I try to transpose the kid from that photo on the pool deck onto this Benji. He's got that same slouch, like your father's still leaning on his head.

Benji hands me an ID. My first driver's license. I'd only passed the test the second time. Auntie Opal had been promising I could move in on my eighteenth birthday, so I'd listed her address; my parents' had changed month-to-month, a rotation of motels on the beachfront, depending on who was dealing and how much the bail was. Your father had asked for it in Dasharath.

"I thought Unc was dead."

"So did he."

"He used to hum that way to me."

"He's contagious."

I drop the license in the weeds. Benji nods.

"Unc told me your son could help me."

"Help you what?"

He tugs a strand of his hair to his mouth with his left hand and slides it between his teeth like he's flossing. "I couldn't stop being me."

It's the same with Cathy, or any of the other recidivists at Doro's clinic—less obviously, with anyone. You can change a habit, but not the desire that drives it. Relapse is only as far off as your discipline's length.

"Just get Ezra to the starting line," Benji says. "The rest's me."

"Don't come."

He bends into the pickup.

"You were going to show me something."

"Did." He points to my legs. "Seventeen-minute 5k. That's what those can do."

Ezra

Shiela stands a prosthetic leg on the floor beside Casper's cot. A stiff cylinder of dull plastic.

"Where's the foot?" Ezra asks, shaking off Percocet-laden sleep. His tongue feels fat with the drug. He'd borrowed one for his fatigue, another for Casper's pain, and a third for Benji, thinking it might slug him down vicariously.

"This one's just for the assessment," says Shiela.

A cramp clenches Ezra's left gastroc. "You can come back."

"We've put this off for too long." She gavels the tile. "Let's wake him."

Ezra yanks Casper's big toe till it pops and falsetto-says, "Got your piggy."

Shiela takes her hands off the prosthetic, which seems staked there, freestanding. Ezra pictures her lifting Casper like a Play-Mobile toy. She puts her hand on the stretched side of Casper's neck.

He pounces awake in a kind of plyometric sit-up. "You again."

Dr. Walsh shoves through the door. "Just poking my head in. How's that AMPPRO?"

Casper's head tips back to his shoulder.

"We're getting there," says Shiela.

Walsh nods at Ezra like he'd been the one speaking. "Got a big brick workout in the a.m."

"Age-grouper," Casper says.

"Is he sweating?" Walsh asks. "Ezra, did someone bring you the Cleocin?"

Casper's forehead does look polished. He swings his kicking

leg off the cot and points it at Walsh like an accusing finger. "Want my bug back."

She palms Casper's forehead, squinting at the monitor. "Ninety-nine eight. I'm getting a nurse."

"You're a doctor."

"Surgeon. I'm not authorized for med dispensation."

Ezra pictures Walsh's jaw unhinging to spout Cleocin like a Pez.

"Y'all be good. I've got a phlebectomy in t-minus…" Walsh flourishes back her sleeve to flash her digital Timex. "Minus. I'll grab that nurse."

She jogs for the door with deliberate form, pulling her legs under her hips meticulously.

"I'll go on and mark you down for sitting balance." Shiela gashes her clipboard with her pen. "I say we go ahead with the assessment, if you feel up."

Casper storks himself standing on the right leg.

"Not yet." Shiela unpockets a stopwatch. "There are forty-two tasks we'll run through. Only attempt the ones that you're confident and comfortable with." She taps Ezra's chairback. "Sorry, hon. Got to borrow this."

He groans to his feet.

Casper toes up on the right foot.

"I'll put that down as single-limb standing," says Shiela.

"Seems qualitative," Ezra says.

"We go case-by-case." She nods to herself more than Casper. "Can you try sitting down for me?"

"Ain't doing nuts for your sake." Casper braces his weight on chair's arms like parallettes, straightening his leg and stump in a gymnast's L-position. He lowers himself slowly like he's milking a workout. "I move for me."

He one-ups each item of her test. Pistol-squats through the timed balance. Hops back and forth over a water bottle with shut eyes.

"Great," Shiela says. "Both of you."

Ezra's hopping, too—too used to being told how to move.

Shiela hands Casper a crutch. He machine-guns it at Ezra, who fakes taking bullets.

Shiela shakes her head. "Y'all two. Let's wrap up with the step test."

She leads them to the stairwell at the corner of the floor. The crutch is too tall to nock properly under Casper's armpit. He flaps it out to clear the floor. Halfway down the hall, he mutters "nuts," and tosses it.

"You'll want that in a second," Shiela says.

Ezra picks it up. Shiela props the door.

Casper stops. "Did I curtsy?"

"Pardon?"

"Ain't a lady. Go first."

Ezra steps through the door. "Thanks. Sorry."

Shiela follows him. The door clatters shut.

Casper inches it open with his crutch. "Want my droops."

"His what?"

"The Percocet." Ezra pulls the pills from the key-pocket of his running shorts. The waistband cuts his knuckles, grit-stiff. The night that he'd stepped into these shorts, Casper'd still had both legs.

Shiela drums her clipboard. "This is simple. Climb, descend. Just two steps."

Casper hops up the stairs two at a time.

"That's plenty!" Shiela calls. "Can you descend?"

He summits the flight and about-faces them.

"Just two stairs," Shiela says. "Go ahead."

Casper totters on the landing.

"You didn't say Simon."

"You can use the crutch," Shiela says.

Ezra jogs it up to him.

"Don't look," Casper says.

Ezra descends the steps.

"Right. I'll just spot him." Shiela pushes the clipboard into

Ezra's chest. Shiela climbs the stairs and stops two steps below Casper. "You can use the railing."

The kid presses the crutch's arm cushion into the top step like a shovel he's testing the dirt with. Scoops it once as if digging a hole to put his foot in. Shiela drops her arms and steps back. Casper lowers himself to her.

"Flying colors," Shiela says

"Save the fag-flag for Atom-Man." Casper hops around her, stomping himself to a crouching stop beside Ezra. "Droop me."

Ezra pulls a pill from his shorts, hands it over.

Shiela holds out her hand for the clipboard. Ezra unfolds the paper before passing it back. Strange to see his own name written on the assessment, the 'z' of it crossed like the body of a '7'. BlueCross has to be onto them. Shiela soft-yanks the clipboard from him.

Casper snorts. "Y'all two ain't gonna to hump."

Shiela shuts her eyes. "I'll have that K-level tomorrow. Can you find your way back?"

She pushes through the door before Ezra can splutter *absolutely*. He lets it fall shut, a buffer for his blush.

"Ain't a boomerang," Casper says.

"What?"

"Benji." Casper smacks his thigh with the crutch. "Quit waiting with your hand out. He ain't coming back."

Casper

I beat RoboCop back to my room, turn that egg face-his rotten. Shiela Petey's left that fake leg by my cot, looking tree-stumped without me atop it. The burger's back on TV. And I can see RoboCop's thinking as clear as the sex gleams through that food when you turn the sound off: he's thinking I'm waiting on Benj. But I'm waiting on him. Hope and hate for him to know it, but long's I got him around I don't even need to weep over who we're missing.

RoboCop can keep the Percs. Benj can stay away. Wish he'd never even given me his secret name. Matter-fact, I'm taking back the *I* he lopped off of it; you're done getting me, Benji. You can't be Unc to me. Shoo to that shed of his and get on shaving them sheep. Get off on it, maybe. Picture Benji haircutting them like his own head. Never knew a ram was a boy sheep till he told—the same animal! Then again, they call men dogs. *You're a good one*, Benji'd tell me every time before he said to shuteye, and I'd shut ever organ on down to my kidneys. Them days I drooped even deeper than Percs, nodding easy because Benji was moving me.

Now it's just Shiela Petey. Ever day she comes and pops me onto that stump. Only she calls my leg *the stump*, and calls that tree-stump of a fake leg *the leg* like it's the very bone of Fido, which Adam the Atom Man said is French for the authenticest thing. Shiela puts my leg in the sock and the stump just sticks. Don't even have to glue or tie it. The *provisional leg*. She says I'll get one more articulate after the stump—my leg—shrinks. I hope that's not Fido's bone. The phantom limb of that tree stump. Fido, fetch! My own body yaps loud enough; could use one less limb talking back to me.

Shiela tries to graft me to that sucker down in her lair where she gives me the therapy. The room's matted and barred and foamed like gymnastics, plus mirrors all over so I can see the fool she's making of me. First day she wanted me to hold onto two bars and walk propped between even when she'd plain-saw me hop in on my own one foot. I squeezed through them bars like they were Wayne Gretsky and Bobby Orr's hockey sticks guarding me. Passed on through them bars so fast I hopped off my stump. Shiela gave me some mumbo about progression and sent me back, showing me a stick-figure on one-them clipboarded sheets. Baby school, if you ask me. And I ain't up for that any more than hockey, gymnastics, or amateur forestry.

Provisional, Shiela kept calling that stump, and it sure did feed me up. I leaned one hand on the bar and un-popped it with the other and gave her a good thunk to the upside with it. RoboCop gulped his snort, but I heard. And Shiela held her head looking at me all speculating like what the 'h'-'e'-Bobby-Orr-and-Wayne-Gretsky's my problem. Folks've been asking that my whole lifelong with me a-chorusing. Benji's the sole soul who never gave no bones about it, or at least kept those bones buried; he just told the training without ever asking or wondering. Every rose has its thorn, the telling goes. And Fido gets his nose poked if he sticks it too close when he's dig-sniffing. That's why being with Benj was like Percs, I reckon: if I ran as hard-far-fast as he said I'd tucker out enough to keep whatever was wrong with me forever-buried.

Yet here's Shiela Petey trying to pull her own wool over me. All them goals stick-figured on her sheet are to goaltend my attention from noticing what I'm missing. She herself fessed it's fixing to shrink. How much? What if all of me scrunches up to my neck and then I'm one-them shriveled heads getting voodooed by witchdoctor Walsh?

Now it's her and Shiela versus Orr and Gretsky tree stumps for hockey sticks, the four-them scraping up the thin ice of my thinking. I need Percs to refreeze them. RoboCop's my dispensary. Pops off that bottle and spanks them out like Pez candies. So much for GU gels and sports performance. He's sweet on Shiela, so I go along and eat all her provisionals to get to the Perc Desert waiting for me.

The menu of items that she checks off her sheet! And the pamphlets she hands me that RoboCop sounds out back in our room. Purpose and process. Goal's to tone the muscles. Reorient the center of gravity. Tasks are filters for grief. He needs tasks worse than I do. I can see the run welling up in him. His veins shrink like my leg from too long without moving, clogging his heart. He'll either blow up or take off soon's he's out the hospital.

RoboCop says you got to mourn a lost part of you, and I don't know if that's the pamphlet or him telling me. What we both know is he's reading to me. Wanting to do me that favor. I nod along for his sake like I'm taking it. That's no bone of Fido, but I don't mind the lie; I can stand letting him think.

Casper gets discharged on the tenth day. Ezra isn't sure how much of that stay was for the limb healing versus the last of the Staph getting scrubbed from Casper's bloodstream. He'd begun to get this sleepless idea that Casper's hospital room was a cell, color-coded according to crime and victim: a white-collar crime against BlueCross. The ivory walls; the azure seep from the TV.

Ezra flips through the discharge papers. The surgery and therapy and the reservoirs of liquid and oral drugs and the P.T. and the room he's taken up, and the shuttle-ride home are all covered. Not a single cent of copay. A siren wells. Ezra winces a glance out the exit, anticipating police; just an ambulance. Duh. He wishes they'd just cuff him.

Ezra hands the papers back to the receptionist. She passes them to Casper. From the way that Casper had stared at those pamphlets, Ezra'd already gathered that the kid couldn't read. But how could anyone make it to eighteen without learning to write their name? Casper Swayze: a ghost in the eyes of the State.

They step outside to swabbed sky. It's God-bright out here, but there's the roomy promise of fall in the breeze. The air feels spacious after a summer toothed with skeeters and tongue-thick humidity.

Casper stands on the prosthetic, tipping the crutch to Ezra. "Minus?"

Meaning how long until his next Percocet. A phrase Casper'd taken from Dr. Walsh; should've taken her Timex. Ezra was thinking he'd have to get the kid a watch, hating that his mind went to this. Was that their dynamic now? Were they exchanging gifts?

"When we get home," Ezra says. "Back. The boat."

"But math the minus."

"Thirty-four," Ezra guesses.

"Thirty-three Mississippi."

"Minutes, bud."

"Minutes." Casper chews the word like he can gnaw down the unit. "Fetch the moped."

"It's impounded."

A shuttle grumbles around the median. The driver kicks out and jogs around to Casper, drumming a clipboard with black-painted fingernails. "Ezra Fogerty?"

"That's him," Ezra says. "Us."

Casper dives into the passenger's side, leaving the prosthetic standing behind him. Ezra climbs into the back. The chassis snorts with the driver's added weight.

"Just us?" Ezra asks.

The driver squashes the gas.

They catch a red light at the intersection by the veteran's cemetery. Casper's cheeks bulge with held breath. The driver works his steel-toed boot on the brake like a kick-drum. The shuttle inches into the crosswalk. "Kure, right?"

Ezra nods, watching Casper's pursed lips and the clock.

"Should've called a boat."

Traffic thuds past, catching some pothole or hump in the intersection. A long red.

"Guess y'all heard about the flash floods." The driver spreads both hands out on the dash like he's sun-drying that manicure. The black on his fingernails looks stamped on, squared and edged. "Hurricane Samuel," he says. "Tropical freaking depression. Named after my ex."

The dash clock flicks to 12:07. Casper's throat twitches.

The shuttle's hood nudges halfway into the lane. A Civic swerves wide and honks.

"Amen!" the driver hollers. Below his steel-toe, the brakes puff.

The light greens. They catch the pothole going over the intersection. In the rearview, the cemetery and Casper's nostrils both shrink.

Three minutes without air and the kid's nose-breathing.

A long stretch along Oleander past a cigarette kind of drag. All self-storage spaces and doublewides in this neck, ash-trails of gravel drives stretching off through smoky pines: Oak Ridge and Riverview and Lake's Edge, streets named by topography, and one corner store named for its pet. Oleander dumps them into the right lane of 421 at Monkey Junction.

"So the elephant," the driver says. "Where do y'all stand far as traps?"

"Hard pro," Ezra says.

"Amen!" Driver smacks the wheel, swerving them. "I say classify them as varmints. Authorize open season. The rednecks will flock, promise. Let the Duplin militia eat off them. Rugs and dinner for the swamp counties. You want a hand getting that off, bud?"

This to Casper, who's chewing the pill bottle again.

"He's teething," Ezra says.

"That's one word." Driver snorts. "He's engraving his whole damn dental record."

The kid's going to get the cap stuck, warp the thread. But no more chance of stopping him than there'd been on the Piston. His face stays as blank-smooth as that day, pedaling on after the flywheel had busted. Where's his brain? The same place. Ezra knows the kid's thinking of Benji.

"Bet y'all could give me both ears' full on traps," the driver's saying. "Couple of closet snare experts. Y'all brothers?"

Casper spits in the cupholder. The driver stares at the gob like he might tea-leaf a fortune from it.

"Sorry," Ezra says.

He shrugs. "Tip me."

The dash clock says 12:19. The ride's not so much going slowly as coagulating. Ezra whiffs the weft haunts of Pinesol and vomit cross-stitched with the A.C. And the Piggly Wiggly attached to the strip-mall Bible college, and the mainland's last fire station, and the Goodwill with the roof in need of the sentiment that was under it, and then the first tire-tracked coyote. A mat of sun-wrung fur and organ on the shoulder. Casper lifts his eyes to the rearview as they pass it. They start up Woody Hewett Bridge in the same order: him ahead, Ezra behind. Only now the kid's looking back. Same motion, different meaning: no Benji.

Casper spits the pill bottle. "Bark on." He means it like a tree this time, surely—they're back to the roots. They've come home.

"You good back there?" the driver asks. "You get carsick?"

Ezra's breathing like he's running.

Casper grins. "RoboCop's getting squirmy."

The kid's right; Ezra's been still for too long. He could use a jog. A helmet to leave his brain in.

"Crack that window," the driver says.

They crest the bridge. The sopping sheet of Kure crumples like soaked paper below them: wadded dunes and pulpy sand college-ruled with narrow streets, carnival rides writhing cursive across the boardwalk, hole-punched by dark shapes on the margin of horizon. Silhouettes as blank, as fixed in their shapes as negative spaces.

"Buzzards," the driver says with the blunt tone of a destination he's announcing. "I'd call that an omen if it weren't so on the..." He taps the bridge of his nose. "Sure you don't want me to crack that window?"

"I'm good," Ezra says.

"If you feel something coming up, you just tell me."

The buzzards hang slow circles, black punctures in the ozone.

They come down to the flood. Water brims out of ditches, blurring the road's shoulder. The shuttle's tires shed snakeskins of water. The plaster Jaws gargles water out front of Wings. The town council looks to've declared imminent domain over every sign along Ocean Street. CURFEW MANDATORY. EVACUATION ADVISED. Iterations of these messages repeated on billboards, restaurants' marquees. The sign outside Kure First Baptist says FLOOD'S COMING. A handwritten retort's mounted on the mailbox of the bungalow next door: ITS YOUR CARBON FOOTPRINT, NOT JESUS'S.

The driver drum-rolls the steering wheel, shaking his head. "God's wrath or the ice caps. Both put us underwater. It all the ends in the same apocalypse, if you ask me." He taps the bridge of his nose again, and Ezra nearly tells him *don't do that;* instead, gulps. "Want me to pull over?"

"No."

"Well, you do, you just tell me. Don't be a martyr about it." The driver presses something on his door, plunging every window. "Had enough heroes for this bus. I am not fixing to have me the same kind of Tuesday."

An onshore gust scrapes fumes off the marina, smearing an internal, synthetic odor, like perfume spritzed in a surgery. Wilting herbs. Rotting beef.

"You can just let us out here," Ezra says.

"You sure?"

"Sure."

The driver glanced at his GPS, Casper's leg. The kid shields his lap with both hands in some knee-jerk the source of which Ezra tries not to picture.

"Sure," he says again.

The driver raises his eyes, brakes, and Casper relaxes—whatever expectation he'd been tensing for averted. He falsetto-sings, "RoboCop's got the squirms!" and jerks his door open, giddy with relief.

Ezra has the prosthetic and crutch. He crams the fare at the driver, yanks the sliding door and it resists.

"Got to wait for it," the driver says. "Automatic."

Casper pogoes on his right leg—hopping for joy, then for balance. His stump flails as frantically as his arms. Ezra catches his foot squeezing around the van door and sprawls facedown, skinning the just-healed skin of his palms. When he shoves up

Casper's struck a tightrope of equilibrium, a taut line formed from the cords of his hamstring and his Achilles tendon. As if Ezra's taken the fall on behalf of him. He hopes so even as he hates himself for the instinct: a part of him longs to even their suffering.

"Y'all good?" the driver asks.

Ezra stands up and turns to him. "Peachy."

"Don't make me drive him back." The guy cackles, winks at Casper. "Keep your brother."

The kid leans through the passenger's window and spits.

The driver presses his thumb down and the side-door inches closed. He presses a button on the console and guitars saw-blade the speakers. A wailing howl rises not far to their west, as if grating against it. The shuttle skids a u-turn and fishtails north up the oncoming lane. The guitars shrink out of earshot, but the howling keeps grating. Another wails up from the south. One frictions off the other, sparking more. The dunes. The duplex across the street—from inside it, Ezra swears, rattling through the garage door. Adrenaline lurches up his throat. But it's not their number or their volume or even their proximity that spills those flight hormones through his bloodstream. It's the fact that, though he searches and spins, swinging his stare with all the blunt force of the branch, he can't see a single coyote. To know they can get this close invisibly. To think they've done so just to put the fear of the preyed-on back into them. And in that moment Ezra knows that staying in the woods with Casper had been the right and only thing. He'd had to ward them off. No more choice than the infection had left Dr. Walsh. If Ezra'd run to call an ambulance there'd be even less of the kid. Casper's extending his stump to balance, holding it straight out behind him. Like a tail, Ezra thinks.

"Varms."

The kid says it like a sentence. He reaches up and twists the pill bottle, clenching the cap in his teeth. He tips it back and spanks out some tablets. Three or four. His throat bulges with swallowing.

Ezra gulps dryly. He offers the crutch. "Trade me? I can hold those."

Casper shoves the pills down the front of his shorts. "Go on, homo."

He hops on one leg for a block. Ezra stops when he falls, offering the crutch and prosthetic. Casper shoos him. Ezra turns down Bromine Avenue and waits just out of eyeshot.

Casper crawls around the corner glare-first. "Quit waiting up."

"I'm running out of arms."

Ezra drops the prosthetic and goes on. A rustle and crunch later Casper catches up on the prosthetic. His acceptance of the thing is the opposite of surrender, Ezra thinks: he only popped it on because he can't stand Ezra getting ahead.

Ezra drops back.

"You ain't getting more into me, Shadefoot," Casper says. "I ain't looking back."

Long droop down Bromine Avenue. October cold. The tree cover steals all summer from the day. They wade through pools of chill, the shade sapping Ezra's body-heat like floodwater. His hands and feet are cold from a week of scarce eating. His heart thuds blunt and low. He carries Casper's crutch across his chest like a gun. Buzzards' heads drip down from branches and the rain gutters of trailers, necks curling like faucets, as if their beaks spigoted the water ponding the yards they lord over. Their belching squawks. The decoys they've displaced from porches bobbing in standing water, plastic owls and rubber snakes set out to stave gulls. The buzzards are less skittish. Casper keeps clapping his hands in failed efforts to spook them, stomping his prosthetic. *Provisional leg.* He's moving as fast as Ezra on the thing. There's something feral in the brainless way the kid's adapted to his new body. Ezra remembers the trapped coyote chewing its leg. Remembers Ma telling him not to get histrionic. When Casper begins to slow it seems less a failure of his anatomy than the Percocet catching up; he lists more than stumbles, catching himself on Ezra's chest. Keeping his hand on the crutch. Ezra passes it to him.

"Just to hold," Casper says. Ezra nods. Casper braces his weight on it. "Clam it."

"What?"

"Hush."

"Didn't say—"

"But hush your eyes."

Ezra shuts them.

"Never asked for no caddy," Casper says.

"I know."

Ezra listens to his progress: crunch of his right foot on the gravel, crunch of the crutch, then the longer crackle of the prosthetic leg scraping ahead. Crisp sounds like the dry chords of an accordion. Ezra counts out fifteen of them. When he opens his eyes, Casper's only one lawn past where he's standing. His shoulder blades bunch the same second Ezra takes a step. He drags the crutch faster, doesn't look back. Ezra keeps having to stop to keep from pulling even. Casper's ear tips to his shoulder. Ezra thinks of a teapot. Thinks he can see the Percocet welling up in the kid, a loosening that begins at the base of his stride. His right leg seems to drip down from his torso. He trickles himself over that crutch. Ezra feels a similar liquidness in his legs. Something's wrong with the quads; the muscles feel flexless, like the fibers have turned into ligaments. He Jell-Os along on tendon and cartilage. Their progress—this day—his brain—is profoundly slow. No. It isn't a matter of pace so much as clarity. He's become accustomed to the abstraction of exhaustion, his months with Benji blurring by like a view of a landscape through a foggy window.

"Quit gawking." Casper's swiveling in the center of the cul-de-sac, using the prosthetic as the axis. "Hear your pants-ants from here. Go run some-that squirm off."

Crackling friction between that stump and prosthetic. Ezra wards the sound-image of torn stitches. He lands on a worse picture: the kid compassing just like this the night he'd stepped in the trap, spinning in fevered search of Benji.

Casper quits rotating, needling his stare at Ezra. Pupils pinched from the Percocet. "Truck's gone."

"What?"

"Truck's gone. He ain't here. Save your craning."

Ezra shakes his head.

"Don't let on like you weren't." Casper spits. "You're the pot, thinking I'm the one he's got leashed."

Is it the kid's anger that turns Ezra, or the source of it? The need to disprove or look away from his claim. Benji's the one who'd held him under that waterfall of exhaustion. How was that submersion any different from the Percocet washing over Casper? God's wrath or the ice caps. A flood of dopamine either way. And Ezra isn't sure if he's running toward or away from that recognition, bouncing back up Bromine Avenue for the first time in two weeks.

"Have the headstart!" Casper hollers. "I'll count to infinity!"

Ezra's legs move by a stretch reflex, a rubber band snapping back: he runs himself slack, as if motion itself is his settled state. Glad he'd stopped short of the boat. Better to duck out before getting all the way back to that cabin. Casper'd called it home. The longer Ezra can put off putting his feet up, the longer he can delay confronting the fact that at some point in their absence he'd started thinking of it the same way.

A slogging run up the beach. North across the slanted sand with the pier growing in front of him and no sense of distance or time or goal beyond reaching rib-bursting effort, breath and blood songbirding this return to exertion. Like that he's fourth-grade again, chasing a stray ball out of bounds at recess. Catching up to it and leaving it. Those earliest runs with the excuse of lacrosse, lapping the fence-line at recess with a toy stick and a ball pretending he was practicing cradling. Ms. Jill had watched his orbits from the camping chair where she reffed and convalesced her long-torn meniscus. She'd crutched around for all five years Ezra'd spent at New Dawn Elementary. *Drop the stick,* she'd told him. He'd ninety-ninth percentile-ed the mile at that spring's Presidential Fitness test. 5:20. Ms. Jill'd thought her thumb must've bumped 'pause' on the stopwatch. Had him run it again the following Friday. That time she'd clocked him at 5:16.

The next morning, Ezra'd been barreling back from a run and nearly collided with Ma at the mailbox.

"Woah there," she'd said. "Morning."

He'd turned and watched her trot off in taped-up tennis shoes. Those shit-kicker New Balances had been the most suitable footwear she'd owned in those days; hadn't run a day in her life, or covered a mile at a clip in all those days combined, according to her own hyperbole. He'd inspired her into the sport. It was all him, in her words, ever since. But Ezra's mind pans farther back than all of that, zooming in to those first steps beyond the lacrosse ball—the moment when the object had shifted.

He runs without sense of far or hard. Under the pier; through the swathed chill of the carnival rides' sand-stretched silhouettes; beyond the boardwalk and marina to the end of the island. He only folds over when he runs out of beach. Hands-to-knees, then knees-to-sand, and then he's prone on the bank of the inlet with his senses scrunching and the shadow of Woody Hewitt bridge cowling the inlet. His legs bulge with the first dull pulse of soreness, throbbing like a sigh climbing. The twinging he'd felt in his quads before starting had simply been a lack of this— freshness a sensation so strange that he'd mistaken it for an injury. His legs have absorbed the work he thought he'd squandered swinging that branch, or at least wrung out the last of the fatigue.

This is just baseline, maybe. For a year he's been walking around on quadriceps prone to buckling, gingering his way down steps and curbs. Most folks lived their lives without that sensation. All it would take to join them would be stopping persistently. Then the butter-slide of the easy life: his days would congeal and clarify, thick and tooth-sticking as ghee. All those pamphlets he'd read to Casper talked about purpose as a method of mourning. Folks used to don burlap to do that, hire professional wailers, chair-sore their asses sitting shiva for a week. You needed a task to contain your loss so you could check off the sentiment as 'complete.' Item processed. Running after a goal let you burn off the grief with your energy.

But forget that, and the squirms—just tricks to work up starting inertia. You run beyond them like that lacrosse ball, Ezra thinks. The pursuit itself becomes the object. At some point he'd lost sight of this—the motor of his own legs moving under him—staring ahead at less compelling things: Casper's back, Ironman rankings, personal records. His own gasping reflection in Benji's Oakleys. The weary warmth he feels now beats it all. The tidal flow from freshness to exhaustion, his pulse springing and neaping. Ezra lies in the inlet's shallows, savoring the precious estuary of his own energy. And aside from being starved and cold, and itchy from brackish water lapping him—those salt crystals rough as a cat's tongue—and the buzzards smearing the sky, and the coyotes as invisibly everywhere as the tideline of bilge odor hanging over the marina, the fullness of their absence as claustrophobic as Benji's—Ezra's as puppy as Casper. For the first time in a long time, he feels animal happy.

He fartleks home. Backtracks staccato, in surges and jogs, accelerating and lapsing according to whim. Sometimes he walks. More than once, stops. He hurdles the railing of a beach access and sprints up a protected dune and there's no sheriff in this ghost town to stop him. Just buzzards and coyote wails breeze-rolled like tumbleweeds. Only one other soul that he sees from his sandy summit: a single sunbather shivering. She lies prone on the deck of a beachfront, unstrapped from her bikini. Elbows up to stare back. Ezra notices her breasts clogging the space between her and the deck.

"Yeah?" she says.

"Sorry."

He turns and jogs. Pauses. She's flopped onto her back when

he turns again. A sideview of boob spilling into her armpit. His stare sticks like it had on Shiela at Casper's therapy, the parallel bars brushing both of her lusciously wide hips; something about pressed flesh. Ezra'd spent every one of those sessions in a state of ambient horniness. Typically training blunted this. His twenties had mostly been one flaccid flop of exhaustion, his testosterone drained by training. He's too used to all his heartbeats going to his legs. Strange to have enough blood to spare for his penis. He stares at the sunbather staring up at the sky, wanting to say, *you don't know what this means to me.*

"How about those coyotes?" he tries.

"Fuck off."

He siphons the blood back into his strides. Passing the pier, he latches into a tempo. About half-marathon pace, lactate thresholdish: that liminal effort at which hydrogen ions start accumulating. Not to train. Just to feel it. A welling numbness in the calves and hip flexors. He grows limb-dumb, clumsy with fatigue. Clings to rhythm to keep his pace up. Aligning breaths and footsteps, the sand and his gasps crunching—one noise seaming to the other, or sinking under it. Calming himself with a system of smoothings. This starts with those muscles at the backs of his ears, pinched and small as a restaurant drinking straw's crumbled wrapping. He lets them lapse and stretch. Cheeks next. Shoulders. Hips. Smooth the task, too, to the beach just in front of him. This step. This step. This step. Concentration a kind of reduction. A litany of refocusings. Isolating each stride until he startles back to the end of Bromine Avenue, alarmed at their sudden sum; also, at the Sprinter van parked in the cul-de-sac.

Ezra pulls up and turns how he'd come, then turns back to the van. The road runs to it like an equals sign, as if this is his effort's product. Bigger than the popup camper. Backed in. Parked near enough to look like they're hitched. The door's open on the driver's side, a wetsuit hanging off the sideview like a pelt. Below the door are a set of glutes wrapped in bike shorts, legs propped up on the door's inside. Ten empty toes curl over the open windowsill, waggling greeting. "That you?"

"Me."

"Well come the hell over. Let me count them."

Ezra takes sweet seconds doing so.

She's lying on a yoga mat, shaved to the epidermis. Like she'd razored her top layer of skin off with her hair. That vascular. That sinewed, and the flayed kind of sunburnt. A poster cadaver for a lesson in starved anatomy. She grips Ezra's left, then right ankle, raising the negative spaces of shaved eyebrows. "BlueCross must've counted wrong. That's two." And checks her watch. "I got four more minutes draining. Then I want a hug."

Ezra gingers down beside her, still fragile-legged.

She tips her head back toward the popup camper. "Who's stud?"

Ezra looks that way and sees Casper asleep on his Bianchi. Straddling the top tube with his right leg and prosthetic, leaning with the bike. His left shoulder propped on the sidewall of the popup's nylon extension. Crutch wedged under that armpit. The kid's head, of course, sideways, a plumb-line of drool dangling. He seems both posed and slack, somehow, contrapposto. Opiated to sleep.

"Sure. Later." She pats the ground to her left. Mud clings to the back of her stubbled head.

Ezra elbows down and swings his run-sore calves up beside hers. Idea's to elevate the feet for fifteen minutes, letting gravity flush waste products from your legs. All the hours they've quartered just like this. Here they are all over again, just her and him.

She bumps his right knee with her left. "There you are."

"Hey, Ma," Ezra says.

Casper

Then here's the her of him.

I was just fixing to ride the bike. Guess them Percs must've hit. Like a scene just fell out the day's movie: I un-dip from a droop and RoboCop's gone-got cloned in the feminine. She's thin-bald to the point of resembling a medical condition. Sheared sheep to his ram. Big-ass van bumpered up to the camper with the driver's door flapped and the two-them leaning their legs against it, fishhooking their feet back like bait at me. I ain't biting. Never took nuts from no one. But RoboCop. Way he cranes toward her. Way she cocks the sideview through the dropped window with her heel and he ghosts the same motion, so you'd take him for the clone, only God needed a man's rib to make ladies. Pebble-skip of her talking. Sinking splash of his laugh. Other thing about a man's that he was made to take the lead, but it took a thin minute for that to turn into him pulling the cart Eve was sitting on, and her steering. Reined him right on out of Eden with the snake as his bridle. A flood and a cross later ever straight sop's bending knee for them and leashing their fingers with rings. Adam the Atom Man clued me to all that. Said he thought fags were better off; said that with my own hand stroking on him. Swear he was as pot-calling as RoboCop. Least his Eve was imaginary. To see Robo's heel tracing this lady's; to hear the rock-plop his laugh. Could've sobbed. All heart-hopes I'd got when RoboCop was rubbing on my foot in that hospital were sinking like that rock of his laughing. I was just fixing to ride the bike, then the droop, and in the time it took my head to tip up I'd sussed that this lady was holding his leash. She had him sit-and-stay. His heart-hope's kenneled in her ribcage. Sum of that-all was as hard a swallow as crotch, and sore as a stiff kick to it. Stiff as this bicycle my own crotch seems-been kissing on, dent-bending around its top tube like sucking lips. I was just fixing to ride it—which I'll get to—but first I could've sobbed. Because I heard-saw that this lady had her fist taut on RoboCop's leash, and so long as her grip stayed gaumed on him RoboCop couldn't be my Benji.

So I nib a Perc. Another. Don't hoot if it's been enough hours; my brain hurts. Leaking ache all through my organs. My own heart-hope's trying to keep sinking, only it's already bottomed out in my knee. Nigh on to dropping out of me. Them stitches yapping with my ever blood-beat. One more Perc and I'll get on with that ride. I'll get onto this bike. Keep tipping when I try. I crutch one hand on the camper and swap-pop my crutch to my other armpit and tick-tock between them, trying to strike a balance. Striking it like a second hand, passing it in an instant. I shove off the popup and lean onto the crutch. Shove off the crutch and lean into the popup. Lucky I'm out from Shiela Petey's funhouse of therapy. Couldn't stand my reflection in them damn joke mirrors seeing me. Just trying to ride. But first, droop. All this work-up and I'm yapping for more Perc. I still down a second. Bite off the cap and catch the two-them craning gazes at me.

RoboCop stone-throws his voice back; he's weighted and sunken it. "Meet Ma."

He'd done took half my name for her. Mama's what Benji called me. Now I know what Adam felt like getting his rib God-snatched. And his livestock. The name-taking alone gets my goat, herding it off for that damn leash-clinging Eve of a sheep. Now I'm meant to meet her? She's got more leg, and a van. Not to mention she's the one barged up here in the first. I gulp a third Perc.

"Naw." She can damn well meet me.

Ezra's pupils go pinball. "That's Casper."

"8:20." Lady says it like she's renaming me.

I get back to tick-tocking that bike. More tip now than strike. That perch of balance keeps narrowing as the Percs widen through me.

"Come now," Ezra says.

"Gonna ride."

Lady snorts. "Looks like it."

I slack back against the popup. Still fixing to, but a Perc first. One more droop. Slurp it down, then my senses. Pinching squint. Yapping nerves hushing quiet. I'll ride sometime. Still fixing.

M a

I fuel you with week-old orzo unwedged from the Sprint-er van's fridge. The resistant starch will bolster our gut flora. The serving size is pre-portioned—2,100 calories' worth in ei-ther 36-ounce Tupperware, enough to replenish three hours of aerobic cycling. Don't even try fitting the container into the microwave. That's by design, darling—can't be taking in BPAs. Anyway, heat wilts the basil.

You scoop the stuff up with your hands. Your hair drips into the bowl, tangled beyond the scope of a comb or shampoo. The last time it got that blonde and long, you were running laps of the playground at recess.

"Pop a squat," I tell you, and bring you the small spoon.

It's all I can do not to ask what else you've eaten and how much you've moved, to try and balance your physiology like an equation. We sit on the couch. You swallow each bite like a horse pill, without tasting. I chew mine forty times. When I was at the height of my equalized gluttony—those 160-mile bike rides balanced by family-sized boxes of granola—I'd been chew-ing each bite 160 times, nodding off more than once before fin-ishing. My stomach capacity was too big for my heavy eyes, but my waistline stayed tight. Riding all day to earn those gut-aching feasts had seemed worth it to me. Doro said some folks are wired so that eating gives them sex-level doses of dopamine. Others get it from exercise. I don't think that your fix comes from either of those three. You eat staring out the back window.

Casper's snoring on the boat deck. His stomach plunges without expansion, as if even his inhales are lung-hollowing. The summer I spent with Doro in Peru, my own stomach was just such a basin; I was pregnant with you, but no one would've known it. I thought you were my Tulpa. Maybe that's how you're seeing Casper—staring like the only thing trapping him in these three dimensions is your concentration. I used to look at your father that way, but judging from my trip to West Memphis, his existence predated me. The way that his hum haunts my mind, it seems more like he's my anchor.

"He hasn't eaten," you say.

"Don't take on the responsibility."

You bring the Tupperware back up to your face. Can't hide behind hunger. Kid might just fit into your teenaged tri-suit. Remember how all of your want was fixed on the finishing tape at that age? I'd begun to think you might stay that way. It would've been better, maybe—or at least risked less pain.

You stand with the Tupperware held at half-mast in front of your stomach. "I'll see if Casper wants some."

"You need those calories."

"I'm not hungry."

"Bring him mine." I swear I can feel the olive oil seeping out of my stomach as I stand, pooling into paunch. If I could just wring out that skin like a napkin.

I follow you out to him. Stud looks like he's decomposing. The dark blurs the edges of his form in the shrinking way that a carcass decays. Horseflies spore his stump. The stitches at the end of it stretch like a spare mouth that he's breathing through. That would explain his aerobic capacity.

You set the orzo beside his stump.

Stud sits up, tipping his ear to his shoulder. He flicks the Tupperware off the boat deck. I crouch in the dirt, invert the container.

Stud's spit lands to my left. "Go back to baby school."

"Dude," you tell him.

"Tell RoboPeep to quit crying."

But I can't. Cannot stand seeing food gone uneaten. "What-ever antibiotics they've got you on probably massacred your microbiome. The orzo's got resistant starch. It'll replenish your gut flora."

"Shucks ingredients. I'm fixing to ride."

I pinch soiled grains of orzo out of the dirt like worms.

You stoop beside me, grab the Tupperware. I drop orzo into my cupped palm.

"Mom."

"Just a little more."

"You're not going to eat this." You carry the Tupperware into the camper and rinse it into the sink.

Stud hollers, "Still fixing to!"

Your eyes still stuck on the kid in the rearview.

"How're the legs?" I ask. "Scale of good to gravy."

You shut your mouth and eyes. Your cheek bulges with sucked food. I could get out of my wetsuit in the stretch of that silence, grab my bike and wheel out of T1.

"I left my race in those woods," you tell me.

"That's productive fatigue. Feeling fresh this far out is bad news. You still want a little weight in the leg. Means you've still got all those bricks in your system. Mortar's drying. Mark Allen almost pulled out of Nice in '95 because his calves were tight on the warmup. A dip and a spin later he's on the Riviera, clicking off 5:30 miles." You'd handled that DVD until your fingers scratched DJ-skips into the footage—Allen appearing to teleport past Luc Van Lierde for the lead.

"I don't even want gravy. I'm not even worried, I mean." You reseal the lid onto the container. "I'm doing thinking in split times."

"The will comes back, Love. Discipline's like your body. A part of it. Just needs some recovery."

"Is he breathing?" you ask.

Casper still looks to be on the carbon cycle's back nine, or the opposite end of your timeline—shrinking to your size at ten, nine, eight. My gaze was wall-eyed in those days: one on the training log and the other on the grocery list. Both on the second item, sometimes. Working for those weekending Piggly Wiggly trips after that week-ending training session, our shoulders too worn from ocean swims to carry the food into the trailer. Just tossed bags into the camper's fridge and stuck the receipt under the SETUP EVENTS magnet as our checklist. We ate by expiration dates, checking off perishables like accomplishments. Mondays were all greens, cruciferous stuff through midweek—stomach-stuffing dishes for minimal calories. How I love that third-cup-of-coffee buzz that comes from the starved brain, the cortisol dump of a negative energy balance. All the Computrainer time trials we rode on depleted glycogen, staring at the silver-surfer avatars on the Dell monitor with our sphincters muttering under the hums of the windtrainers. All the shits I unclipped for, real and fake—some feigned just for breathers. But you—Love, Champ, my second Tulpa and onlyborn son— you stayed as steady on your wattage as the racing weight you maintained.

"That's one less body between you and the finishing line," I say.

You laugh—less at the thought, it seems, than at me. "I'm retiring."

You shove the orzo into my lap.

"You broke through the cocoon," I say.

You cut the sink. "You talked to him?"

That I'd stood face-to-face with him seems best to leave off. "He called."

To say you were in record shape, zenning. That the monk work was done: you were out of the shop and fine-tuned. I tell you that part of the truth. Not the way that your father's voice had hummed through him, or how your father had let himself die to me in Nepal, then gone back to a sheep farm in Arkansas where he'd raised Benji instead of you. I'm with Benji that far: better to spare your headspace. You've gone twenty-six years without knowing your father. That revelation can wait until after the race. Later, maybe. I tell you I'd begged Benji to let me speak with you, that I'd left Tetlin that same day.

"Tetlin." You say it like a name.

"That's just where I was passing through."

You grab my phone off the counter and fend me off with one palm, plugging the place into Maps.

"The drive's seventy hours," you say.

"There were detours."

I'm not just talking about my training stops and dip into West Memphis. It was an eleven-hour drive to Kure from Arkansas—too long to go without moving.

I'd been cruising through Raleigh with my mind on a good long run spot when the BlueCross Rep called about follow-ups. Pulled over at Duke Forest while he baritoned on over disarticulations, squinting at the trail map. Your leg was already gone, how I saw it; there was nothing that rushing could do. I took off on a sobbing twenty-two miler.

I pick up after that part. It's true that I'd floored it from there on. Made it from Durham to New Hanover County Hospital without peeing. Ladders everywhere in that atrium, ending in midair—what were they working on, nailing the ambience? The lady at reception stood out of her chair like I'd told her this was a holdup. Didn't even ask who I was there for; must've seen the *you* in me. I'd just missed you, she said; you'd just been released.

"I piddle into the cul-de-sac and here's Stud. First thought was I'd walked into a cripple colony." Of course I remembered Casper from last year's Chapel Hill Ironman; just hadn't recognized what was left of him. Benji hadn't said a word about the kid—not his infection, not his cohabitation, not who'd been who's carrot. Not who needed who.

"Detours," you say. "I could've used you."

You had, Champ: put Casper down on our insurance policy. "You could've called. It's a quarter for a payphone."

"I was distracted."

I wish I could admit that I'd been distracted, too. That I still am. But I'm the only parent you have. All your life I've worked to make you feel like my love's locus. You can't know that most of my waking moments are focused on food.

"I told you I'm done racing. Cold turkey." You hang in the doorframe with both hands, leaning out like you're waiting for me.

"What were you up to when I got here?" I say.

"Just running."

"Huh."

"Just moving."

"Sounds like tepid turkey to me."

We're excavating an old scene. All the midnights you dared me to talk you back onto the tightrope. You're peering over the side now, perched safely on exertion's plunging ledge; have fled the plummeting threat of the effort—the purged mindset it takes to cover distance and distance and distance at a clip. I'm past shaming anyone into anything.

"Ma," you say. "Push me. Please."

But you know like I do that effort comes from you. Suffering's easier; you just weather whatever's imposed on you. No one's making you dig deep in a race. It's up to you to choose pain.

"It's called a residual limb," you say.

"What's that?"

"What they left him with. The thing under his knee." You curl your pinky in farce of Stud's stump.

I slide my hand down the abacus of your vertebrae. You always seemed one short of the standard torso. I always felt like it hadn't formed by a failure of my own concentration. "Let him snooze."

My Timex chirps its warning alarm—my window for post-workout refueling long-lost. That had been some long run of a final pit stop: twenty-two miles over Tobacco Road's rollers mulling over the BlueCross phone call. The thought of your gone leg spiking my cortisol. Still kept it aerobic—6:50 pace and nose-breathing. The fat-burning zone. My pulse stayed too low to tap into glycogen.

I put the lid on my orzo and stop the watch alarm like it might quit my thinking. You're the one asking where I was, but you've been by my side for twenty-six years without seeming to notice the way that food's eating me. Remember when I spilled my Ultragen after Bandit's Challenge and cried over it? How I stopped at five different Subways on the way back to find one that served the rotisserie chicken because that was the one sandwich that matched the macronutrient totals I had left to eat?

"Who's Doro?" you ask.

"A friend."

"You were with him in Alaska."

You say *with* with an inflection that extends its significance. "I saw him, if that's what you mean."

"Is he my dad?"

"God. No." You're all him in that doorway, your voice pulling me closer like the hum that had charmed me to your father. He must have passed down that magnet. How do I tell you that you're the reason for these coyotes? That it's built into your blood, which you just might share with Benji. Your father. His uncle. "I made a promise not to talk about him."

"Keep it," you say.

And go out to Stud.

I un-lid your Tupperware and add my orzo to it and eat every PowerBar stashed in the center console. You know how in the best moments of racing you become so part of your discomfort that you forget there's another way of existing? As if you were born with your lungs searing and legs aching and intestines knotting that way. I can get that way with a binge. My splitting stomach becomes homeostasis. There are moments where I swear it seems like eating and that pain are unrelated.

I call Doro. Straight to voicemail. The opening riff to Imágenes's "Caras Nuevas" backs the recording of his greeting. That summer I spent with him in Peru, the song had trickled out of every boombox and storefront. Doro lets it play for full seconds on the recording before speaking. "You've reached me. I'm sorry you missed me. Recovery is a journey. It allows for steps backwards and meanderings. No matter where you're starting, friend, it's my honor and calling to keep you company."

Doro's phone is probably do-not-disturbed because he's sitting in on group therapy. He just might be prompting affirmative snaps for Cathy.

I airplane my own phone before he can call me back. That Nature's Path granola is like crack (it's the cane syrup—9 grams of added sugars in every 3/4-cup serving). There's a four-pack of the family-sized boxes in the pantry. At Tetlin, Doro was fond of reminding us that sugar triggers sex-level bursts of dopamine; so does a novel experience. A prolonged period of deprivation cues the dopamine receptors to hypersensitivity. (Picture what bliss I'd been in when he'd brought me churros and pollo a la brasa to stuff myself with after months of deliberate starving; impossible not to get addicted to all of it—the dramatic depletion, the excessive replenishment.) We weren't addicted to bingeing or purging; we were addicted to the dopamine release. Doro said there were other ways to jostle those chemicals, besides the one in his original analogy. Jogging. Nicotine. We didn't have to kick our addiction; we could just pick other avenues to get our fix. Anytime we got the urge, we were supposed to fall back on our favorite alternative. (I'm sure this went against Dr. Reyes's professional opinion, but she turned a deaf ear with her meditation bowl—Doro was probably paying her like a philanthropist.) The Tetlin CVS couldn't restock e-cigs and Nicorette patches fast enough. I'd stuck with jogging. I've got that and my safe space and tactile mindfulness to cope.

I try to achieve the wise mind, ramming my rationale mind into my emotions, but I ran twenty-two rolling miles this morning, and my safe space is too sandy, and we don't have any Play-Doh—just 98.8 ounces of Pumpkin Flax granola and Auntie Opal's glass centerpiece bowl.

I pop all of four plastic bags of cereal open and mound it up the way I've seen trash clog a culver. I top the heap with four scoops of vanilla whey protein, drench it in milk, and dig in. Every bite's a dopamine landmine. I eat until each pumpkin seed feels like shrapnel in my stomach. I keep going. There's still more in the bowl.

And I know that I'll pass the night sweating from the sheer effort of digesting, sleepless. Might as well hop on the Computrainer as soon as I finish eating. I'm too stuffed to get down into aero position, so I'll have to pedal sitting up. The granola presses down on the vegetables from the orzo until they gestate into something less flora than fauna, a bloat more zygote than cruciferous. It shifts like it's kicking. I shut my eyes and pretend back to Peru, where I laid in Doro's apartment and ate until I grew full of you.

Casper

Still fixing to ride. Just the sun's scampered off in my nod. I nod off and on getting greased with the lardy light of the moon. My gone leg's yapping at it. That van's still out front, taller than the camper. Ms. RoboCop's still squatting, dag-nab Eve of a leash-yanking sheep. Little Miss RoboPeep. Ha. I pry my way across the deck to the cabin. Worm on down into that dirt dark, the packed air warm with stink. No RoboCop. Little RoboPeep's herded him off from me. And my gone leg's yapping, but his gone-ness yaps louder. You know you're at home if you feel safe to sleep. That's why I got hope when RoboCop nodded off at the end of my cot, because it meant I'd homed his heart; Adam the Atom Man said your heart's your home's nuclear. But now he's denning down somewhere different. His heart's beaten away from me. That's the thought sends me spanking the pill bottle. And me nigh-on to thinking he'd hold me; should've known. None gaum onto me hard enough. Not Adam. Not Benji. None-them yapping ghosts. Though the hurter truth's that I'm the ghost. I'm the one wafting off. And RoboCop can't hold me because he's as shapeless as I am, which I saw in how eager-easy he posed like Little RoboPeep. Just took this long to swallow. Needed the lard-light of moon to grease that hard truth smooth for me. A haint needs a place to haunt. Well, I ain't got a place, and I'm doomed to waft till I do. Which is why I've got to move on. Still fixing to.

But first, hush this yapping. The Perc muffles that and the squirms. But it just covers them up, like how you can drink water to trick off your hunger, slurping enough for a stomachache to distract it. But your starve always comes back. Like that. In the dirt-dark of that cabin I spank the pills out the bottle and wait for the pills to spank me back. Spank me down like Whack-A-Mole: me ducking out from under, even as they hit. Hunkering into a hole of a doze. And I dull and warm and slow and the hours pass like wrathful footsteps going over (all the basements and closets under stairs that I've hid from them, folks stomping down with belts or phonebooks or claw hammers or boners urging for something to hit), time holding my lonely like an echo. Not even Perc can rid that part from my dreams. Through the full droop of my doze I know I'm alone. That cabin's just clog-full of empty.

Ezra

Casper's gone from the boat deck. The moon shimmers off a trail of sweat leading to the cabin, a smear as pale and wet as a butter-pat melting in a skillet. Ezra gets a vision of buzzards scraping the kid off of the prow.

"Dude?"

The door shuts.

Ezra jogs a circle around the cul-de-sac, then another, coughing the dirt stirred from his first trip. He curls around back of the camper. The cabin door's open. He pries himself up to the deck and crawls into an odor so strong that his scent gets ditched by the rest of his senses: mildew, pus, melted plastic, and the reek of stale beef and cheap Coppertone—Benji's scent. He'd never seen the guy eat or apply sunscreen.

"You can't be him."

Casper's voice sounds underwater. Ezra falls to all fours and crawls, feeling like he's dog-paddling. Something smacks his hand. He grabs it—a wet, flailing, annelid thing.

"Quit off!" Casper hollers.

Ezra's holding the kid's stump. It feels more gruesome than Ezra'd thought; plainer, maybe. Bundle of skin and tibia. Why hadn't Walsh made a clean cut at the knee?

"Pet yourself," Casper says.

Ezra braves his hand over that cruel lump. "Does it hurt?"

"The inside still sores me."

Ezra lays his head in the space where the kid's shin should be. Ma'd always said that caring was a shit motor, but it worked great for brakes. His skeleton feels downshifted, his vertebrae the cogs of a 38T chainring.

"Robo," Casper says.

"Yeah?"

"You sleep?"

"We're talking."

"Oh."

"Go ahead."

"It's just this thought's gnawing me." Casper sits up with a lip-smacking sound: his sweat-wet back and the sleeping bag parting. That separation seems the opening enabling his speech. "What if I'm still tick-tocking?"

"The bike?"

"I keep tipping."

"There's no rush."

"Sure. Got four livelongs."

The Ironman; Casper still thinks he's racing.

"Asking could I hop stairs," the kid mutters. "Fixing to hop 140 miles this Saturday. Fixing to show Bobby Orr and Shiela Petey."

The pill bottle rattles. Ezra swears he can hear space in that sound, an indication of its dwindling contents. Damp crunching.

"You can swallow those," Ezra says.

"I gag easy."

The chewing turns to chattering. Ezra presses his back to the floor, sealing any space for shade to sneak between him and the carpet. Benji's voice comes as wet as a breath on his neck.

Heard once of this lady rescued a whippet with shot hips. Rescue's PETA-speak for prolonging a dog's misery. Throw Fido in an apartment with no yard space where it can't do what its muscles and nerves and centuries of breed-memory scream for it to do. I think of the angst. They think of the cute Christmas card. Anyway, this lady. She had to go out of town for a week for some dog-fucker rally, whatever ass-sniffing PETA thing. Well, she measures out a week of food for Fido. Okay, cup a day, and how many...? Kidding. Pours it all in the dog bowl. She gets back and her floor's smeared with puke, streaked with blood. Down the hall, another smear and more streaks. On she goes, mourning that new hardwood, probably. There's Fido with its tongue out, dead and teasing. Dumb shit scarfed all that food in one go. Ruptured stomach. Bled out or puke-choked. A dog'll eat as much as you put in front of it. It's all now. No such thing as pacing. Parable of the clean bowl, Tootsie. Now moral me.

And Ezra'd answered not to eat all the tuna, and Casper'd answered to forget how far you had left, and Benji's Oakleys had reflected the kid as he nodded his agreement.

Ezra rolls over. Casper sucks the pill bottle like a thumb—but not his. Ezra's name's on the prescription. Sunrise wells in the bottle, drowning three tablets. Two weeks before the next refill. Ezra leans over the kid.

"Can't hold me." Casper opens his eyes. His cratered pupils seem struck, as if Ezra's image is the very impact hollows them. "You ain't home."

"We're in the cabin, dude. The boat. They let you out."

"You."

Ezra drags his palm over Casper's head. The kid moves against his palm's pressure equal-and-oppositely, grinding his stubble against Ezra's callouses like his teeth. Who's flattening who?

The kid's empty pupils two holes Ezra's falling through. And how far until they strike something; and what will it be? Trying to talk to Casper is like stumbling through a basement, and that basement, besides being lightless, is full of past hurts. Some of them—racing, Benji, varms—Ezra knows. But others are as grossly strange as Casper's stump, things he doesn't want to touch. And Casper sits somewhere across that darkness.

"I'm fixing to move," he says. "You ain't home to me."

M a

Off you go. But Champ, I was still working up to what I need to tell you. You know how I am about getting started, inching into lane six at Sloop Point in December. Always better to dive in and sprint.

There was a time when I was so afraid of food that I almost lost you; a time, even, when that fear made me think that I wanted to, but that was just Unc's spirit taking hold of me. There was a time when I carried all three of us. This is the story of the man who should have been your father—the one who helped me know how to keep you.

Souls don't come in fixed quantities. Unc would say that a Tulpa forms when a body's too small to hold its own feeling. Your Auntie Opal used to keep me up with stories about the Dybbuk, which she'd called—in English plainer to me—Clings: dislocated spirits that hitched themselves to former lovers until those old flames carried out their wicked machinations. I preferred the Ibbur, a righteous spirit which compelled its host to carry out some unfinished mitzvah. I've thought that your father was one, then the other. I'll let you decide who to trust, then who was what. I've seen enough to believe anyone could be anything. The world isn't as scientific as I'd like for you and I to believe.

After that stadium collapsed on your father in Dasharath, his spirit hitched itself to me. Limping out of that hospital in Nepal, the air in my throat coagulated with something more choking than rubber smoke; the best way I can word the sensation is like if a scream acquired texture and weight. That was your father's Ibbur breathing through me. The last thing he'd told me was to leave him, so I got right back to moving.

Auntie Opal's dreidel landed on Peru. I chucked it in a ditch with the Atlas, bought a one-way ticket with LATAM, and boarded the flight carrying nothing but my passport and you.

I brought four rules with me to Lima. The fourth was your father's plea to forget him. The third was never to mention you. I passed the flight in the lavatory to honor it, blaming diphtheria and turbulence for your kicks. Not flinching was the second rule; the first—the foremost—was to make a mitzvah out of moving. I walked out of the international terminal, through the cram of cabs, south of Callao down the coast road. Cliffs lifted the city to my left, wire grids spanning the loose rocks and clay on their faces like hairnets. The northbound lane flanked by orange signs: ¡Precaución! ¡Desprendimiento! To my right, lunulas of beach cuticled by jetties of crushed construction debris. The Pacific seemed clutched under those knuckles of cinderblocks, as if the city was trying to pin down the ocean. Doro would've said it was going the other way—the land trying to crawl out from the buildings built over it. I might've believed him—but only later. Right then I was still cruising for something interesting, moving faster than stand-stilled traffic on the Malecón.

Buskers hopped onto the hoods of halted vehicles and juggled Inka Kola bottles. I wanted to be near them, or be mistaken for one; back then I had this hope that if I brushed up against enough interesting shit, it would start to rub off on me.

A handstanding man walked between cars on his palms, pinching a sawed-off gallon jug between his bare feet and sing-songing for alms. His baritone belonged two continents east: the same sweet note that had drawn me under that Dasharath grandstand.

I dropped my whole wallet—the real one—into his jug. "Hello, Tulpa."

The man balanced the jug on my head like a crown. He cartwheeled to his feet. His forearms were bigger than his biceps, as if all the muscle in his arms had been squeezed. His knuckles were scarred in a pattern like the teeth imprinted on a mouth-piece.

He had to be something I'd conjured from missing your fa-ther—the exact shape of my longing and grief.

"Tulpa," he said. "Qué significa en inglés?"

"Tulpa," I said. "It's a concept." Here's what I was thinking: if an Ibbur was a stowaway spirit, and a Tulpa was the runoff of someone's emotions, maybe I'd just longed Unc back into being.

He took the jug off of my head. I'd been afraid to touch it. "Me llamo Teodoro," he said.

"It's Tibetan, I think. Nepalese."

"Escucha. Me. Amo." He pressed his thumb to his chest. "Te. Adoro." He pointed that thumb at me. "Me amo. Te adoro. Repeata."

"Cute joke."

He plucked my wallet out of the jug. "Nice offering." He took out every *sole* I had and handed the money back to me. "But you should be the one to add it to her altar."

I assumed that he meant Santa Rosa's. "No cathedrals. I don't do guidebook shit."

"Bueno. One of those." His voice raised octaves in English, as if he'd regressed before puberty. He had the nasal accent of someone from one of those cold, middle states—one of the -*ota*'s, maybe. "She oft strays from the beaten itinerary."

"I like to walk until I'm lost."

"Your sandals show it." He wedged the sawed-off jug be-tween his feet, kicked into a handstand, and palm-walked off be-tween lanes. His back muscles striated like an animated anatomy poster. His sunburn was as pink as exposed muscle. I could count every sinew shifting through his skin.

"Are you a gymnast?" I asked.

"Thirty pounds ago."

He didn't have a gram of fat on him from his scalp to his soles. The mass would've had to come out of his organs, his bones. What's an absence weigh? Could loss be broken up into units of souls? I'd left Dasharath swearing I was dragging that, the summed absence of Unc's ghost.

Doro palm-walked away, whistling tunelessly. The noise was just one sustained note, like a treadmill belt without anyone running. Sounded like it was coming from under me. I jogged after him, feeling like I'd fall off of something if I didn't keep up.

I followed him south down the coast through the skyline's ebbing shade. As the sun wested, the city's shadow shrank. Doro was claiming I'd parted the clouds. I told him to blame the equator; had shown up in Lima on a sunny assumption, clueless about the convection that pinned the city under fog from Barranco to the foothills east of Pachacamac, where he said we were aiming. I told him I didn't want to hear it, picturing his ribs as the rungs of a ladder I was climbing. The sky was my aspirational destination. But I did know those bones of his like that baritone.

"A Tulpa," I said. "It's basically a thought's corporeal manifestation. Like an emanation of longing."

"You're calling me dreamy."

"No."

"Didn't think so." Doro balanced on one hand and pinched the skin under his nipple with the other. All his brawn was in his shoulders and arms; his chest was so muscleless it was slatted with ribs. "I've got too much flesh on me."

A cliff thrust out from the coast in front of us, figureheaded by an open-armed statue of Jesus. Either arm was as long as the statue was tall—about steeple-height. Doro hand-sprung over a barricade into a tunnel bored into the cliff's base. The passage funneled us out to a rocky bay. This gulp in the coast was called Herradura for its horseshoe shape, Doro'd tell me later. It looked more like an ashtray. Trash bobbed in the whitewater. A burnt-down hotel perched on the rocks at its south end. A domed building rose from its southern leg like a stubbed toe.

A set of steps climbed the cliffs at the center of the bay. A streak of sludge sweated down them, smearing across the rocks to the shorebreak. He took the staircase on his hands. Vendors perched on the landings that elbowed each switchback, crouching beside quilts pinned with wooden flutes or gypsum statues or alpaca-hair bracelets. Each twitched to their feet when Doro passed and tossed a trinket into his sawed-off jug. Every landing had that same rotation of items laid out in the same order like the matching beginnings of a board game. The wares piled up as uniformly as the strata in the jug, matching the streaked clay of the cliff face.

The stairs topped out at a brick alley spray-painted with warped faces. They seemed smeared by the thickening trickle of sludge. The alley slendered into a brick ditch. Bungalows with broken bottles cemented across the tops of their courtyard walls. Cats soft-pawed between their barbs. The sludge socked my ankles, gloved Doro's wrists. Fragments of Styrofoam polka-dotted it. The ditch rose out of the brick hostels of beachside districts, past glass slashes of hotel facades. It dipped below a Metro crossing and widened out to a paved culver. Half-built tenements topped its slopes. Naked children squealed and splashed in the stream. Hunchbacked women in too-small hats rinsed cloth diapers in it. A one-eyed man sitting on a birdcage full of hamsters pulled out a rodent and dropped it in Doro's jug.

We moved farther inland. Broken TVs and takeout boxes and hubcaps covered the culver's slopes. A hill of trash clogged the culver. We climbed it, debris scuttled out from under Doro's hands and my feet. I thought the stuff was shifting with our movement, but we stopped at the summit and the trash kept on sliding. I turned around. A chihuahua dog-paddled at the base of the mound. Children waded through the coursing trash as calmly as a shallow end.

Doro pointed up to the foothills, where shanties were toppling. "Pachamama's stomach is rumbling."

We stood for a silent while, watching those buildings' rooftops go jagged.

"Pachacamac," I said, thinking of this district's name. "The goddess, or the place?"

"The same. Pachamama's the land. It's up to us to feed her."

Doro pointed from my hand to the mound. I tossed the cash down.

He packed down the spot with his left foot, disappearing it under the shifting debris. His second and middle tarsals margined a sun-blurred tattoo: *don't lose it, you'll use it.*

I had the sick hunch that the message applied to you, reinforced by the way he was staring at me.

"Who died?" he asked.

I thatched my hands over my stomach. I wasn't showing yet, but his pupils had this gleam like the monitor of a cat-scan—like the reflection of a projector that was slicing through me.

"I know an heir when I see one," Doro said. "So who'd you lose? A husband?"

"Just my aunt," I said. "It's just me."

"I figured you'd inherited something." Doro nodded to my sandals. "The shitty footwear's what gave you away. You're wearing worn-out like a decoration. Classictrustafarian . A real vagabond forks it over to stay in good shoes. And they sure as shit wouldn't toss off three hundred fucking soles. I knew vaulters who could've eaten off that for a full Olympic cycle." Doro curled four fingers under his ribcage. I got this sick picture of him hitching them up, exposing his lungs like the middle segment of a telescoping lens.

"We can go back for it," I said.

"It's Pachamama's."

"Aren't you hungry?"

Doro took off at a flimsy sprint. His legs looked like they weren't used to his weight. The faster he moved them, the slower he went. I walked comfortably alongside him, stroll-for-stride.

We took the culver back to the bay. By the time we reached the ocean, I was straining, too. Doro plodded to a domed building at the southern end of the cliffs. Its cinderblock facade was charred the exact color of the blood blisters blooming where my big toes were pinched by the straps of my Tevas.

Doro led me through a toppled set of double-doors into an atrium. Pulpy brochures and ash rugged the floor. The back wall was missing a Jeep-sized section of brick. Tarps stretched across holes in the ceiling beams. Instead of all the things I should've been puzzling over, I remember wondering why those tarps weren't patching the walls; back then I didn't see how anyone could put shelter before privacy.

I followed Doro through the hole in the back wall. We entered a circular space rowed with the plastic frames of reclining theater seats. A pile of cushions was heaped to the left, aligned below a crescent-shaped crack in the roof.

Doro tugged a sleeping bag out from under the stripped upholstery. "It's no hostel, but it's got a roof. Mostly."

I bellyflopped onto the cushions, glad for the first time in a long time to be finished moving.

He spread the sleeping bag an arm's length away and laid flatbacked, staring up at that crack. That dome looked like a cracked skull. "Where are you getting lost to tomorrow?"

"Somewhere with anticuchos."

"Can't help you there. It'll be el mismo for me." Doro shut his eyes. "Tremor's coming."

Ash and dust dandruffed down from the dome.

"Don't you eat?"

Doro sucked in his stomach. A cave of shade formed under his ribcage. He wedged the sawed-off jug into it. "Vicariously."

That jug stayed stuck in his torso as he hummed to sleep. Even his snoring sounded like singing. It felt less like his voice was coming into my ears than reaching in and pulling all my nerves out of me. I've never felt less of myself in myself—all mind and no body. Even if I'd wanted to run, I had no limbs to leave.

The next day we carried Doro's sawed-off jug from the Malecón to the trash mound, taking on offerings. Doro chalked up every tremor to Pachamama's rumbling stomach. A man at an anticucho stand by the Metro overpass dropped four slick skewers of meat into Doro's bucket, and Doro handed them all to me.

I scarfed three all at once. Gnawed the skewers. Splinters stuck in my gums. I swallowed the blood. I offered Doro the last one and he swatted it off. He said he wanted to suffer with Pachamama, but I had the feeling his martyrdom was more for me—for you growing in me. If a Tulpa came out of someone, wouldn't it know what other things their body was harboring?

Doro dragged his sleeping bag under the hole in the roof. Said that way the rain would wake him. I laid on those seat cushions a body-length away, debating how much of my first rule I was breaking: I'd been moving, but moving through the same place.

"What about an Ibbur?" I asked.

"Is that English?"

I explained it to him how Auntie Opal had told me: a spirit that compels its charge to complete some righteous deed. Doro wanted to know what mine was, but I didn't yet have a sense of the mitzvah Unc expected. Maybe when the time came I'd snap to it reflexively.

"I'm awaiting instructions."

"I bet this is it," Doro said. "Feeding Pachamama."

Seemed like he was the one I needed to get to eat.

We kept racking up trips to that trash heap and back. Not once did Doro touch me. Not once did I see him eat. He swatted off every anticucho I pointed toward him, said skewers bothered the scars on his gag reflexes, but I was starting to feel the real fix he was after. There was a serenity that came with starvation. My life narrowed down to the next footstep, whichever trashy patch of ground laid between me and stopping. Flopping down on those seat cushions became bliss. I wasn't happy, but I was peaceful: I didn't have enough energy left for grief.

I'd lie down under the hole in the planetarium's dome and watch the clouds smear the real stars like a projector screen, waiting for showers that Doro swore were coming.

He promised that the air could only stay this laden for so long before raindrops dewed together through the humidity. We'd get a monsoon before the Feast of Santa Rosa closed August. The floods would flush the trash out of the culver. Only then—when Pachamama was quenched—would Doro have his feast.

Every time a tremor popcorned that debris, he blamed Pachamama's indigestion. I nodded along like I had to your father's stories of Tulpas, only without the credulity. I didn't point out that our offerings were only stuffing her more, or that flushing was what you did with shit. I had a better metaphor for what was stuck in that culver. As summer sweltered itself out, the tremors bucked those foothills like you kicking inside my belly. I dreamed the cliffs of Herradura into spread legs. Something more than trash was crowning; more than a new season, or a Tulpa, even. It was going to slide down the culver like a birth canal and come breathing into the bay.

Then, on the penultimate day of August, a procession of three-piece-suited Catholics shouldered Santa Rosa's plaster effigy across the overpass shading the culver.

"Half a million children in the pueblos jovenes are starving, and these cabrones feed a statue." Doro tilted his head up and spat. "They stuff the alms boxes and leave Pachamama starving."

"I thought she had indigestion."

"We're trying to trigger her gag reflex." Doro pointed up the culver. "We want all of this to get upchucked."

The Metro slowed out from the left side of the overpass. The men slanted to the edge of the track. The effigy slid off their shoulders and plunged, shattering on the bank of the culver. Shards of porcelain swarmed up. My left cheek felt bee-stung. The procession leaned over the railing, cursing, jousting prayer-clasped hands.

Doro picked up egg-shaped hunks of foil nested among the cracked pottery. Candies. He dropped them in the jug.

"Rain's coming," he told me. "Let's feast."

We ran back to the planetarium. The west wind peeled the clouds off the horizon like a sunburn, baring a strip of gloaming as pink as new skin. Doro dumped the jug into the dent that I'd left on the seat cushion. Foil eggs and withering hunks of anticucho scattered.

"Go ahead," he said. "Eat."

"You."

Doro put two more cushions at either end of that one, forming a crescent. He inverted the jug at the end of the cushion nearest me and stood an Inka Cola bottle at the end of the one in front of him. "I was like you," he said. "Mistaking living for moving." He pumped his arms. "Took the world at a run. It was all one big inhale for me, but that's only half of breathing. Try exhaling. You've got to let it out."

"I'm trying."

"Not how I mean." Doro pressed his thumb into my bellybutton. I broke my second rule then; I flinched. Maybe he broke one, too—that was the first time he touched me. "You're starving more than yourself," he said.

About that third rule, the one where I swore not to think of you: a Tulpa is born from concentration, so it made sense that you'd disappear from my belly if I kept you out of my head. Out of sight, out of mind, out of my life and body. For years, I blamed your father's spirit for willing me to vanish you. Told myself I'd mistaken his Dybbuk for an Ibbur: every step that I'd taken gathering food for Pachamama—thinking he was driving me to do good—had actually served atrocity. But that want was all mine. A feeling is a curse, not a crime. That much I believe.

I pointed to Doro's foot tattoo. *Don't lose it, you'll use it.* "Don't lose what?"

"Weight. Lunch." Doro said. "I used to run the bath when I purged. The toilet was in the corner, across from the tub. I'd have to swing my right leg out of the bath so I could reach the toilet to vomit. Hokey Pokey. I'd put this foot down on the bathmat and see the message."

"Did it stop you from purging?"

Doro rubbed the words with his thumb. He'd never punched

anyone; those knuckle scars were his own molars' imprints. "You seek help and they sentence you. When I fessed up to Coach, she called the ambulance on me. Off the team. I got locked up in Behavioral Health with the cutters and car exhaust huffers. I sprinted suicides in the hall. They locked me down in my room. Okay, jumping jacks, handstand pushups. The orderlies strapped me down to my bunk to keep me from moving."

"But you got out."

"I'm here, aren't I?" Doro said it like he was really asking.

He had to be my Tulpa, but maybe the one that came from my hunger instead of my grief. Maybe you're seeing Casper that way. Don't take on that guilt; don't mistake it for caring. Shame's never won anyone's heart or races.

"We're the same," Doro said. "I'm no vagabond, either. My dad's got a stake in the gold mines in Ayacucho. He's up there now, disemboweling Pachamama. Thinks I'm holding it down at his condo in Miraflores. I never even picked up the key." Doro peeled gum off of a wadded napkin and used it to stick an anticucho skewer to either side of the Inka Cola bottle.

"Cristo del Pacifico," I said.

He'd made a map of Herradura from the seat cushions. The bottle was the statue. The jug was the planetarium. I piled a line of trash across the central cushion, halved another anticucho skewer, and propped it off of the cushion's inward edge for the staircase. Raindrops embroidered the seat cushion.

"We've both got work to do," Doro said. "I'm not who you want me to be."

He scooped up a handful of trash, pressed it into his mouth, and chewed.

I walked out of the theater. The atrium was grouted with fragments of Styrofoam and Inka Cola caps. Litter rimmed the clifftop, clogging the staircase that switchbacked down to the bay. Something skeleton-looking was snagged on the top landing—a runged jut of white like a whale's ribcage. A stream of trash and sludge water-fell down the stairs to the bay. Debris bobbed like cigarette butts in the shorebreak. From my bird's eye, the vista looked like a giant ashtray.

The flood was shin-deep on the stairway's upper landing. Couch cushions and Inka Cola bottles eddied around the skeleton-looking thing. Its bones proved aluminum to my touch: an intact set of roofing gutters. I crouched at the cliff's edge.

Doro leaned down beside me. He wiped his mouth with his hand. His chapped lips looked as rough as his callouses, as if eating had taken the same toll on him as palm-walking. "Stay."

"I can't heal you."

"You can heal with me."

I wasn't ready to admit that I needed to. For nearly three decades I'd swear that your father's Dybbuk was the only thing plaguing me. Then I got that call from your phone and heard him humming through Benji. Unc couldn't have been in both of us; everything I've ever done has been up to me.

"You don't know who you are until you're standing still," Doro said. "Until you make yourself empty."

A tremor shivered the stairs. I swore that my spine was conducting it, a pang splitting my stomach. Loose rocks chattered behind their nets on the cliff face. Something slashed the backs of my calves. I fell onto my hands, the roofing gutter jabbing out from under me.

A pang split my stomach. If I could stay this hungry, I remember thinking, I might just have room for you.

"I used to have this idea that calmness was a container I had to squeeze into," Doro said. "Now I know I'm the container."

"Let's fill you up."

He pushed out his stomach. It bulged like a turtle shell, convex and sectored by his flexing abdominals. "There's no room."

"We'll make some."

"I promised I'd never do that to myself again." Doro said it like a request.

That might have been the first time all summer that I knew what he needed from me.

"You have me," I said.

He tipped his head back like a Pez dispenser. I swore I could see every toothmarked bottle cap and jasper amulet and finger-printed centimo that we'd brought Pachamama high-piled in his windpipe, but I was the one choking up. I crammed my thumb and forefinger into his mouth and tried to pinch his uvula.

He hacked. Nothing came up. I pulled my hand back and rubbed his spit into my palms. I felt like I could've walked miles on them. Wish I could say that I'd gone up the coast to Callao International and left Doro trembling. Instead, I asked, "Why won't you touch me?"

"I was afraid of breaking something."

I never did ask what he meant: breaking something in him, or in me?

He hailed a taxi to Miraflores. We stayed in his father's condo for three weeks. Doro brought me arroz aeropuerto and tubs of canchita and pollo a la brasa on beds of fries that were as brown as raw potato skins with dripped grease. I ate until I was showing, lying on a futon he'd pushed up against the wall-to-ceiling window. I could see clear up the culver we'd walked so many times. The overpass had collapsed in the earthquake. Dammed rainwater and trash brimmed behind it, spilling over into the streets of Pachacamac. Doro told me about the double B.S. he had waiting back at UA Fairbanks—nutritional science and psychology. I started to feel like his case study. As soon as I'd stored up enough energy, I told him it was time to leave. He said he'd gotten me into this mess, that it was his duty to extract me.

He applied his allowance to my plane ticket back to the States. We took the same LATAM flight to Miami, first-class. The stewardess smiled at my swollen belly and told us both con-gratulations. Doro ate the wrappers of his complimentary pretzels and biscotti and passed their actual contents to me. We pained through customs together, then parted ways. He flew back to his gymnastics and bio classes; I connected through Raleigh to Wilmington. Our plane bounced down on the tarmac and my water broke. Seventeen hours later I was holding onto you.

Doro isn't your father, but he gave you the chance to become *you*; in that way, he did give you to me. A father, a son—both looked like ways to get stuck. You get that, Champ. Stopping lets the tired catch up. Understand this, too: it wasn't you that I didn't want, but what you might bring up. I was afraid you'd teach me to love stillness. That inertia was all I ever wanted the earthquake to shake out of me.

Twenty-seven years I've been trying to keep you to myself like a secret, wondering why it feels so important that I do. Here's what it's taken me nearly three decades to think: I dropped my real wallet in Doro's jug that first day because I wanted to stay in Peru. All summer it was that, not you, I refused to admit to—the way I was taking to Doro and the narrowing habits of starvation. We could've put off the rest of our lives with our shrinking routine. The only thing scarier than stopping moving was the idea that I might actually enjoy doing it. That's why I really left Tetlin. The phone call from Benji was just an excuse.

Doro'd asked me if I was leaving because you needed me, or because I wanted that to be true. Maybe the same goes for explaining him to you. I want to air it out, but hearing it might not help you.

My feet are still sore from walking that culver. My blisters didn't close up until I was finished nursing you. I swore I'd never run until I saw how you took to it. Maybe that's the only part of all of this that you need to hear from me: you don't lose what moves you, so don't be afraid to test the brakes. That workout can wait. So can Stud. Come put your feet up beside mine and let's count ourselves lucky: just your legs and mine, intact and in spite of—two by two.

Casper

Haunt off, RoboCop. Got my own ghosts to conjure. Go snug in your own grave, I ain't Fido; be your own bone. His going leaves a full hollow like an echo. I gulp a Perc but it don't dwindle that hurting. My heart throbs in the root of my stump.

I crawl out of the cabin. The Piston leans upside the back of the camper, its glint scabbed with rust. Did I mention roots? That sight tugs me under the roses I'm waiting to catch whiffs of last Christmas, Benji shake-waking me before RoboCop grinning mistletoe. Lips as prickly with chap and kiss-asking as them very leaves. Dragged me out the cabin saying Santa left something.

I winced out to hand-hurt cold, all blood clumped in my vittles. The boat ladder sword-sharp on my bare feet. Then the yard. Froze sand stings special, ever grain like a skeeter biting. What I'd give now to feel them chewing on ten toes. All I gave then was a proud hoot that Benji'd woke me but not RoboCop. Maybe also a moan, but my hooting heart drowned it out because Benji'd chose me. There you go: Fido's bone.

Benji stood upside a shin-high square with a tarp over it. I coal-walked to him on my tiptoes, only them coals was cold. Sand good as glass on my fascia. Know I said skeeters, but it sharpens the longer you go. Them grains even stick like glass. Glass comes from heatening sand. Melt it till the atoms stampede to steam and then cool them stuck, the pluses and minuses hugging each other so the nuclears scrunch. Shape that glass hollow. Pour in sand and you have yourself a thing that holds itself, making and keeping its own shape. Should've been a glassblower. Not saying I was pining so in that moment, because them days I did believe Benji was the gel packet holding all my carbohydrate-like energy. Now I know there's more than move in me. I got fat and meat and ribs stuffed with empty where RoboCop and Benji echo.

Though I will fess some regret. Oh, to glass-blow that hourglass and flip it so that time trickles back with the sand. The hourglass and I are ditto like that, come to think: it's made of what it holds, just like me. But I'm branching off on one too many tangents. Hazards of these Percs, or maybe just the always of me.

Benji tore off the tarp and reveled me with the contraption Santa'd abandoned, an old bike of RoboCop's with the windtrainer clamped on its back wheel like that trap yapped my leg off, but that wasn't this, and all I was then-thinking was that Santa was Benji, wishing I could show Tammy Galarde he was real as Fido's bone. Even in my past I was still looking over my shoulder.

Tammy'd shown me her presents in her attic Christmas week, block-stacked in the back of her Pop's closet like Legos. FROM SANTA written on ever last. I'll fess my eyes got to watering. She called me a baby for not knowing, so I showed her the grown-up thing. We were just getting to the wet part when her Pop came home. Caught the two-us rubbing right there in his closet.

He punched the police first, then hung up and rumpled his hair like deciding. He called Ms. Ida. *Your*—and he stubbed, not sure what I was to her, how to call me—only that I wasn't her son. Starting and starting over. *He violated. He showed. What he did to.* Could not get it into a sentence. Tammy thumping around her room where he'd sent her. Me gulping snorts, because who'd her Pop think showed me rubbing?

But also a quease. Ms. Ida swore me that rubbing was just for us. Said they'd take me back to Trask if I even whispered our sacred secret. Bye waterbed. Bye track meets and Tammy Galarde and the Parsley Middle School swim team. No more afternoon runs sweating out the chlorine I'd sponged in the pool that same morning. Beads sharp as glass shards, me savoring that cutting sting. No more of that, and no more eating when I was hungry. I'd be as gone as the g-sound in Ms. Ida's lasagna.

I would not go back to Trask, that damn bedbugged museum of a children's home. Could not give one more tour of the former plantation. Was finished handing out fascinating slices of Appalachian History. Them cotton collars they necked us in. *Garments.* Posing for photos in Merrill Trask's Historic Weaving Room. Could not invite one more clot of diabetic tourists to try their own needle-pricked hands on the loom. Past asking them to make a purchase in the gift shop, where all proceeds go to the home. We the children craft each of these beautiful souvenirs. We the children are beautiful souvenirs. Please take us to your beautiful home. But it was picturing the look on Ms. Ida more than the threat of Trask that was squirming me. Her eyes leaden sad. The heft-ache of them weighting and shaming me. How her hug would hurt more than any ruler, belt, or nail-prickled plank I'd ever been spanked by. That was what made me dash for the sliding door as Pop Galarde wrathed and paced. Out the yard and over the fence with my quease ebbing just like when a race starts. Before's the hard part. All the sick's in the waiting.

And that *was* the start. I ran the sun out the sky. Went until I wasn't fleeing Ms. Ida or Pop Galarde, just chasing the sweet air I lunged up from in front of me—playing like I was PacMan, chewing a path through the night as I moved. And it seemed I'd never be sick or hungry or ashamed so long as I kept gulping breaths off the platter of ground I was covering. That was how I epiphany-ed the fullness that fast-moving can give you. I towed the sun back up, too. Came out on the shoulder of I-40 and kept right on going up it, traffic slurping past, diesel burps and rubber and crumbs of cigarette butts backwashed off big trucks. Reckon I'd've kept on that way if I hadn't come up on one-them semis cooling its brakes. The driver sunning himself in a beach chair off the side, squinting at me or sunrise. Red chest wooly like a Brillo Pad. I could've swerved wider. Could've passed around the other side. Instead I kept coming until he tipped his hat at me.

That squirt drove clear to Hickory gripping the top of

his window. Got himself a tan-line that stopped at the second knuckle of his left hand. Then we pulled off for the night and he reached across with it, wordless, and pressed my ear into his lap. Held me like that the damn night. So I remember his tan line. Had a long, sweaty chance to study it while I inched the wallet out his pocket. Didn't even think to check the center console or glovebox. That's where they keep the best stuff. Pills. Pipes. Shards in Ziplocks. I was happy with just the wallet that first time, and I tiptoed out the side and ran without so much as a snack from the truck stop. Had to rid all the squirm I'd built on that drive. Went on and on and kept going. Pausing sometimes; hope-looking for a place to stop, but not finding. Not even with Adam the Atom Man.

But Benji pulled the tarp off that Piston he'd pieced for me and I curled up in front of the hearth-heat of his feet, the hurt-cold sand warm as home.

He soared his stare off my shoulder like a parrot. "Pedal some."

And perched said stare on the boat deck in ward-wait of RoboCop. Please. RoboCop would've stayed tombed in that cabin if we scratch-dragged the boat to the inlet, rolled it over, and let it glug down to Davy Jones. But Benji wanting to keep this contraption a secret only warmed me: he'd picked me.

So I crotched on and rode. Benji punched up the watts till the flywheel snarled louder than my growling stomach. My stomach gulped my brain and my lungs and I was all legs, pedaling until Benji yanked the plug and palmed my head to quit me. His sunglasses reflected RoboCop, who stood in the cabin door stroking his lymph nodes.

"Quit that," he said. "Hurts my neck."

I straightened my head. Getting down into my legs takes me back to that first run to I-40, when the trucker burst in my ear and I climbed out that cab tipping my head.

This morning I could pop the whole skull off without either-them hooting. Just the Piston, me, and them sink-necked buzzards curling circles over the yard, drip-squawking like their heads are leaks. Must've whiffed my stump. Plus the Piston looks a carcass leaning upside the camper like varm-picked bones, or like yesterday how I propped after getting the bike tick-tock-ing.

The bike's bolted to the windtrainer, holding it so you can't tip. If I were just to fix the broke part. And then I epiphany! I hop out that cabin and giddy-spin, dizzy with the now-knowing of how I can ride.

Making it to the Piston takes a sweaty mosey. I do it by a trick I eavesdropped off the sprinters back at Trask, a drill the coaches called rolling. Make-believe your heel's fixed to a wheel, take a bound, and rotate it, sucking your heel up to your butt and yanking your knee up and out and reaching snappingly for the ground with the leg you just sprung from. Dangle and lim-pen the other one. Them twitchy 100 runners would cross the infield like that ever day of track season. Course, Trask's infield was an old cotton plot, and the dirt track that lapped it was short by a few lanes and meters. Our warmup was plucking crabgrass. My run was never done until I'd left lunch on the backstretch. The cardboardy retaste of box milk and the watered-down con-diments they let you squirt as much of as you wanted from the pumps. I always ponded a whole plate of just ketchup and A1, even after Ms. Ida was putting three squares and a snack in me. Tammy Galarde said I drooled half what I licked down my chin, maybe explaining why not even she'd sit with me. And she called *me* the baby. But she always dropped her raisin box walking past.

There I go into Everywhen, working myself down to snivel-ing.

Anyhow: rolling's the trick to fast hopping, and that's how I made my way to the Piston. Must've looked some fool to which-ever varms were lurking, but dare them all to race me.

RoboCop's egg rotten if he thinks he's fixing to beat me Saturday. Seen that poster-him cracked on the curb last year. Shattered. Humpty Dumpy. Might reckon he's patched up, but the cracks'll come back soon's he gets out in front. He'll see that empty road stretching and leak. In the lead it's just the edge of your own hurtening and heatening that you're chasing. Got to run till your gut drops. Your innards splat on your pelvis and you keep on, containing it, holding yourself in. That's the part that scares RoboCop: not even the hurtening or heatening or holding, but the thought that he might do all that and still not be fastest. That's the fear rotting him. He don't know the way you can't sniff your own stink, but I've whiffed it. Ever livelong that dies off before race day it reeks stronger. And him thinking them buzzards came for me.

And me coming back like a buzzard, sprawling out with the weight of remembering. Lord, how my mind swerves. Blame the Percs. Blame Benji for up-and-offing, leaving no one telling me. Next thing I'm facedowning in the yard with my splinters all through my good leg's balance muscles. The ankle and shin sore real quick from rolling. I crawl back for my peg-leg. Gonna need it for the Piston anyhow.

But the Piston. The bikes' aluminum bones rusty like bits of skin withered to jerky. Like to see one-them buzzards break its ugly beak trying pick it. It's rust-stuck to the camper's backside right along with them herbs ditched by Benji. Me as wither-left as the plants coffined in them boxes. All-us. I give the Piston a yank and it stays. Lean my full weight back to pry, dangling till my grip gives and I slip. A shard from that busted flywheel bites my ass where I hard-sit. That steel's blown-bent like a popped blister. The ergometer's no-go, but the bike wheel might still spin. Hub's fixed to the windtrainer with bolts like it's just waiting to get lightning-struck back to life. And my legs got just the lightning. But a Perc first. Got to droop. My mind's yapping up too many wrong trees. Just that last clot of pills in the bottle. I set to spanking after it, but my slobber's gaumed it to the bottom. Try smacking it loose on the camper wall and the screen door clatters open.

"Don't have to knock." Little Miss RoboPeep noseys out at me.

"Didn't."

"Huh." Hanging off the frame like a third door, sweating a

new hue for her tri-suit. Spandex dark with the same dampness polishing her skin. Irks me that she's gone-got a sweat going before me. "Well, you can come in whenever."

"Nuts."

"I'll just leave it propped. It's hell-hot in here."

"Your sake."

"Yep." She stays hanging. "Some contraption."

I go back to the pill bottle, trying worm my tongue down the tube.

"Heard how that happened. Heard you pedaled the whole heat of hell into it. 500 watts for how long?"

"Slough off."

"Well, your lactate threshold must be ridiculous. I'd love to get you in a heart rate monitor. Put you on the ergometer, test your FTP."

"Hate being numbered."

"Heard that, too."

My tongue's all cut up from the bottle. I quit that and try cracking it on the edge of the windtrainer. Her just dangling out the doorframe, spectating me.

"Got a spare in the van," she says. "And a toolbox."

The pluck on this lady! Nerve like Shiela Petey. No wonder RoboCop got all hot-bothered by her. Your worm crawls toward what's familiar. Ms. Ida taught me all about Oedipus and the reverse-birth urge to burrow back in the womb. But hard to picture Little Miss RoboPeep ever fitting RoboCop. Thin as screen door she's impersonating, hinging out the camper and dangling. "I've got twenty minutes left on the Computrainer. Want to hop on when I'm finished?"

"Nuts."

"Well, it's yours to ride. If you feel up to it, feel free."

I chuck the pill bottle at her. She ducks. The bottle soars into the camper and smacks something.

"I'll leave the door propped," she says, shutting herself in front of it. She pushes an old shoe between the frame and the screen. Hear her cycling shoes cluck across the vinyl. Hear them snap into her pedals like one-two buzzard beaks. Then the squawk of the Computrainer's motor revving up with the steady gust of her pedaling.

And my stump's yapping. Ought to go after that pill bottle, but I couldn't stand her catching me taking her invitation. I tip back over that Piston and tug on it, but her words keep chewing me. *If you feel up to it.* Like feeling's the thing keeping me. *Up to,* like I'm slumped under some mood. As if it's my own mind instead of equipment restraining me.

I irk a turn, take a lap of the yard to unthink. Gonna ride. Piston's not going nowhere. Just my mind. I crawl around-side of the camper, around-front and find RoboCop's footprints. His track crosses over a slew of paws. Looks like the varms had themselves a damn square-dance in the cul-de-sac, yet RoboCop's steps show no sign of stooping or looking. Blind old him. He looks for the varms and gets skittish from not-seeing, but you can't spot one dead-on. The trick's to look around and not for them: see the paw prints and scratches on doors and holes dug under fences and tipped-over trashcans. A varm's like a ghost that way. You find it by the disturbance it causes. Got to go by how it haunts since your stare passes clean-clear through its body.

But I keep ground-eyed over RoboCop's footprints. Trace them up to the front of the camper, back how I came, and then backer, backing around to the boat. So that was no Everywhen I'd been dreaming. Must've been the real RoboCop come to sleep with me last night. Hope flutters my heart, but I'm bothered, because I just know some other hurt's fixing to fly-swat it.

And that Computrainer's still squawking. The screen door huffs with Little Miss RoboPeep's pedaled-up breeze. It rattles out and back to squish the shoe propping it. *If I'm up to it.* The nerve on her. Gonna ride, just first got to droop. Got a steepening need. Ever time I gulp a pill is like giving up to gravity. RoboCop's afraid to go over his own edge while I've done cannonballed off of this one. Still waiting to land. Maybe I'll splat on the same road where RoboCop cracks and leaks. That picture's enough to fix my fixing to. I go on in, nuts to Little RoboPeep.

There she perches. The humps of her spine poke up through her tri-suit like callouses worn by too long riding into a head-wind. I can count ever one. Her aero-helmet points back at me like a wrung-necked rooster's 180 ed beak. And ever upstroke of her pedals flicks stinging skeeters of sweat back at me.

"Just getting the Percs!" I holler.

She don't turn. Not taking nuts from her. Just getting the bottle. I look all around the camper floor for it and don't see. I'm skittish to put my foot down inside till I spot it, like I'll swerve if I don't keep my eyes locked where I'm going. Then the chirp of a watch alarm. She sits up, the humps of her spine ebbing, and slides her sockless feet out the shoes.

"Ezra still asleep?"

"He up-offed."

"Huh."

She unstraps her heart rate monitor like a bra, unpeeling the top of her tri-suit right in front of me. Ribs you could climb like a ladder. Them sprawled shoulders of RoboCop's. Her heels leave ponds on the vinyl with both steps she takes toward me.

"You want on?"

"Just getting the Percs."

"Right."

Now it's me hanging in that doorframe like the screen.

"Seen them?"

"When I ducked them." She does this bird-shrug, scrunch-ing down her neck. "But not since."

I put my peg-leg, then my good foot through the door. The floor's warm-wetter lava, the vinyl hot with heat seeped from the Computrainer and slick with her footprints, like I'm walking on her body heat and brow-sweat. Wobbling. Tick-tocking. My heel slips and I catch myself on her bike seat.

"Want a hand?" she asks. "A leg up?"

This lady. I give her a fart of a glare. Waft a real stink-eye toward her, clenching my eyelids like sphincters.

She takes it like a wink, winking back. "A spare set of eyes, maybe."

I rest for a gasp, draping over her bike. Looks like a hunk of Martian technology. Brake cables veined through the top tube and electric shifting. Power meter crucified on the handlebars, the suffering of her ride blinking Christly on its screen: 90 minutes at 200 watts and 130 rpms— Roadrunner cadence. No wonder the Computrainer was squawking.

"That was a recovery ride," she says. "Easy spinning."

I kick off my peg-leg and side-mount the bike easy. Just swing my leg over the saddle and *hup* and I'm perching. That'll quicken my transition split. While RoboCop's trying to stomp off his wetsuit I'll be upping-out of T1 and pedaling.

"Didn't land around there," she says.

I'm irking the right pedal around, working my foot into that shoe. Don't even have to loose the velcro. The inside's warmdamp as a snatch on your first thrust; feels as good, too, riding how I been fixing to. I whir up a squawk and a gust, heat rising up my legs like my worm before bursting.

She comes up beside me. "I had it on ergometer. Punch plus to up wattage." I swat her hand off when she reaches. She says, "Sure."

I punch plus. The Computrainer drops its hum, the flywheel bearing down on the back tire. My right knee grates against the resistance. Watch my cadence slump. 60 rpms. 50. I try and churn it back up with her hovering.

"You're all downstroke," she says. "Quit stomping." Staring at the power meter like she's the one pedaling. "I pretend I'm scraping shit off of my shoe. Helps me engage the hamstring."

I punch plus. The Computrainer snugs to the wheel and try-stare that cadence up. I tug the hoods till the bike rocks.

"What're you training?" she asks. "Doing sprints?"

I cover the screen with my hand. It's her looking that's weighting it.

She stands on. Despite all her tiny, the lady can loom. Casts a shadow ten times her size like one-them anvils over Wiley Coyote. She held 200 watts with her legs Roadrunnering. I'm huffing at 210 with my heart rate about equal to it. A laptop's altared on the table in front of the bike. Mark Allen gashed with static like a varm dragged its claws across the screen, froze in hurt like Little RoboPeep's bleeding Jesus.

"Can't claim to like what y'all did with the place," she's saying. "Half the island's underwater. Gotta go to the mainland for takeout, not to mention these coyotes. Some plague you dragged in. You and Benji."

I quit pedaling. Before I can dismount she pets up my shoulders. My lungs beat my squirm: I sigh first, because that's how Benji settled me. Mark Allen's wearing Oakleys as big-bright as his on the laptop.

I chomp the screen shut and buck up. "Hell you wearing that helmet for?"

"Safety."

I knock her a bonk on the side.

She unbuckles it. "I'm getting my neck used to the weight."

I knock a better bonk on her buzzcut and hop off after Percs. Roll and fall. I all-fours around in hunched search. She crouches down, too.

"Don't help."

"Just draining my legs."

Her back damp-smacks to the floor like fast humping, then clunks like the headboard that fast humping jostles as she slings her heels up on the wall, her ribs bold as the slats of the bed frame. I crawl on, thinking of all the things she can fuck. Turn and tell her some: a cadence, her spaceship bike and Computrainer.

Another bird-shrug. "De nada."

Then the front door gets knocked.

"It's your house!" she hollers, thinking it's RoboCop.

But RoboCop knocks a beat. This was one rap like a gavel. And I'm crawling for the backdoor before I can even figure the feeling I'm hopping from, whether it's fear or rage or joy squirming me.

Second, single knock. "Town census?"

Some jasper. Only as I still down do I brain what was throbbing my nerves: the thought that it might be Benji.

"I'm here to ask a few short questions, sir or ma'am? And invite you to tomorrow's town hall?" Hollers all that like asking.

Little RoboPeep checks her watch. Next checks me. Her narrow neck sprouts and bends, vining with tendons. No wonder she's got to used-to the helmet—lifting her head off the floor seems a strain.

Fallow days when I'd been just as weak: stretches where I'd grown so rump-sore or queasy from bursting that I swore myself shut and starved off alone. Without steady eating I frailed corpesish. I've held still for days. Patches where my arm hairs froze to the ditch where I wallowed, too starved to even gumption enough for shivering. Hunger always sent me back to bursting strangers. You quit one pain and another fills in. My throat amphibians at the thought, that old frog Mr. Sob hopping.

"A few short questions?" says the door.

Little RoboPeep's head clunks back to the tile. "He's coming!"

Hard gulp and I bellow it open. Sun comes through brightloud as shouting, muffled by this lank-haired feller acting dude. Clipboard underarm like he's fixing to surf on it. Instead, he pops it up-front his face. "Hello? I'm a volunteer representing the Sloop Point Homeowner's Association?"

"We're not donating," says Little RoboPeep.

"Absolutely." Feller flips back a sheet. "That's great! Because actually? We're just asking you to contribute your opinion." Talking in a stretched tone to show he's reading. Wanting us to know, *this is less cool than me.* He flips back to the first sheet. "Hello? I'm a—wait. As you likely know, our island is overpopulated by coyotes. Our community has been forced to combat this threat with ineffective and dangerous measures, including poisons and traps."

"Fuck a trap."

Feller drops his clipboard and for the first time he looks at me.

I grip the doorframe and wag my stub-leg at him. "I'm the

choir, preacher."

"Shit. What."

"Run into one. Chomped my leg so bad they lopped it."

"Seriously." All the ask flattened out of him. Staring at the gone where my foot ought-be. He pats his phone out his khakis. "Why didn't...shit. Gotta get you in front of a camera. Would you mind?" He squeezes a picture

"Absolutely." Little RoboPeep says. "We don't consent."

"Wait. Your name." He flip-squints through his pages. "You're Ezra Fogerty?"

"Shut the door, Stud."

As I do, he sneaks a picture of me.

Little RoboPeep drains a sigh. "There goes our serenity."

Which where'd my Percs get to, so-speaking. I turn to search, but sap, all squirm sloshing out of me. Soreness wells up my bones. Picture the plunger pushing that first dose of medicine out the syringe, the nurse telling me to look off even as my eyes were on Benji. And I saw how the needle went into my shoulder in his Oakleys, but I knew his eyes were closed behind that reflection. Because here was something getting in that he hadn't told, tainting the pure *him* that he'd put in me. I drip down slow and puddle on the vinyl, no skeleton left to hold me. Seeping nose. Pulse going like the last mile.

Across the floor Little RoboPeep rolls up her eyes for an upside-down view of me. "Your ticker's on the Richter, Stud. You're shaking the floor with that heartbeat."

Ezra

Just a run. Ezra just has to keep his brain in his body. To put it back, after handing it over to Casper; best way to do that's to get moving. So he'd left the kid on the boat and jogged out of the cul-de-sac. Caught a tailwind coming up Bromine Avenue—a rare offshore—and his legs had just masted out from under him, his strides billowing.

He hits Ocean Street outrunning his lungs, in oxygen debt already. Lactic acid welling in his fingertips. Sprints across the road to the beach access into caution tape, tearing through before turning to slow. The wind-stretched strands like tentacles groping toward him. Trying to pull him back. He sees the backside of the sign he's just sprinted past, orange with warning, and takes a wrong comfort from it: government-sanctioned panic. He starts back down the access, then stops, not really caring to read it. Enough to know that he isn't the only one getting histrionic. But what turns him the other way is a sharper, darker instinct that he still can't quite name. He runs onto empty beach and into an urgent Atlantic. The offshore wind raises eyebrows of whitewater above furrowed swells, waves cresting in front of him skeptically. He dolphins under their troughs. Pushes off the sand and springs up and streamlines back under the next one until he's clear of the shorebreak and swimming. Only shaking the sucking cold as he slaps into stroke. No goggles, eyes open, saline glazing his seeing. Stirred sand hides the bottom from him. The water shattered with sunlit salt crystals. He breathes with his chin tucked into his armpit, swimming straight out without sighting. Stabbing going. Still waiting to get a handle on what's thrusting him. Groping for the hilt of that urge or compulsion.

A hum bulges up to his north. He gulps a choke of water when he turns that way to breathe. A squint's glimpse of a boat slashing chop at him. The motor's hum dins and stutters. Snorts bilge as it quits. He detects the hull without turning toward it, by some primal awareness of large, lurking things. When he hears shouting, he stops lifting his head to breathe. Tucks his chin, churned his strokes, and strikes a forearm. Fingers fish-hook his chin. He drops his legs to tread, swatting at the seeming dozen hands grabbing him. They drag him up thrashing, scraping him. His shorts catch on the barnacles callousing the hull. They slide off his hips and he kicks them free. The shorts jellyfish out as they sink, doming and billowing, and he's naked on the deck with a sheriff's badge on a barrel chest bulging over him.

A sheriff's hat's racked on the zinc-thick face above that, its brim low as the eyebrows and mustache over the top of the mouth flicking spit down at him. "Navy commercial?"

"Sorry."

"Asked you something." The sheriff's hat turns. "Towel! Jesus."

One flutters down on Ezra's lap.

The sheriff swabs his face with a palm. "I asked if you're one of these SEAL wannabe assholes. Did you see a Navy commercial or what?"

"Sorry."

"Where'd you get in at?"

"Bromine. The beach access."

"And you missed the sign. And the caution tape."

"Sorry."

"You mentioned." Second swab with the hand. "Well, the water's contaminated. There's a goddamned health advisory."

The deck brims and tips with life-vested deputies, enough crowded neon for a respectable clown car. Sun-warmed water sluices over Ezra's head. He looks up at a gallon jug and the deputy dumping it. Some stings up his nose and he drops his head again.

"It's this LiquaTox folks have been marinating their lawns with. I've been saying—swear—all it takes is one good rainfall, then the runoff. That's what you were swimming through. Why we pulled your dumb ass out the water." The sheriff tosses another jug in Ezra's lap. "Here, you keep dumping this. Where the hell were you swimming to?"

"Nowhere."

"Nowhere."

"Just swimming."

"Nowhere. Well, you got pretty close. You're a mile offshore. We only swung out this far for calm water."

"Sorry," Ezra says.

The sheriff swabs his face again. His mustache seems to slide closer to his upper lip. "Citation's two hundred dollars. I'll just go write that up for you."

Ezra's skin has already sun-dried, though the towel's still sopping. He skids it over his thighs anyway. A mile straight out had felt more like a pool's length, even with his running shorts bloating up like a dragsuit. He'd only noticed their resistance as they were slipping off of his hips. The same ones he'd run after Casper in, and had sat and slept and fermented in ever since. Jesus. He looks off the back of the boat, at the zippers of wake opening behind it. He stands up and leans over the motor. Looks closer. And finds the urge that sent him swimming all that way. Not Benji or Casper or spite or shame—just his own reflection slicing away, parting with the chop spread across the water's surface. The only thing propelling him had been him.

A raking shout from the bow, but he's already leaping. Dives into a streamline, flutter-kicking past the wake. None of that grogginess from past stints without swimming, that numb skew that land-lock typically causes in his stroke. He's all urge and churn and no destination but his own nerve endings. Craving every organ's and sinew's sensation—freshness and fatigue, thrill and wince, contraction, relaxation. Breaking smoothly through walling exhaustion, holding form and velocity as his limbs brick-stack with lactate. Just to feel that; to *want* to feel it.

The boat curls back and four deputies fish him out with the sheriff shouting down and Ezra's gasp-laughing. Can't get a hold on an inhale, even after they've cuffed him to the railing. The sheriff goes to the bow for a water and cough drops and comes back for a second round of shouting. Wanting to know who the hell, demanding ID. Threatening arrest, misdemeanor, and Ezra snags enough breath to say sorry. To keep saying it, turning his laughter to chanting. Drowning out the sheriff and the swell-slapped bow and the stuttered mow of the outboard until his own voice is the only thing in his skull: an echo, but not a reflection. All his. No more care for Casper or duty to Ma or Benji's words tainting him. A near year since he'd collapsed in Chapel Hill, waking in the medical tent with that mullet dripping over him. Seeping in. But Ezra's sweated him out. All it took was moving for movement's sake to get his brain back again.

They dump him off at the marina in a parachuting pair of swim trunks, the Coast Guard sizzling through on the radio. A trawler'd been spotted scraping up shrimp off of Bald Head. In this water! Dumb or poor enough. The sheriff holds the receiver to his ear, palm-swabs his face again. Doesn't offer Ezra a ride home. Doesn't take him to the station, either. "Keep them," he says—the trunks apparently his. The boat whisks off and leaves Ezra on the dock with a citation plastered to either wet pec, shouting sorry.

Someone hollers, "bastard!" and lays on a foghorn. Buzzards shatter the sky at the sound. Ezra brandishes his middle finger around, scanning the boats for the culprit. 'FOR SALE' signs rise like white flags from pilot's decks. Prices crossed out. *Best offer. Call for details.* At the prow of the *Sea Saw,* a wicked figurehead: four coyotes hanged from the bowsprit.

"You're kidding," Ezra says, meaning it. This really does seem a parody, a hyperbole of bad tidings—more the entrails themselves than the doom they portend. Kure's rotting.

A stranger in your home, or you in a stranger's; add to those horrors finding home stranger than you'd left it. Worse to've been there for the strange-ing. Ma'd bought their plot for dirt-cheap and gotten what she'd paid for: spoiled ground. Ezra'd been sixteen when the Dow Plant shut down, held his breath through the deflating economy. Neighbors moving out. The dirt stinging his nape when he laid back on it to drain his legs, putting his feet up on the Sprinter van and watching the ocean advancing. More feet of beach sandbarred after every hurricane season. Hitching the boat to the camper to the Sprinter van in air poppling with ozone, raked by sideways rain, joining evacuating traffic with their conga of mobile homes. Splashing back down Bromine Avenue through all the things that the storm surge had dredged up. Chairs and lawn mowers. Doghouses. Sheds. Rain gutters stripped intact off of houses. All of this bobbing like offerings against the flood. Fewer and fewer folks coming back with them. Roofers and landscapers and septic trucks replaced by insurance adjustors. Ezra'd lived on it, through it. This island had been sinking as long as it had been home.

He finds a drum set in the dock as he runs. Mid-and-high Toms in the planks, then the aluminum ramp cymbaling under him. Tarsals clattering with each impact. The jarring charge of it in his shins. Past the closed dock-and-dine joints onto sidewalk and asphalt. Condos on the beachside. Rounding the nadir of Marina Avenue's horseshoe swearing he's melting the road, welding onto Ocean Street. He'd look back at the same view he'd found aft of the boat: his passage a clasp by which zippers of wake opened, asphalt loosened to liquid from the sheer heat of his speed. But Ezra knows better than to look over his shoulder. He stares where he's going. And swears Casper's in the glare where the sun ripples road, the light bending the same way that the kid's head tips to his shoulder.

He chases that vision home. Keeps it pinned by his eyes all the way down Bromine Avenue, where Casper tumbles into three dimensions in front of him. The kid's speed-wobbling up the road on his prosthetic. A cameraman and microphone-waving lady jog after him. Ezra can hear the crunch of the lady's ordered speech a block off but can't quite shape the words of it. Casper doesn't glance back. A news truck's lozenged in the throat of the cul-de-sac with its doors hanging open, parked in an apparent rush. The slant looks haphazard, but its placement seems strategic—obstructing the exit.

Ezra keeps running, bluffing for the cul-de-sac. He diagonal-eyes them as he comes: cameraman with more makeup than the lady, who's spray-tanned the hue of sourdough crust. His concealer seems to smear under Ezra's gaze.

"Just a soundbite," Sourdough's saying.

When she jousts her mic at Casper he takes a back-arching bound, sucking his right leg under and ahead of him like a long jumper's forward-reaching landing; landing with the collapsing force of one. His butt bounces off the road at the same time as his hamstrings. The prosthetic skids off. The cameraman stumbles over him, lurching into a prolonged trip.

Ezra's a mailbox away. Hard swerve as he levels with them. Sourdough jumps back, her mouth shaping a shout, and Ezra pulls up on his front foot, pivoting uncertainly. What had he meant to do: bite her? Only in his lunging had the lacuna of his intention occurred to him.

"Bfagh!" she hollers. Voice on broadcast delay.

The cameraman comes out of his stumble without tripping, circling around. "Got it! Still rolling!"

Casper's rolled onto his stomach. His arms buckle when he tries to push himself up; breath-knocking bellyflop. The hairs on Ezra's shins stir with the shove of air leaving him. He eases his hands under Casper's armpits and feels thronging heartbeats. Kid's torso's crowding with blood, like his veins can't keep up with his arteries. "Dude."

Casper seems asleep. His stump twitches like a dog wagging its tail at a dream. Sourdough looks at him, Ezra, him. "Brother?"

"Bystander."

Ezra props the kid against his own legs, gets him sitting. Has to flex his calves to keep from getting pushed back by that pulse. Talk about ecloses. Their image swells in the camera lens prodding toward them: Casper on the ground, Ezra bouncing in place. A near-perfect inversion of the day Benji'd tied them to the truck.

"Who're you?" the cameraman asks.

"He's the brother. I said." Sourdough pops her neck like knuckles, at the prolonged pace of a threat. "Can we use you?"

Ezra looks down the dunes of his abdominals at the top of Casper's head. The blonde aftermath of that buzzcut like the stubbled rays of a sun fuzzed with heat. It rises as the kid leans off of Ezra's legs.

"Droops rolled," he says. "Down to one-some. Just the wad."

Sourdough wafts her mic at Ezra. "If you'll just talk for a sec about the coyotes, then go into your take on what happened to Ezra—"

"He is!" Caper shouts. "He's the one called the wee-woo."

"The ambulance?"

Ezra nods. The cameraman backpedals, twisting his lens.

"So you were there with him?"

"Swung the varms off the nightlong." Casper rocks back and forth like he's trying to roll up to his feet. And Ezra can't kick him quiet—can't speak—because he wants Casper to keep putting words to what he'd done. "He stayed," he says, and Ezra puts his hand on his buzzcut; coming from Casper, that's as good as thanking him.

"Take us through that night," Sourdough says.

Casper's chin bounces off his chest, his teeth clicking together. "Hush!" Looking down at his stump. He slaps the bandage, opens his mouth, and retches. The bile falls out like a ribbon unspooling—the thread-thin contents of an empty stomach.

A splutter of dirt-churning tires, then sharper friction. The news truck slides out of the cul-de-sac with a din like a utensil gagging a garbage disposal. The sound clenches, the truck listing on its chassis.

A slammed door. "Gah–damnit!" Ma hollers.

She's backed the Sprinter van into it.

The cameraman cranes out from around his viewfinder.

"It's already hit, Mitch," Sourdough says. "Keep rolling."

Ma apologizes into sight; rounds the fender with her hands lifted and trots up the road toward them, shouting, "Sorry!"

Sourdough sighs. "One soundbite, I'm asking."

Ezra scoops Casper off the road. Forks his right arm behind the kid's knee, left behind his shoulder blades, the kid's torso sagging, and hunches over that caving stomach.

"Get that, Mitch."

Mitch puts the prosthetic into Casper's lap. Casper in Ezra's arms. Kid's lighter than the deputy's swim trunks.

"I mean the shot," Sourdough moans. She stabs the mic at the kid and he bites it.

"Sorry," Ezra says.

"Sorry!" Ma shouts.

Mitch walks over to meet her.

Sourdough squints at the toothmarks on the mesh screen. "This forsaken island. Never should've left Charlotte." She underhands the mic into the ditch and stalks away from them, muttering.

Ezra carries Casper off the road, away from the news truck. He takes the crunching cover of brush around back of the camper. Casper's nose is running in watery sheets. His snot pools in the webs of Ezra's fingers. He has no shirt or spare hands to wipe the kid's face with, so he lifts his head to his chest and smears it on his skin. The kid's nose squeaks like a chew toy.

"Use a droop," Casper says.

"Take one."

"Did. Just the one-some. The wad's left."

"They're not on you?"

"Rolled off. Said."

Ezra burdens toward the boat.

"Camper!" Casper hollers.

Ezra leans toward the backdoor instead. Drapes him on the couch. Ma's already brought the Computrainer in from the Sprinter van; the bright mat of sweat under it proves that she's ridden, too. But her bike's gone. He watches through the front window as she roots through the Sprinter van, taking in the physics of the collision. The van had impaled the news truck with its bike rack. The truck's side door puckers around the rack's prongs, its *Star Witness* logo enjambed. The van appears unscathed at this distance, cushioned by its spare tire. The rack itself is conspicuously empty. Ezra can see Ma's Cervelo through the van's rear window, seat-belted into the dinette—secured for a premeditated impact. She'd been running interference for Casper. Ezra watches her cramming across the front seat, loving her for it. Mitch stands cradling his camera by the driver's side and nodding at her filibustered apologies. Ezra can hear her from here. Every word etched as clear as if it's his own eardrum her voice is chiseling into.

"The lizard one. Ginko? Got a paper copy somewhere in here. If not the console, the glovebox. If not, I'll pull it up on the computer. Where's my phone?"

All those backstretches and finishing chutes he's run down with her shout reaching him in the round, bulging out from the cowbells and blurred cheers. His ears attuned to her voice by some mammal law of maternity. A coyote pup learns its mother by sound, knows her howl before its eyes even open. Before it even stores her scent in its snout.

Ma drags back out of the van with the laptop. "I'll just pull it up."

Mitch has his phone to his ear—maybe calling Sourdough, who's disappeared.

Ezra turns back to Casper. "Who sicced the press?"

"Cheryl. The damn home-own 'sociation." Casper's ear hits his shoulder. "Droop please."

The bile's dried to a damp shadow on his shorts, more like

spit than puke. Kid's stomach that empty. Nothing but water and salt to vomit. He doesn't writhe away when Ezra checks his pockets for the pills; he sighs, actually. A silent breath, but Ezra feels its passage stirring goosebumps on his arms. He leans in and slices his arms through the couch cushions.

"Quit looking for. Look around." Casper's voice snot-damp, congested.

Ezra turns back toward the window. Ma's pecking at the laptop, Mitch peering over her shoulder. "I tried caps lock. Bear with me."

"Rolled," Casper moans. "The floor, Robo." And taps his stump like a foot on the cushion.

Ezra gets down on all fours to check under the couch. Only dust bunnies snared in Band Aids. He feels around for the bottle anyhow, his arm gaining a wooly sleeve. Crawls away with it fraying his sinuses, sneezing.

"Guys and I," Casper says.

Ezra tries to drop below the dust cloud, lifting the skirts of each piece of furniture as he belly-crawls through the camper. All he turns up are new allergies. Den to the bedroom and back to the couch like this. He grabs the edge of the end table and pries himself up to his knees, shaking the table. No; backwards. The table's shaking him. Ma's phone marooned on a Pine Island 10k coaster, an incoming call spasming, staticking him with panic.

The phone goes still the second he grabs it. The screen's runged with new message notifications. The senders read like exclamations: *WANDA BLUECROSS. ERNST WHEELSDEALS.* Ma keeps her phone on caps lock, uses folks' jobs for surnames. Banners ladder up to his own fainting face; her lock screen's that picture of him curb-stomped in Chapel Hill. The topmost—the missed call—is an exception. Just *DORO.* A voicemail notification tops the screen.

Ezra exhales. What had he been expecting? His own name at the top. Benji'd taken this picture of Ezra, and he'd taken Ezra's phone, so if Ma'd gotten a call from him, it would've been

Benji's breath oozing through the speaker. Benji'd caterpillared into Ezra's home, body, and brain. No wonder he'd held back hammering down that boardwalk, letting Casper sprint past him: pushing to his own limit would've exposed the fitness Benji'd spun into his sinew. The man's in and of him. Benji's made Ezra his cocoon.

He drags his thumb across the voicemail's notification banner, punches in his birthday for the passcode. The lock screen shakes its rejection. Shakes again when he enters Ma's. He tries 0954—her Ironman P.R.—and it opens.

The transcription of Doro's voicemail is garbled. *Hey Jew saw remiss your call list end…*

Ezra hits the play button.

"Hey you. Sorry, missed your call. Listen."

Ezra presses pause. The voice is vaguely male, maybe Canadian. Ezra pictures a mountie pointing Ma in the right direction to keep from picturing an ice-fisherman netting her in his arms, leading her into a shivering tryst. She'd said she'd taken detours. Maybe she's been secretive instead of sexless—or Ezra's spent his whole life oblivious. Better to stay that way. He hits 'delete.'

And scrolls, matching up the dates of messages with the days. Casper'd gotten out yesterday, the twenty-third. Wednesday. Take away ten days in the hospital. They'd lopped his leg on the thirteenth. So Casper'd stepped in the trap on the twelfth. Benji'd left that same evening. He flicks down to the date and there it is, Ma's name for him: CHAMP. Incoming call at 11:33 p.m.

He pictures Ma fumbling for the phone, reaching out of whatever race she'd been dreaming. Strange that she'd even picked up. Always slept with it off; then again, she'd always been sleeping a bedroom away from him. Had she been leaving it on up there in the Yukon in case he called? The idea of her losing sleep for him burdens him—and the guilt that he hadn't reciprocated. He'd been too exhausted to spare any anxiety beyond the next feat Benji was going to demand of them in training. Benji'd called Ma the same night that he'd left; she'd picked up expecting

Ezra and gotten a treatise on Ezra's fitness instead. The call had lasted fifteen minutes. They'd talked long enough for him to race a 5k. Imagining that conversation is as taxing as running one: Benji driving off in Casper's truck, telling Ma how he'd gotten Ezra into shape. Any record Ezra set would be spoiled by him. The worst thing Benji'd done, Ezra thinks—hating the thought even as it occurs to him—was tainting his fitness.

The front door sucks open.

"No good'll come," Ma says.

Ezra jerks back and trips. Sits hard on Casper's stump, but the kid's sealed with sleep. How long's he been dozing? Ezra's thumb's hovering over 'CALL' on Benji's contact information. He hot-potatoes the phone into Ma's reaching palm.

All she says is, "Snoop."

Outside, Sourdough's brooded back. Mitch walks a slow pan around her with his Nikon, lensing up the damage done by that bike rack. They seemed to be broadcasting. Eight months of Ezra's life had gushed past before the clog of that hospital; now his life's flooding again, events rushing past too fast for the narrow seconds holding them. Ezra floats off the couch by the welling pressure of them.

"Not a word—" Ma starts.

"Just biking."

"Huh."

"Just to the pharmacy. Casper's sick."

"Noticed."

"It's withdrawals. Those Percocets fucked him up. I'm getting him Advil. Tylenol. Something." Too rushing much, the waterfalling plunge. "He lost the bottle. Make him space it out if you find it. Cut up the tabs. Refill's not for a week. That's assuming Blue Cross doesn't catch on." Spilling panic down the steps.

"Have a good workout!" Ma hollers.

Casper

But I'm only playing sleep. Shut eyes soon as Little RoboP-eep's phone got to quaking. Couldn't stand watching RoboCop quake along with it, the shakes going up his arm like the Holy Spirit through the old Doctor Reverend when he was casting out demons. Only RoboCop was trying to reel a demon in. Soon's he snatched that phone I knew he was fishing for Benji. So I fake-slumped. A sleeping dog's let to lie. Guess what old one I learned that from? The Doctor Reverend. If I heard him peek in on me I'd let on like I was conked and listen to him stand panting, laying hands on himself instead of me. Strange how there's a sacred sense around sleep. If you let on like you're snoozing deep enough even folks who feel fine and right coming into your body won't wake you up. Guess my demons stayed lying right alongside the dog in me. Never could figure if the Doctor Reverend was quaking from Jesus going down his arm or the demon slithering up it, but he sure did quake when the burst squirted out of him. And so long as I let on like I was conked he stayed in that doorway, keeping his prayer-pattycaking palms off of me.

RoboCop stood there good and long at the couch foot the same way. Waiting long after the phone quit its trembling. Me faking leaking sleep, gulping snot even as it glazed my face. Then the door banged and Little RoboPeep onstaged and dear Rob-oCop got to hem-hawing for my sake, worrying over me. Up-offed to get Percs, leaving me and Little RoboPeep.

I risk a peek at her. See her hunching over that phone like it's a map to the potluck she needs to eat all of. She should try Ms. Ida's lasagna with biscuits in the crust. Called that private

Eye-talian, count of it'd take a detective to find the spinach hidden in the middle right alongside the 'g.' Little RoboPeep's acting like she might find some in her phone, flitting her thumb up and up off the screen.

"Don't sit up," she says without straying her gaze from it.

My head-to-toe's yapping, but I've got to crunch up. Can't have her thinking I'm listening to what she tells me.

She swings her foot up and presses it to my chest to stub me. "These people. Try caps lock, he tells me." Glancing out the front window, then back at the phone. "Was Ezra gonna call?"

Not saying Benji's name—or *him*, even. Making the same mistake as RoboCop with the varms: thinking looking or saying straight-on will summon him. But talking around him makes the shape that holds his ghost. In he floods to that quiet. Up to me to plug it shut.

"Benji?" His name takes up the same space he was haunting, sounding wet from my slobbering nose.

Little RoboPeep squeezes her phone like to keep its speakers from hearing. Being fair, I have heard that phones sponge up all you say to some cloud to rain back down as junk-mail and sidebar ads and search suggestions. In spite of all I grudge her, she's earned a fair take. She fended off the clipboard feller till that fat news truck rumbled up, then fended back the microphone lady and cameraman, whomping talk at them the way RoboCop whomped that branch while I squirm-snuck out the backdoor. Should've hunkered in the boat cabin, but the squirms were something awful plaguing me. Soon's I took off up the road Mama and Paparazzi spotted me. Made a culpa. No fault of Little RoboPeep's. She might still be holding them off with her jaw if not for my squirms, which I've known all along will be both bookends of me. Ever since starting out the Galarde's backdoor I've been clued to it. Moving'll prove as grave as it was womb, carrying me clear through ever volume of autobiography between.

Little RoboPeep is clued, too. Reaches one-them towels

from the stack by the Computrainer, reaching back without tipping or taking her foot off of me. She drifts dust-like down. Bends the leg pinning my chest till the knee gentles onto my throat, not denting my breathing.

"Don't drown, either." And smears the snot around my face with that towel. Wearing a t-shirt big enough to sail with. See her breastless chest through the gaping collar. Ribs showing like a throat's layers through an open mouth, the ridges of each deeper layer smaller-ing. I peer through to the unzipped top of her tri-suit hanging husked off her hips. She slices her hand where it puckers, feeling. The Percs rattle in the bottle as she dredges them up, my teeth chattering harmony.

"Found this on the porch. Must've soared through the window."

More like dropped into her pocket. Probably had-hid them from the time that I chucked them, but I let her lie sleep.

Taking sweet time opening that bottle. I watch-wait her twist for sugary seconds, wanting a let at it. But my headaching's out-yapping my talking. Finally Little RoboPeep sticks the bottle down at me. I bite onto the cap. She twists when I clench like a pencil she's sharpening. Yanks back and I gnaw and it comes shaving, stripping threads as it frees. Back of my head smacks the couch arm. She waves me down as she stands, showing she's coming back. Like I've got nerve enough left to lift. I watch her off to the kitchen, the all of me yapping. She chips the wad of pills apart with a knife stuck down in the bottle. Spanks some out the bottle and comes back. The speck of Perc on her palm's nit-scant. I'd snort, but I'm afraid my breath would whisk it off. I long a look back at the bottle. Too far.

She holds out the Perc-speck without saying or smiling. And the news is out front. And RoboCop's up-offed, but he's coming back with more Percs. A speck's worth might tide me. So I lick it off Little RoboPeep's palm and lay back and let on like I'm conked, the only dog left to trick being me.

Not that he'd meant to ride to Hampstead. Just that Walgreens and CVS had been boarded in truce on either side of Ocean Street. (Walgreens marquee: CLOSED FOR SEASONS. CVS: CHECK THE CHICKENS ACROSS THE ROAD.) So he stomped the pedals over the summit of Woody Hewett, descending to the mainland on a carless road. That asphalt as barren ahead of him as the best-case version of race day. He swung out of the bike lane without shoulder-checking and tucked his chin to the handlebars, a wind-piercing needlepoint of knuckle and nose. The Trek shivered with speed. He glanced down at the handlebars to check his pace, but Benji'd stripped the power meter months ago. A roadside speed check ahead. He smirked the chain to the big ring and sprinted. The sign blinked 37.

Then Zenning. All lung and leg until the horn belches behind him. A Honda swerves past, straddling the median and eructing weed smoke from the windows. He sees its bumper stickers before it lets up on the horn. EVOLVE. (CO)EXIST. Marijuana leaf. Silhouette posed in a mudflap girl's parody, pot-bellied and trucker-capped. PROUD PARENT OF A LANEY HIGH STUDENT.

That collage is good for his bearings. He's needled clear to the haystacked end of the county. He stands to sprint through the last stoplight on Gordon Road, an intersection famously hated for the wink-speed of its yellow. Past that, the asphalt throats out to I-40. He swerves into the final Shell station before the highway and takes the lot's back exit out to Retail Loop.

The route offers the best riding in three counties: forty miles of freshly refurbished road. The pave came in anticipation of an outlet-flanked gated neighborhood. Development halted in the midst of deforestation, but not before Tanger had erected signs for the yet-to-be-built complex. A totem of logos for Adidas and Auntie Annie's and Levi's and Eddie Bauer stands stranded at the edge of the asphalt. The promised businesses could've dressed an army of Asher Roth wannabes—and stuffed them with enough pretzels to fill out their sagging jeans. Each brand name is basketball-goal sized, advertising hundreds of acres of barren dirt. Ezra pictures those hypothetical frat-rappers buried.

A pace-line of roadies approaches in the southbound lane, lifting fingers off the drops to offer shakas and peace-signs. The WheelsDeals lunchtime group ride. The hulk hunching his shoulders in third wheel breaks formation and u-turns. The word PHUKET is stretched across the back of his jersey, slanted by the alternating shift of his shoulderblades. Wispy. Ezra brakes. Wispy soft-pedals, glancing back like he's waiting.

"I know what you're thinking," he says.

Ezra coasts up beside him. "I was trying not to, so save it."

"The Phuket people fucked up my ticket. Some shit with the time change."

"You're not racing?"

"They're resolving it." Wispy says it with the detached speed of a mantra he's been chanting. They're both wobbling their handlebars to keep from tipping, inching along at walking speed.

"What about you?" Wispy asks. "Benji's got you biking in a drag suit?"

Ezra's still in the sheriff's swim trunks. He stutters, "Accident."

"I take it he doesn't buy into tapering."

"I'm just turning over the legs."

"That's all there is to it." Wispy claps Ezra on the back. The edges of his huge palm overlap with either of Ezra's scapula. "I'm just glad that you haven't gone missing."

"What's that?"

"You didn't read the *Slowtwitch* thing? I sent you the link."

Wispy frowns. "Maybe don't, actually."

"I haven't had my phone with me."

"Redacted, dude. Come take some pulls on the pace-line, get that neuromuscular recruitment. What're you weighing these days?"

Ezra sucks in his gut. "Something."

"Well you shrank. In a good way. Like in your frame, even."

"Shucks. Thanks."

"You know who you look like?"

"My Ma shaves her eyebrows."

"I was going to say that kid who smashed Chapel Hill last year. You remember him? Casper Swayze?"

"Wispy!" someone shouts.

The WheelsDeals guys are waiting in the shade of the Tanger sign, prodding bike computers and fishing energy gels from their jerseys.

"You're holding up the peloton," Ezra says.

"You, too."

Ezra clenches into his aerobar. "I brought the wrong bike."

"Another time." Wispy u-turns again. "I'll be seeing you, anyway."

Ezra unclips and watches him thrash into a sprint. His knees fly out to the sides at disturbing angles at the top of each pedal stroke. The roadies teeth the tops off of energy gels and lift them in toast of Wispy, or Ezra, or those never-to-be-garbed Asher Roth wannabees.

"Pour one out," Ezra says.

And hammers north until he's zenning again. Aero position all the way out to the asphalt's fishhook end. Past that, the road lies unfinished. His parched tongue feels as rough as that gravel. All four of his water bottles spurt dust when he squeezes; he hadn't filled up before leaving. He licks sweat off his forearms, turns around, and small-chainrings twenty miles back to the Shell station.

The clerk hollers, *shirt!* before Ezra has the door open. He steps inside and grabs a "Laney High Parent" tee off the rack, noting the absence of the word *pride*.

"Shitter's just for customers," the clerk adds.

Ezra squints at the medicines self-contained in displays, card-stock wasps and rhinos folded up from the backing of boxes. Rising as stiff as the erections they promise. "Y'all got Advil?"

"Look left."

Ezra walks all the way down the counter and back before spotting a travel pack of ibuprofen tablets. "Anything you can chew?" Picturing Casper grinding those Percocets.

"Dip," the clerk says.

"But medicine. Kid's stuff. Gummies."

"That's it."

It's three dollars a bottle. He'd stuffed a twenty in the sheriff's swim trunks. Fishes his first citation from one pocket, the second from the other; turns both pockets out before seeing the bill crumpled and damp-stuck to the first ticket. Ezra must've passed double-digits of pharmacies, and here he is buying six travel packs of off-brand ibuprofen.

The clerk tweezers his cash with two fingers. "Where've you been?"

"The hospital."

The clerk gags as Ezra turns. Noon on the wall clock as he leaves.

He rides home under the height of its heat. Gust-whisked grit stings his back, its impact indistinguishable from the ache of his sunburn. A tailwind, at least. College Road is a straight shot to Kure, but more red lights. He swings wide on the beltway. The asphalt ripples like hills under the sun's brightness, a set of distant rollers that he never reaches: a trick of the eyes and the memory. It's a flat ride until he hits the incline of Woody Hewett Bridge.

A few jerks of the handlebars and he summits it. The ibuprofen chatters like Casper's teeth in his pockets. The urgency of the mission he'd departed with returns the way nerves reclaim a limb pinned-and-needled with sleep. Ocean Street passes as one white blur of lactate. A hurt later he gasps back to the camper.

No news truck. Buzzards sharpen the sky.

Ma comes out of the Sprinter van with her shoulders up to her eardrums, shaking her arms out like she's just set down something heavy. "There he is."

"Packing?"

She slams the side door shut as he dismounts, as if concealing evidence. "You worked up a sweat."

"Likewise."

"Not a competition." She's still bent with the weight of whatever burden. Yet to shake that work's muscular hangover. "Not today."

Back to that subject. Probably—actually—still on it. Her thoughts most likely hadn't ever left the Ironman. If Casper's mind's a basement, Ma's is a wind-tunnel: all thought gusting in one endless direction. Ezra stoops to thumb gravel off of the Trek's tires. "Walgreens was closed. And CVS. I had to go into Wilmington."

"Huh. I figured you rode down to South Carolina."

"Took the beltway."

She pinches her watch, the timer chirping as she stops it; he can tell by the sound which function it's set on, like an ornithologist narrows birdcalls down to species. "For four hours."

"What happened to the news?"

"Gathering reinforcements. They left in a tow truck, but they got footage. They'll break the story tonight, then we'll get the stampede. Bet we'll get every station from here to Topsail. Gonna have to charge for parking."

"Too many vehicles to back into." He picks at the gravel, feeling like he's cleaning the grooves of his own synapses. An ape-brained comfort to this: as reciprocally soothing as grooming. "Everything's happening."

"As it tends to."

"I mean too much at once. What—" He throat-catches the

question Benji'd loved fishing out of him. *What the hell?*

—*will we do?*

—*am I doing?*

—*did* you?

Ma slow-lowers herself to the van's footboard. "Compartments, Love. You don't run the bike course. One thing and one thing and one thing, like racing."

"So what's first?"

"Catch our breath. Pop a squat." She pats the footboard beside her. "Savor stillness while you can."

Ezra leans his bike on the van and sits. A year ago he'd never have risked the stiffness. Yoga, foam rolling, ice baths after every session. All habits he'd left in his helmet for Benji. "I did do that. The Chapel Hill bike course. I was running."

"How'd that go?"

"You know." It had led him to Benji. "You commemorated it," Ezra adds, remembering the photo of his Chapel Hill collapse wallpapering Ma's phone. "He took that picture. I came to with him waving it at me." She draws her feet up to the floorboard, adopting a gargoyle's perch: heels-to-haunches, chest-to-knees. "What'd he say when he called?"

"What I told you. You're fine-tuned. His work's done."

"You said you started driving back that same night. How come? He must've said something."

"When'd he take your phone?"

"Thanksgiving."

"Thanksgiving?"

"I told you."

Ma swallows her legs with her shirt. "*Going AWOL.* That was your last text. I took that as a consensual arrangement. I thought you'd been sneaking looks at it. I was getting *read* receipts."

"You were messaging him?"

"You. Your phone. I kept mine in my bibs in case you replied. Every pothole I hit I took for it vibrating."

"He had it. And my laptop."

"I didn't know."

"You left me with him for eight months," Ezra says. "Four percent of my life."

"You're rounding up." Ma tucks her chin under her collar, turtling up against it.

Ezra pictures her hunkering like that in the collapsed stadium in Nepal. The posture's both juvenile and geriatric. It makes Ezra want to cradle her. "Quit bunching up like that," he says.

She spits her shirt.

He can't quite clench his jaw. "Your phone would've been more aero on the top tube."

"Hindsight." Ma grins. "It counts if you miss someone like that, too."

Which leaves Ezra gaping again. That he'd been mistaking his shame for anger; that she'd seen it before he did. This woman from whom he's gotten it all. Mother enough to usurp the splattering contribution of his nameless father, tying each chromosome's shoelace for him. All the days they'd spent double-knotted: stirring at 4 a.m. and tiptoeing into each other en route to the bathroom, twinned toothpaste stains on their shirtfronts from talking while they brushed. Yet Ezra'd blinked off the eight months they'd spent apart, or slept through them.

"It's like I was underwater," he says. "Like I was swimming under all of it, holding my breath."

She rubs his arm like she's trying to steal static off it. Her legs stretch out, flush with his. He looks at their matching socks and sees the ground stippled around them. The cul-de-sac's crowded with paw prints.

"What'd you get Stud?" she asks.

Ezra rattles the ibuprofen out of his pockets. "All they had."

"At the pharmacy?"

"How's he doing?"

"Sleeping." She pulls the pill bottle out from under her shirt. "I gave him like a tenth of a tablet."

"You found—"

"Had them. Caught them. He threw them at me."

"You didn't—"

"Hush." She back-fists the van's side-door. "He's in there."

So Casper was what she'd been carrying. Ezra pictures her tending to the kid. Should've been him.

She karate-chops his shoulders before he can stand. "I figured we'd bug out before the press gets here, but Stud's snoozing. Let him keep on while he can." She tips the Percocet bottle over like an hourglass. "Gonna get harder once he's out of these."

Ezra squints at the scant grains of crushed tablets. "Christ. He's got to stretch that out for two weeks."

"But not yet. He's sleeping now. It's all the same lesson, Love. Nuance. Finish the bike before running." She gropes under her shirt again, slides her phone out, and presses the home button, wafting the lock screen in front of him. That picture of Ezra's crumpling. "That's what this should've taught you."

The sidewinding way that he'd fainted: knees, hips, spine, and head bending an 's' shape, like a snake scraped off the pole of its caduceus. He snatches at the phone even as she hands it over, grabs her whole open palm in his fist. He looks down at it, then up at her standing. She flips their hands over and slides hers out of his.

"Just don't eat it," she says, tapping his chin.

It's the fourth time today she's stolen his jaw out from under him.

Ezra folds the phone in his hands, half-minded to hand it back. But she's already turning.

"Regardless of whatever voodoo fuckery Benji got up to, he did get you fit. Not making a moral claim on his method. All I'm saying's that he brought you this far." Talking over her shoulder, like Ezra this morning. Deadringer. Same blueprint. She'd been right about this much: Benji wasn't the motor. Benji *built* the motor. He'd built Ezra, the lungs and legs that he moved with. Ezra always sinks back to that fact, or that fact wells back up—

rising in him. "Your lungs show through your ribs, Love," she says. "I can see the speed on you."

So how can't she see that speed's toxic?

The phone cold and sweat-slimy as an eel in his hands. As likely to starting writhing. He puts his ear to the van's side door, listening for Casper's snores. The kid could hold 4:30 miles and keep his breathing quiet, but his gasps shook the whole cabin as soon as he fell asleep. Talk about living egregiously. Had Benji developed that habit in Casper, or had he brought the kid here because he'd already had it? Seven and a half months since that pickup with the Christmas lights had honked down Bromine Avenue. Ezra'd stopped running to watch it pass, turning to cock an eyebrow at Benji. That had been the first time he'd asked *what the hell?*

Now an interrogative throb rises from the van, a curled hum like a bug trapped between the door and his earlobe. Ezra presses closer and pairs that up-tone with his pulse. He's hearing his own heartbeats seashelled in his eardrum. Tour de France cyclists got their veins so sludgy with hemoglobin that they had to climb back on their bikes in the wee hours and ride to keep their blood from clotting. A full night's worth of stillness risked a stroke. Talk about fragile fitness. You could only live like that for so long before crumbling. Ezra's poised at that same urgent peak. He has too much blood. A bursting need to keep it pumping.

He stands on legs like guitar necks, the ibuprofen bottles clattering out of his lap. Bends and his hamstrings clench as if capo'd, taut from the abrupt shift between sprinting and sitting. A cooldown was rule one. Flush lactic acid. Ebb the heartbeat. He walks his palms up his thighs, tipping into a shuffle. He jogs across the coyote-tracked, tire-gashed cul-de-sac. Casper's child-sized stomps dent the gravel.

Then asphalt. His strides lengthen with traction. Coming up Bromine Avenue opening up like that first run after his post-Chapel Hill wallowing, following Benji's original instructions—*bust a nut*—and each next step's another second he isn't unlocking Ma's phone. An avoidance he's been perfecting for the near half of his life: swinging around time, trying to pass outside every bout of exertion. You don't slog through an Ironman; you forget you're doing it. See that tactic displayed in the smooth game faces of all the greats: Mark Allen, Peter Reid, Crowie. Casper. Their eyes nearly shut, their chins tucked as if praying. Holiness is a matter of being set apart. That's what they did, removing themselves from themselves when they raced. *Brain in your helmet.* But here's Ma telling him to stick it into this second, staying so present you forget all that's left.

Like that, Ezra's thudding onto the sandspit of Kure's south end. He used to run out here at midnight and curl up to sleep in these dunes. So much for a cooldown. He's put four more miles behind him already, retracing the route from his and Casper's last brick without meaning to. The last beach access is hexed over with caution tape. This time he reads the sign: *BEACH CLOSED BY ORDER OF NEW HANOVER COUNTY HEALTH COMMISSIONER.* Leans his chest to the tape and tears through. On the sand he turns north and left. The pier looms, pelicans topping its pilings like headstones for the crap-trapped coyote. Or Casper. That brick had been his last workout on two legs.

Better those ghosts than the one in Ma's phone. A low burn in Ezra's left forearm from squeezing it. He switches the phone to his right hand and shakes the burn simmering. The pier grows as if feeding off of his approach. The humid caws of birds perched on it—buzzards. Spring traps anklet each piling. Ezra shivers under the pier and turns around. Something cool drips onto his forehead. He wipes off a rusty, reeking smear. Sunscreen and turning meat.

Benji.

He slows back around. Frays of ground beef hang from the buzzards' seamed beaks. Ezra's sweat itches. He's walking, unlocking Ma's phone. *Calling CHAMP.* It goes straight to voicemail, his own dumb falsetto chirping instructions: "You've reached Ezra Fogerty, professional triathlete. Leave a message if you already sponsor me, or if you're offering. If you're looking for an interview, learn to read. The contact form's on my website. That's blogspot-dot-EzraFogerty-dot-Triathlete." His tone so down-the-nose, his voice cracking in this recording he can't even remember making. Has Benji listened to this? The message prompt's beep roils Ezra's gut like a starting gun.

"Hey." The word comes curved instead of straightedged, more ...*buddy* than ...*bastard,* the actual antonym of his intended tone. Ezra stubs his tongue on his clenching teeth, stubbing on the point of entry. Every silent second thickening with his blood. It wells in his legs, laced with lactate, curing them stiff as planks. A burning fatigue catching up. He tips into a trot, but too late; his stopping's already kindled it. He hangs up.

What had he wanted? For Benji to answer? Then what? Fill Ezra's ear with apologies? With his wet wheezing, at least. That absence had kept Ezra sleeping lightly last night as much as anything. He'd grown used to dozing with the white noise of Benji's mouth-breathing.

Ezra tries pumping his arms and the burn leaps to them and he knows now that it'll be one long char back to Bromine Avenue. He'll show up bone and embers. The buzzards squawk taunts and his skin itches and he can't lift his knees any higher. Strides sopped up by the sand. Still holding Ma's phone.

He slows and thumbs the home button, getting a record-stacked glimpse of open apps. A *Slowtwitch* article's open on the browser. "Meltdown in West Memphis." An exposé on Benji's training compound. Ezra's eyes stumble over the text, his legs stumbling up through the softer sand. Arkansas sheep farm where Benji'd been raised. Three of his athletes found running themselves to exhaustion, institutionalized and declared triplet head cases. A fourth blamed Benji's folk magic, claiming that he'd quit the camp before being fully indoctrinated. A correspondent had tracked down another of Benji's former charges in Shreveport, an ex-ex world champion who'd warded them with a shotgun from the porch of his trailer, offering up one sound-bite—to rack off. Was this why Benji'd taken Ezra's phone, in anticipation of the story breaking?

Ezra's eyes stick on the pictures. Pastures blooming with spring-shor sheep, their stalky legs and pale flanks lending them the look of cotton. Wind turbines blend clouds and light on the skyline. A clapboard house. The police tape flossing its porch rails looks structural, as if applied to hold the crooked beams in place. A crumpled water trough. Tire-tracks gash the ground around it, their treads dulled with fresher tracks: paw prints. Ezra hurdles the captions without reading them. A sun-rinsed image of a man and boy on a pool deck. The man brows his eyes with a binder, propping his elbow on the boy's head. The boy stands with the sudden, uneven height of a preteen—all shin and throat, slouch-ing. A dangle of stopwatches reaches his bellybutton, the cords crossing his torso as if stretched by the weight of the timepiec-es. He leans forward at the seeming verge of stumbling. Those sunglasses. That jagged mullet. He can't look so hard at the man standing next to him. Knows those long cheekbones and rain-cloud-colored eyes from somewhere important, but doesn't want to place that face any more than he wants to read.

Ezra closes the article before finishing. He pulls up Face-book, toe-dragging for the next beach access. His footsteps make lathered squeaks on the sand. He has *Benj* in the search bar, sug-gested pages unhinging. The two consecutive Benji Newtons at the top are both wrong. The profile pic he's looking for is an Oakley lens from kiss-close, the camera too tight to recognize any facial features. Ezra'd mistaken the image as an aerial view of a lake for months before noticing the crow's feet in the slit of beach at the left edge, reinterpreting that sand as skin.

Baffling to reconstruct the photo's origin: the phone or cam-era held up that close, the blinding flash. Had Benji taken the picture himself? If not, who'd he told to take it for him? Scrolling all the way down his wall (no statuses; all 'at'-s and tagged posts), Ezra'd found this image at the rind of it. First and only photo he'd ever uploaded. His page was twelve years of shout-outs and shared posts without a single comment or 'like' from him, giving nothing back but the spitting image of whoever had looked at it—just like that mirrored lens in his profile photo. The instructions pinging into Ezra's messages had been the only proof there was an eye behind it at all, watching him.

The two Benji Newtons the search bar turn up are a horse mask and a shirtless skateboarder, not this. Benji's profile is either blocked, gone, or gone private. Ezra pulls up Messenger. Ma's latest message to him came two weeks ago. Picture of her bike propped on MOOSE CROSSING sign; up a road walled with hemlocks, an actual moose twists its head in the exact pose silhouetted on the sign. *Like my painting?* Ma'd written. Another week before that, a picture of her Hoka landing on a root-knotted sector of singletrack. *Tricky footing,* she'd written, followed by sneaker, peach, and flame emojis like ellipses. Then, three minutes later: *my mind's on you, Champ.* He scrolls up through eight months of such, all with *read* receipts. Benji'd been in Ezra's phone. He'd seen everything.

Ezra splinters still on the beach access, leaning on the railing. He checks his own profile for tampering. No new posts since May, when he'd turned his phone over. But Benji'd logged into Ezra's page, worn that green light by his name like sheep's clothing: every time that chat box had shown Ezra was online, Benji'd been behind the screen.

He slashes the app closed. He winds up to throw the phone and something ticks in his shoulder. He pauses with his arm cocked at half-mast, still staring at the sandy summit he was aiming at. The slopes are stippled with coyote tracks. These dunes are fenced off to keep folks from accelerating the ocean's work, eroding the fragile sand with their flip-flops; now the coyotes are slackening the slopes with their paw prints. Ezra pictures them flooding the beachfront, spilling into vacant duplexes. How Benji'd come into the camper and banished them all—waved off Ma, then cabined Ezra and Casper, leaving the camper as untouched as a trophy cabinet: proof of what he could make them do.

Ezra searches Find My Phone, sweat slurring his typing. Wipes the screen off and logs in. His phone's last ping was ten days ago in Kure. He clicks the map where the location's pinned. A green patch south of the cul-de-sac; the woods around the bromine plant. He clicks the sidebar to reveal previous pins. The phone had pinged once in Topsail the night previous. A clump of pins at the end of Bromine Avenue before that. So Benji'd left them, then slunk back. Had he been in the woods watching Ezra swing the branch? One more glare disguised by the coyotes'.

Ezra strains down the beach access, stride dilapidating. Ma says you have so many matches. No matter how hot you can get them, there's only so many in the box. That box being your body; the matches, your legs, lungs, and nerves. He lurches through more caution tape and comes out by the marina. The hanged coyotes windchime below the *Sea Saw's* bowsprit, picked to bones. Buzzards perched on the prow napkin beaks in the crooks of their wings.

He shuffles south down Ocean Street the same way he ran earlier, a straggling parody of this morning. Stares that pin on the phone into growing. Holding it out like to transpose it on the road, afraid it'll vanish without the weight of his looking. But the harder he looks, the more he sees around: hotel facades bleak as gravestones. Boardwalk closed. Claw marks crosshatch dumpsters behind restaurants, the disemboweled bags of garbage cans. Tumbleweeds of breezed trash. The old Quonset hut of Town Hall, its corrugated tin spitting glint like a spring trap's jagged teeth. The marquee's been modified since this morning. TOWN MEETING NOON TOMORROW. TRAPS POISON COYOTES.

Yard signs crowd the mulch in front of it, stock-printed with the same message. AGENDA: APOCALYPSE. WE STAND WITH EZRA FOGERTY. And a picture of Casper.

A surfer-haired kid's planting more signs up the road. Ezra slants toward him. Kid turns at his panting and steps back. "You okay, man?"

Ezra looks at the sign he's just planted. One of those plastic-and-wire deals, the mass-printed political kind. His name capitalized atop a picture of Casper. "Where'd you get that?"

"Made it."

"The picture."

"That guy lives in Sloop Point. Lost his leg to a spring trap. You local? You coming to the town meeting? Have a sign." The kid hands over a pinch's width of the stack. "We've got to urge the town council to take substantive action."

Ezra's still examining that picture of Casper. Kid's standing in the doorframe of the camper. Same running shorts he'd had on that morning, and the morning before, the stump dangling out with all the wrong flaunt of an erection. Something meant to be covered up. The picture's faintly blurred, like the camera'd been moving. The edges of the frame blindered by fingertips.

"You took this." The news truck obstructing their driveway. Casper fleeing the scene. "You called the reporter."

"Culling's the most humane solution." The kid's reading off of a clipboard. "I've actually got a petition. Would you sign—" He drops the clipboard digging through his pockets. "Got a pen?"

Ezra slaps the signs out from under the kid's armpits. Kid looks down at them, up at Ezra. "What the actual—"

Ezra's gone before the rest of the question. Eyes pinned to the pin showing his phone on Ma's screen. He moves himself onto that map: his own progress represented by a red pin. Just his phone. Then the insurance, the reporters, and Casper. One thing and another and another, all leading back to this one. All because of Benji.

He's in sight of Bromine when the first news truck scrapes past him. Knots tie in his hip flexors the second he surges. He's falling forward just like Chapel Hill. *Hips forward, Tootsie.* Second news truck. He cuts between houses, through backyards, into brush, crushing shrubs. Poison oak scrubs his shins. A gash clears through the scrub ahead of him: one of the plant's runoff ditches, swollen with water as dark as a contusion.

He wades through the trench, thinking not to leave footprints. Ridiculous. Coyotes don't stalk you; they set out bait and wait. That first one he'd seen reeling into the woods. The dozening pack of them lurking in the trees. That was when Benji'd told him about Shadefoot: how it haunts people's tracks, grows into their brains through their gaze the moment that they look back. Ezra swears the breeze combing his nape is breathing.

The ditch curls south and he slops out of it, the red and green pins bobbing closer. They conjoin into one point on the map. Ezra wedges Ma's phone into his waistband, goes down on his palms, and crawls. Sandspurs prick his hands. He bumps into a branch.

His branch. The bark's cracked where he'd gripped it. He holds it just like that and rolls to his back. The sumac's tousled from Casper's crawl. Ezra shuts his eyes, listening for mouth-breathing, waiting for Benji's hand to pet his head. Tensing to swing that branch.

A long nothing. Then, a stare's weight; a watched sense. He props up on his elbows, opens his eyes, and looks into it.

A coyote hunches at his feet. Its right forepaw's poised as if halted in mid-stride—like he's startled it. Yet it's the one that stealthed up. Seems to be trying to breathe quiet. Its dry snout cracks as it dilates. Its raised paw quivers gently. The hind-leg on that side's stalked hard behind it. For a sick second he thinks the left's missing—that this is the coyote from the pier, escaped from the crab trap—then sees it kicked straight back, parallel with its tail like a bird-dog's: pointing at him.

Ezra crab-crawls away, tight-gripping that branch. A cool firmness strikes his tailbone. Tallow eyes kindle the brush behind it. The coyote's paw hovers over his phone. He snatches it.

That Ironman-brand case with the chewed edges. He sets his teeth to the plastic, a pre-race ritual he'd forgotten or replaced; suppressed, maybe, after seeing Casper grinding his teeth. The coyotes multiply in his periphery.

If his phone is here, and Benji'd had his phone, did that mean Benji had been here the night Casper stepped in that trap? Had he crouched in the bushes and watched Ezra swinging that branch, one more pair of eyes among the coyotes? The thought's rougher to rub up against than the coyotes' dead-skinned stares. They circle closer, pinching him like a grip. No, a spring trap. You take what you can from what hurts you; you apply that tactic.

Ezra drops the branch and stands. The first coyote's still pointing at him. The rest seem to close in without moving, drifting through the trees. Ezra limps nearer to the pointer. It holds stiff. Touch-close. He reaches down, waiting for its jaws to shackle his wrist—but feels thorns instead. The coyote's fur is briar-sharp. It presses its head into his palm.

"Settle," he whispers.

And drags his hand down its backbone. His thumb and pinky rub either ridge of its hips. He's heard Carolina coyotes are bigger because they have more wolf in them, but this one's so narrow. It clenches its branch in its jaws and lifts it up to him, and he knows like spoiled food—-with the same wrenching certainty of inhaling rot's scent—that this one's part dog. The coyote—the coydog—whimpers itself sitting.

The rest of the pack swirls around them, clinging tight as a fog. Ezra grabs the branch from the coydog. He swings it and his right leg cramps, thigh and calf lockjawed. He falls.

The coyotes come forward one at a time to bite the coydog. They nip its flanks and retreat. Their tongues spill like they're retching their intestines. They bite without tearing, methodically. Ezra thinks of Benji retreating after comforting Casper, extracting every strand of his fallen hair from the kid's sleeping mouth: the coyotes move with that same precision, serving some delicate, hidden end.

The coydog lays its head between its forepaws. It inhales as they loosen their jaws, its sides swelling as if striving to keep the fangs in its wounds. Like their teeth might plug the blood. The woods crowds with wet yelps and parched pops.

When Ezra tries to crawl, his cramp leaps. He rocks arch-backed in the dirt, biting down on his phone. Sour-sweetness of Benji's sweat on it. Mulchy scent of organs. A hair strangling his tonsils. He coughs meat and sunscreen—someone else's air leaving him. His spluttering slumps to a hum.

The coyotes are gone in a slash of haunches. They saw off through the brush, leaving Ezra feeling halved by his back's spasming. That serrated hum. He swallows.

"Shit-faster-you-getting-this?-better-be—" A lady skids out of the brush, shouting a sentenceless stream. She kicks off running shoes, throws down a pair of heels in a dice-rolling motion, and fights into them. "Shit, Jesus. You good?" she asks Ezra.

"Just cramping," he says around the phone.

"Don't move. Shit." That last at her sock-feet in her heels. "Roll, Heidi. The ticker tape'll cover it."

A lens thrusts out behind her, then the lens-shaped gape of a camera lady. She offers Ezra a hand.

He rolls prone and walks his palms toward his knees. The coydog's bellied down in the dirt, that hind leg scythed back like it's pointing. Ezra picks her up and she doesn't resist. The length of her back barely spans his clavicles.

The camera lady reaches out like to pet him. "Jesus, sir. What can we—"

"Benji Newton."

"Mr. Newton—"

Ezra spits the phone. "Not me. Put the camera on."

The camera lady has her phone out instead. "Is 911 for dogs?"

The reporter hops a heel loose. "Roll, Heidi. Mr. Noonan—"

"Benji Newton. Benji Newton brought the coyotes." Ezra hoists the coydog in his arms. Its head and tail flag, but that hind leg stays stiff. "Find him. He did this."

Heidi shoulders the camera. The rank flash of that lens. That sunburnt creep in the bike jacket who'd stumbled up on them in the woods and snapped a picture. *Did you do this,* he'd asked—meaning Casper. The spring trap. And he'd taken the picture and Ezra'd snatched the phone. His own phone. He'd called 911 from the emergency screen with no sleep and the spinning keeping him from noticing and dropped it in chase of the sunburnt creep. Must've stolen the phone from Benji. No. He'd taken that picture; Benji'd sent him.

Ezra's running. Scissor-striding on stiff legs to keep the hamstring from cramping and leaving the reporter fighting out of her heels.

He tantrums into a cul-de-sac jammed with news trucks parked as skewed as toppled dominos. The Sprinter van shivers at the top of the circle, reporters elbowing up to the driver's side. One starts for Ezra. The van's backdoor slits open and Ma's hand darts out, beckoning, and Ezra feels like his ears are congesting as he pushes through the blooming camera-flashes and mics sprouting toward him. His foot on the bumper and someone grabbing his arm as Ma half-bars and half-props the backdoor. He scrapes the grip on the shutting door, which slams on a braceleted wrist. The door bounces back enough for the hand to shrivel through and Ma shuts it again, leaving Casper and the bicycles and him.

Ma wedges into the driver's seat. Ezra smacks the backdoor when she gasses it, hard-sits on the floor. Casper's buckled into the dinette, curled around the booth snoring.

"It's not a pet-friendly campsite," Ma says into the rearview. "Better claim she's for therapy."

The coydog bleeds in his lap. She mops the floor with her tail like she's trying to clean it. It spills in thin streaks, from shallow punctures: the coyotes had bitten softly. Wounding with the gentleness of healing.

"Got a name?" Ma asks.

"Shiela."

"Huh." Ma slants across the center lane onto Ocean Street, leaning on the horn. "A service coyote. I'm stoked to hear Stud's take."

Casper's stump lifts and falls like breathing. Ezra pins it with his hand. Casper doesn't stir. The huge bulge of his Adam's apple sinks down his throat like an actual fruit that he's swallowing. The kid had said he'd gagged easy.

Four bikes are buckled into the bunk beds: Ma's, Casper's Bianchi, both of Ezra's—the Trek and his Felt DA, the tri-bike forbidden by Benji. The ride's RoboCop from spokes to shifters. Deep-dish wheels. Aerobars brainstemmed by a new power meter. Ezra eases the coydog off his lap, bracing up to the bunks. He slides his hand down the Felt's top tube. The chainring's lubeslick, the cassette bright with grease. Ma'd tuned it.

"That seat angle's aggressive. Might feel like a prostate check when you're climbing, but it's a lot less frame to lug than that fossil you've been on." She lists over the center lane again, watching him in the rearview. "Wasn't sure which you'd want, so brought both."

The rest of Ezra's gear, too. His helmet, transition bag, and racing flats are stashed in seat-backs, his tri-suit draped off the headrest. His citizenship and surname are stamped on the seat of it as per Ironman regulations: FOGERTY USA. Like his ass is a municipality. Ma'd packed like he was going to race. And Ezra understands then that he is; somewhere in the ache of this day he'd decided. Ma'd known before he did.

He plops into shotgun.

"There he is," she says.

"Here we are."

Ezra plugs his phone into the charger lolling from the center console. It rattles the cupholder in a cute mime of electrocution. The battery icon crimsons the screen and he jerks the cord out, afraid of what it'll revive. First a shower. A drive. Then—Jesus—an Ironman. One thing, and one thing, and one thing.

The main drag sucks back in the rearview, buzzards sipping from brimming ditches and the spat glint of spring traps and yard signs with his own name attached to Casper's image. He tilts the mirror down. The kid and the coydog wagging stump and hind-leg as if dreaming in harmony.

"Don't microwave the cajones just yet, Champ." Ma points to her phone, which has slid front-and-center below Ezra's waistband. "You'll be using those this weekend."

He drops it in the driver's side cupholder. "You knew about what Benji did. The water trough. The missing athletes. Why didn't you—"

"Jack up your cortisol? You were stressed enough." Ma stomps the brake for a yellow light, bracing her arm over his chest. "I'd've brought it up after the race."

Only from Ma is this a viable excuse—she who bans use of the word 'lose' in the twenty-four hours leading up to a triathlon; they'd spent plenty of mornings fishing through his backpack for absent PowerBars or goggles insisting that the nutrition or equipment had *gone missing,* the way a vase breaks itself in Spanish.

They roll through an empty intersection at the edge of the marina. Ezra stares at the soiled water. His skin itches. His organs.

"I thought this whole AWOL was your prerogative." Ma's talking through her collar again. "I figured: Champ's twenty-six, he wants to try space out." She tucks her left leg up to the seat, sliding it under her shirt. "Far as I knew, you were reading those messages."

"You said that." But she's justifying to herself, not to him. Hearing that dredges a sob in Ezra's throat, like pulling up a fishless castnet. He pictures his anger as water straining through the mesh.

"I'd've come home at a hat-doff. I was waiting for your when."

"I know, Ma. You'd been putting off that trip for too long. Benji just brought it up. I insisted." Ezra swallows. "You left for me, not for him."

Ma eases her leg out from under her shirt. A kidness in her

like Casper's, how their feelings are so legible in their anatomy. Maybe their bodies are easy to read because there's so little of them—a limited vocabulary for mastery.

"You really want to hear what else he told me?" she says. "When he called?"

"Can't risk histrionics."

"First of all, he told me you were zenning. His word. Fine-tuned." Ma snorts under her collar. "Then he started talking some Halloween shit about footprints. Something with islands and eating hair."

"Eating hair."

"Yeah. Or feeding it."

Benji's hair sticking to Casper's heel. His lips pressed there. "He kept sucking Casper's cut," Ezra says. "Humming to it."

"The cut?"

"It sounded like a spell. Like he thought he was casting one. Casper gets these nightmares. And Benji'd sort of, like..." But Ezra remembers how carefully Benji pulled his hair from the kids' mouth and swallows, afraid that explaining will fracture something. "What'd he say about hair?"

"It's a poor source of leucine." Ma winks.

Ezra stands, steps between the driver's and passenger's seats.

"So the guy high-fives monkey paws. He thinks his humming summons interdimensional entities. What's the harm if you don't believe?"

"You do."

Ma turtles into her shirt again, sweating it; Ezra's turn to see through her. She's treating this like her lampoons of his rivals, watering down threats with humor.

"Champ. What I said about motors—"

"I remember," Ezra says. "Go. You've got green."

He braces on the headrests as she gasses it. Cement fills his thighs. It sets when he lowers himself into the dinette beside Casper. A soreness that won't crack before Saturday. He'll race with today's work stiffening his legs. That idea's strangely soothing: if he falls short, he'll have this excuse as his safety net. No matter how hard he races, he won't see the true limit of his fitness; with that, permission. On Saturday he can push himself off the edge.

Ezra dozes. The coydog's tail brushes his feet. Casper's stump swishes his thigh the same way. Ezra can't tell whether Ma's voice sinks into his sleep or rises from it—the first words of a dream. "Use him how you want to."

Ezra gets the sense that she means Casper just as much as Benji.

Casper

Next I know the van's rattling, my head yapping with ever bump. I sit up. The yapping pours down like by gravity, pooling in my gone leg. RoboCop's curled there like he's playing prosthetic. Pressing his knee up against my stump like if he shoves enough our kneecaps might confuse and make one bone for the both of us. Boy could use a good rub-a-dub. Itchy stink from him. I poke his pockets for Percs and get empty and he don't bat an eye. I poke harder. All the times I've stirred to things I wish I'd slept through, folks leaning and panting over me. Shouldn't wish waking on him, but I do.

"Up here, Stud." And there's Little RoboPeep's arm craning back, rattling a bag at me. I hop up and the van bucks and floorboards me. She glances all her worry back at me, but I hear the snort she gulps back. Bet she meant to catch a bump. "You good?"

"Nuts."

I crawl up front, rattling like the pills that got to be in that bag. Wiggle up into shotgun and she yanks the bag past my reach. Stuffs her hand in, pops a cap, and takes one. One! And the wrong color. It dulls a pale maggot in her handing hand. Better than the gnat-speck she last gave me. I slurp it off her palm and set to gnawing, taking a gander of our coordinates. I-40's westing out the windshield, one-them woodsy stretches. Pines so tight you could catch a branch going by. Shattered cones and needles all along the shoulder. I've hitched through this neck once or twice. We're a gas station shy of Duplin County, I reckon. And I've got a hunch where we're aimed.

"Chapel Hill," I say.

"Chapel Hill," she says back. Both-us looking at RoboCop's head resting on the table in the rearview, our own two foreheads at the bottom of that mirror like dunes.

"He won't do it."

"He'll do it."

"But not faster than me."

"Put money on it. You have any of that? Any cash?"

"You reckon he can beat me?"

"He'll have better weather this year. Cooler forecast."

"Then I'll have it, too."

Little RoboPeep's eyebrows hop up to the mirror, or the shaved streaks where they should be.

I spank my stump on the seat. "Soon's he saw me tick-tocking that bike he reckoned he had me. But I'll figure how to perch before Saturday. And still lick him if I can't." Her still hoisting them bald eyebrows, heightening the bar of her belief. Then I see we've been talking in separate directions: her meaning my time from last year, thinking I can't beat it. Thinking this year RoboCop might beat me. "I could crawl the whole damn bike and marathon and he wouldn't pass. He can't take the lead from me."

Them eyebrows of Little RoboPeep's. Pale patches of skin in the shapes of them, like two Band Aids ripped off after too long in the sun. Ms. Ida had her eyebrows tattooed when she got shut of plucking the real ones. The left curved higher than the other, to where she always seemed to be cocking it at me. Never got around to telling her. Never had enough mean in me.

"He can't hurt like I can," I say.

Little RoboPeep's face droops at last. She's been into my Percs herself, maybe. Her lips curve down like she's fixing to bad-news me, and like she's not sure if I'm not used to it. As if life ain't been one continuous ticker-tape of tragedies. Maybe she susses that, because she sterns her voice low instead. "Seatbelt, mister."

Which we both snort at. Hers uncorks a chuckle. Her

chuckle cracks my grin. Then the two-us are both leaking laughs till the root of my gut cramps, them same thrusting muscles that push the burst through the stem.

"Got a friend," she says, gasping her breath back.

"We're still inching up on acquaintances."

"Meant the dog." She whips her thumb behind her. Takes a second for me to crane around where she's pointing. My view smears when I move—a little melty with fever—but then it pools into seeing. A varm's leaking at the back of the van. Bleeding itself a dog bed, hind leg thumping a mock of me.

"That's Shiela," Little RoboPeep says, one-upping the mockery. "She's Ezra's." Just rubbing it in. Wiping it all over the butt of this joke, the stink of which leads me.

I crackle up ragelike, then it hits me: Little RoboPeep's fishing for a rise. Won't give her the smirk of biting. Let that varm flaunt that spare leg and be RoboCop's Shiela. The Percs are fixing to hit anyway. I'm nigh-on to drooping. Not yet, but it'll come. So I slump in anticipation.

"We'll dump her at the next rest stop," Little RoboPeep says. "Tell Ez she made a run for it."

Fixing to conk right through the rest of this ride. The fact that I can gives me a plush feeling. Because even with the varm back there and Little RoboPeep up here I did sleep in this van, and that means I'm home. Take that plush and times it by the Percs and I'm fixing to be a damn bomb of fuzz-feeling. Soon's that pill hits, that is. I lick the powder off my teeth, biding.

Ezra

A shuddering squeal wakes him. He presses his face into the table, eyes shut to trap the last streaking scenes of a dream. Humming shears; a ram bucking against sweaty hands; a shed furnaced with panic, a hundred bodies bleating the same herded heat. The tin walls absorbing and containing it; the mens' shirtless backs griddle-marked from leaning against the corrugation. Someone else's siphoned memory. The images evaporate, but he can still hear that bleating. Something's stuck on his tongue. A curl of blandness across the tastebuds, like a hair. None when he spits. He rakes his teeth down his tongue, then his fingernails. Nothing but the taste of it—rather, the patch of taste's absence. He drags out of the dinette, his swim trunks squeaking the seat.

They're parked out front of a Love's. Eighteen wheelers crick around the corner, jack-knifing their hauls into spaces. Their air brakes are the bleating. Ezra knows this station. He's uncoiled nervous shits in the abductive glow of its handicapped stall on plenty of mornings. He and Ma always filled up here before the Wolfpack Triathlon, a race just close enough to justify driving up the morning of. They're in Fuquay Varina. The near side of Raleigh. He's woken up 150 miles west of where his eyes shut, traveled a third of the state in that prolonged blink. Fingers crossed that he'd cover distance the same way on Saturday.

But he's clumsy with soreness. He stilts into the bathroom and unsheathes a rusty blade of urine. His arms and chest are crusted with blood. He starts searching for cuts before remembering the coydog. Goes back out to the aisle and sees her blood on the floorboard. Trails it to the side door. The window faces a Hardee's behind a patch of crabgrass. A blur passes the window, then another. Ezra slides the door open, untinting his view of things. Casper's speed-crutching away from the coydog. He swivels and slips, sitting hard on the weeds. She overshoots him and hooks back. Ezra climbs out on clenching hamstrings. He sits into a groin stretch to exorcise the haunt of that cramp.

The gas station doors part for Ma, who wields two gallon jugs of water toward him. She wedges one into his crotch. "Shiela's aero."

"What?"

She nods to the coydog, who's sprinting circles around Casper. Right. He'd named her.

"I told him to tie her up by the Hardee's dumpster," Ma says. "I was going to tell you she jumped out, made a run." She sighs down to his eye-level by way of her own hamstring stretch. "Too late?"

Casper's snatching at Shiela's orbits. She swerves from his grasp, yipping giddily. Runs so low it looks almost like crawling, ribs mowing the crabgrass.

"She is aero," Ezra says.

Casper lunges at her from his knees. Her barks shallow and quicken, hiccupping yips; they leap pitches and fray. A sharper sound joins it. Casper's barking back at her. Kid and dog just as puppy with play.

Ma knocks her forehead off her knees, nodding. "Too late."

Casper

Still biding for the Perc to hit. Still hadn't when Little RoboP-eep pulled off the road, curling us down the ramp of the Fuquay Varina exit. Halted upside a gas place I done been at. Maybe not this one, but the brand. Red heart on a yellow sign like a flipped McDonald's logo; nights I spent squinting out against that glow. Pockets stuffed with what I could scrounge from a glove-box or center console, spitting a burst's taste. Ever gob I hocked tallowed in that sign's glint. Leaving a trail of saliva for them to chase when they woke, but not sweating it. None-them truckers could keep up. They might huff across the lot some, but they'd quit soon's the lactate started welling up. The loot I'd taken from them seemed less worth chasing once the hurt started to heaten. So maybe I ain't been to this exact gas place, but I know it.

And I happened to be second-thinking myself, my will smearing with fever. When was that droop coming? Where'd Little RoboPeep put them Percs? Probably had them on her. She'd gone back and gentled a resistance band like a collar and leash around the varm. The varm sniffed it, but didn't whimper. Let Little RoboPeep drag-walk her up front. I faked sleep, plotting to scrounge around for the Percs when she left me, but she plopped her chapped hand on my forehead. Said she was going in to get something for my fever and why didn't I take care of Shiela? Shiela meaning the varm, and "taking care of" meaning tying her up behind the Hardee's. "Something" meaning a Perc, if I was lucky. The varm lapped at my stump, lathering up them stitches. I told Little RoboPeep I was cozy how I'd perched. She didn't take that like an answer. Set to whispering about why I had to take care of Shiela, how she didn't want to fall through the thin ice that Ez had her on.

"He's out cold, but I can't risk him catching me." Little RoboPeep wrapped the resistance band around my wrist, but may's well've been clipping the leash's collar-end on me. "With you, he's more lenient." Her hand on my forehead again. "I'm going in. Gonna get you something for that fever." Instead standing waiting over me.

I irked the door open and played up my limp. Easy game, way my fever wobbled the ground out from me. The varm was in on it, too, springing ahead and outstretching the leash. I had to haunch down to keep from sledding after her. The sheer strength of her, or the weak of me. Little RoboPeep set the crutch down real gentle beside me. She went into the store and I bided till the doors smacked shut behind her, the varm still tug-of-warring. I wrapped my end to the door handle and left her to it. Dug through the glovebox and center console but no Percs. RoboCop still spurting snores. I crawled back out to find the varm tuckered slumped, all her play drained from leash-yanking. Small wonder. Looked to be wearing most her blood on her fur. And that sight did spring a leak in my sympathy. I took up her leash and my crutch and swung around-back the van with her claws clicking after me. Little RoboPeep's personal record was the license plate: *9:54IRN*. I swabbed my palm under it, a trick I learned at one-them gas. A door key and ten dollars inside. I took the ten and leaned deep on the crutch. Tipped my head and made sure my reflection in the sideview looked sorry enough, pitying up my limping. Then I went around-back the store where the semis were snoring.

Big trucks park two ways to show what they're up to. Facing the building means no-go. Facing the curb means come knocking. Bandanas on the sideview to tell you what to bring. Green's uppers. Yellow's downers. Red and purple's you; go to those ready to climb into the cab and get used. Red means it's your mouth they want to leave a bad taste in. You guess what part purple is, and the kind of squirm that giving it leaves in you.

But that's from meaner times. Today I was buying. Picked out a sleeper cab with a yellow bandana and watched myself grow toward the sideview. Out stuck a hand. I handed the ten up and it shrank back and I waited. Tried the door after a lapse.

"Coming up!" a voice hollered.

Then the hand poked back out and dropped three pills down to me. I tried to catch them like grapes in my mouth and missed. The voice muttered. I crouched down and snatched them off the pavement and gnawed them down, tasting a chalk-staleness I knew from somewhere. Didn't place it till I'd swallowed already. Something about how the powder gaumed onto my tonsils minded me of track meets at Parsley, and that's when I knew that trucker had done got one over on me. These were no downers. Not even weak stuff, but the opposite: I knew that chalk-staleness because I used to trade Ms. Ida's lasagna for Tammy Galarde's Ritalin before track meets. (How that girl could eat a Tupperware full of it and run! Deserved a blue ribbon for digestion. And I did give her some. And she did tie up a necklace of them and wear it. And we were friends the way Little RoboPeep will never be with me.) I spat static and bit my tongue, my teeth already chattering from the memory of the Ritalin. Sheer anticipation of that buzz. A giddy feeling swelling up that I resisted, like someone you don't want bringing you to bursting: that squirming moment of straining against your own nerves, your brain hating the pleasure welling up in your body. I jabbed my fingers into my mouth to gag, hard-leaning on the crutch, and the varm yanked at that second. Pulled the leash right off my wrist and charged off. Leash must've conducted some-that Ritalin. Her tail back as a lightning bolt, fur jagged with static and dried blood. My crutch clattering on the concrete beside me. She stopped upside the store and looked back at me wobbling for balance—waiting, wanting me to chase. And there I was hopping to keep from sprawling, meting out that inertia. Running's controlled falling on two legs, but there's less control to it on one. The varm took my stumbling for chasing and darted off and I plunged, my leg rolling right on out from under me. A snort from that yellow-bandana'd truck. I crawled back to that crutch and let it conduct my grudge, because your mind's all pluses and minuses of electricity. I crutched on around front after Shiela and next thing I was the nuclear, breaking my own ankles in the weeds with her spinning cartoon-bird circles around me. RoboCop and Little RoboPeep stretching by the van, watching.

So now it's all four-us back in that home of a vehicle. The Robos are up front, and the varm's in my lap in the back with me instead of leashed by the dumpsters at Hardee's. I never had the chance to figure out whether I meant to do that, leaving the varm how Little RoboPeep wanted me. But the varm don't seem to grudge me, lapping at my stump like a damn scoop of chocolate ice cream. Except dogs die from chocolate. Lasagna, maybe. Little RoboPeep winks at me in the rearview; no grudge from her either. She did choke me some Tylenol for the fever, and the Ritalin's jittering out the worst of the yapping, so I brush off my own grudge about her holding out on the Percs. That's how a home works: you ditch your dirt on the doorstep when you get there. We left ours at the rest stop instead of the dog, kicked off with the thought of all the bad tastes I used to spit. Maybe that's what Little RoboPeep's winking at—our troubles passing. I catch her wink in my hand. Put it to my lips like the kiss that she's good-as blown me, because now we're like that: a four-pack of family.

Ezra

The jitters hit Ezra as soon as they leave I-40. The van rolls off the exit ramp onto Highway 54 and he's back on the bike last year, slow-cooking his thighs up the slow rise to Franklin Street. A false flat's more painstaking than switchbacks, a simmering hurt. Thinking you're coming up on level ground, straining up an incline too subtle to see. It's that way until Raleigh Road rises like a black tongue lapping sky. Two nights before the race and Highway Patrol's already posted warning signs. LANES CLOSED SATURDAY. EXPECT DELAYS. The grass stretches of shoulder are ruptured with messages from civilians, preemptive puns and backhanded encouragement. *Worst Parade Ever. Go (Your Name Here)! Chafe Now, Party Later. Seems Like A Lot of Effort for A Free T-Shirt.* The snark and frequency of these densify as the road steepens toward campus. *But who has the ball? I'd rather watch Duke play.* The Tar Heels leave a big footprint; in Chapel Hill, where basketball season casts a yearlong shadow, the municipality has carved out one weekend for triathlon, that esoteric feat of persistence. The Ironman Corporation had the wisdom of putting their race two months before the start of conference play, when even Woody Durham's ghost catches its breath between this fall's prospects and excuses or celebrations from last season. For one Saturday every August, the basketball-starved student body trades their jerseys for volunteer vests, for body paint down frat row and wet t-shirts on the lawns of sororities and coolers testing tailgates' weight capacities, a day-long dry run of alcohol tolerance and noise complaints before the prolonged finger-crossing of UNC football season. None of those spectators gave a hoot about the slow-twitchers slogging past them, and that went two ways. With a hundred miles in your legs, you just couldn't be bothered. You'd slid low enough on Maslow's hierarchy to where your mouth was watering from the actual lemonade coeds were dumping on each other, not their sopping chests. What a waste of hydration.

"Don't burn your match yet." Ma's looking at him in the rearview again.

"Huh?"

"You're head-racing. Save the cortisol for Saturday."

"Right."

"Do it for the sake of the seat. You're leaving a sweat angel on the upholstery."

But driving over the course is like dragging a match over his nerves. Ezra's heart hummingbirds as if he's already racing.

"Try breathing," Ma suggests.

He does, and gut-deep. His lungs have that carved feeling of exhaustion, the bronchia scraped out like pumpkin seeds. If he'd lifted his shirt a glow would've passed through his ribs like a Jack-o-lantern's grin. "I feel like shit."

"How big's the bag?"

"Shit," he repeats.

"Better than being it. At least you're at the stage of a simile." Ma culls her speed for a spandexed jay-jogger. A half-wave of thanks from the runner. Ma thrums the driver's side window with her knuckles like aquarium glass. "There you go. Spend your mind on some ogling."

But Ezra'd only been watching her strides, thinking she needed to bring her hips forward. A strange satisfaction in that. Back to the chemical castration of fatigue. "Heel-striker," he mutters.

Ma bends his ear like a price tag she's checking. "Yep. Still my child."

"Y'all?" Casper hollers. "Shiela needs a pitstop."

Ezra sees the kid with the dog in his lap, half-standing with her claws scrabbling at him.

"Ope. Yep. She's going ahead." The kid sits back with his shorts darkening.

Ezra feels warm from watching, a comfort he's ashamed of—like heating up his wetsuit on cold swims with his own pee. The kid's being gentle with something.

They plunge down 86 onto Fordham and slant into the turn lane for Morgan Creek State Park. They'll swim in the reservoir. They'll molt their wetsuits on its south bank, straddle their bikes, and shiver out of the campground over root-crinkled asphalt; on the return they'll be sopping with the opposite problem, the heat of the day's work. Then the run. The finish line's already erected on the west bank of the reservoir, a vault of pomp where speakers throb under-palm of an Ironman Incorporated emcee. Eighties rock sluices off the van's windows. The gathering looks like a rave at this distance: flashes of skin-tight Lycra and bright powders in bottles, electrolyte concoctions that would likely shine like glow-sticks under a blacklight, inflatable tube-men flailing. The emcee pitches free merchandise into the crowd with the meticulousness of a guy who'd had somewhat of an arm once, a probable ex-relief pitcher for wherever J.V.

The campground's a shantytown of just such former second-stringers. No one who could throw ever bothered to run. No one who could run fast bothered to run far. The cross country flops turned to swimming. Then you had these compression-socked klutzes who'd resorted to a competitive outlet centered around excessively burning calories.

They roll past propped camper doors bannered with drying wetsuits and cycling bibs. Still-frames of crossed compression socks, farmer's tans, hair turreted by bike helmet vents. Each glimpse like the scrambled panel of a triptych: every subject, come Saturday, will subject themselves to martyrdom.

Ma cracks Ezra's window. "You good?"

"Just threw up in my mouth."

"You need to stop."

"Nah. Swallowed it."

"Stop stressing. You'll wring out your adrenals. Race later, rest now. Here. Point me." She knocks his head with the campground map.

They scrape into the cul-de-sac the kid hotboxing the gatehouse had marked for them. The road's called Three Point Circle, greened with the kid's fingerprint where he'd pointed at it. Ezra sniffs and smells weed. Sniffs again. A little slump would be good for him. Maybe he'll walk back up to the gatehouse to do some deep-breathing.

"This us?" Ma asks of the lot coming up, already flicking her blinker.

"Yeah."

She pulls past and backs in with hubristic speed. Their slot's a tombstone of pavement with a septic hookup. Jagged picnic table. Couple pines listing in like they want to take the seats. An Airstream hitched to a pickup left-flanks them. Ohio plates on the pickup, though the Airstream's are Missouri. The guys crossing their shins below the camper's awning glare at the pre-race festival on the far bank.

The mustached one points across the water. "You folks here for that?"

"This one." Ma flicks her thumb back at Ezra, who up-nods reluctantly.

"So you're the try athlete."

"Sorry."

"A hundred and how many miles?"

"140," Ma says. "Don't remind him. But if you bet, put your money on Fogerty."

Shiela spasms out the driver's door and Casper tumbles out of the sliding one, hopping off of the prosthetic. His piss-soaked shorts squeak as he moves.

Mustache's mustache raises with his eyebrows. He turns both at his buddy. "Did our slot say no pets?"

"Service dog." Ma flaps her hand at Casper, who's hopping for the water Shiela's already splashing in. "He was in the shit in

Ramadi. Lost the leg." She cups the flapping hand to shield her lips from the kid. "*Pee tee ess dee.*"

Mustache makes a sheepish, back-of-throat sound.

Cleanshaven pulls his shins out from under his. "Yeah, Tim. You're an ass. Sit with it." He stands and waves vaguely at Ezra. "Good luck at your try-a-thon."

Shiela's dog-paddling after Casper, who's broken out in full freestyle. Ezra walks down to the water and watches the kid wrestle it. Hours back he'd been laminated in fever. What's gotten into him since? More than Tylenol or Ibuprofen. Maybe he'd swallowed some of Ma's philosophy. Can the kid get so *now* as to forget withdrawal?

Ma lunges up beside him in a walking hip-flexor stretch. "Nice neighbors."

"Don't think they'll lend sugar."

"Your try-a-thon." She snorts. "At least he didn't tell you break a leg."

"Doesn't seem to bother that one." Ezra nods to Casper, who's specking across the water.

"Losing's better than breaking."

"And you call me histrionic."

"I never claimed immunity." Ma lunges wider, sighing at the dull pop of some joint returned to its socket. "Go save your dog."

Shiela's swiveling back for shore, flailing blurs of her forepaws. Tipping her head back against her own splashing. Ezra wades in.

He swims slow, muscles coarse with this morning's effort. Each combing stroke catching knots of sinew. Afraid that pulling too hard will leave them with split ends. The reservoir passes pristine, fishless and sand-bottomed below. He can see right down to the sunken logs frowning with his strokes' distortion. The water's clear as a lens, but its warmth connotes filth, like a stagnant pond's conflation of germs and heat.

Shiela's yelps skip a pitch, and Ezra places the sound—her bark's an echo of the Piston's flywheel before Casper burst it.

He lifts his head to sight. Coming up on her now. He shifts to a scull, sinking his legs. Below the sun-warmed surface the water temperature drops in neat layers, stratifying his torso with cold. He casts them off like the inverse blankets, shedding his shivering instead of insulation. Touches sand with his tiptoes. Shiela writhes placidly when he grabs her. He hoists her overhead and wades back, feeling cleaner as he goes. Walks up on the beach with Ma slow-clapping, a low burn in his shoulders.

He sets Shiela down on the sand. She licks his scabbed palms when he tries to pet her. The lake's rinsed the blood from her fur, or Casper'd scrubbed it off. The kid's halfway across the lake. Dusk and distance have reduced him to a bug; his arms antennae, skimming the surface. Ezra doesn't blink, afraid he'll dart off. "You gave him something."

Ma quits clapping. "Me?"

"He was laid up. Couldn't get a word out this morning."

"Way of the will. He's a dog."

"You sound like him."

"This again." She turns back for the van, crunching up the beach. "I'm getting the chicken started."

Ezra hangs off his spine, exorcising the haunt of that back spasm. The muscles of his nape burn from keeping his gaze up on Casper. He squints at the silhouettes on the far shore, searching for his reflection—but of course he won't find those Oakleys in this dusk, at this distance.

"You want rice?" Ma hollers. "Jasmine or basmati?"

Ezra stands up, punching the hurt from his vertebrae. "Are you making a plate for him?"

She's already ducked into the van, deaf to his accusation. He'd hate to picture that dinner table. Better to leave Benji in his helmet. Ditch the man and his brain.

Casper

Water don't grudge the stump. Sure, stings first, but then them stitches pucker. Kick up a couple chopsticks with my good leg and stump the way Ms. Ida taught me. Try-pinch the water between my feet like one-them sushi rolls. Them days I had a tendency to let my legs sink. These days I got less leg but a new heart-hope buoying. Flick my head back and see Ma and Ez spectating. Flick ahead and see jaspers studying. If there was a ditch I could swim in along the whole bike and run I reckon I'd beat the course record easy. Truth's I'll have to hurt some. Gotta figure how to perch the bike, too. Big to-do list. But I can let later lie. There's another difference between Ez and me: he's got to get to it, but I never gave a hoot how long Benji put off what-all workout he was putting us through. Me, I could put my feet up right there on the starting line and count sheep till the pistol shot them down. Nod off and nod on and still beat him. Not bragging, just fact-ing. Just getting cozy in the smacking of my quickening heartbeat.

I hunker back to last year's race in my head. All them age-groupers making a fight out of the swim, swinging their arms ever-which. Twice I got my goggles kicked off and kept moving while I bobbed, fixing them with that wake-making melee still pushing me. One big brawl out to that first buoy. Third time my goggles got kicked off I just let them sink. Swimming squinting a blur of the bottom. Remember I was thinking how sand's ground-down fossils, how Adam the Atom Man said one day I'd wake up with a mouth full of it I kept grinding my teeth. Wondering if I'd spot him watching. Knowing not. But I couldn't quit peeking the crowd for him when I ran up the beach.

Then I'm scraping that very sand with my fingernails on the far shore, getting manicured with ground-down fish teeth. I start wading. Fires Halloween the staring faces of jaspers like I'm the haint summoned from their spooky stories.

"You swam from the far side?" one-them asks.

And them saying is me seeing. I stand in the shallows and look back. Too dark to spot our campsite, but here's the difference between Ez and the Atom Man: I know Ez is still over there chasing his gaze after me.

"You racing?" that same jasper's asking.

I start hopping for shore with the lake falling off of me. When it drops past the stump them fire-lit faces Jack-O'-Lantern. Their gaping mouths stretch and warp with flickering horror. I wave the stump up at them. I trip once and the asking one half-stands like to help.

"Don't touch me!" I holler. Couple more silhouette heads whip this-a-way. All them visors and compression socks and energy gels they're sucking like a bong-hit of carbs, out-Robo-Copping even Ez. I just tip up and hop off. Gonna show them. Fixing to drop all their jaws. They'll be picking pine straw out their teeth Saturday.

I take the road around the reservoir, that crinkly scab of pavement. Keep catching toes on the roots speedbumping up through the asphalt. Keep sprawling. Work up a good bleed on my palms, like I been playing patty-cake with Ez or petting Shiela. I swam the reservoir in a snap of my fingers. That same distance is a whole encore on one leg. My palms clap and clap against the pavement. After enough trips and falls I just crawl, fed-up of getting bullied by gravity. Folks lean over, offering me their arms, which I chomp at and swat. Pretty soon they quit off. My reputation seems to beat me. Time I come around the east bank folks stand to poke the fire or droop their heads, faking busy or sleep. I can hear their voices dropping off ahead. They rise up again once I'm past them, very edge of earshot. I go off through the bushes to the softer pine straw, lapsing down on my belly. Slide on out behind the gatehouse and taillights sting me. There's a wrench, then a screech. I open my eyes at the pickup stopped about a foot shy of my skull. The driver's door opens with a thick waft of weed. A kid steps out after it like that smoke's shadow—his narrow ass wispier than the fumes.

"Goddamn," he's saying. "Goddamn, goddamn." Looking at where my gone leg was, like he's thinking he squashed it off. All frog-eyed, his voice croaky with smoking. "You good? You gucci?"

"You didn't do nuts."

"Yeah. I didn't feel a—right. Glad you're gucci." He turns toward the truck, back to me. "Listen. Can I, like. You want something? A ride?"

Maybe he did bump me, because some part does feel broke in my throat. When that old frog Mr. Sob hops, I don't even try-gulp him.

"Goddamn, man. You good?"

I just pry on over the tailgate and weep.

"Woah, woah. You can sit in the cab. Come on up here." The kid runs around and opens the passenger's door. Runs upside the driver's and beats me in. He's leaning across shotgun by the time I leak in, digging through the console. "I got Kleenex somewhere. Where to?"

He reels back and hands me a hanky. I stuff it in my mouth just to grind on, just to chew. And the yapping's fierce all a sudden, as if the Ritalin was only holding it off like a bowstring, building its power ever second it stretched it back. I point north.

"Know the lot?"

But Mr. Sob's clogging all talk out my throat.

The kid watches me, his red eyes wide with deciding. "You smoke?"

I nod.

He reaches back into the console and comes out with a lighter. I pop the glovebox before he can lean over. Pull out a shrink-wrapped lump of nugs.

"Goddamn," kid says. Then he rolls a real tight one for me.

We drive around the lake and I sip the joint. Kid's talking the whole time, but the kind of talk that's like quiet. Listing off his life like a song he's half-humming. Mindless stories I don't hear a word of. Only words in my head are the ones I've been quieting ever since I first tipped the bike, what I've known this whole time below speaking: I'm not fixing to race the Ironman. I can't even perch the bike. But even as I think that, my sobs ebb. This is real scrunchy indica that I'm drinking. Right quick I'm low-breathing and narrow-eyed, and not once do I pass it. I smoke down till I'm chewing the roach. Hit and hit and hit.

The truck's stopped, the kid eyeing me. The windshield's all pines. We drove out of road. "Did we miss it?"

I lean over and plant a kiss on his lips.

"Goddamn!" he hollers, jerking back, and I kick out of shotgun before he can so much as shoo me to go. Step out and sigh up the whole night, my chest wide with the warm well that comes after deep sobbing. Despite the smoke pinching my ribs. Despite the ashes tickling my throat. I swat at the headlights as the kid backs his truck, grinning into the blind that they leave as he goes. The road's wobbly under me. I let myself just tip over. I'll find my way back to the van, but later. Sweet to know that Ez will keep on watch-waiting, that he and Ma and Shiela won't go without me. More than Percs can hit. More than moving can droop you. There's plenty-things to sip and gulp that'll rid my squirm without the hurt of racing. I can put my foot up without even using it; without even wanting to. Why'd I want to move anyhow when I found a home finally?

Ezra

Every worst day of Ezra's life had been the eve of an Ironman. The amp and pomp of trademarked pre-race festivities.
The sponsor tents hocking massages, foam rollers, acupuncture,
fungal extracts and carbohydrate gels and all kinds of last-min-
ute supplement suggestions, and the bike showrooms prowled by
ex-roadies whose commission and attitude equaled that of the
salespeople at a sports car dealership. The DJ and emcee narrat-
ing over it all, working the finishing area in their own endurance
feat; they'd banter and throw t-shirts and spin dawn to dusk, then
be back at 3 a.m. Saturday, jawing on until the last finishers strag-
gled in at midnight. The whole event made more jagged with
the migraine of a light training day. Hard to relax when there's
pressure to do it. Harder when the riff to "Enter Sandman" keeps
warbling over the lake at you.

That's what Ezra wakes up to, squinting at slashes of sun
through the blinds. He can feel the slats of warmth where light's
landing. Can sniff something rubbery. Casper's still curled in the
dinette, asleep. He'd slouched up after dark last night, about an
hour after Ezra'd started worrying; had come from the road instead of the lake. "You run back?" Ezra'd asked. Casper'd just
shaken his head and reached for Ezra's plate, taking both baked
potatoes he'd been putting off eating. Kid ate them cold and
plain, biting into them like apples. He'd squirted ketchup in
his mouth and sat down and Shiela'd pooled herself in his lap,
whimpering histrionically.

"Naw," he'd announced on the back of a belch. "And ain't
fixing to." Then he'd laid back on the dirt and conked out.

"Fixing to what?" Ma'd asked. "Brush his teeth?"

"Race." Ezra'd known like Ma'd known when he'd decided the opposite, the same knee-jerk way he'd seen the dog in Shiela. "He's talking about tomorrow."

They'd both watched the kid's ribcage yawn like a jaw. His pelvis and legs seemed a tongue he might draw back up into it. Ezra'd yawned, too.

"Acceptance," Ma'd said, nodding finally. "That's stage five. Stud figured out how to grieve."

So why couldn't Ezra staunch his own sadness? He'd carried Casper and the dog into the van fighting it, laid them down, and let out one snorting sob. Felt the need to buckle the kid into the seatbelt, for some reason. Which is still on. Ma's monologuing outside. 10 a.m. on the microwave. Ezra's never liked waking late; never would have, if not for the Whack-A-Mole exhaustion Benji's training had beaten him down with. Rising after dawn leaves him thinking of all the training he could've gotten over with had he rolled out at the crack of it. Not that there's any today. No; a whole placid afternoon lays before him, which he'll wade through with the vague sense of killing the same idle time he's craving. On the outside, this day will look a lot like the one after the Ironman, but Friday's resting is spoiled by the task yet-to-come. He'll put his feet up the same way on Sunday, but only then—after the effort's behind him—will it feel like luxuriating.

So you check that your backup goggles are in your race bag for the twelfth time and scroll blindly through your phone until your thumb-muscles burn from the motion, then you prop that arm over your head to try and flush the lactate, wondering how many seconds you've just added to your swim split—every ache, every knot and throat-tickle magnified. Rhetorically speaking. Ezra's phone is buried under crumpled PowerBar wrappers in the cupholder. He doesn't want to see what else Benji'd been up to. A wolf clothed in his contact info. Another shit thought to step off the wrong side of the bed into. Pile on the ordeal of packet pickup, where every athlete will converge to collect their Ironman-issued race kits: the paper numbers for the bike, helmet, and run belt, the digits matched on the swim cap and stick-on tattoos—all that, plus a digital timing chip to strap to your ankle. A bag full of identifications. To get his, Ezra will have to wade and trip through fifteen hundred other athletes rubbernecking for rivals or toddlers lost in the forest of shaved legs, or—most optimistically—an available bathroom. Then the press. *Triathlon Insider* will be there, and *Slowtwitch*, and local access, all buzzarding around the table set aside for top competitors. The Ironman people will want soundbites from the contenders. It's just short of a press conference. The din and jab will get him more amped than the countdown on the beach—which he might not be conscious for, honestly. He tries not to think about that 4 a.m. alarm, steps outside. Sun as sharp on his eyes as the pine needles on his feet.

"The whole run with his helmet on," Ma's saying.

Tim the mustache tips a kettle by their fire pit. "Why didn't he ditch it?"

"Leaving equipment outside of transition's a DQ. Besides, that would've proved it was an accident. This guy, Wispy, he had to act like he'd meant to do it."

"What'd he say?"

"Wanted to get a step ahead out of transition. Reckoned he'd lose half a second unbuckling the helmet."

"That's inane."

"That's Wispy. And here's Champ. Pop a squat, Love. Have some rooibos."

"Hey," Tim says, standing on an olive branch Ezra'd missed the extension of—sounding sheepish.

"I'm good. About to swim and spin."

"Huh."

"Just a shakeout. Flush that shit feeling."

He goes back in for the bike and goggles. The Felt's warm to his touch. Its wheels spin with a wet tick, like a big cat at the cusp of purring. He props the bike on the van and lays out his equipment. Number belt, racing flats, helmet balanced on the aerobars. Relics sanctified by the sweat of past efforts. He hikes his wetsuit with Ma craning her neck up from downward dog.

"You're defeating the purpose of that pose."

"There you go." She drops her chin back to her chest. "Self-sabotage. You get that from me."

He drills through transitions, dolphining out of the shallows stripping his wetsuit, stomping out of the legs as he buckles his helmet. Leaping onto the Felt DA, he's adrenal again. Palms sliding off the straps of his cycling shoes as he squirms his feet in, clipping the roots that bulge varicose through the asphalt of the campground road. He pedals, swerves, coasts, and swipes at the Velcro, groping to cinch it. As he passes on the gatehouse, he's still wrestling with the left strap. He unclips and put his right foot down to yank it. Mocking applause from a campsite behind him.

He stomps the pedals, fleeing wolf-whistling. Quick spin. Twenty minutes. But whipping up North Columbia, he's still out of the saddle; catches himself and sits back, upshifting, mouthing, "Idiot."

His average wattage is 400 on the power meter. He soft-pedals, urging that number down like he might erase the exertion from his legs as it sinks.

He'll have to ride long enough to flush out the lactate—thirty more minutes at least.

Right onto Cameron to dodge the tumult of Franklin Street. Coasting downhill through old campus, the road cobbled with bricks that had been buildings in older centuries. Sprawls of lawn ribbed with oaks thicker than the columns facading the halls. Students sit in the booths of their roots, laptops trayed on books, both-handed texting. The air's full of Friday. Ezra detects the buzz without absorbing. He hadn't thought twice about a gap year after high school. He'd been on the cusp of his pro card. Why not go all in for a season? Another. Eight years later he was still on that cusp, an amateur without an hour of college credit. He'd never even applied. Cruising through campus now—the end-of-summer swell, the sex and blush of it—he wonders if he'd given up more than a diploma. He'd always had Ma, the camper-full of her company, but maybe lonely had other rooms. Now he has Casper, or Casper's with him; he's come in and filled up another one.

East Cameron dips down to Raleigh Street, running into Country Club Road past the intersection. The light's yellow. He downshifts and goes for it, the Felt's deep-dish wheels whomping—his effort, for once, in stark agreement with gravity. He sucks past cars that are already braking. His view of the intersection's blindered both ways: the trellised walk of the arboretum blocks his view to the left, a head-high cobbled wall to his right. To brake now would lock the tires and send him somersaulting. The light changes. He spears into the intersection a hairline of a second later, making it by the grace of that built-in beat between red and green; making it, and then clenching the brakes for the pickup fishtailing through a right turn off of Raleigh Street. He jerks left on dumb nerve, skipping over the curb and plowing into a bush of azaleas. Extracts himself with the truck's draft still stinging his neck like a peeled scab. A jogger's stopped on the far sidewalk, head-shaking-staring. He follows the guy's gaze up the road at the truck. A white pickup. Ezra gets a smeared glimpse of the blank tailgate before it disappears around the curve. Bumperstickerless, a camper shell on the bed. The sideview mirrors furred with some colorful debris. Flowers?

Christmas lights.

Casper's truck. Ezra's decided it in his legs before his head, because by the time he screams he's all out of lungs, out of the saddle and sprinting after Benji. Country Club climbs past Forrest Theater, a stone gulley that looks fit for an older English than Shakespeare: more an altar for druidic sacrifice than a stage. The cobbled stone's crowded by hunkered oaks and chodey pines. Ghimgoul Castle looms a click through those woods, haunted by a headwounded spirit; then there's the old college cemetery across the road. Ezra climbs through four centuries of hauntings, chasing a more urgent ghost. He summits at the intersection of

South Road and looks both ways for the truck. No sight of it left or right. He keeps sprinting straight. The road steepens and he thrashes his bike and now his scabs really are peeling, the scrapes on his palms opening up. Never going to heal enough to see the lines; his fortune seems to unwind with those breeze-spat threads of blood. Country Club gravels and narrows into Laurel Ridge. He keeps on at risk of his race tires. The road dead-ends at the LDS parking lot and Ezra masts himself over the handlebars, panting back to his senses. He'd seen a white pickup with colors on the mirrors. Sunlight. The clown-bright sponsors' logos on his own tri-suit reflected. Had it even been a Toyota? His average wattage is back over 300. The ride profile looks like the terrain that he's climbed: a flat bracketed by two jackknifes. He's been riding for forty minutes, and he'll need another thirty to cool down properly. He watches his chest heave in the glass facade of the church.

"Idiot," he says to it. "Fucker. You just ruined your race."

And waits for some Mormon to lean out and chastise his cursing. But none comes. It's a goddamned forsaken Friday. Ezra's less mad at the fatigue welling up than the relief of the excuse that it buoys. He's treating his body like his uncharged phone in Ma's cupholder, afraid to see what's in there—the fitness that Benji'd put in. Afraid to see Benji in there: whether Ezra goes in, down, or out, he always dead-ends into him.

He's back at the campground by noon. Wheels the bike into the Sprinter van and gets highbeamed by Ma's eyebrows.

"Just a spin," he says.

"Huh." She leans out of the dinette, eyes his palms. "Did you take it through a blender?"

"Shower," Ezra says.

"You're going to turn some heads at packet pickup."

"Shit."

"Longer we wait, the more swamped it'll get."

"I'll just rinse off."

"Better knock."

The bathroom door swings open before Ezra can get to it.

Casper hops out, grinning Christmas. Beady pupils. Perspiration quartz-ing his forehead. Looks polished. And Ezra knows in that instant that Ma's let him have the rest of the bottle, because the kid could only get this smooth with Percocet. "I'm the ringworm!" he hollers.

"The ringer." Ma points at him. "That's Love. And you're Stud." She rubs Ezra's head.

"What?"

"You're racing as him."

This because of Ezra's fumble with the insurance. Bad idea to be seen front-running an Ironman on two legs a couple weeks after one was amputated. High likelihood that Blue Cross has a sponsor tent around somewhere. Employees racing, certainly. If that doesn't clue them, there'll be his name next to his two-legged picture in the press—assuming that his performance lives up to his legs. Ma monologuing it all as they inch around the reservoir, dodging joggers and cyclists. Folks coming back from packet pickup wearing their race t-shirts like trophies, the back bold-printed with the word ATHLETE. Once they cross the line, they'll receive another one that says FINISHER. In the meantime, their intent's the best boast they can make; anyone racing is serious about showing it. They pass arms already sporting race numbers, calves tattooed with the Ironman logo. Ezra scans those arms for single digits. Race numbers are assigned based on your seed, which is determined by your world ranking. Ezra's was 140th at the time of race registration, putting him third on Chapel Hill's race roster. Casper's fifth place from last year had lifted him to 98th. Ever since registration had closed, every time Ezra'd refreshed the race roster—keeping it open despite knowing it wouldn't change—Casper'd been seeded first. Now Ezra will race with his number. One. A target. A prediction. A jinx.

Ma swats his thigh. "This is exposition, not accusation."

He nods like he's been listening.

"You did the right thing. A good thing."

"Thanks."

They're pulling up to the race site, as close as the van can get. The road's coned off ahead of them. NO PARKING signs every foot or so on both shoulders. A volunteer's already waving Ma on with a stuffed Mickey Mouse glove. The registration tent towers at the far end of the race festival, a big top dwarfing the sponsor booths in front of it. Ezra will have to walk through that gauntlet.

"Be surgical," Ma says. "In and out with your head down. And your mouth shut. And this." She slaps a ball cap on his head, masks him with sunglasses. "Not so much as a 'no comment.'"

"Right."

"I'll be right here, filibustering this ass." She up-nods the volunteer. "And try to calm the hell down. They don't deserve your adrenaline."

Ezra's searching the rearview for Casper when the kid's head pops up beside him; he'd been riding in the floorboard behind Ezra's seat.

"Can't come," he says, sounding sorry.

"Gonna give it to him?" Ma asks.

Casper drops a ziplock in Ezra's lap, its sides opaque with duct tape. "Take me."

Ezra peels open the bag. Wet in there. Damp. A rubber-band-ed stack of IDs. He pulls them out: the top one says Casper Swayze. The picture's the kid, at a squint. Buzzcut. Debatably brown-eyed. The height—five-five—about six inches gener-ous. Close, but not him. And even less Ezra. He looks down at Casper, the kid, a boy who'd once answered to Mama as well as Mama-less, and then back at the IDs. They're neatly, fist-thickly stacked. He slides some up high enough to bend the tops back. Bearded men, wrinkled women, impossible aliases. Souvenirs. Trophies? Another thing crowding the room of Casper's memo-ry that he regrets bumping into. The bag's insides duct-taped as if concealing them. Ezra wishes they'd stayed that way.

"Don't grudge you," the kid says.

Ezra nods.

"Have the record."

Ezra shakes his head.

The volunteer smacks his hand on Ma's window. She gives him a thumbs-up, plus the middle finger of her other hand. "That's sign language for sock and buskin." Then, to Ezra, "Better go."

So he takes the I.D. that says Casper, then hands back the ziplock and the stack. The kid grabs Ezra's arm instead, prying himself up and Ezra down in one motion. Both of their elbows braced on the center console, faces kiss-close.

"Me can't beat me," the kid whispers.

Ezra nods again.

Casper

Me and Ma watch him off. I crawl on up and curl in the warm of his seat. Curl, too, in the warm of the rest-them Percs she gave me. Said she'd trade the bottle if I let him race as me, but I'd've done it anyhow. Strange how your where changes your want: how scared I was of getting made into him in that hospital! Squirming at them machines pumping me, RoboCopping me up. But in this Sprinter van where the four-us live, we're square. And I told the truth: hope he takes the record. Know he can't, but still want him to. Wanting's the least I can give Ezra, because he done gave his name to put me in 'surance. Watch him off, slouch-shouldered yet nerve-tall, bouncing on his tiptoes how he walks when he's antsy. I.D. pressed to his chest with both palms, both-handed holding it. Getting his blood on. The boy who got the Percs and the home I'm now curling in for me.

"One for me?" Ma's looking at my bag of left people. I pinch it tight-shut and she laughs. "Kidding."

And that vest buster's hammering his big-gloved hand on the window through this whole, hollering about a ticket. He leaps back as she gasses it into reverse. We shrink him driving back.

"Fill the buster!" I holler, greasy-gleamy off Percs, plus the caffeine pills and Tylenol I rooted out the glovebox before Ma snuck up with the bottle. Burping up three flavors of powder, smearing and shining along.

Ma backwardses into a carless campsite and jerks into drive, forwardsing out of it. We take a lap up to the gatehouse, round it, and come back. My bud from last night sees me and ducks under the counter. Nuts to him. Don't need him. Shiela's still whimpering back-under Ma's seat. I put my hand down and she suckles. A dog calms by dragging its tongue over rough. Folks see them chewing fur without knowing they're anxious, steering clear in fear of fleas. If they just put a hand out them dogs would smooth right on down. Got a bag full of people I ought've told that to. A bag full of could-of-been-different. Well, I'm done making that mistake, so I tell it all to Ma, from the chewing on up to the smooth.

"Well, you're welcome," she says. I'd left off the straight-up thanking her, but she'd heard right on through.

We're still trickling through the cyclists and joggers when Ezra steps out the crowd looking garbage-disposed. His hat's slanted incognito, but he's still walking on that bounce. I even beat Ma to spotting him. She hefts her eyebrows when I swing my door out. Then he's in, both-us scrunched in the one seat. How opposite we used to far-end the truck bed riding in it! Never again. That went right off with Benji.

"Get it?" Ma asks.

Ezra sighs about five minutes of built-up breath. "Got it." The cab fills with the unsaid of all the cram he's just gotten through. "Almost didn't."

"Yeah?"

"The address on the I.D. didn't match registration. The lady asked me to confirm the one they had."

"And you did."

"Lucky guess." A long quiet crams into one second. It's me he's now-looking at. "You put us down as your home address."

"Yep."

"Registration closed December first. You came after Thanksgiving." He halts talking. "You weren't even there yet."

I don't know where he's stuttering toward, so I just whisper, "Turkey."

Ezra shakes his head. "Did he say you'd be staying with us?"

"Never mind," Ma says. And her hands beat his eyes to the phone in the cupholder.

He shuts his like he's both kinds of beat. "Is it night yet?"

"Twelve forty-five."

He whimpers. And I get a dark thought. I prod his fists and his chest. "Got me?"

"What?"

"Casper." Thinking that maybe it's like a bar, where when you can't say what's on the card they take the I.D.

"Sorry." A sweet time he's fishing it out his bike shorts. Warm and sweat-slick as a flounder when he hands it back to me. I take a lick and warm, too.

"Disgusting," he says, but his tone meaning the antonym.

I hand the card back to him. "Keep me."

He takes it. And now the quiet's too thin for the time, a second's silence I let stretch. We park back in the campsite to find our neighbors bringing wood to our fire pit. Ma gets out to greet-thank them, and only then do I work up to telling Ezra what I was fixing to. "Benji promised a home for me."

"He said that?"

"Honest." The answer I'd throat-held since he asked.

Ezra nods and not-looks at his phone in the cupholder, watching Ma light the logs our sugar-lending neighbors dumped off. Tim comes out the Airstream with teabags and a Heineken, an eye-twinkle like he's aiming for a back-slapping afternoon. But in the van it's just a quiet like glue. Me and Ezra stick to silence because we don't need to say nuts. We're cozy enough with each other for that. Shiela paws up on the center console to snug me and I hoist her on up. She fits just perfect across the two-us. Ezra puts his hand down and lets her lap his scraped palms. I stare long-hard enough I can see his sweating quit. Watch his pores tighten shut. His breaths narrow, and I know I gave that calm to him. First time I've ever seen him put his feet up before the hurting's done, yet here he is lounging on race's eve on account of me. He gave me his name, and I gave my droops to him. Feels warm to feel equal. I'd like to keep that heat going—the two-us hot-potato-ing good back and forth, making kin out of kindling.

Benji

You hadn't meant to hit Ezra. Hadn't meant to be here at all. You'd driven off from West Memphis with your heel aching, waiting to live up to Unc's promise that you'd dissolve. Without Tootsies listening, there was nothing to keep you in your body. Should've gone like noise in the forest with nobody around. A rule that Unc hadn't even managed to follow. His bones drowned in that water tower. Should've held your breath and joined his skeleton, but you had better bones waiting. If Ezra looked back, you just might be able to borrow his. With that, your will to leave him be had snapped. You'd driven to Chapel Hill to wait for him.

Four days humming to summon Tootsies, hoping that they'd show. Drinking Cheerwine by the liter in the backs of gas stations. Busking by the McDonald's drive-thru. You tossed out every Big Mac. You could've used the kid's credit card (not his, but the one that he'd had), but there was no quench in paying for it, in not seeing what they'd do. Folks walking your way before you even looked at them. You told them you wanted money for cigarettes, bullets, wine, a timeshare, a motorcycle, and they still opened their wallets. The manager came out to shoo you and went back inside having offered you his spare key. You only took that as a trophy. Never could stand a bed. Unc's idea of A.C. had been propping a window. The clapboard got so stuffy in July that you'd slept outside, leaking naked across the dirt to let the ground drain your body heat. Soft slosh of Unc shifting in the trough beside you.

But here in Chapel Hill as summer wilted into fall it was cozy in the pickup. You haunted back to the same Shell where you'd first seen the kid last year, parked there and waited for his ghost to catch up. Gas station sunsets through the windshield, backlit car exhaust butter-wiping the sky. That podunk aurora. Then starless night, the station's lights blanching clouds' bellies. Staring at the square glow of the pump canopy to keep from nodding off, keep that image of the kid's leg in the spring trap from coming back. Not the ghost you'd wanted.

This year it was Ezra riding past you, bombing his bike through the yellowing light of that intersection. The shivering speed of his breathing. Ribs furrowing his tri-suit. For a stupid second you'd mistaken him for the kid: that same numb face, fragile with effort. Beautiful. Then you'd seen both his legs. You'd already been turning. Him cutting in front of you too fast for you to brake; you too breath-taken by him to think. Had to stop him from racing before he ran holes in his feet for you. Or you'd wanted to break him, greedy to see how much hurt he'd hold and keep moving. Hard to trace the origin of a reflex. You ran him off the road and he crushed into the bushes and when you glanced into the rearview there he was, sprinting after you. The ram in him. The cure he thought of you concentrated to poison.

Idle the truck up Franklin Street where traffic cones already orange the right lane like Jack-O'-Lanterns to set off the bike course. You're the loose spirit they're warding. Back over one with the pickup. Stake out a spot. Feel yourself in Ezra's fitness, his welling blood. Tomorrow you'll evaporate from him, or flood farther in. Up to him. All depends on whether or not he looks back for you.

M a

A disorder inhibits daily functioning. Case in point: how I wince not to weigh out the portions for our fajitas. Instead of calculating the macros of those tortillas and chicken you're sliding around, I estimate your hair's drag coefficient. They say a stray brake cable can lose you a minute over an Ironman-distance race. The difference between a high-and-tight and a zero-guard shave has to be worth something.

Stud slumps into camp, reeking of weed. Shiela yips over to him and sneezes. He pats the air inches left of her head.

"Nice swim?" you ask.

"Think he took a sauna." Stud's as dank as the wafts I'd caught off that hotboxed gatehouse at the entrance to the park.

"Pop a squat," I say. "Bet you're hungry."

Stud shoves a pinky into the guacamole. "I ain't eating varm upchuck."

"Try it on the peppers on onions."

"The salad's supposed to be green, not the dressing." He flicks the gob of guac at Shiela.

This is who you've been living with. Hope you've taken notes. Tomorrow you're going to play him.

Before I can muster the gumption to tell you the plan, your chin's drooping. Rice stubbles it. Your plate slants in your lap. Shiela sneaks licks of the chicken and guac.

I grab her jaw, try and pry it apart with my hands. "Spit it."

She whimpers, but clenches.

"Let off her." Casper swats my arms. "Not like Ez was using it."

I itch to weight out the uneaten food and force-feed you

every missing calorie. Your loose jaw is what stops me; you gape the way that baby-you used to sleep. Those sweet dreams ended the evening before your first triathlon. I've gotten too used to drifting off to the noise of you grinding your teeth.

I ease your mouth shut.

You blink up at me.

"Go on and bed down," I tell you.

You stand like the sixth hour of a long ride after pulling over for a number-two pitstop. Stare for a bonking second at your watch. "It's six."

"Honor your Circadian."

You set your plate in your camper chair. Eight hundred un-eaten calories. At least a hundred grams of lost carbs.

"I've got a gallon jug of Gatorade Endurance pre-mixed in the fridge," I say. "Try and get that down before morning."

You list into the Sprinter van. The hair on the back of your head is bunched into a grid of knots shaped just like your helmet's vents.

I jog after you. "How about a buzz?"

You doze off on the toilet before I can get the electric razor plugged in. I lift your chin off your chest. It droops again. I buzz your head down to the pate, the guardless clippers mumbling into your skin. Every pass across leaves you looking more like the kid. You become him in shafts of bald, transforming by razor-widths.

I ought to wake you up and tell you who your father is. The pain of listening to you recite what Benji did, brushing it off to keep you from sweating it even as my heart longed to let you know that I'd suffered the same charms in Nepal. You'd read that *Slowtwitch* article; surely you'd recognized yourself in that picture of Benji's uncle, or him from that photo I kept in my tri-suit. Then again, you've never been big on mirrors. Maybe my knowledge makes the resemblance obvious. After all, you've never been in a room with him.

Your cut locks release sneezy wafts of chlorine. Through the window, Casper's watching like he wants to put on the *you* I'm taking off. I picture him sweeping up the hair and nesting on it. Once I'm finished, you don't even rinse off, just crawl into your bunk and unlive.

I dustpan and trash-bag your hair, set the Gatorade you forgot by your bedside. No way you'll drink it. So much for a steady carb up to top off your glycogen. I take a sip, then another, then a chug. The Orange Endurance formula tastes like the Tang Auntie Opal used to dust margarita glasses with at our Passover pregames. The concoction sustained me through many a Seder, lip-syncing *The Women's Dayenu* after tasting the sparkling trace of tequila and citrus.

Before I can holler *dayeinu!*, the Gatorade's drained. 831 calories. I don't need that energy; I'm not racing. I swear I can feel the sugar rushing for an outlet through my bloodstream—a throb in my veins like the one in your head after too much caffeine. If I don't siphon it off, it'll get stashed as muscle glycogen; once those stores are topped off, anything left will get stuffed into fat cells. Nothing to do but get moving. I've got work to finish anyway.

I pull out your race belt out of your transition bag. My hand brushes the Clif Bars in the inside pocket: Chocolate Chip, Crunchy Peanut Butter, the most average flavors (500 combined calories). Everyone knows to go for the ones with the longer names: White Chocolate Macadamia Nut, Chocolate Almond Fudge. Iced Gingerbread's fine, but you get those sharp chunks of dried something. The less you can see of that climber on the front of the packaging, the better the taste.

Your race belt fits me more snugly than usual, and that's not just the Gatorade's sodium bloating me. You look even tinier than your typical racing weight. Anyone besides your mother would say that you dead-rang for Casper. I remember your father, your truer spitting image, but it's not me you have to trick come race day.

I center the race belt on my pelvis. Casper stands by the

campfire. Shiela darts from him to the water and back, but the kid's watching the van door like he's waiting. I tuck the run number inside my running shorts and pull on a medium Ironman Chapel Hill technical tee. The shirt's baggy enough that the hem covers the race belt. I step out into sticky evening.

"Delilah," Casper says.

"Come again?"

"Hell'd you Samson RoboCop for?"

I slide my hand over his buzzed head. A warmth moves toward my fingers, and I picture that as his thoughts—his synapses responding to contact like the light those plasma orbs you used to fondle at the Discovery Store. "I Caspered him."

I jog out of the campsite and take the road west. Pine branches slat sunset. It's not even dark yet and folks are already emptying gallon jugs over their fires. Tents zip shut. Athletes slide grocery bags over their bike seats on the four-percent chance that it rains tonight. I never quite got that convenience; your ass will already be soaked from swimming by the time it hits the saddle. There's a supreme selectivity around comfort with triathletes. Our crowd's the type to run a marathon with the beds of their toenails blood-blistering, then bitch about the distance between the finish line and parking. As soon as the race is over, all toughness gets cast off.

This finishing chute is a hundred-yard gauntlet of plastic barricades screen-printed with race sponsors. Time Out Biscuit Company. Weaver Street Market. Ventum. Roka. Active.com. Half of the logos are local restaurants, and the other half fashion the kind of equipment it takes to burn all that Carolina comfort food off. Just past the chute is a twenty-six mile marker. I love how they do that—like you need to pace yourself for the final .2. Not even I give a hoot about my split time within sight of the finish line. I trot over upside-down chalk slogans.

MACCA MODE.

Get Burly, Jessa!

Just don't lie down scrawled atop a chalk outline.

The asphalt bends around the lake, its pave growing as bumpy as gravel. At the twenty-fifth mile marker, I turn around. I retrace my steps at race pace. The chalk phrases. The Rolodex of sponsors flanking the finishing chute. I pull your bib out of my shorts and sprint across the line wearing your number. No matter what happens, you crossed the line first. Casper did.

This is my secret, vicarious superstition, carried out since the days you were racing the draft-legal circuit: sneaking across the finish with your bib. I'm not saying if it helps, but it's never gone well if I skipped it. Remember USAT Nationals in 2011, where you overshot the first turn on the bike course and took a two-mile detour? Remember how it had been raining the whole week leading up to the event? I'd skipped my ritual that time to stay dry. Never again. There's your answer to why I insist on running and riding outside during hurricanes.

The eve of Chapel Hill, the finish line had been closed off and security-guarded. I wish I could say that had stopped me— to take on the blame—but I'd hopped a barricade and charged the line at a pace fast enough to jack my heart rate into Zone 5. I'd done my part, I'm saying. What happened at that race was all you.

I trot back toward the campsite with my legs feeling like I'd covered the other 139 miles of the event, waiting for the ritual's usual warm-skinned afterglow. Getting it done should leave me with the same peace as a key workout completed. Instead I've got this twitch like a sugar rush, but preemptive.

I might beeline for your transition bag and borrow just one of your gels. A Honey Stinger. Squirt it onto that Peanut Butter Clif Bar, maybe. I'll be doing you a favor by downing the solid food—sparing you the risk of G.I. issues. You'll think Casper got into them, but won't ask the kid questions. Tomorrow morning I'll swing into the race expo and stock you back up with liquid nutrition.

A disorder interferes with daily functioning, but it's after sunset. Something about daylight spoils stuffing yourself; all my best binges have been moonlit. They've come without witnesses.

I call Doro. He picks up so abruptly after the third ring that I get the feeling he'd been making himself wait for that many, as if holding off for that long would suggest something. What? That he hasn't been biting his fingernails waiting to hear from me? I picture him gnawing down past his knuckles, until the only thing jutting out past his wrist-wraps are bloody stubs. He'll be pinching the phone between his ear and shoulder.

"Granola or cereal?" he asks.

"Clif Bars, actually."

"Dr. Reyes is leading guided meditation. I'll put you on speaker."

"Don't." So he'd taken his phone off of 'Do Not Disturb' for me. He'll probably be pacing the same hall where I'd heard from Benji. "Ez is racing tomorrow."

"I take it he wasn't indoctrinated."

"Listen. If you want—if you're up—why don't you fly down?"

A gong drolls on Doro's end of the line. He makes a noise in his throat that might be meant to mock it, but I suspect otherwise. He's built himself into himself up in Tetlin—manifested an airtight version of his vision in the selfish way only available to the hereditarily wealthy, ruling out all but dramatic irony. Maybe some Tulpas come less from focus than funds.

"I'm not flying across a continent to watch your son blur by on a bike."

The cinch in my stomach feels like a living animal thrashing. My want for him to come—for him to want to come—seems as separate and severe as a rat gnawing through me. "You said you wanted to meet him."

"I wanted you to bring him into our discussions. You can't heal until you get to the root of the wound."

"My wound has a root?"

"We both know how this started."

"We do?"

"Forget it. I'm assuming."

"No. Tell me what you're assuming."

"This is just me saying what I saw."

"Go on."

I swear I hear Doro preparing to drop his voice, a convex silence of the type that suctions out quiet right before something deafening. "You weren't ready for him."

And yes, Champ, that's true. I did entertain the idea of not having you. The same animal part of me that took to starving might even have planned for it, but you of all people ought to know how imagining quitting something can actually help you follow through. Isn't that why you toyed with early retirement so many times? Knowing you can makes it easier not to.

I pull the phone away from my head like Doro's words might be attached to it. A horsefly darts in the space between my ear and the screen.

"Eva?" Doro says.

"Are you telling me that my son's the root or the wound?"

"I shouldn't have. That's up to you."

"You're the root."

"I'm absolutely complicit. I was stuck in my own pattern, and you picked that pattern up, but only because you were already coping with something. The literature shows that these patterns get perpetuated. This is me trying to help you and Ezra."

So that's what Doro's after: not us, but a way to purge his conscience of what he thinks he's done to us. I'd mistaken a tether for an attachment. "You wanted him to fly up to participate, didn't you?"

"Have you shared your journey with Ezra?"

How can I, who have no problem calling you into the bathroom to show off a well-sculpted bowel movement, get so shy when it comes to explaining how I get practically body-snatched by food? Maybe I don't want you to feel guilty for not noticing. You watched me bike more miles in July than the Tour de France cyclists to burn off serving bowls of granola that took actual hours to consume and did nothing but offer me blueberries. I don't blame you, but I bet you could talk yourself into responsibility. I know all about the traps we can make in our minds: you've seen me weigh out garlic powder, counting the trace calories in seasoning.

"What airport would I fly into?" Doro asks.

I hang up. He calls back. I airplane my phone.

And plod back to camp. The van's sliding door's all the way open. Casper and Shiela are gone. You sprawl solidly in your bunk, swelling your blanket with the throbbing breaths of deep sleep. The sound spools around me like sea breeze. *Safe place*, Dr. Reyes would say. I already jogged, and I still don't have any Play-Doh.

I'd rehearsed every coping strategy at Doro's clinic without ever considering the underlying assumption: for any of this work, I had to not want to binge. I've been through enough workouts to handle the discomfort of a stuffed stomach, and the last mirror I ever bothered to look in was your father's face before we got crushed by that stadium. He saw me that completely: like a reflection. I only ever went hungry for the anti-anxiety and performance benefits. But my nerves are impossibly knotted, and you're the only one racing. Give me one good reason not to eat everything.

I mean it, Champ, please.

The fridge light strikes me like a U.F.O.'s abducting beam—I blink once and numb, get sucked senselessly in. The only feeling part of me seems my tongue. I eat shredded cheese out of the bag by the gasping handful, then finger the tub of sour cream empty. I rinse my mouth out with the leftover lemon juice and spank El Paso taco spice onto my tongue and unscrew the lid of the Gatorade Endurance powder and chew it by the crystalline, clumping scoop, eating too measureless much to even estimate calories.

When I slink pull the Clif Bars out of your transition bag, you're still sealed with sleep. I squirt two Honey Stinger energy gels between the bars, sandwich them together, and throw them both in the microwave. You twitch onto your stomach. The bars and honey heat into a single hunched lump. I pinch them out with a napkin. What I need is JIF peanut butter.

I cram my wallet into my pocket and jog out of the van. Has to be a jar left out on some table. I jog by campsites, refluxing what I've eaten. My stomach fists around everything I've crammed into it, shaking with each stride.

In Dialectic Behavior Therapy, Dr. Reyes had talked about food as the most dangerous addiction, a thing that you biologically need to keep using; you can't cold-turkey quit, she would say, but the summer before you were born, Doro and I had both tried. For the twenty-seven years since, I've been his disorder—interfering with his daily life. Seems like he's kicked the addiction. Maybe we like each other better estranged, when we remember the versions of ourselves who'd been compatibly weak.

I stop at the dumpster. The lid's bent convex, as if something hot had swelled out from inside. I slide open the side door, expecting seat cushions. Tied-off grocery bags crammed with banana peels and the cardboard-colored packaging of designer organic nutrition bars whose wrappers probably cost as much as the fair-trade ingredients. My trash bag gapes on top of the heap. The top's torn apart like it's been punched through, drooling chicken juice and shreds of fiesta-blended Great Value cheese. Ezra's hairs are stuck to the plastic. I hadn't taken it out. I clench my Clif Bars in my mouth and lean in.

"Polo!" someone shouts from across the street.

I jerk back.

Casper's standing beside a pine, hitching his shorts. Shiela sits where his shin should be. He rubs her head with his stump. She rolls her eyes back, panting ecstasy. "I had to take Shiela out," he says. "And me."

The Clif Bars are too thick to bite through. When I try to spit them out, they catch on my teeth.

"Wasn't lurking," Casper says. "Wouldn't do it in a dumpster if I were. It's a pool game, and no one made you Marco first-place."

"Did Ezra ever say anything to you about me?"

"Just ever secret." Casper hops into the road. Shiela moves with him, rubbing her head on his stump. I jog over. He stumbles and plants his arm on my shoulder and we stand like that in the middle of the street. Shiela gives me truce eyes, tail flagging. Your hairs are spooled around his left hand.

"You took out the trash."

"Shiela. She dragged out the bag. Caught her getting after that green-ass dressing." Casper glances at my stomach in the way Doro had—with the casual speed of a hunch's confirmation. Like he knows what's inside me. "Guess she beat you to it."

"Yeah."

"I usually ran it off before. You've got a gut on you, holding it down after. Or maybe you're trying to lose it."

"Not like that."

Casper nods. "I'd rather keep as much me in me as I can. Even if I'm stuffed." He shuts slowly, like he's biting into something savory. "Adam the Atom Man sure loved watching me eat. He'd take one bite out his Hot Pocket and hand it over. Them cheesy innards dripping like a duck getting field-dressed, all glimmery with his spit and the grease. Reckoned he wanted more me to hold onto. Bet he fed me up to 120."

I don't like the glimpse that this gives me. "Can I practice telling you something?"

Casper bends up and down on his leg like he's testing it. "How long are you jogging for?"

"I was done."

"Shame." Casper nods to my race belt. Yours. "Take it off. You're fixing to tank my ranking, 9:54."

"It's a superstition."

Casper shudders.

"But I can't hold all-us three."

I unbuckle the belt and hand it to him. He wipes his fingers on the bib number, greening and whiting it with guacamole and sour cream. Wouldn't put it past USAT to dock you for some kind of cleanliness penalty. He clips it around his waist as gently as if it were a nerved part of him, lifts his hands in mock victory. I picture a world where he's two-legged, the two of you stride-for-stride. I think I'd be ringing the cowbell just as hard if he were the first one across the line.

"You were fixing to fess," he says.

"I'm having second thoughts."

Casper gives my stomach that glance again. "Ez don't grudge you none."

"For what?"

"He always needs someone to grudge. Was me when I showed up. Then it was Benji. Then it was Dr. Who-all at the hospital. Should've been Shiela Petey, but he was conniving to hump with her."

"I doubt that's true." You're like Doro that way—a spiritual eunuch.

"I'm just saying it's your turn to take some. Ez ain't rough to you off of nothing you done. Not yet." Casper winks at the Clif Bars in my hand. "Shucks Honey Stingers, but I'll take one. We're teamed." He bites through them as easily as a slice of white-wheat Sarah Lee. "When Ez goes hungry, blame me."

Ezra

Ezra wakes infant, born again with the first chirps of watch alarm. He lets it chirp on, basking in the depth and breadth of his rest. Not a dream he can recall, nor a single stirring for water or pee. Casper pillows his face against the sound in the bunk under him. Shiela barks against it. Ma comes back from the front of the van and presses the button to quit it. Doesn't say a single word, just keeps a long hold of his wrist. He sits up rubbing slug-trails of sleep. A baseline warbles over the water. Ma opens the side-door and it thickens, twining with guitars and asides from the emcee. His armpits and his palms stay dry. Not the slightest twitch in his stomach.

"Ez?" Casper's porcelain whisper.

"Yeah?"

"You sleep?"

"Just my body." Ezra hangs his legs off of the bedside and waits for his nerves to spill into them. Waits for Casper to speak.

The kid ducks out from under his legs. Stands up and looks at him, deliberating.

"What's up?"

Casper darts one hand into Ezra's lap and pinches his penis. "Wormhole!" he shouts, but his shout cracks. He hops off with Shiela siphoning his excitement, climbing him with her paws.

Ezra can't find the Clif Bars in his race bag, but snatches a full box of PowerBars from the center console. He drips into the bathroom and takes melted bites, drooling them soft enough to swallow without chewing. Perches atop the toilet for an empty time. A knock.

"It's 4:45, Love."

"You mean Stud."

"Right." Clotted pause. "When were you planning on heading over?"

He stoop-stands. His legs aren't sore, just blunt, as if kneeless. Has to sort of swing them ahead, wondering if this this what walking with a prosthetic feels like. He opens the door for Ma and leans back against the sink.

She pokes his bare shoulder. "You're not numbered."

"I was waiting for you."

"Likewise."

She already has the stick-on tattoos in her hands. The tradition goes way back, applying each other's numbers. For smaller races you'd just Sharpie them on your shoulders, then a mark on your calf to show what division you were racing: "O" for "open," "N" for "novice," or your age for the rest of the field, who compete in four-year increments. Ma'd insisted he write her age tiny to fool her competition, the number scrunched up in the crook of her knee. But the Ironman stick-ons are standardized. She soaks them onto his shoulders with a washcloth. "You good?"

"Can't tell yet."

He watches her hunching to the washcloth in the mirror, making a show of the task to avoid his eyes. "He'd be chewing up hemlock and trying to spit it on me."

"Who?" Ma says.

"Funny. Here's the fucked thing. There was probably a point where I'd've let him do it."

"Brant Secunda had Mark Allen picking up dead birds off the side of I-5."

"This is different. Benji did something to me. Like, physically."

Ma let the washcloth slide.

"Anatomically. My lungs feel like—I don't know, like I'm getting someone else's breathing."

"He fed the hair to you." Casper's standing in the doorway like he's been there a while.

"Hey, buddy," Ezra says.

The kid slides his jaw around, debating saying something. Someone knocks on the van's side door.

"One second!" Ma hollers.

Casper's already hopping to get it. She groans up and Ezra follows, the stick-ons long-stuck. They'd been drawing it out.

Tim the mustache steps into the van. "We're not interrupting?"

The buddy—boyfriend?—steps around him. "We're rolling out. Saw your light on and wanted to wish you luck." He stabs Ezra with an envelope. *Your competition* is hand-written on the front.

"Thanks."

Tim says, "You're supposed to open it."

Ezra teethes off the top and dumps out a card. The front says *get well soon*. Inside's a stick-figure runner kicking up cartoon-curlicues of speed, the curlicues coiling around other stick-figures behind him. In equally curlicued cursive, looping under this: *Sorry for smoking you.*

"Like the hairdo," Tim says. "You look streamlined."

Cleanshaven nods to Casper, who's leaning in to squint at the card. "You look like your brother."

Tim and Cleanshaven both go to shake his hand in the same jumbled second. Tim adjusts his trajectory to Casper, who doesn't take it; he's flipping the card back and forth like the figures might animate, smearing the ink with his thumb. Sweating. Ezra sees that and gets the morning's first blurt of adrenaline. Casper's nervous for him.

Tim gives the kid a hesitant shoulder-clap. "Nice to meet you. And thanks again for your service."

The emcee's voice cuts clear across the water. "We are one hour out, folks!"

Ma checks her watch like she doubts this, but nods. "Better mosey."

Ezra makes for his bike and backpack. Out the door before

he realizes he's still in his boxers. He props the Felt and grabs his tri-suit from the clothes-hanger he'd just walked past. Drops trou right there in the campsite, without a glance from the folks jogging and pedaling past. The nylon clings as close and weightless to him as the stick-on race numbers. Seems to dry into his skin when he zips it. He folds over his backpack and excavates it, re-checking for everything. Shiela noses over and sticks her snout through the zippers. Ezra's loading the bag back up when he spots Casper's I.D. in the side pocket where he'd stuck it. He pulls it out now and examines the card.

The emcee's voice grows out of the sound system, someone punching up the volume. "Fifty-five minutes! Let's have a hand for our athletes!"

Shiela stiffens at the whoops warbling over the water. Out goes that back leg again. Ezra slides Casper's I.D. into his tri-suit's inside pocket only bone-knowing why, feeling the rightness of this in his marrow. Ma's still jawing with Tim and the other one in the van. She won't come out to send him off—another tradition. Any final well-wish or sentiment is another match burned, just like the lactate built up from sprinting. A heat that'll stay hearth-ed in his chest through the day. Too much weight on those words. So he shoulders his backpack without waiting. He's straddling the bike when he hears the soft smack of a single foot coming down on the sand.

"Ez?"

Casper. Ezra can't turn. But his stomach rolls when he realizes what he'd been too drooped to respond to the first time: Casper's twice called Ezra by half of his real name. He listens to the kid hopping through the sand, a sound like sitting down in a beanbag chair every time his heel's landing. As if relaxing his way toward him. Taking a load off with each near-landing. Ezra feels breath on his neck before the palm on his shoulder. Casper seems to pry himself level with Ezra by that hand, coming sideways into sight. Shiela quits her point and leaps up on him. She walks her paws up his stomach and he leans hard enough that Ezra has to stagger his legs to keep from tipping.

"Grown soft on the varm," Casper says.

"Me too."

"Naw. You got hard." Casper snorts. "You named her for Shiela."

Ezra nods, trying to preserve the fragile bulb around him. He'd begun to picture the calm encasing him as a lightbulb, his adrenaline its unlit filament. Has to hold off on flicking that switch. The lifeguards are still adjusting the buoys in the reservoir. He looks past them, at the flood-lit starting line on the far bank. It'll be easier there than here. This—Casper—feels brighter, more worthy of fear. The kid's breath and hot hand strobe with fever.

"You take anything yet?" Ezra asks. "This morning?"

"Naw."

"Start with Tylenol. You can do Ibuprofen two hours later."

"Kay."

Despite the flirt of rock riffs and the chatter of Ma and the athletes spinning past, the whole dawn is suddenly both very empty and entirely full of the two of them. Ezra's stomach turns again. Steady. Not yet; not for this. The wrong motor. So find some jumper cables and conduct it. Ezra knows Casper's been trying to tell him something all morning; the problem, maybe, is that Casper doesn't yet know what it is. They stand like that long enough that Shiela settles down, pooling herself around Casper's foot. But the kid still leans on Ezra for balance. Runs his other hand over the stubble on Ezra's head. The first hiss of his whisper's drowned by the emcee.

"Fifty minutes!"

"What'd you say?"

Casper shakes his head—but had whispered, Ezra's sure. Ezra cups a hand to his ear like to trap the sound in there, echo it back how a seashell holds the ocean. "Bark on."

"Naw."

"Not today. At the pier, remember? When we saw that coyote. You said bark on. What's that mean? Like a dog?"

Casper's hand slides off Ezra's neck. "Just something he said."

Of course. The phrase was as empty as Benji wanted their heads; the kid had only been echoing him. A sharp clacking gores the air. What is that? Cicadas? No. Casper's teeth chattering. He cups his jaw as if to still it before speaking. "Just asked if your legs was still sleep."

"They'll wake."

Casper nods. "All I said."

But that wasn't it, either.

Ezra rides off from the campsite, trying to decipher the smothered word that he'd whispered.

No luck on that, nor his legs. He pedals the Felt with dull thighs, wind funneling through the furrows Ma's jerky work with the clippers had etched into his head. The breeze steals his body heat. He pulls off to pry on gloves and a beanie and catches someone staring at his shoulder—that race number like a promise of ranking. He zips into a windbreaker to cover it as much as to quit shivering. Adds his helmet and sunglasses. Now he's wearing most of what he'd stuffed in his backpack. He rides on with it half-open, the loose zippers smacking. Spins past campsites pungent with flatus, loud with the huffs of deep-breathing athletes. The struggle to preserve nerves. Not to burn matches yet. Why isn't he working himself into a knot? He brakes into the race site and stumbles dismounting, still yet to shake that dull from his thighs. Racks the bike and dumps his backpack and folds over it and lays out his equipment in quarter-time.

"There he is." A long-waisted guy leans beside Ezra, looming all the more for his stooping. The top curls of 2's hook above his arm warmers. "Hey, buddy. Remember me?"

Like Ezra hadn't crashed into the man's subtle brag a mere fortnight back.

Wispy.

"But Phuket," Ezra says.

"That never shook out. I blame Delta's luggage fee. $3,000

US to fly international with a bike box." Wispy's tossing down his own run gear on his racing mat, speaking without looking at Ezra—less conversing than burning off nerves. "Some show you put on last you," he says.

Ezra snorts at this blatant assholeishness.

"Trying to knock down that course record?" Wispy asks.

"Just racing."

"Well, I'll have my eyes on the rearview coming out of T1. Give a wave when you pass me." He stands with a showman's groan, propping a hand on the top tube of Ezra's bike. "Looks like you upgraded the ten-speed."

That lights the morning's second match; Ezra jerks up as if cringing back from his own adrenaline's kindling. Wispy'd actually mistaken him for Casper. All it had taken was a race number and a buzzcut, maybe a little of Wispy's nervous distraction.

"Break a leg," Ezra says.

"Same to you." Wispy ducks back down to adjust the tongue of his left running shoe. Ezra jogs off, sinking into it. A long juke around the bike racks to exit transition and then he's cutting between campsites, stomping and tripping through the brush brainlessly. Just like that night before the branch-swinging. Here he is at the cusp of a similar exertion, the earthen enormity of it surfacing like a tectonic plate.

Just a shakeout run. Little warmup. The stupidity of this ritual, putting miles in your legs before an eight-hour race. Of course, it's really nerves that he's running from. Trying to keep that spurt of adrenaline from catching up. Needing to save that for the far and dark stretch of asphalt at the end of the day. There'll be plenty of nadirs between, and unpredictable ones: darkenings of the mood that will start as the recognition of all the road left to cover. At some point in the second lap of the bike that darkness, like a front-lit shadow, will shift. He'll start feeling the hurt of all the miles behind him. But he'll have to stumble through each of these blindly, saving the matches for the marathon. Coming up Franklin Street there'll be plenty of kindling;

passing through Carrboro, even. But then he'll be out on the long lonely of Dairyland Road, his own breath lowing like the cattle so conspicuously missing from the spans of grass surrounding that cracked asphalt. Hills that crest and roll like the ocean, so much so that one might believe the herds have sunk under them. Those empty miles would leave the staunchest skeptic gullible— even those who weren't woozy with exhaustion. How easy to sit down. Just to slow. Take a few extra minutes to finish; take second. But if he wills himself correctly, he'll loop back into town and the crowd and the long downhill back to the campground will finish his work for him. That last 10k will be sheer inertia. It's the marathon's middle miles that worry him. Out there on his ransacked legs and alone he'll need every one of those matches to keep his effort from extinguishing. But not yet. Damn it. *Slow.*

He catches himself gasping, his own breaths pulling him out of his head. He's run the loudspeakers to a shrunken hum behind him. Left the campground for the bowels of some neighborhood. The cloned facades of ranches stretch like a barbershop's mirrors on either side, approaching the seeming asymptote of infinity. One of those developments folks move into while the contractors were still building. Somewhere there'll be cul-de-sacs of empty lots, paved driveways leading up to gravel heaps. He swivels, unsure which way he'd just been moving. He tries to navigate by the loudspeakers. Runs toward the thud of that music until it divides into guitars, drums, and stomps, recombining into that old sporting anthem of Queen's. If they're playing that they've to be close to the start. He speeds up, afraid to check his watch. Cuts through side-yards setting off dogs like alarms. They chase him down the insides of their fences. Rounding a garage, a BMX bike swoops in front of him. He throws his hands out to buffer the collision and winds up halting the bike's progress, gripping the rider's shoulders. She looks about ten. Princess dress, Converses, helmet with mohawk spikes. Flashes her braces—baring her teeth.

"Sorry. Sorry." Ezra lets go as she growls at him.

"What the goddamn are you up to?" Her tone like she's asking for his drink order.

"Just lost."

"Join the club." Her eyes climbing him.

"I'm Ezra," he says. "Casper. I'm Casper Swayze."

"Don't give a goddamn. And your name's weird. You want breakfast?"

"I ate."

"You look goddamned starving."

"Thank you."

"My sister was anorexic."

She slides the buckle of her helmet over her chin, setting it in her teeth, and Ezra almost weeps—so fragile, so fraught with the prospect of the effort ahead of him. He used to chew his helmet buckle just like this, slaloming through the bromine plant's trenches on his bike until he'd gone far enough that could honestly say that he hadn't heard Ma calling him home for dinner. His mental image shifts into Benji chewing his mullet.

The girl lifts her eyebrows at him. "She cries randomly, too."

"Got to go," Ezra says.

"How come you were running? Are you trying to burn calories?"

"Not really."

"Bull. How come?"

"You know where the state park is? Morgan Creek?"

The girl flicks one thumb behind her. "You're literally a block over. Goddamn. So how come?"

"Late for something."

"What?"

"A run. Sorry."

Ezra can see pines behind the houses across the street. He takes off for them, funneling through another side-yard, and feels the music like a headwind as soon as he passes into the trees. Has to lean into the sheer resistance of the loudspeakers. He fears a glance down at his watch: 5:54. Idiot. He'd just jogged for half an hour. Four miles, probably. He's due on the beach in six minutes and he hasn't even finished unloading his backpack. He catches a volunteer's stiff-arm as he aims for his bike rack.

"Transition's closed, sir."

"I just need my goggles."

"Blanket policy, sir."

Ezra leans around the guy, pointing to his spot on the bike rack. "My stuff's literally right there."

"Don't shout, sir."

"I just want my goggles, please." And swim cap. And wetsuit. And timing chip.

The guy glances over his shoulder. "Blanket policy."

"I'm stepping around you."

Another volunteer's jogging over, saying, "Sir?"

"The Final Countdown" cuts out for the emcee. "This is the last call for our first wave of athletes!"

Ezra shoves past the first volunteer, jukes the reinforcement, scoops up his goggles and swim cap—too late to hop and yank into the wetsuit—and even as the guitars fray back out of the sound system and he swivels back for his stuff because *idiot* his timing chip's still in his backpack. He straps the chip on his ankle with the volunteers grabbing him. In a last ditch, he unzips his windbreaker; once they see that their grips loosen. They turn their extraction into an escort, their voices stubbed by his swim cap: *Got to get you...coming through...*

As they guide him down the coned-off path to the beach, the same one he'll be running up after swimming—the clock as against him now as it will be then (three minutes to the start!)—Ezra honestly thinks that he could lie down in the sand and fall asleep. But takes his place on the shore, in the front row of bristling and huffing and arm-circling athletes. One minute out. The crowd chanting the countdown. The athletes' antics slow. They palm their goggles into their eyes one last time, dropping to crouch. The whole start line's gone still with thirty seconds to go. The music cuts out. Had Ezra missed the national anthem?

He looks around for a flag, the bayonets of marines. Instead sees a guy in a Carolina blue three-piece suit raising the starting pistol, holding his loafers. He stands on the sand in his sock-feet. Idiot. Ezra moreso for noticing. Dress socks. Jesus.

When the gun fires, he's still staring. Doesn't even hear it; only knows by the smoke. He stands stoned for a long second, straight-backed and stiff-legged while swimmers sprint around him. Then he turns toward the spectators strangling the starting corral. Ma and the kid clarify from that crowd as if their faces are enclosed in a magnifying glass. The kid waves. Ma points toward the lake. Ezra turns back, his feet sinking in the dampening sand. The swimmers' serrated arms blading out. The line of them stretches halfway to the first buoy. The race numbers on their shoulders passing him are climbing, the middle of the pack parting around him. He stares at a *174* swinging back and catches the elbow attached in his mouth. The culprit plunges ahead without turning, anonymous in the stampede. Ezra sucks his teeth. *Now.*

Then he's tipping and thrashing into the thing. Punching strokes. Water splashing the back of his throat, thwarting his twists for breath. He swims a long time without sighting, just streaming through the crowd. Smacking his hands on the legs of the swimmers he's passing. His goggles and swim cap pinching his head like a zit; striving to burst it, break out from the clog of bodies. Keeps his chin tucked until he reaches open water. Lifts his head and sees the wake of the lead pack already hooking past the turnaround. A long stretch of still water between him and its tail-end. Four buoys. He tongues his split lip, tasting sunscreen instead of blood. Yet his finger's red when he touches it. He stretches his strokes out and smooths, cycling through his anatomy. Breathe and reach and no *next*, only an ellipses of separate instants—*now* and *now* and *now.* The buoys arcing with the curve of the north shore, hooking back. His hands flashing under him. Slit's glimpse of the Sprinter van when he breathes to his right. Each left-sided breath he can see the lead pack, those ellipses of swim caps. The buoys bend back around and he's aiming toward the starting beach again. That sand as rinsed and pale as the skin around Benji's eyes the last night Ezra'd seen him, the first time the guy'd lifted his Oakleys. All that time he'd mistaken the lens for a lake in Benji's profile photo. Aiming into the guy's eyes. Thinking that as his fingertips gouge the sand. He's swam too far into the shallows, could've been dolphin-diving for yards now. Add that loss to the minute he'd stood stuck on the beach. He high-knees out of the water fumbling for the zipper of his wetsuit, peeling his cap and goggles off in one *puh* with his free hand. Right. He wasn't wearing the wetsuit. No wonder he's shivering. A barbed chill across the stubble on his buzzcut, his shaved head hemorrhaging heat. He runs arm-heavy up the sand. Hating the numb stumble of swim exits, the blood yet to hourglass to his lower extremities. Impossible to look gallant with your strides flopping. And why are folks staring at him? He smears the drool off his lips and sees his spit streaked with crimson. The elbow to the face. Right. Still can't taste the blood.

"It's getting medieval out there," the emcee suggests.

The digital race clock reads 54:50. A minute of that had been him standing on the beach. Ten seconds sacrificed reaching for the wetsuit, twenty for swimming when he could've been dolphining—53:20 without the handicaps. Still slower than last year, when he'd stayed within slap of Wispy's feet.

Ma's voice bullwhips from the crowd. "Get 'em on the bike, Stud! Two minutes back!"

Ezra traces the shout to her face, and to Casper's. The kid's ear sits on his shoulder. Dusk still chills the air, but the armpits of his t-shirt are shaded with sweat. Standing there with a hand on Ma's shoulder, the other scratching Shiela's head, perched between them on his right leg and prosthetic. Ezra wouldn't mind borrowing the crutch. His own legs are still bloodless, phantom pains under him. Casper gives Ezra a look like the scariest part of the movie, grazing him with his eyes like he's fighting his fear to look. The faintest scrape of a glance.

"Make that 2:20 back!" Ma hollers.

Ezra'd stopped moving again. Standing motionless on the rubber carpet leading up to transition, staring at Casper staring past him.

"You good?" Ezra asks. He's abruptly aware of the I.D. in his pocket, the card's edges digging into the small of his back.

"2:25," Ma shouts, "and counting!"

He crosses the timing mat, his anklet chip chirping. His name—the kid's—Casper's—populates the twelfth row of the leaderboard behind the emcee. Ezra tucks that number away. Eleven athletes to chase down, but twelve's the number he remembers, inclusive—the one he'll count out on his fingers as he's passing them later. Because you've got to keep riding like there's one ahead, always. And there is; there's the far-end of your own limit, the specter of the best you can do. Not to mention the kid. 8:20. All day Casper's record will be ahead of him.

Ezra's Felt is the last bike on its rack. The rest of the top guys have cleared out the front row of transition. Ezra stoops to his space, as disarrayed as how he'd ditched it. He grabs a blind handful of gels and a gallon-jug of water from his backpack and inverts his whole tub of drink mix over his aerobottle. Stuffs some gels in his tri-suit and wheels the Felt a few strides before remembering his helmet. How many times had he run through this yesterday? Idiot. He stubs the buckle and clasp for a while, watching the digital clock at the transition exit. Fifty-seven minutes. The buckle clucks into the clasp and he's swearing, loathing himself past it.

But pulls off a fair flying mount. Comes down on the saddle like a pommel, pedaling the exact second that his wet ass squeaks onto the seat. Gets his feet into the shoes within fifty yards. And then it's head, hammer, chainring shifting down. He stays on the aerobars all the way out of the campground, twitching his elbows on the pads to dodge potholes. Hard lean into the turn around Fordham. His inside pedal scrapes the curb. His tires side-skip, but he tocks—Casper's word—and pulls himself out of the fall. Reflux of adrenaline. Another wasted match. He's pushing 370 watts, grinding in the big chainring. A low burn welling in his quads. Idiot. You wanted to hold the hurt in your torso this early. Contain it in your lungs. He upshifts and spins at a higher cadence, shifting the strain to his heartbeat and breathing.

Swings onto North Columbia and the long climb to Franklin Street and spots another cyclist. He's out of the saddle for the climb, straining as the road steepens. Ezra starts to stand, then drops back to the bike seat. *Settle.* Pressure like a hand between his shoulder blades. Back into this pedal-stroke. Adding up *now*'s. The cyclist's disc wheel whomps as loudly as his breath. Ezra rides in his draft until their tires are just-shy of touching, then swings out, lifting his index finger off the bars as he passes. The cyclist looks up the road, thinking Ezra's pointing—mistaking his count. One down. Eleven ahead, out of sight. And not one coyote.

The bike course is two loops. You take Franklin across the train-tracks to Carrborro, past the hoop skirts and co-ops until it trickles into Jones Ferry Road. Take that south down to 15-501, where the lead vehicle waits to escort the leader. Twenty miles snorting exhaust before hanging left up 54, the same climb they'd driven in by—the one that Ezra, last year, had bitten curb on—until you're gasping back through the blurt of Franklin Street. A sharp climb, a long drop, a longer climb. The elevation profile looks like a cursive *z* knocked on its side, a flourish of ligature ascribing that interminable final grade. Do the loop twice. Then your running shoes—but not yet. For now, just the ride. Pedal. Suck the straw. Excavate a gel from the saddlebag for a smear of carbs. Ezra tightens the rosary of his focus to breaths and heartbeats. Shrinks like that until a brave volunteer jogs into the road ahead of him shouting *left!*

The turnoff for Jones Ferry. Ezra clenches the brakes and still misses the turn, overshooting and coasting into a tottering one-eighty. Back around the volunteer, now shouting *fourth place!* Back into his lungs. This early discomfort's slight enough to contain in his chest. The real hurt will come later, a singeing stiffness burning out of his gut. It'll be in his fingertips by the end of the run. The smoke of his own self-consumption will clog his thoughts, blind his eyes, choke his breaths. *Settle.* Not yet.

This first part of Jones Ferry Road is the quietest stretch. Just his pedals and breath and the bleating of dawn insects. Mailboxes beak out of thick-grown pines. Houses set way back up indiscernible driveways. Still early for traffic. When the rare car squirts past, Ezra tucks in behind to get sucked by its slipstream. Swaybacked pickups loaded with manure or feed and one scrap metal rooster sculpture, the bungees binding its rebar talons looking like worms that it's pinning.

They all turn off and leave him riding into his shadow. His silhouette stays figureheaded in front of him, flung long with the low angle of sunrise. He appears to be overtaking that shade as the light climbs. The spilled carbohydrate powder is sweat-crusted and dried on the aerobars, sticking to his skinned palms. His saliva's thick with it.

The road straightens and flattens and the next rider's fifty yards ahead. He'd ridden up on the guy without seeing him, isolated in the course's winds. He's let his wattage lag to 250. He downshifts and churns. This early—near the lead—it's almost easy to forget he's racing.

"Derailleur's broke!" the guy hollers as Ezra overtakes him.

Ezra just glares at his power meter, not a word. Holding 300 watts. He feels the guy tucked in behind him. The passing zone's a single bike-length, and the onus is on the passed athlete to drop back. That usually only happens when a race martial pulls up. Unlikely they'll see one at all on the first lap; behind them there'll be pace-lines of age groupers stretching for miles. So here's this guy milking Ezra's slipstream.

He bears down some. Not a surge so much as a slow-drip, an acceleration too small to notice. The old lactate water torture. Wants to make this chode hurt for it. Ezra hears the chiropractic cracks of him downshifting (that derailleur abruptly repaired, apparently), then the glug of his disc wheel's slowing revolutions.

He makes a game of it. Won't check his power meter until his own pedaling drowns out this drafter's. He rides until he hears nothing but the chuff of his chainring, then keeps his eyes on the road. Little longer. Break it up. Holds himself off from checking until Jones Ferry gullets out to 15-501.

A lump of volunteers beckon him through the left turn, their orange shirts and purpose matching the traffic cones. They'll have the whole right lane of the highway for this stretch. This is the old part of the highway, in Pittsboro. Mowed yards that pout right down to the ditches on the shoulder. Streets named after what's at the end of them: Burkes Farm Drive, Mt. Gilead Church Street, Ellen Road.

The highway bloats to three lanes at the Chapel Hill city limit, growing ischemic with traffic. Lots of SUVs swelling past, domestic triptychs through their tinted windows. Side-eyes from the drivers. Backseats crammed with kids in soccer garb, bent to phones or shouting taunts or waving at him. Folding chairs stowed in the backs. To be sitting in a car sipping coffee, driving somewhere to sit longer: what a different version of Saturday. Musters of stick figures bumper-stickered on the bumpers of these vans like census data: mom, dad, son, son, daughter, dog. Ezra hopes they all lose games of hangman, aware that he's waxing ornery. He's coming up on the first cranky stretch. For the next ten miles or so he'll see the bastard in everyone before going giddy or slanting into self-loathing. His emotions will shuffle like this for the rest of the day, shifting faster with fatigue. At some point on the run, they'll start overlapping. He'd blubber and laugh over Dairyland Road, a sock-and-buskin of conflicting sentiment. And no audience. *Settle.* Except that one: every step he'll be carrying Benji.

Now the burn's in Ezra's legs. *Idiot.* 340 watts on the power meter. Another match. He eases back, but the heat stays. Forty miles covered at a 25.7 mph average. He'd been averaging 24 last year. Casper'd held 25 flat, ridden 4:28. Ezra's sluggish swim and transition had lost him ninety seconds to Casper's split, but he'll ride 4:21 at this pace. That'll have him starting the run with five minutes on Casper. Casper'd covered the marathon in 2:43, meaning Ezra'd need to run—

"Stop!" he shouts, then regrets the lost air. Bounces his helmet off the aero-bottle, gasping his breath back. *Now.* Has to body back down. He grabs the power meter with one hand and yanks. His wattage makes a stuttering plunge, then disappears from the screen. He snaps the meter off the handlebars with one final jerk, swerving. Honks and squawking brakes as he lists into the left lane. Another squirt of adrenaline, kerosene through his intestines.

Huh.

Leave your brain, Tootsie.

Bark on, RoboCop.

That last is the voice Ezra clings to. Conjures pictures of the kid wrestling him in the cabin; flat with sleep; the two of them sucking wind in the bed of the pickup, never more than a few footsteps shy of side-by-side. Maybe that's why Ezra hadn't missed Ma—for the first time in his life he hadn't been laterally lonely. There was Casper to commiserate in the training, their aching as tangled as the mullet that put it to them. Then—with another spurt of adrenaline—Ezra finds the word Casper'd muttered that morning. The one he'd gulped as slyly as a burp, trapping it behind his teeth:

Brothers.

Casper

Not shamed to say I've felt hotter. Ma reckons we'll bike up to Franklin to catch Ez, long's I can perch. But I got this awful cold case of the shakes. Same shivers that chattered me awake this dark morning. Can't work a warm up, yet my pits and forehead are sopping. The ground's already tick-tocking. And I just know I'm fixing to tip if I ride, so I lean on the varm. "What'll Shiela ride?"

Ma squints a good second, then smacks her own forehead like she's the one feeling fevered. "The dog!"

"Ez needs to see her."

"Absolutely."

So sure, I'm shamed some about my condition, but it is true that Ez's sweet on the varm. That he'll want her yapping when he passes. Ma tosses me some-them Tylenol and water and minds me to swallow. I snug into shotgun with Shiela and chew the pills anyway. We van out of the campground at about an inch an hour. My sweat does start to ebb, but my stump is sure smarting. I pet Shiela so it seems she's the one whimpering.

"What's up?" Ma asks.

"Ask her."

Benji sheared rams, and Ma was a sheep, but the scapegoat for all my weakness is this little lap-draping dog. She does warm like a blanket. She does lick my stump. Her tongue tickling my skin covers up the hurt under it.

We inch past the gatehouse, where I see my buddy duck. RoboCops ride out of the campground beside us. Never did see how you could drop a few thousand dollars on your bicycle when you got a potbelly. Ought to save your money and buy less-them burgers if you want to save time. Instead Robos prefer to hem and haw over seat angles and cadence and drag what-alls while they're stuffing face with Hardee's Whoppers. Never gone hungry a day. Never had something to run from, so they jog. That's why none-them can hurt like me. I roll down my window and spit at them with all my hate.

"I told you not to chew them," Ma says.

It's a crunch of cars all the way up to Franklin. Ever other spectator's got the same idea as us: roost up at the corner where the gargoyles perch the big church and catch who-all you're rooting for riding by on that long slog up from the highway. It's your lungs and legs yapping on the first lap, then the whole of you on the second, muting out even the crowd. Same spot I snatched the lead from Ez last year. Then for a lap it was just me and the lead vehicle, and the guy driving leaned out and hollered back, *who're you?* Which what do you say to that question. Hollered back I'd been asking that, too. Then I poured it on till I could've slapped his bumper and he stomped the gas to keep from out of his slipstream. Like I needed to draft. And I'm tiring, my limbs ladening just from minding back to that race. Could not pay me to hop a mile, how I'm feeling. Too cold to move. Shiela shakes my hand off her head and snaps at it. Blood like a bunch of ladybugs in her fur. I got to petting too hard, scalping them scabs where she got bit. She hops out my lap and curls to the floorboard where my left leg ought-be and I think I'd take her as that leg's replacement, because the varm's got born juke in her.

But I do not envy after them cyclists streaming past. Want to tell them Percs would get them the same place they're aiming without the gear or the daylong moving or the Port-a-Johns or the race entry fee. They're all really doing it for the droop that comes when they're done: how after it's over you can sag down wherever you are like it's a jacuzzi, cozy in the leftover heat of your moving. But that'd mean less Percs for me. And I'm already waiting to get more. Already I'm eyeing the CVS up ahead as Ma pulls past closed meters, cones thwarting her parking.

We cross onto MLK and can't find a spot. Turn into a neighborhood where ever other yard's gotten converted to a pay-by-
the-day parking lot. But it's Bethlehem all along. College kids
half-stand out their folding chairs, waving us past. Then Ma
squawks the tires, swerving us down a block. Pulls into a damned
Hardee's parking lot. Swear I hear the universe snorting.

"What's your order?" she asks, braking into handicapped.

"Nuts."

"Someone's got to eat something."

"Shiela's hungry."

Ma comes back with a chicken biscuit and a receipt. Puts the
receipt on the dashboard like a parking permit. Then she scoops
a scatter of old tickets out the glovebox and pins them under the
windshield wipers. Shiela's got her ears cocked through this all,
sniffing after that biscuit, which Ma's set on the hood of the van
like a taunt. At last Ma brings it around-down to shotgun. Lays
it right there in the floorboard and she gargles it, more drinking
than eating.

Now we're posted. Ma hops back in and I tip back my seat.
We can see the bikers coming by a block up. It's the tail-end
riding out now, the real totterers.

"Look at this snail," Ma says. "Got his helmet on backwards."

I watch him pedaling, his knees going wide ever time they
rise up. Nightmare for the meniscus. My stump's still yapping
too loud to conjure a good joke, but Ma's punchy—maybe from
nerves for Ez. "Or his head," I say. She cracks up.

We settle in for some heckling. If Ezra's going good, we'll
see him at nine thirty. I'm only getting worser, solacing myself
by pretending I'm draining some-his hurt. If that's the case he'd
already be coming by, because that block up to Franklin Street
looks longer and more booby-trapped to me with ever next minute passing. I grow Ez-like as the clock climbs, squirming at the
prospect of walking. Wanting to get the hurt over with. I swing
my door out at nine, Shiela and Ma whipping their heads to me.

"Let's mosey."

"Little early."

"Gotta stake us a spot."

"Huh." Ma glances up the block at my looming lie: it's just the last stragglers trickling by, the crowd thinned in proportion to the athletes. "When'd you take that Tylenol?"

I shrug.

She spanks out two of the grainy others, the tabs Ez brought for me. "It's fine to chew these."

She dredges a couple camper chairs out the back while I do. Red and a green. "Want one?"

"Naw."

She sets the green by the sliding door. Then the crutch.

The mere seeing it grudges me. I kick-spit out of shotgun. Ma slides her door back and steps down with her chair. I lag a look at it. The fabric kind that scrunches up, like the ones Ms. Ida brought for my swim meets. Ma reaches back and pulls the green.

"Want the red one."

"I'm bringing both."

"Lemme hold it."

She hands the red over. I prop it under my left arm.

"Go on," I say, and she goes.

I go slower. Got the chair in one hand and the other leashing Shiela. I lean into the chair when I swing my full leg, planting my one foot and dragging up the peg-leg, swinging the chair past it to prop the next step. She's got the idea the chair's bait I'm laying out. Ever time I prod it down she lunges, wringing her neck on the stretchy band of her leash.

Ma glances back when she comes out on Franklin Street. "Want a hand?"

"Got them."

"I can grab Shiela."

I quit coming till she turns, then anger the chair down all the harder, which just rowdies Shiela. Dog's leaping and pawing and gnashing that stretchy band—puppy-hearted, but barbed with varm's fangs. This stretchy band's about chewed through. I mind to tell Ma that soon's I get up to her. She's peeking back again now.

"Don't look!" I holler. Won't be a circus for nobody

She slows back around.

I toss off the chair and wobble on with Shiela pouncing circles. The stretchy band tangles my peg leg and yanks it out from under me. Next thing I'm sprawled and she's dragging slobber over my stump. The stitches split and I kick at the sting, but hit her. She hunches back whimpering. My shame out-yaps my gone leg. Shiela was just puppying. Following instructions, even: stitches did look like one-them dotted lines showing where to cut. She backs off, the stretchy band slithering out my grip. Before I can reach, Ma's forking her wrists through my armpits.

"Quit off. Grab the leash."

Ma takes a step and Shiela shirks her. Ma lunges and she dodges, snaps at her arm.

"Motherfucker," Ma whispers.

A growl bubbles up in Shiela. I lay my face down and crawl toward her, head-hanging all the weight of apology. Her growl drops. She sniffs my arm as I lean it out toward the stretchy band. Then Ma lunges to stomp it and off Shiela darts. Ma's foot comes down on my reaching fingers.

She jumps off. "Oh, Love—"

I swat off her hands as they flutter down, pointing my stomped fingers after Shiela. "Go!"

But Ma just braces one hand on her bald brow and takes a knee. Takes a breath like the front-end of a sob, only holds it instead, and that gulp tugs at me like a leash. To leave her head-hanging here would just tear my heartstrings. I long a look up the block after Shiela, then look back and pet Ma.

"Go," I say again, but this time like *go on*.

She just shakes her head. And for the first time I think of all the yapping cocooning her: the wrong 'surance, Kure getting flooded with ocean and reporters and varms, and biking through

Alaskanada stranding Ez with me and Benji. Only Ez wanted that. And me. I'm trying-chew all that into words when Shiela sniffs back to me. A hairy-footed pair of flip-flops slaps up behind her.

"This your dog?" A man stern-staring down, bald above the ankle. All hair from his head to his legs seems slunk down to his feet. "She ran right out onto Franklin. Glad there wasn't traffic."

I gaum an arm around Shiela.

"Saw y'all at the campground," he says. "Nearly came over and said something. You know this—" he lifts the stretchy band—"this *freaking crap* is hurting her. You try putting it around your neck." But puts his own head through the end. "Ever tried that?"

"Just extension cords." That gets Ma and him staring alike at me.

The man shakes his head, which tugs at the stretchy band, which hoarsens Shiela's panting. He ducks out of it and drops it to me. "Buy a *freaking* leash."

I tell his back to have a blessed day. My head, stump, and shame are all yapping, but no grudge. I start to wonder if I only ever used anger as one more crutch, a thing propping me up when I had to keep moving. But now I got a home to get still in. My own place to stay.

I hug all my sorry into Shiela, then turn some comfort to Ma, but she's already standing. Let her fork hands under my arms.

"This okay?"

I don't swat. She gets me up on my foot, then sticks the peg-leg back under me. I let her take the leash, too. She ducks under my arm and we walk up to Franklin that way. The green chair's open and sweat-damp up the back. How long was she waiting while I wobbled? She eases me into the red chair. "How's your hand?"

Bruises swell the fingers she stepped on. The pointer's nail cracked like lightning. "Got the other. But my stump's yapping some." I kick it up and flick blood.

Her hand covers her mouth. "Gonna grab the First Aid kit."

"And Percs?" My voice jumps out when she turns, like her turning's what's tugging it. "Don't leave me!" Shout that before I even catch up with the feeling. She covers her mouth again, turning back. "Gimme Shiela." I pat my lap and Shiela hops up on me.

Ma squints at us settling. "Got her?"

"I'm holding on."

She unhands the stretchy band. "I'll be back in a sec."

I squeeze my arms tight around Shiela. Hugging something feels like getting hugged when you're fragile, the same cozy comfort. And I'm fragile. Fixing to drift. So I squeeze a whimper out of Shiela. I let on like I'm holding her, but really she's holding me.

Shiela's ear perks. Her throat tenses with hearing. She jerks her snout south for long seconds before the cheering and cowbells louden to me. The crowd still around lean off the sidewalk, flapping signs as the lead vehicle norths along Franklin Street. The road behind it looks empty. Only when the car pulls even do I see the lead cyclist ducked up to its bumper. Not Ez. It's that stretchy-band-built feller Wispy. His arm warmers hitched up to half-cover his race number, just showing the fishhook out of the 2. I snatch a glance of his face smooth as sleep. His eyes good as closed, too. Drafting off that bumper he's ducked up to, not-seeing. Not a race martial to cite him. The driver's not saying nuts, either.

"Learn a bike length!" I holler.

Wispy stays hitched to the car's slipstream, zenning.

Then Ez. Shiela gives a sniff and a jerk and I feel him through her, feel his welling hurtening and heatening like ever instant I ran ahead of him. Never had to look back to know how far he was behind, nor hear his slurping breathing. I could tell how big my lead was by tightness—how a muscle bunches tighter against a stretch, this sinewy tension tugging backer with every step I stole ahead. Now I feel his coming like a cramp easing, the opposite. Shiela's straining in my arms and I'm losing my grip because the nearer Ez gets the less squeeze I have left, my muscles are giving all their contracting to his. I tangle the stretchy band round my arm as he whomps into view, looking like he's got all the hot I haven't been feeling.

Slurping breaths. Bloodbearded from his split lip, hurt-heat rising off him like steam. And I don't got enough *go* to stand or clap or cheer, even. He might still down if I shout for him anyhow, like the start and swim exit; then I epiphany that it's better for him not to see me. I skooch the chair around on the sidewalk. Shiela's bursting with yapping and wagging her whole spinal column. The chair's legs scuttle and it tips. My noggin cracks off the sidewalk and I'm looking at sky, headache and sun just bright-blinding.

I chest my chin and look past squirming Shiela. Ezra throttles them aerobars with both hands like that branch. That night the trap bit me. Hurt so big it choked out all my senses except that bunching distance between him and me. Ez's closeness smoothed my lungs down just enough to keep breathing. I sucked the air flung by the branch he was swinging, cozy in the space he was clearing for me. My arms loose. Then the gone weight of Shiela.

She bark-bounds after Ez and he goes glanceless. Doesn't seem to hear, even. A few folks make to chase her and a few stoop to me. Even as I swat them off and watch Shiela go I can't trim my grin because Ez is zenning. And I know then that he'll ride right past Wispy. He won't be scared to lead; might not even notice he is. All he'll see is my ghost reeling him. I ain't stupid. I know that's what he's chasing.

I tip up to my foot and peg-leg and watch him speck, shrinking even smaller than shrinking Shiela. The folks who made to chase her have long circled back, walking toward me with the shrugging shame of the dusted. I wobble past them with my peg-leg jabbing into my stump, but all my yapping's as gone as my clumsy. In one sudden I'm rolling into a run. Set my stare onto dog-Shiela and roll, moving how I been fixing to ever since first wanting to show Shiela Petey.

Ezra bends gone up the road and dog-Shiela slows. Throws a glance back in feel of me coming. Her tail jolts. She shakes herself like tired's water she can flick off her fur, then low-runs up a side-street.

I slant off the road to try and hypotenuse to her. Cut through some woods sliding over pine needles. Reckon I'll head her off a block up. Roots and weeds gnash my good and peg-leg and swallow me back into that night I stepped in the spring trap. They break me down to that time's raw components, the brainless effort of fevered moving. My head fills up with heartbeats. Thoughts of Ma and Ez drown in my thumping blood; I'm back in my old home, the den of my body. I just run. Quit even looking for Shiela. But then I mind why I'd run into those other woods in the first place: I'd been looking for Benji. That squirming thought spoils it. I fold over with my stump full of my heartbeat. Swear I can feel the work-hurt even past it, down my gone calf to my foot's ghost.

No sign of Shiela. I walk out the woods calling for her. Long tangle through bendy roads. Lumpy hills crowned with houses. Knotted streets. My sinking pulse beaches my chill and next thing I'm wobbling, shivering. Cheers smear down a rise. I turn up the street and see cyclists flashing. I tip toward them and whiff meat and sunscreen. My gut plunges.

Here's my truck.

He sits on the hood, the whole front sagging under him. Parked on this corner like he's been waiting. Worse: like this is where I've been coming.

"Hips forward," he says, them damn Oakleys spitting me back at me.

I try-halt, but my reflection keeps going. "Where's Shiela?"

"Who?"

"You got her." The squirm in me just knows. "Give her. What'd you do."

Benji holds his palm out to me. And I'm trying not to come

with ever bone even as I watch myself grow in the mirrors of his Oakleys. I put my head down and he rubs it.

"Missed that," he says. His callouses prickle my buzzcut. And I squirm even as I press into them, hating that I missed it too. Strands of mullet spit-stuck to his lips. He pinches some into his mouth to suck. "Saw RoboCop."

"Don't call—"

"Didn't. And he wouldn't've heard if I did. He was zenning when he went by." The hair in his mouth curls with his grin, looking like strings lifting his lips. "I thought he was you."

"Is."

Benji drips off the hood. That damp hair. That dribbling basketball belly. I wag my peg-leg, baiting him—daring him to say something. Fixing to lay all my rage on him soon's he does. Soon's he glances at it, even. But I can't see where he's looking.

"Quit them glasses."

Benji walks around-side the driver's. I lurch after him on longing, but grind my peg-leg into my stump to squish the need.

"Gonna drive on out to the run course. Gotta get to him." Benji swings his hand at the wall of the truck bed and swallows. His hand drops, but I know he was fixing to tell me to hop in. Both us want it. But I'm not about to let on if he isn't.

"Give me Shiela."

I peer into the truck cab in search of her. Burger wrappers and food crumbs in the seats. Another turn of my gut to picture him making that mess. Aside from his hair, Benji never let us see him eating. Thought of him chowing down in my truck— Adam's truck—makes my insides feel filthy. Then the picture worsers: what if he was feeding someone else all that food? Letting them sit in the passenger's like we never could, telling them what to eat. Telling his secret name. Feeding the hair to them. A shame-hate brews from my filthy feeling. The same brimming rage I felt finding that picture in Adam's phone, that fist-pinched dick under texts I was glad I couldn't read. I swung a double-edged hate at him, cutting myself with it, too—because

I didn't even like touching him, yet up came Mr. Sob's toady friend jealousy. A toad's a landlubbing frog, and jealousy's like dry crying—a crinkled heat hurtening my windpipe. Hurts twice that to think of Benji bossing someone other than me.

"Coming?" he says.

"Shut of being told."

"I said if you want."

I'm still beg-baiting him to look at my stump, but them mirrored lenses hide his eyes behind more of me. All our time in Kure was just like that: like he was looking out my own eyes, using my head as his living room. Knowing my ever craving and squirm like its furniture. His hand slides off the bed. The smear of damp from his palm matches the one on the hood where he was sitting. "Did I find you a home?"

I nod.

"Do you like it?"

I try not, but the truth hops up. "Yes."

"I never made you do anything. I only invited you."

And he's right. He only ever named what I wanted, sometimes before I even knew it. He swings the driver's door open. Climbs in and I stand there, itching to hop into that truckbed. I lean on the hood, kicking off my peg-leg. Mopping my stump over the damp left by his sliding. The grill nicks my loose stitches.

He's still got the driver's door open. Talking through it. "She'll come back if you leave her."

"What?"

"Your dog. If you gave her a home. She'll whine right back when she sees you're not chasing her."

I hoist my stump up on the hood, lay it out like a hunting trophy. If he'll just look. When he does, I don't even know what I'm fixing to do.

"Can't ride up there," he says.

"Ain't coming."

He leans his head out.

"Don't want to." Hating that I do. Hating more that he beat me to knowing, which is exactly why I *do* want to: hard not to follow someone who shows you to you.

"Should I back up, then?" he says.

I let my stump slide off the hood, but stay leaning on the truck.

He tucks his head back in the cab. "I'll just pull around." But his door's still open. Truce.

"Ever get a ram that couldn't get up?" I ask.

"What?"

"After you shaved them. Did one ever fight out all its run?"

"The rams," he says. His eyebrows hop up above his Oakleys. "Forgot I told you."

And real sudden I see another first: now it's me sitting in the furniture of his head. He gave me a thing more secret than his name when he told about them sheep. Wonder if he'd even meant to. I think back to the dank drive to Urgent Care when he'd whispered it, probably thinking me deaf from fever. "Well, did you?"

"Not once." His voice kisses me. "Only for you, sweetie."

Then his door shuts. I hop off to the side holding my peg-leg and just wobble. Still wagging my stump, daring him, fixing to. Shame-hoping he'll suck it like my heel, maybe. He rolls past at the same pace as he drops all the windows. Brakes when the shotgun-side one's level to me.

"Thanks," I say. "For the home."

Only in the after of those words do I know that thanking him's exactly what I've been fixing to do. Feel a long-fraying rope snap. Watch my head slant in his sunglasses. I lean into the window, but only to pop my peg-leg back onto my stump. Then I'm perched on my own two.

Benji slants his own head like he's trying to keep my reflection from spilling out the lenses. "I only invited you."

He rumbles to the intersection with the left blinker twitching. As he stops, his own window unrolls. He sticks his fist out, then three fingers, like he's tallying ghosted varms—only now he's counting something live and new. He keeps it hanging through his turn, out-of-sighting up Franklin, and nothing tows at me. The rope's snapped. I let him go without the slightest wish to move.

Benji

Driving out to the run course—away from the kid—as leg-hard, as lung-sharp as running. Mustering all your *here* not to plunge into the cocoon. Can't look back. The kid's stump. How he'd dangled it in front of you. Urgent for you to take that hurt and hold it. You'd bitten his leg off when the picture came into your phone, gnawing it every time your eyes closed—digesting that mangled fact for two weeks. Whirlpooling into the Everywhen. Bobbing back up in the wake of Ezra riding past, sweat-damp and heart-cramped from long-waiting. Then the kid was rubbing his head on your hand again, the prickle of that stubble conjuring the past months back up as richly as a scent-memory. And the waft of what he'd asked. That question like a phero-mone from a sex gland, a pungent flash: why and when had you told him about the rams running?

Your last spring on Unc's farm had been dawn-to-stars swel-tering. Zone Championships fell on shearing week. Unc stayed home while you covered morning practices, claiming he'd squint-ed into enough sunrises. His cataracts were as pale-bright as their accumulation: seemed to flare when you looked at him. You squinted at him through your sunglasses. The swimmers squinted at you while you laid out their workouts—a thirteen-year-old who'd been swimming in the slow lane two years ago giving na-tional record holders instructions. You brandished Unc's binder, pretending to read. But you were giving them a steeper taper than he ever had, plummeting their yardage to freshen them for the end of the season. Back to the farm by eight to sweat with the sheep. The tin shed ovened with a hundred head's flailing heat. And you fresh off the pool deck, your own sweating neck itching from hay dust and chlorine. You never knew which work you were scratching. The swimmers squirmed with the dissipating fatigue just as badly as the rams sweating under their fleece. Both were hard to keep your hands on. The swimmers were sneaking in extra yards, craving snug exhaustion; even if they weren't doubting you they'd've done it, eager for the blanketing warmth of soreness. They'd've sabotaged their own races for the sake of that fix. You didn't blame them: you still pinched your toes, running the dawn hot in chase of fatigue every morning. But Unc called the whole squad out to the farm for a lesson when he heard them complaining. If they were going to squander their recovery, they could do it more productively: let them help wrangle the sheep.

Unc gave you the shears. The first ram thrashed into a panic as you stepped into the corral with it. Unc blamed your blood— said they could smell the coyote you'd come from—but thrust the gate shut with the blunt shove of a lesson; it was you, not the swimmers, he was set on teaching.

The ram roiled in its wool. Its withers rose like chop through its back. It took four swimmers ten minutes to exhaust it. You waited until it settled under their combined pin. None looked all the way at you when you drooped the shearers down to it. You kept on your sunglasses. The wool frothed off the ram's flanks as pale and wet as the spittle it gasped. All fight seemingly panted out of it. But as soon as the swimmers let it up, the ram bolted, rushing through the gate before Unc even had it half-open.

Unc nodded after it. "That one still had some run."

The lesson: exhaustion was always a decision.

The rest of the rams went the same. Surrendering to fatigue and the shears, then sprinting as soon as the swimmers stepped away. Unc hung a tenderloin in the shed and it cured by the heat of your bodies. You buzzed a piece off with the shears. Unc licked his own sweat to salt it, but your sweat left your throat raw from chlorine. Gum-cutting, tongue-parching jerky. Wool coiled across the rusty shears, inverse of the blood coiling between your clenching teeth. You sheared every sheep; a hundred writhing heads of them rushing off as soon as they were let up. Gnawing your jaw sore on that tenderloin. The front of your neck and the throats of your wrists cramping equally. The work was done before you'd chewed the meat down enough to swallow. The sinews curling like split ends inside your cheek.

That was how you learned they'd always have more to give. There was an accord between the beaten brain and nerves: the brain believed the nerves' burning exhaustion. Fatigue settled them like a blanket—exactly what stilled the swimmers. They were cozy in the lie of their perfect exhaustion. Like Unc's magic, knowing it spoiled it. When had you told the kid? All those nights words had snuck through your hums. The hair spell. The cocoon. He'd been holding as much of your hurt as you'd held his for him.

You'd never meant to tell him. You'd never meant to let Ezra swallow your hair, either. The wrong reflexes. Those lies were its own kind of blankets: like the sheep, you couldn't rest if you believed you'd intended. But it had slaked something in you to see both of them still moving.

The dumb throb of Ezra's nostrils when he'd ridden past you, taking the lead without flinching. A position you could never quite coax him into. Always figured he'd needed something in front of him. There'd been that greyhound track in West Memphis where the rail broke; your whippet ran blindly past the pack while the rest growled over the lure. So you'd spelled some of that same stuff into Ezra. Part dog, but some ram in him too.

Then the kid. That strut of a run he'd come up to you with, brandishing the gross stump in front of him; he already hadn't had enough limbs to keep up with his motor to begin with. How'd he ever settle down if he knew there was flight left in him? He'd lost his leg because of you. For you. Chasing after you. That photo of him caught in the trap is still trapped behind your eyelids. Displayed, maybe—you'd thrown your phone out the window less because of the kid's mangled shin than the pride it brought you as proof of how far you'd pushed him.

Of course, you'd meant to tell him about the rams: you'd been greedy for him to keep moving. Shadefoot can never settle down, either. Only exists in footprints. Curl your toes on the gas pedal, shrinking into the kid's. A tendon-tug to hunch into the shape of him. That means you've almost ruined Ezra; he let you into his bloodstream when he looked back at you. His every heartbeat spreads more of you through him. You've got to get him to stop moving before your burst him. You've got to fill him more completely. No different than gasping water your first time in Unc's cocoon, your will thwarted by your reflexes. You've known how to save him all along, but your greedy needs kept you from doing it. One more trick on yourself. Just a little longer. Another mile. Another month. More of you welling up, the fitness you put in him accumulating. Magic only works on those who don't know how it's working. All you have to do to break the spell is explain yourself to him.

Drive the truck out to do it. Jostle across throbbing asphalt, oak roots bulging like a pulse through a wrist. Past the patchouli cloud fogging Carrboro. Out to the empty sprawl of Dairyland Road and you're sobbing to see him; whether you stop him or push him on, you know this will be the last time that you do.

Ezra

The hurt's reaching his cajones. It's welled out of his lungs and muscles by now, brimming under his cuticles, seeping into the last of his extremities. He's back on 15-501, urging his wheel toward the bumper of the lead vehicle. In the car's rearview he sees Wispy a precise bike-length behind him, a barnacle of Lycra and carbon fiber attached to the legal end of his slipstream. Fine. Ezra's too concave to be bothered by the guy, low in the flooding hull of his body.

The lead car honks and parted a pace-line of ten-speeds. They're lapping the first of the stragglers. The etiquette's to move right, but these riders swerve clumsily to either side, wrapping Ezra in a gauntlet of gasping cheering. Ought'v'e saved their oxygen. These folks won't stumble in from the marathon until midnight. Ezra can't picture moving for seventeen hours any more than they can conceive covering the course at his speed; in that mutual bafflement is a kind of allegiance.

A lady in a singlet sloganed *Iron Granny* hollers, "Kill it!"

"You!" Ezra hollers back; wincing, revises. "Beat me to it!"

The first and the last. He speeds past cyclists with Reese's Cups taped to their handlebars, a guy eating a peanut butter sandwich with one hand. He'll see that again on the run.

"Want a bite?" he shouts as Ezra zips around on him.

He turns it down with a thumbs-up.

"On your left!" Wispy hollers, swinging wide to pass.

He's put a bike-length between them before Ezra can brake to drop back. Idiot. He's let his pace slouch again. Wispy's shoulders rock with the full-body force of his pedaling. Ezra bears down, but carefully. Steady drip. The road lifts and Wispy surges blatantly, standing out of the saddle. Ezra stays seated, but the asphalt between them is shrinking. He slows out of the passing zone and the hurt ebbs from his fingertips. Could've held his breath at this pace. So he downshifts. Before the gears even bite into the chainring he's bridged the gap. Wispy glances over his right shoulder like he thinks Ezra might try to sneak around him, fulfilling his own unsportsmanlike prophecy. Ezra passes to his left just as fast as Wispy'd whipped around. Ezra watches him bob in the lead vehicle's rearview, still standing. Sees him plops back into the saddle and shrink. His helmet, then his head, then his legs rise above in the plane of the rearview as he falls back, appearing to be ascending. Takes Ezra a few seconds to sift the true physics from this illusion. He's deep enough in now, every sensation frayed by the strain of breathing and beating. *Miles to go before...sixty seconds' worth...* The Frost and Kipling conflating. The words tangle and repeat with each pedal-stroke, another rosary brushed by his cadence.

15-501 leaves the church-and-house part of town, thickening through strip malls and gas stations. El Cazador. Coin Laundry. Big E's Pawn and Gun. Apartment complexes like barracks. Shouts smear out of passing cars' windows. Kids lean out flashing peace signs and probable gang symbols. The highway bends back up to run flush with I-40. Neat rungs of noise-buffering pines behind the buildings to his right, buffering the scrum of the interstate. Billboards rise past their canopy like eyebrows. Soon he'll be hanging that awful left onto Raleigh Road, fighting that last awful climb up to Franklin Street. But now. *Now.* It's just him and the hurt out here.

And Casper. The kid's ghost fills every empty inch of the road ahead. The sheer weight and shape of an absence. What was it the kid said about the coyotes? Don't look for, look around. See them in the paw prints and holes dug under fences. Look at the kid's leg, Ezra's body; don't look at those texts on the dead phone and see Benji. *Overload, Tootsies. Born skittish.* It always whirlpools back to this, Benji's voice eddying in his head. Just like those nights in the boat cabin: Benji, Casper's ghost, and him. Ezra isn't ready to be alone with them again.

So he lets his breaths settle. He slows. Leaning onto Raleigh Road he throws a glance back like a cast. Wispy's less than a speck on the road. A half-mile back, maybe. But Ezra swears the guy's head rises as he turns his: fishhook swallowed. Ezra sits up, gulps a gel. Stands to stretch, sighing the clenched backs of his knees. He coasts until Wispy sinks back into the plane of the rearview and finds his legs caulked when he downshifts again. Wispy rides up and tucks in an exact bike-length behind him. He'd been right behind the lead vehicle's bumper when Ezra caught up to him, a reasonable moral distinction: there's a difference between drafting off of a car and getting towed along by another rider, easing your own burden at the expense of their speed. Ethics aside, Ezra's glad for the company. Not quite next time. Ditch him on the run. Maybe. For now he wants Wispy right here to drown out his own insides, that anatomical symphony composed and conducted by Benji.

They stay like that through the crowd and the climb. Wispy rides loose-jawed while Ezra grinds, unable to shake the stiffness from holding up for him. He wobbles the handlebars, swerving his trajectory. Wispy keeps sitting up like he thinks Ezra's dodging obstacles. He's soft-pedaling, but refusing the lead.

The sky drips right down to the road when they reach Franklin Street. Tar Heel country. In this neck, all outdoor activities are excuses to sport Carolina blue. Sweatshirted folks spill banners off of sidewalks to goad or greet them. Ezra doesn't read the banners' slogans. Doesn't look twice at t-shirts tied tourniquet-tight around Kappa pledges' scant midriffs. That his own waist is smaller than any of theirs is the only thought the sight stirs. His own hurricane effort's all that he's hearing, the crowd's shouts drowned by the gale of his breathing. The lead vehicle drops onto Cameron and he jerks after it, arcing wide enough that his outside pedal clips the far curb. Wispy cuts past on his inside, leaning low through the tangent. His shout splits the storm in Ezra's head.

"Lost count?"

A blank of noise before Ezra chisels the words, his brain as sluggish with English as a second language. Another beat until he catches the gist: he'd been riding like he was about to start a third lap, aiming straight past the turnoff for the campground. Shit. Idiot.

They're coming up on the end of the bike. Like that, the weight of the miles behind him burden him again. And here Wispy is with his ass shoved way back on the saddle, slanting into curves like he's skiing, trying to open up a gap on the downhill. Ezra lets him have it, used to this. They go on while you lag. There's no rope to drag him over the asphalt today. He'll accept the comfort of the position he's cozy in: second. The number he'd've worn if he'd been racing under his real name.

Wispy's gained a hundred yards when they level onto the Fordham. The lead car pulls off at the gatehouse and his disc wheel vanishes into the campground.

Ezra makes the same turn and enters a dome of commotion. Cowbells and vuvuzelas, Twisted Sister on the loudspeakers. The pines trap the cacophony like a blister under their canopy. The emcee's shouting, despite his microphone. "Give it up for our race leader!"

Ezra can't see Wispy up the curve of the road; can't yet see the transition, but swears he hears Wispy's feet smack the ground as he dismounts.

"It's our swim leader George Wispler first off the bike. George, nice seeing you again."

Ezra's scanning for Casper and Ma in the crowd, off the aerobars and soft-pedaling again. Idiot. Needs to bring himself down, back into his body. In a minute he'll have to jump off of the bike and remember bipedalism. Then the run. *Now* the run. The transition entrance looms before he's gotten his feet out of his cycling shoes. He has to unclip and put a foot down at the dismount line. Hops on it as he fights to free the other shoe, straddling the bike. He winds up in a split with the bike laid down under him. Wispy's bobbing toward the exit already, running like he's forgotten the past five hours of swimming and cycling.

"Record pace!" the emcee hollers.

Ezra wobbles into transition. The furrows between empty bike racks seeded with running shoes. His own are still in his backpack. He hooks the Felt on the rack and braces his forehead next to it, the world going white as he bends to fumble with his cycling shoes. Okay. Velcro. Unzip the backpack. He plunges through the wrong compartment for a while before finding the racing flats. Leans hard into the rack to stomp into them. Sitting would be so much easier, but he wouldn't get up if he sat. He slaps and tugs at the tongues and shuffles toward the exit.

"Casper Swayze!"

The emcee's voice striking Ezra like a match; finally, a punctual one. This is his next time. The ground he's covering becomes a wedge. Each next step he takes widens. Coming out of transition he's reached some semblance of a run, shedding stiffness like snakeskin. Shoves the timing clock to keep from reading it. A volunteer lunges as it tips. Ezra rasps, "Sorry." His anklet chirps over the mat and the emcee cuts across the soundtrack with his split.

"Shut up!" Ezra shouts. Desperate to get brainless.

Out of the campground, Wispy getting taller ahead. His legs bend like fangs behind him. That long backbone. Those gnashing strides. Two for every one of Ezra's, yet Ezra's running right into that underbite. He tucks in out of habit—all those miles behind Casper. But this shoulder's too tall to look over. Wispy's huge back censors the road ahead. Ezra doesn't even see the aid station until it's beside him. Wispy grabs every cup. Ezra reaches and misses the tardy one that gets shoved at him. The volunteer sprints to keep pace, spilling it as she thrusts it at him. The cup's empty when Ezra tips it back. He tosses it at the upcoming mile mark. Wispy checks his watch, disguising a look back as he flares out his wrist. But Ezra catches his glance; also, a gob of Gatorade-sweetened spit.

Past the gatehouse together. Up Frat Row toward Franklin. Lawns pimpled with solo cups, earmuffed with dueling sound systems. Cackles and shrieks and nods and bird-chested freshman sloshing beer on them. The grade steepens. Wispy's strides lose their bite, flowing like ribbons behind him, Ezra half-stepping to keep from tangling in them. He sneaks another look at Ezra over his shoulder, checking his watch again, and Ezra gets the hunch that they're nearing the next aid station. He comes up on Wispy's right shoulder, sliding between him and the curb. Sure enough, the volunteers are right there on the corner. Fraternity brands on every arm stretching cups at him. Ezra grabs the first from a guy with his volunteer shirt bandana'd around his head. Wispy reaches his long arm across Ezra's chest instead of dropping back, holding it there like he's restraining him. He knocks the next three cups out of the volunteers' hands before grabbing the last one to quench himself with. Ma's old tactic. The friendliness Wispy'd approached him with in transition—the grudging fairness he'd shown dropping out of Ezra's slipstream—has corroded. Extremis has him ruthless, cruel with fatigue.

But Ezra's steady. Yes, heavy-legged, balloon-knotted intestines, but not straining. He drops back, taking chopping strides, yet his feet now hit the ground at the same rate as Wispy's. The guy's form is going the same way as his manners. His long legs push him just as upward as forward, his calf tendons bunching and contracting under his skin like springs. More like Slinkies, maybe. He seems to be folding backwards more than progressing. But Ezra hangs back. There's a lot of road left. Plenty of miles run head-on into the misery.

They turn left onto West Cameron. The brickwalk's coned off for them, though they have the whole street to themselves. The crowd's still watching the bikes go by a block north on Franklin. Wispy keeps catching his toes on the bricks. He folds lower each time he stumbles, as if falling in increments. Now

Ezra can see over his shoulder. A cozy view to the t-bone with Merritt Mill Road. Banks of live oaks and cottages. The cheers and whir from Franklin Street spill down every intersection, a din that they wade through like a stream. Then another block basking on the brick walk.

He rhythms off Wispy's shoulder all the way to the turn. Wispy lists off the brickwalk and into the road, stumbling into a surge. Ezra actually relaxes as he checks it. Opening his strides is less work than half-stepping; feels more like stretching than accelerating. They're coming up on the third aid station, Wispy hugging the curb. Isn't going to give Ezra an inch on the inside. Running right in the gutter. This time he doesn't lift the watch, just looks over his right shoulder. Ezra steps out of his eye-line as his head turns, swinging left to pass him and the aid station. Doesn't reach for a cup. He runs Wispy's footstrikes out of ear-shot, surging against the full strain of his pace, and he knows by the way his intestines cinch that it'll be one streak of hurt from here to the end, which could be a finish line just as well as a ditch. No more now, no more next time, just this. He's alone with it. The lead's his.

Off of Merritt Mill into Carrboro, startling the few patient spectators who'd already dragged their chairs out here. Clucks of dropped cowbells, sighs of wind-stolen posters. Wafts of patchouli and stares from the dreadlocked hula hoopers out front of the co-op. A couple cat-calls.

"Try yoga!"

"Slow down, man."

Out of the main drag onto Greensboro. Greenhouses and cottages. The aid station at the four-mile mark. Not looking at the digital clock. Not needing to shout at the volunteers screaming his pace at him because he's back in the basement of Maslow's hierarchy, bottom of the steps with the door locked and soundproofed. And the lights off. Him and the furniture of his thoughts. The dark shapes of questions he starts to bump into.

Where are Casper and Ma? He hasn't seen them since the

swim. No way he'd missed them. Regardless of how deep he's burying himself, Ma's shouting has always bored through. And wan Casper, fevering sweat through his t-shirt. How bad can withdrawal get? Ezra's slowing, watching the kid shrink again—but this time it's the stakes, not a score, that has shifted. Hard to hold 6:30-mile pace wondering if something's happened to Casper; hard and stupid. Crabgrass pinches the sidewalk out from under him. He spills into the bike lane. The bike lane trickles into a narrow shoulder. The asphalt cracks and sheds the shoulder's white paint. Ezra thinks of the kid's splitting stitches. The asphalt dips and rises through the hills like a suture. Dairyland Road closes his strides out from under him.

He grinds down to a trot, grating his heels on the pavement. His brain's left his helmet for the E.R., Casper back there again. Ma dealing with the insurance. Shiela stuck in the sprinter van, overheating—when had the clouds parted? He hadn't noticed the sun under the oak-shade on West Cameron. But out here on this stovetop asphalt, its greasy heat spills molten down his shoulders. The hurt's grown too big for his body to hold, leaking into the day. Ezra stops, all those matches burnt out of him.

Turning around feels like inverting. All his blood sloshes into his skull. He could run back into Carrboro, hitch a ride to the campground, but what then? Would Ma have left him a note? His own phone's uncharged in the Sprinter van. Hers is in the woods by the bromine plant. Is it really so impossible that he'd ridden past her without noticing? They'd just spent eight months apart. Maybe his radar for her cheers has gone dormant. He's being histrionic. He'd watched Casper caught in a spring trap and crawl it off. Kid could handle a fever.

Ezra spins, trying to shake off the image of Casper in another hospital; instead seeing him smearing though the sumac, dragging his trapped leg. Crawling away from Ezra as much as the coyotes. *Leave,* the kid begged. Ezra hadn't listened then. But here's his next time. Let the dog lie. Hold the hurt like that branch and keep swinging.

Hard swallow. He turns back around. Bears down on the uncovered road, striding under and over shadeless rollers like a needle through skin. Closing the wound. Every step a new stitch. Back to the system of smoothings: ear muscles, jaw, shoulders, neck—wearing through that old rosary. Casper's voice joins the beads, warping with each turn. *Leave. Lead. Me.* Fading. *Brother.*

And then Ezra's a hermit in his hurt. Nothing but his own footstrikes stranding down in front of him. The jar and ache of each contact. Falling farther as he pounds down the back of a roller and spots his reflection smirking up from the base of it.

A white pickup's stopped on the road. Ezra watches himself grow in the rearview. He spills toward it, running at the edge of control. He's gathered up so much speed by the bottom of the descent that he sprints right past the truck. He coasts along the flat until his legs are back under him, urging himself to keep going. *Don't look back. Don't give him that.*

But even in the din of his effort he hears the low buzz of the unrolling window. Works like a finger pinching his ear. Ezra hooks around and sees himself again, trapped and twinned in the lenses of those Oakleys. The sun and the road and his body are all swallowed by them. Benji leans out of the driver's side window and hums.

Ezra pains toward the truck. His feet feel like dead animals, nerveless weight he's dragging. All those nights he'd stood outside while Benji hummed the cabin air shut around Casper, swearing he was hearing smothered sentences. Now he's inside that hum. But it's a language lower than words Benji's speaking. The stale rake of strained breath across the tongue. A damp so warm it scarcely feels wet. Sunlight splitting the lip of a water trough. And it seems less that Benji's producing these perceptions than summoning them; they're coming out of Ezra. They pool against the insides of his eardrums and well up his throat, stinging the backs of his sinuses. Ezra folds over and retches and sees urine melting down his legs in tallow streams. Thick and dark as candle wax. His vomit sparks off the growing puddle of it, flame-orange with Gatorade. Stomach acid an exact match for the fake-sweet fruit flavor.

More senses coming. Turning meat on his tastebuds. Bleating behind his eardrums. A searing tightness rolling up the backs of his heels. Someone else's pains leaving him. They strain toward Benji's hum like something they've been estranged from—the rent ends of a torn muscle conjoining.

Even as Ezra aches, he swears that he's healing.

Then it's done. Benji swallows his hum and Ezra slumps into the side of the truck, emptied. But not by exhaustion; it's his own soreness that's left him. He can't stand without it. He's been running on stiffness, held up by tightening joints and tendons.

"I had to leave," Benji whispers. "I well up if I stay. I'm poison."

"Casper's leg's gone." Ezra says, cutting his confession out from under him.

Benji suckles the ends of his mullet.

"You did that. He stepped in your spring trap. He was looking for you." Ezra's speaking plainly—his breath settled already.

"There's a larger system," Benji whispers. "A spell on you. You swallowed the hair. I tried not to, but reflexes. I'm sick."

Dairyland Road compressed and contained in those sunglasses—every mile Ezra has yet to cover appearing behind his reflection like one more thing he's dragging, the deadweight of the task ahead. Add to that the too-muchness of all that Benji'd done. And there's no way to break it up like a triathlon, to isolate it like the insurance and the Percocet and the coyotes, because Benij seeps into and spoils it all, defying compartmentalization. The guy's LiquaTox. He mars the ground Ezra stands on. Ezra finds him without looking for him, even looking away. Even not looking back. And he isn't being histrionic. He leans through the driver's side window and Benji doesn't move. Their cheeks brush.

"What happens to Shadefoot?" Ezra's voice feels vacuumed up, the question coming to him at the exact rate that he asks it.

"If you don't look back, I mean." All the times these past weeks he's pictured the person as the victim, but maybe he's had it backwards.

A spit-wet strand of Benji's hair sticks to Ezra's ear. He knocks on Ezra's chest just like a year ago, pressing Ezra back to his cot in the medical tent. Ezra stumbles back from the truck, as feeble now as he'd been then. He coils down on the asphalt. A frayed heap.

"I wanted to see what you'd do," Benji says.

Then he gasses it. The tires lisp off the road, spluttering for traction. For a scrum of a second Ezra actually thinks the asphalt's melted to tar—the pavement's that hot, boiling the backs of his hamstrings—but then the truck throttles off, flicking exhaust back like a scab. Ezra crinkles his knees to his chest and shrinks. His face in the sideview looks just like Casper's. He watches that mirror: the kid pulling away from him again. But won't chase it.

His pulse ebbs. He doesn't sob. Doesn't stand. Just sits on the road feeling emptily fresh, grasping for the first time the full scale of his fitness: he's overcome six hours of effort with a minute of rest. Benji'd really fine-tuned him. But he'll never see the extent of his handiwork; Ezra will let that motor rust just to spite him. He turns from the truck with the feeling of a long-fraying rope snapped. No. Benji was never towing him; he'd always been behind Ezra, pushing him, making tracks to put his feet in. With Casper ahead for so long he'd hardly noticed the wet breath behind him; he's been looking the wrong way at momentum. Ezra settles on the burning pavement. The truck's rumble slumps to a hum, then to silence, and not once does he look back. He just sits. He just stays.

By the time I run up on Stud, I'm nigh on to bonking. He stands in the barren mulch bed of a brick ranch on Crest Street, face pressed to the front window. A black iron Treble Clef is mounted on the span of wall between him and the front door in the place of a house number. Rain-soaked cardboard boxes implode on the crabgrassed drive.

I'd left him for one second. Gone to grab the First Aid and come back to find him and the dog gone. I've run down every block between here and Franklin, hollering for him and *here-girl*ing for Shiela. Down Merritt Mill Road where the t-bone of West Cameron Avenue splits. Past the parking lot of the Hunt Electric company, fenced in with barbed wire like a gravelly prison yard until the sidewalk disappeared, into this rolling neighborhood at the next right. Here Stud quivers. No Shiela.

I jog up to him, trying to gather enough breath to catch. The mulch bed's scattered with tiny plastic shards that look like the broken-off hands of Lego people. Stud leans into the windowpane, shaking from those toes to his shaved head. Looks as if a current's been conducted up his one quivering leg—shivering like he's standing on a wire live with electricity, but broken-off Lego arms are the only things exposed in the sand of that mulch bed.

I'm too deep into oxygen debt for all the things I ought to shout at him. Too afraid of whatever he'll say to any question I might ask. Where he's been. Where Shiela went. What it is that's brought him to this spot where he's shivering.

"Thought I lost you," I heave.

Still seems like I might've. Stud leans harder into the window, blind and deaf to me. The pane conducts his shaking.

I step up beside him and cup my hands to the glass. Stacks of plastic armchairs pillar the room. The shadows between them look rusted, dappled like sunlight's coming through holes in the roof—but the house is two stories. I crouch, trying to see ceiling. Not much better off than the runoff-washed plot where I'd raised you. I've passed nights in plenty of nastier squats; maybe that's what Stud was plotting on, casing this spot to sleep. Expecting that I'd left him—or planning to leave me.

Abandoned places have always seemed sacred to me. Auntie Opal said that holy places were set apart from people, but I've always felt more reverent toward places people chose to leave— the traces souls leave in places that haven't always been empty. A feeling has an echo. You can leave a sensation in a place, walk off from some overgrown emotion—call it the creeps or a Dybbuk or a Tulpa. In Dasharath, then Peru, then Tetlin, then West Memphis, I'd tried and failed to let go of my own.

When I'd left Doro the night of that earthquake, I knew what I was doing: turning my back on him was the best way to guarantee that he'd always stay with me. When your father had begged me to forget him, he'd been trying to spare me from the same.

Stud hops back from the window. "Ain't home," he says, "and ain't sweet."

"What's that?"

"It's too big for just us and Ez." The kid's voice thins like a split end."Shiela offed."

"We'll find her. Bet she's back at the van."

"Naw. Benji fed the hair to her."

I remember the hair of your father's I'd choked on. Had he pictured that as some kind of charm? Bet he'd passed it on to Benji. Benji had said that Unc was contagious. He'd caught you and Stud up in those superstitions. That's enough to guess what Stud means; better not to confirm it with his clarification.

"He offed to boss someone else," Casper says. "I don't hoot.

Let him spill about sheep."

I step back and catch his sparse reflection in the window-pane. His clavicles jut up from his shoulders like loose bolts. The sinews of his little muscles unwind when he breathes. He seems at risk of disassembling, like a soapbox derby car that rattles apart the moment it coasts past the finish line—as if the only thing holding him together was moving. I pray that's how you're racing. Until you've given all there is, you won't quit. Better to get all that agony over with once than approach it over and over and back away; one and done beats a decade of .98's.

"I don't grudge him," says Stud.

Neither do I. We can't choose who we believe. Benji was only doing whatever he'd learned from Unc, thinking that was the right thing for you. That's better than I can claim.

"He had to take my truck," Stud's saying. "I was like to up-off in it. Now I'm stuck with you."

"Want to go in?"

"Naw. We'll miss Ez."

Only when Stud says it do I check: my Chrono's stopwatch has the race time at 7:30. You ought to be twenty miles into the marathon, by my ballpark—meaning we missed you in T2. I must've run just as far searching for Stud. Three and some hours of running gone by in the time-suck of exercise. Hard not to tally up the energy I must've burned (a conservative 8:30 mile pace would put me around 700 hourly calories). That's not your father's Dybbuk or Doro's Ibbur compelling me—it's just my own instinct. Hope you've been as caught up in every next step as I was. I'd been living up to my third rule from Peru: I'd as good as forgotten you.

The wincing pomp of that Ironman finishing area. The Jum-botron scrolls with the bike times of athletes coasting into T2, their splits flanked by division rankings. I keep my eye out for any-one in my age group. "Sweet Child O' Mine" warbles through a pair of basketball-goal-high speakers. Compression-socked spectators line the path around the lake, holding their hand-made posters overhead for shade. Stud and I slide along the barricade lining the final straightaway. My cowbell clanks pace with our cadence.

Stud stills it with his stump. "We ain't arming salvation."

He's had both hands locked around mine ever since we climbed out of the Sprinter van, squeezing like he's trying to keep himself from shaking.

"You okay?"

"Just holding off on the droops." He sticks out his tongue, the tastebuds blanched with pale powder. "I'm running right through these."

Percocet. We'll have to do something about that, and the insurance coverage, and Shiela, and Doro, and who your father is—but only after you break the tape. Problem-solving takes periodization.

Gracie Winters's bike split flashes across the Jumbotron, two hours behind mine from last year—and she's in first place for women 45-49. That Kona slot would've been mine.

Stud follows my eyes. "I was fixing to dip under eight."

He rests his head on his forearms on top of the barricade. It bounces; his whole skeleton's still shaking. Harder to watch than the seconds piling up on the race clock. To take the course record, you'll have to be in the final mile. I try and conjure the fatigue you must be feeling, but you can't recall the depth and breadth of that sensation. Only way to get your body back to that place is racing.

Ever since hanging up on Doro last night, I've kept my phone airplaned. I swipe the setting off. Five texts from Doro stack up on my screen.

Can't offer those rooms (admissions influx).

We did what we could to give you the map. Best luck with your journey.

Hope all's peace and victory for you and Ezra.

Don't be a stranger if you don't want to.

Joy, D.

There's a part of me that's come to depend on the idea that Doro was losing sleep over me. Selfless love begets selfless love, but never reciprocally: picturing him tossing and turning freed me up to adore you just as restlessly.

Before I took off, he'd asked whether I was going home because you needed me, or because I wanted you to need me. I think he was projecting; I could've asked him the same thing about bringing me to Tetlin. I wasn't his unrequited love—I was his self-imposed responsibility. I came, I stayed, I absolved him. Mitzvah done.

"Knew he wouldn't beat me." Stud nods to the race clock, moaning the words like a bad feeling confirmed.

8:20. The record will stay with the kid. Somewhere on Graham Street or Columbia you might be using that as an excuse to let up and bring it in easy. I quiver my cowbell to conjure you.

The soundtrack crackles silent. "Our first-place athlete is approaching the finish line," the emcee announces.

What does *approaching* mean—a mile out? Within sight?

Applause erupts around the lake. The emcee drops the mic in a solo cup and fumbles with his laptop. The opening notes of "We Are The Champions" prickle through the speaker.

Wispy slows into the finishing chute. His legs flop in front of him. He veers between the barricades to high-five the spectators, and by the way that he's taking his time—the fact that he's not glancing back—I know you're not close to him.

He grabs a U.S. flag from a fan, as if this is some kind of world championship instead of (sorry, but frankly) a second-tier, non-destination, late-season race.

Wispy twists his visor forward to display the Headsweats logo and puts on the sunglasses stashed in the back pocket of his tri-suit—a walking manikin for sponsors. He hoists the finishing tape and pauses for the race photographer.

"He got him," Stud says.

"Ez got himself. His brain got his legs."

It's always been in your head. Your discipline and preparation are monk-like, but you always find a reason to back off during the event. All the races I've watched you cross the line with more left to give. The tank isn't really empty unless you're crawling at the end. In that sense, your DNF last year was the first race that you hadn't quit.

Wispy loiters around the finishing area, offering race officials unsolicited handshakes. Six minutes later, a guy in a too-tight tri suit strains across the line. Wispy crumples him into a hug. The next pro crosses in 8:39, pulling off a pair of ice-stuffed latex gloves like Torbjørn Sindballe.

"Next time," I say. You've missed your P.R. and the podium. A scrunching in my gut gives me a hunch that's the best case. I shove up to Wispy, swat away his huge handshake. "Seen Ezra?"

"Did he start?"

Right. You'd been Stud to Wispy. Of course he hadn't recognized you running by: when you're that deep in the hurt and drained of your glycogen, it's hard to see or think clearly. Your competitors are just race numbers, just bodies.

Stud hops up to us. "She means Casper Swayze."

"I passed him out on Dairyland. He was sitting like he pulled something." Wispy lifts his sunglasses at the kid. "Wait."

I yank Stud away.

He pounds his head with his free hand. "Shucks me. Wasn't thinking."

"You're cool. Wispy's got the spoils distracting him."

"Not that. Ez."

"We know where he is."

"But he ate the hair." Stud's face shrinks around his wince. Seems like he's lost more than the leg; he needs you like an organ he's missing. "What if he went after Benji?"

Left off of Cameron onto Jones Ferry Road. Back up the 54 to skirt the clog of downtown Carrboro. The brick houses and churches give to overgrown pastures, spit us onto Old Fayetteville. Athletes plod down the middle of the left lane, blindly tired—hoping a car will rush by and put them out of their misery, maybe. Stud's eyes shut like he's praying. I put my hand on his stump. He presses up, but not like he's fighting my grip. More how a dog leans into the hand rubbing it.

"He'll be there," I swear. "Just him."

A quarter-mile up Dairyland, there you are: legs spread, leaning back on your palms, staring shut-eyed at the sky. Smiling. I stumble out of the van and lose my legs. It all falls out in one breath: Shiela gone, Stud lost and found, Benji.

"Saw him," Stud says.

Your eyes open like they're spring-loaded. "Me, too."

You brace your hands on my shoulders and prop yourself standing.

Stud hops toward you. You totter toward him.

"Knew you'd quit."

Stud spits a pill into his palm. He drops it in your hand and you swallow it. I'd like to tell you to stop, but I'm pretty far from permission.

"Fess something," Stud says. "I never really was fixing."

Your legs have left streaks of sweat on the road. I stretch my own out on top of them. "I've got one. A confession."

You turn my way. "Ma," you say, like you're only now seeing me. Your sunburnt lips split when you grin. All I can do not to wipe the blood off your chin. "I'm retired! I quit!"

"Listen, darling. There was more to my detours."

"Not the time."

Maybe you're right; maybe it never is. A Tulpa feeds off the concentration you give it. It might make me nauseous, but I'll go on holding Unc's in.

"I was with your father in Tetlin," I lie. "His name's Doro Rankin. Short for Teodoro."

"I don't want to hear it."

"You can meet him."

You limp over and offer me your hands. I can't take them.

"Ma, you're plenty."

You take my wrists and pry me to your feet. Now I'm the one shaking. I press my chin to your shoulder. It jackhammers your trapezius. "He wasn't worth knowing," I say.

Some secrets are stomach-aching.

Stud tugs the van's sliding door open. "Giddy up, Robo-Cop."

You plant your left shoe on the footrail and pause. "Just two steps."

He snorts. "Okay, Ms. Petey."

I've never felt farther outside of a joke. You must've shared things with Stud that I won't ever get to hold. This is why I ought've left home—to give you room to grow beyond my knowing. I should be happy, but I feel like you're missing something. The more that you share yourself with others, the less of you there is left to know.

I'm only so held up by my body's dimensions because I want it to be the perfect size for my soul. In West Memphis and Peru and Tetlin and Nepal and Auntie Opal's flood-insured grave, I'd let parts of myself spill over. I'm spread too far and wide for anyone to really know—not Doro, not Unc, not even you. The best I can do is love what's left of you with my remainder.

We're all different degrees of alone.

Benji

You don't find the dog. She just prances out of the pines as you gas up at the Shell station. Red resistance band dripping from her jaws like prey's blood. She tips her head like the kid; like Ezra shrinking in your rearview, brimming with untapped fitness. His sweat still slicks your hand. You just put out your palm and the dog wags over to you.

Rub the short fur of her snout with your fingers. Close your eyes and feel it into the kid's buzzcut. One replacing the other. Replacing is following, the second thing chasing the absence preceding it. Filling the deficit. That's racing. Gravity. Pursuit is the universal instruction. Stroke until your fingers numb to its texture, like a word hummed until it loses significance. Sorry. Cursed. Reflexes.

Cures and poisons can both be diluted.

It's a straight shot east to Kure on I-40. The Interstate nocked between feathery pines. The pines pinched by rainclouds as whorled and padded as fingers, each hill the road climbs rising like the asphalt is a bowstring drawn back by the sky. The piedmont drops out from under the truck with all the undone tension of an archer's release.

The dog slathers her head in your lap as you drive. Check her over. A pointer through her haunches, but the equilateral ears are all coyote. Used to get mutts like her in the pastures, coydogs that Unc's sheppies had sired. Unc had grudged them more than the full-blooded coyotes. The sheep would catch the scent of a coyote and start bleating, but those mutts must've smelled like the sheppies. The sheep let the coydogs trot right up.

Woody Hewett Bridge cranes over the inlet. Swerve off the

road and drive under it, parking in the wet-cool gulp of its shade. A mudbank barbed with ditched fishing rods. Stranded cars. A *no swimming* sign. Hazardous waste; unsafe concentrations. Sit with one hand collaring the coydog, feeling inside your own throat. The traffic's hum above. All those vehicles passing over you, anvils and anvils of suspended weight. Set cruise control to twelve—race-pace—and kick the door open. Spill out with the coydog flowing after you. The inlet gargles the truck. Shadefoot leaves no tracks, nothing to show his coming or going. Mud sucks Ezra's flip-flops off your feet. Trot up the bank on stiff heels, coydog chasing. Up Woody Hewett Bridge. The shock of its sudden grade. All the times you'd pushed Tootsies over it. Jog up it with the slope straining your Achilles tendons, the dog whimpering after you. Slapped by the drafts of passing traffic. Glass and hubcap bolts prickling your bare feet. Then they numb. Don't look down at them. At the summit the coydog perks her snout, bounds ahead—she's smelled home.

Trickle down to Kure. Boarded storefronts. Parking lots ponded with flood. A breeze shatters the water's surface and the sun catches the chop as bright-sharp as shattered glass. Drip into a ditch deep enough to swallow your strides. Hide your feet. Melt down Bromine Avenue. The mud pit of that cul-de-sac. The home you'd made but stopped just short of taking. Don't go in.

Squelch around to the boat. The planters gutted behind the camper. Your herbs trampled, but some leaves plucked. Grin to picture Ezra testing them. Crouch by the broken Piston. The flywheel's shrapnel brindles the ground. Press your cheek to it. Your tongue. Suck in taste of the kid, the blood and sweat you'd wrung out of him. The coydog pouncing through the mud. The mutt. Shiela.

Unc taught you that coaching took empathy: you had to nerve-know the solipsis of exhaustion, that lonely moment when your own body becomes the world of hurt holding you. He showed you when he put you in the cocoon. Showed you that cruelty took empathy, too: you learn to hurt someone by following what hurts you. So what's cruel and what's coaching? There must be a moment where pushing them becomes paining them. But there's always been a cataract around your intentions. Whether you want to hold their hurt, or hurt them so they'll need you to hold it; whether you left to keep from ruining them, or to see if they'd follow you. Another lesson of Unc's: the worst punishment is taking. You can add chores or a belt to a back, but what hurts more is an absence. No hair. No lunch. No one looking at you.

Take the kid's leg and Ezra's win out from under them because a wound—like a sutured tendon, or a beach split by a storm surge—grows closer when it shuts. A stiffness. Scar tissue. A cure follows sickness. Healing follows wounds. The larger system you hope you've been serving: to make them need you, then leave them, leaving them no one but each other to lean into.

Got to drift off before they get back. Climb the boat ladder and the coydog leaps up, whining behind you. Scoop her up. Cradle her in one arm and she laps your wet cheek. Your hair sticks to her gums. Lean away and it stretches like strands of spittle; you're already in her, it's you that she's drooling. Pull the door and the cabin sighs your breath. The carpet clumped like sore tastebuds. Step onto your tongue. Let yourself swallow you.

The last coydog you'd fed your hair to. Your last spring on Unc's farm, the morning after the first shearing. You'd woken to him weeping into *The Tibetan Book of the Dead*. He tore out the pages and ate them. You jogged off from the clapboard with your wrists and cheek muscles aching. Gums cut from the jerky. Head smarting from Unc's lesson.

Then the mutt. Limping down the south pasture's slump when you ran up on it. Took it for a loose sheppie until it hackled. It sped up and you followed, socketing your heels in its pawprints. It sprinted and stopped and you trailed it. You caught up and it sprinted again. It didn't turn around. All the way to the nadir of the pasture like this. The fence tilted west and rose up a long slope. The coydog panted louder. Stopped. When your toes scraped its heels, it snarled around and clenched stiff, its pupils vacuuming you into its throbbing exhaustion. Spittle as solid as salt on its lips. You tugged a strand of hair from your mullet and held out your palm; all you did was offer. The coydog licked the sweat, swallowing your hair with it.

When you got back Unc was knocking on the water trough. You let him out and he ran his hand over your drenched mullet and licked it. "This shit," he said. "Still at it."

You weren't sure which shit he'd sniffed: your running or the hair spell. But knew not to ask. He stepped out of the trough. His exit left a slice in the water that kept widening, and a pulse was pushing you. Unc didn't force you into the trough any more than a cut forces blood through it. All he did was leave room.

The bloated warmth of that water. Unc's hum. The lid's hinges cackled rust when Unc shut it, and then it all stopped— the dampness, the humming, even the dark. Glass shards pricked your hands when you groped the trough's edges. You pressed your palms in. Pressed your heels to the bottom and headbutted the lid, desperate for friction to confirm you were solid. But the sting and impact dissolved, then the water, then your skin: it just drifted off, or your insides ebbed back. That trough could've been your ribcage. Coyotes' squeals blended with your breathing. Then the lid opened. The light dragged in the rest of your senses: your stinging hands, the reek of your urine. Unc kicked the lid over with his heel.

How long had you been in there? An Everywhen. A lifetime how the grub flies, the maggot sprouting wings: the exact length of a transformation. You'd felt what it was like for your body to become the only thing holding you, and that was better than any charm or system. That was what dogs and RoboCops and kids all ran up against—the same internal, anatomical limits. As soon as you took the lead it was just you, lonely in extremis. A state your stiff heels had kept you from ever swimming or running to. But Unc had shown you. And you'd gone to the pool deck that day without his binder to hide behind and sent the swimmers racing toward it, knowing for yourself what it was like. Sprints off of the diving block. No stopwatch. No thought of tapering. The swimmer who drove you home had to set cruise control, her calf cramping when she pumped the gas.

You came home to Unc's hum. He crouched in the yard with the coydog across his lap. The mutt you'd fed your hair to. Unc had hummed it to sleep. He was doing something fragile to it. Looked to be plucking something out of its eyelashes. The sun caught the gleam of the needle between his pinched fingers.

He was stitching its eyes shut. He wept up at you. "I have to find a better way to be."

That was when you'd known you'd had to leave. Not because of the pain Unc inflicted so much as the pain he took in doing it: the fragile work of stretching out the mutt's eyelid, the precision of threading that needle. Could've just cut the coydog's tendons. Run it over. Thrown it in his cocoon. But Unc savored the effort. He pulled the coyote's eyelids out, making a tiny pleat of them. The thread sank and surfaced and it was you he was pushing it through. He didn't turn around. You breathing over him as he stitched.

Thirteen years you'd chafed with the myth that he'd made of you, Shadefoot stories swelling blisters of his cheeks. The coyotes you'd come after or from. His speeches scaring other swimmers away from you. He knew just how to hurt you, and that was a kind of comfort: proof of how closely he knew you. You'd never asked why he'd kept you. The etiquettes of magic and love: don't name the larger system. But here you were, seeing Unc's. The only larger system he served was his need to be needed, to hurt a thing until it came to him for a cure; to make for himself, in this way, a space. And you were the same. You'd known his grudge against coydogs when you'd fed your hair to this one, what he'd do when it followed you to him. You were as bad as Unc.

You stood there until he swallowed his hum. He dumped the coydog off his lap as he stood up and it pawed at its eyelids, shrimping its tail under it. You went inside and gagged a backpack with clothes and cash and Unc's binder, but no stop-watches. Came back out to find Unc shut-eyed in the trough. Drumming the lid. All he said was, "Shut this for me."

You'd caught a ride up to the Zone meet that weekend and coached every swimmer to gold. Folks kept thinking you were someone's kid brother. You just smacked the front of Unc's binder. Head coach. At thirteen.

You still throw up before haircuts. You still can't wear wool. You still don't look back, afraid of the footsteps you won't see. You can't quit a reflex, but you can cut a tendon. You'd backed the van over the trough, but you still feel its tug. Without Unc there's no one but yourself to trace it to. The urge was always yours; all Unc had ever done was shown you to you.

Spit yourself from the cabin. Disgusted. The coydog curls atop Casper's sleeping bag. If you can just let her stay here, make a home with Ezra and the kid. Pluck out a strand of your hair and just hold it. The coydog tips her head. The coyotes' squeals thicken the air. Their voices gill in and out of your ribcage. They filter through the trees the same way. They'll lead you back to the old Dow plant when you turn around, through those trenches that maze like the scars on Unc's chest: something to hold you. Ditches that once funneled toxins. You'll spread through them, diluting into air and liquid—present, but too faint to poison them. You won't have feet to put through the door, but maybe you can still find a way to waft in.

Drop the hair. It swirls in the air suspended by light and breeze; the coydog lifts her snout, waiting. If you can just snatch the hair—let them have her, turn around—

The coyotes' squeals welling now. The hair floats on that sound. Let it hang. Leave it up to the dog to follow you.

Ezra

They're all kinds of people. Gradients, maybe. Ma, Benji, the RoboCops clunking into WheelsDeals mistaking Ezra for Casper. Is he burnt out, injured, off-season? What had happened at Chapel Hill? Wanting to know why he'd quit at the front, abandoning a record day. He stays silent until their stares break, snapping to his old race photos that Ma still keeps hanging. They'll nod at that sad afterthought. *Shame about him. The leg. How's he doing, anyway?*

Ezra guts his race gear from the camper. Goodwills his running shoes, sells the bikes, trashbags the trophies. He strips his posters from WheelsDeals and Ma puts up clearance signs: ALL MUST GO. FIRE SALE. HELP US LIQUIDATE. Without Ezra's face as decor, the questions about him stop coming. And the RoboCops. The staff dwindles to him and her.

All fall it's one thing, then another. The town council declaring coyotes a nuisance; the motels booking like it's summer. Ma puts a sign up at the corner of Bromine Avenue with an arrow that says WASCALS THISAWAY. She charges twenty dollars for parking. Fifty for permission to hunt on her property. The woods behind the camper blurt with ordinance. Every shot gives Ezra that race-starting squirt of adrenaline. Wrong that a starting pistol scares him more than a rifle.

Folks shoot out of truck windows. When they hit their mark, they don't stop. The varms are poor eating and worse lawn ornaments. They decompose under long-rusted FOR SALE signs. When Hurricane Bertha floods Bromine Avenue, Ezra takes Ma's kayak to WheelsDeals, paddling around flood-bulged corpses. The storm surge only ebbs to the dunes.

Ezra sits out the rest of that racing season. He surfs some, sangrias more, and tacos himself ten pounds above racing weight, basking in the aimlessness he'd been so afraid of. Hasn't run a step since plopping down on Dairyland Road. He'd sat in that spot all afternoon with his timing chip on, trying to scrape a strand of Benji's hair off his tongue. Wispy'd run by and said something like, "Sucks," without so much as glancing down at him—solipsistic in his own exhaustion. Other pros panted past, then the amateur Kona aspirants, squinting up the road for calves labeled with their age. The sloggers gave way to the plodders, then the sandwich-eating, walking back of the pack. Iron Granny clapped Ezra on the shoulder like she thought he might get up and finish, but Ezra stayed put like a Shiva, sat even as Ma braked up in the Sprinter van. *Waiting at the finish, she'd gasped. Missed you passing. Thought we'd lost you.* Ezra'd chanted *Casper.* Only when the kid hopped out of the van had he moved. The kid tipped his head as Ezra stiffened up to him. Heavy sweat, but one piece; as much as he'd woken up with that morning.

All he'd said to Ezra was *saw him.* All Ezra'd said was, *me too.* That was it. They haven't used his name since.

But Ezra's still chewing him. Swearing hair's stuck to his tongue. His mouth stays dry from spitting. Waking snorting the turned meat and sunscreen backwashed through the window with the breeze. Goosebumps spark up on his unshaven shins. The hairs rise like matches. A low heat climbing them, a simmering question. What's he missing? He'll walk out back telling himself the real answer: it's not the exhaustion of Benji's training he's longing for, but exhausting himself with the kid.

Casper's got his bark on. Face shucked with sunburn. Ribs like tree's rings, rooted to the boat's pilot chair. He still sleeps in the cabin, though Ma keeps the pull-out couch bedded. He still chews the necks of the pill bottles Ezra brings from CVS. Not a hoot from insurance. When the kid goes to the doctor, he's Ezra. Ezra's taught him his signature, given him his ID. Casper winces before the doctor even prods his stump. Still yapping, he says, and the doctor refills his prescription.

When Ezra's driver's license is up for renewal he takes the kid to the DMV. The photographer looks at the ID, at the kid, and back at the ID. "You grew." All he says. It's that easy.

In the new photo, Casper's head is tipped sideways. The kid's face next to his own name. Ezra reroutes the prescriptions to Walgreens. The kid hops in to refill them. Never crutches. Never the prosthetic. Just the left knee snouting out of his shorts, the residual limb like snot dangling. Ezra dangles over the moped, understanding how the kid might've dripped between file cabinets, vaporizing in sinuses of the State.

He's the ghost these days. The only thing in his wallet is Casper Swayze's license. That, and a picture of the three of them: the kid and him tangling around Ma, her finishing picture from Ironman Savannah. They'd shouted themselves hoarse as she ran through the strangle of cowbells and balloons to a P.R. There they are tipping their heads to her shoulders, prop-hugging her—mirror-imaged. When Ezra mounts the boat, the kid's head tips the way.

"You again," Casper says, spanking the pill bottle.

One pill gets Ezra's head gaveling to his shoulder. He droops the folding chair beside Casper, sinking into the same fugue he'd been chasing with training. Only now he doesn't have to exhaust himself for that fix. The plush warmth of the Percocet smears his days just the same. The high feels like sunrise inside his skin. A basking warmth lulling him to a doze, radiating. They sunburn side-by-side on the boat deck; ear-to-ear, sometimes. But they're still not as close as those months they'd urged through Benji's workouts. The kid leading, Ezra chasing, but together: conjoined in those Oakleys. They'd shared the adrenal bond of prey. When he dozes on the boat deck, it's those workouts he blurs back to.

He only stirs when the kid kicks him. Ezra's sore as he unslumps. The breeze smothered by noon sun. The kid standing in front of him, flicking Ezra's forehead with his stump. That scar's grin. The kid's.

"Let's stroll," he'll say.

He hops across the cul-de-sac on one leg and Ezra trots next to him, a half-step behind. If Ezra ever noses ahead the kid will just surge. But only for so long. Soon—after a block on a good day, but usually yards—he topples.

"You good?" Ezra asks, knowing not to offer his hand.

The kid'll swat the air anyway. "Not taking nuts."

Aside from Ezra's home, insurance, and identity. But this—his own movement—is the last thing Casper has, the pride of the hurt he can hold in his own body. So Ezra leaves him how he wants. He walks home and lets the kid come back crawling.

Casper

We're all each other. I'm Ezra. Ezra's Stud. I used to be
Mama, but now we got Ma, and she calls both-us Love. Got a
picture of the three-us in my Ziplock. Just that and my license.
Our license. My face under Ezra's name. And a hunk of his hair
from the night Ma buzzed him before the race. Felt wrong dropping that in the Ziplock with them other I.D.'s. All them homes
that wasn't, that deck of un-futures like leftover Tarot cards you
don't draw. Well, I drew the right one. The good one. So I tossed
the whole rest in the lake that very race eve and ain't missed them
since. Not Ida, not Adam, not the Dr. Reverend. Not even Shiela. Always known not to look behind me. That's how longing
catches up.

Sure, I still itch some for training. Mornings when the breeze
hits my spine like a tailwind, my stump gets to twitching. Ditto
Ezra. I instinct awake before he comes, waiting out on the boat
deck with the whole day dawn-blank in front of us. Ain't a thing
I'm fixing to do. I pass him a pill and we droop.

But my damn stump always wags me standing. I tip up and
let it wag over Ezra as he jerks with sleep. Way his legs suck I
know his dreams are tugging him to run. How he stiffs up I
know he's sore for more Percs. He'd rather pop another than
come with me. But when I hop out to the road he always ups
and afters me. When I tip he always asks if I'm good. And when
I shoo him he always leaves. Lets me show how much hurt I can
hold. He walks ahead, but he's seen-known I'll always be leading.

I used to think I could live in instructions, thinking the only
way to stay home was to move. Then I stepped into that trap
and saw the home I'd run into. I crawl back and back, ever time

taking my sweet time doing it. Because I'm cozy in the knowing that Ezra and Ma will be draining their legs upside the Sprinter van, waiting. Yet seeing them still jumps my throat frog. Got to swallow a sob ever time they wave me over. I smack my good leg flush with theirs, then my stump. And the honest is I'd give the good one to stay this way: the three-us here togethering. Fixed.

ALL-CONSUMING
A CONVERSATION WITH
MASON BOYLES & JAMES MCNULTY

Hey, Mason. We at *Driftwood* are so excited for this novel publication. I've been pitching it as one of my favorite debut novels, and I've been telling the truth. You've crafted something really special here, and I can't wait for more readers to experience Ezra, Casper, Benji, and Ma.

I'm equally stoked and grateful to you and everyone at *Driftwood* who helped this project come together. I always believed in this book's meat and bone, but it took your editing eye to chiropract it into the more fully realized version that readers will be encountering.

Like many of the best writers, your language teaches the reader to read it. While tricky at first, the language—particularly Casper's voice—becomes easier and easier to follow as the reader becomes more immersed. Talk to me a little bit about the style of writing here.

Everyone develops phrases unique to their personal shorthand, and Casper's and Benji's voices are more dramatic extensions of this tendency. In both cases, the extremity of their dialects is a product of them spending so much time living in their respective own heads. Casper hadn't spent much time speaking to anybody before he started getting comfortable around Ezra. Casper's language is also a product of the rhythm of exertion—you can't spend that long pounding pavement without the physical effort punctuating your thinking. His cadence has staccato moments (foot strikes) as well as spans of breathlessness (a V.02 max effort or the interval between swim breaths).

When we published your story "Myopic" in our magazine, which was my first experience with your writing, I noted in our interview there the "alienating specificity," or perhaps *extreme realistic accuracy*, inherent in your style of writing. That story was about Thai politics and drug smuggling, which is

perhaps more unknown to readers than state-side triathlon communities, but the topic is still relevant here. How do you come up with the voice for your characters—in particular the specificity and nuances of their original dialects and vocal tics?

I give them the space in my brain and on the page to hear them talking. *Bark On* began as a short story in a limited third POV. On a visit to Tallahassee for FSU's PhD program, I woke up at 2 a.m. in the University Motel with Casper literally talking his way out of a dream. The rhythm of his language was a matter of escalation—the further that I got into his voice, the more right it seemed to push his tics to the extreme. I wrote the first two chapters from his perspective that morning. His voice gave it the narrative drive and dimension to grow into a novel. Benji's clipped interior cadence emerged from his exertion of control— even his thoughts must be disciplined down to fragments, controlled to keep them from spiraling to the things that he tries not to confront (the aspects of his past and personality that drive his arc of action through the novel).

Is dreaming crucial to your writing life? How often does a character or story emerge from a dream?

Casper's emergence was an exception. Dreams aren't often directly generative for me, but their odd logic and abrupt pivots can be more broadly stimulatory—sometimes a good reminder to prioritize surprise in revision. I'm disciplined about sleeping and tend to have vivid dreams.

When we spoke after *Driftwood* offered publication, you mentioned you had personal experience with triathlons, and that real experience helped lend specificity and accuracy to the book.

I threw everything into triathlon from the ages of ten to eighteen. Mostly this meant twice or thrice daily training, tracking every gram of food that I ate, and maintaining a full-body shave. This novel wouldn't exist without all those years of 5 a.m.

workouts and race mornings spent in my dad's FJ Cruiser blasting Skillet and Queen. I burnt myself out before I got to college, but I continued to swim, bike, and run recreationally. It wasn't incidental that these recreational sessions began to lengthen when I was drafting this novel. By the summer of 2021 I was regularly biking 100 miles or running twenty or more miles at a time, and I figured it would be a shame not to hop into a race. I wound up competing in the USAT Ultra-Distance National Championships and decided that was enough competition for me, for now.

Can you speak more to how this background influenced the novel—specifically Ezra and Casper's interior landscapes?

Ezra's and Casper's respective pasts both draw from a combination of my own memories and old anecdotes from competitors that stuck with me. Like Ezra and Ma, my dad and I would spill toothpaste on our sweatshirts while we talked and brushed on race mornings. We used to ride the courses the day or week before the race with a MapQuest printout for navigation, and we'd Sharpie our race categories as high and small on our calves as possible. Other tidbits are inspired by triathlon lore, like Casper stealing room service from hotel hallways and leaving his bike outside of gas station bathrooms in the half-hope that some thief might relieve him from finishing training. Ezra's surge around Wispy at the aid station is a tactic borrowed from the 1989 Iron War between Mark Allen and Dave Scott.

Much of the book takes place in North Carolina, specifically Kure. Why did you decide on North Carolina for the setting?

Fiction is always personal, but not always biographical: by definition, it is invented, but all inventions are products of the author's imagination, which often grows out of direct experience. In the case of Kure, I began with a real place and tailored the town in a way that would heighten and contain the novel's tension (the mounting erosion, the seasonal ghost-towning, the abandoned bromine plant overtaken by coyotes). I grew up in the south Wilmington area, which I partially fictionalized as the town of Kure. I did much of my own early swimming, riding, and running on roads and beaches and patches of ocean like the ones that Ezra and Casper frequent, so this setting is inextricable from hard training in my personal imagination. I picked Chapel Hill for the Ironman because the energy of a sports-centric university town felt like a compelling collision with the franticness of a single-day endurance event. The image of athletes pace-lining past tailgaters on fraternity row was too rich to pass up. By the time I enrolled at UNC Chapel Hill I wasn't training for triathlons so much as moving for movement's sake. I spent a good bit of time riding and running on the country highways between the university, Durham, and Hillsborough. So also, and maybe more so, I've always wanted to portray those rolling roads.

Is it important to experience the setting of your works before—or during—your drafting process? Talk to me a little bit about inserting the specificity of location into the narrative.

Kure is a fictionalized version of my childhood home. I imagined a somewhat precise replica of that landscape as the staging ground for their training. The marina full of charter boats, the ruined pier, and abandoned bromine plant are all borrowed from reality. There really is a neighborhood called Sloop Pointe, though I can't speak to their pool policy. Ezra and Casper's longest rides into Wilmington mostly take place on some of the city's most popular training routes. The same is true for the Chapel Hill Ironman. I spent quite a bit of time in Peru, and Ma's recollection of Doro takes place in neighborhoods where I lived. This book is full of places where I've lived, sweated, and walked, but I was living in California and Florida when I wrote *Bark On*. I think that time and distance allow a setting to germinate. Memory is a great fictionalizer, and significant details grow accordingly.

There's a supernatural component to the book, a focus on tul-

pas and Shadefoot and other bits of mysticism, that may sur-prise folks who came to this book thinking it was only about athletes. Could you talk about the inclusion of these elements in the book?

Casper's compulsion to move is its own kind of superstition. Ezra's training and racing is steeped in just as much ritual as sci-ence, a kind of orthodoxy of routine. The same is certainly true of Ma's orthorexic tendencies. That these characters would in-dulge magical thinking isn't a big leap. There was always a suspi-cion of the supernatural in these characters' minds, both around the coyotes and Benji. Sometimes Benji pushes back against the image that Unc raised him in; other times he uses it as justifi-cation for his need to manipulate. As I researched more about thought-forms, I began to think of Shadefoot as the antithesis of a tulpa—that is, a being generated from all that the human mind doesn't or won't think. When Benji first encounters Casper, the kid is running from lots of things. In a less self-aware way, Ezra dodges conversations about his father with Ma. It would be trite to say that Benji feeds off of those cognitive negative space, but perhaps he is drawn to avoidance. I don't know if Benji is Shade-foot or Ezra is his Tulpa, but I know that there are points in this book where certain characters believe those things. Ma's sto-ryline really foregrounded the mystical aspects of the novel. Her pursuit of the truth about Unc and Benji allowed me to portray a (somewhat more) objective perspective on the effect of Benji's persona, on his concrete origin in West Memphis and the nature of his criminal activity.

It was a real pleasure working with you on a revision for this novel. For readers who are curious about the revisions process, what changed as you drafted and redrafted the novel? What could've been, and what *almost wasn't*?

When I first sent this book to you, there were no sections from Ma's POV. You urged me to include her perspective. Doing so exposed more about every character and allowed the book to

confront the compulsion and control from a more psychologically orthodox perspective. Some of the most satisfying sections
to write were her nomadic memories. It allowed the book to
travel to Nepal and Peru, and spiraled into a mystery plot that
lent further richness to the connection between Ezra and Benji.

**Ma's perspective opened the book in a way I don't think ei-
ther of us were expecting, but I think her chapters were a great
addition, and the book is stronger with them. Could you talk
to me about your usual process of rewriting? How much time
does your initial drafting, then redrafting take?**

I've gone from drafting at excruciating pace to moving rel-
atively quickly on my first pass, trusting instinct and escalation.
You get to a point deep in a novel where you're so attuned to
the world and the characters that more decisions are happening in your back-brain. Revisions of Ma's sections were slower,
and more thorough, with lots of back-and-forth deliberating between you and me. A lot of this had to do with giving her the
independent arc that her POV deserved while simultaneously
linking it to the stakes of the triangle between Ezra, Casper, and
Benji. These goings-over were where her relationship to Unc
solidified and her dynamic with Doro shifted. Her starting point
at Doro's eating disorder clinic was the latest addition. The ED
was an issue for her from the earliest version of her character, but
it took the final hour of changes for me to recognize that Ezra's
"latching" to Benji would provide her with the freedom to apply
herself more inwardly and seek treatment.

**Do you often plan out your writing? To what degree do you
outline?**

I outline as I go. Bigger-picture notes get recorded in a
separate document, while short-term planning—notes on that
chapter—goes directly below the draft. This might look like a
reminder for a line of dialogue or something that needs to shift
by the end of a scene. I'll bullet these to be deleted upon com-

pletion. I often see a general shape, but try to stay in the moment—to watch the characters go, letting their decisions dictate the direction of the next scene. A much smarter friend told me that he knows he's writing in the right direction when he deviates from his original vision for things. I value pivots that are hidden in plain sight and surprises that don't strain credulity.

I've been asking a lot of questions specifically about Bark On, of course, but I'd also like to ask some questions about you, Mason. When did you decide to be a writer?

I blame this desolate outcome on my parents' nightly habit of reading me to sleep. We did the *Great Illustrated Classics*, *Harry Potter*, *The Hobbit*, and Terry Pratchett, and regular immersion in those worlds is one of my earliest and fondest memories. I wrote my first story at six, sitting in the front room of my father's law office. My mom had clacked out her master's thesis on that typewriter; I came up with something about Johnny Appleseed. From then on, I would put together short stories and comic books with relative regularity. Lawrence Naumoff's introductory fiction workshop was what got me writing daily during my sophomore year at Chapel Hill. I've been a hopeless case ever since.

What attracted you to fiction?

The magic trick of its immersiveness. The novels I love most pull me fully into their worlds, so that reading becomes like vivid dreaming. It seems like the most central aspect to this is the creation of a consciousness that is compellingly inhabited. The writing must be vivid and specific enough to make the reader experience life right alongside the story's central characters.

What do you need to be able to write?

Adequate sleep, relative silence, and fingers.

Does anything ever gum up the works?

I'm most productive when I stick to my routine. A couple of hours of daily work has always suited me better than creative binging. I find that my focus and motivation are highest in the mornings, so writing is typically the first thing that I do in a day. This also ensures that I get something done before life has the opportunity to get in the way. I'll drink some strong coffee, take a cold shower, pop in a piece of nicotine gum, and listen to 40 hz binaural beats while I'm working to optimize mental acuity.

Conversely, what inspires you? What typically triggers premise or character ideas?

I'm interested in people who have to go against their nature to get what they want. Many story ideas emerge from a single image or scene; for *Bark On,* everything started with the idea of a runner being paced by a truck with a rope connecting them to its hitch. The logical progression is to imagine what kind of person would be driving that truck, and how they'd get the runner to listen to them. Setting is an endless reservoir for inspiration. I'm fascinated with transforming environments: the trash culvers and landsliding slopes around Lima, the eroding barrier island that inspired Kure. The unstable nature of those environments forces urgency.

Do you have a favorite and least favorite part of the process?

I like sinking so deeply into a story that it can surprise me. Both drafting and revising contain different kinds of revelations. The initial writing is obviously exploratory, but you also see new opportunities in early scenes after you've gotten the whole story in front of you. Maybe that's the most satisfying part of writing for me: the discovery.

How conscious are you of the reader when you write?

Delillo's got a line about not writing to an audience. For better or worse, this has informed my approach to drafting. Revision is partially the process of bending the author's vision into something clear enough for others to decipher. This is especially true in a book like *Bark On,* where a deep dive into a triathlon subculture, an elaborate plot, and extreme dialect run the risk of alienating a reader. Your sharp editing eye was critical in preserving the book's spirit while making an inroads toward accessibility.

What writers have you learned the most from?

Michelle Latiolais taught me that enough force can trump anything. Daniel Wallace told me a story could be like a cabinet and gently pushed me into broader reading. Mark Winegardner showed me how structure can be liberating. Kevin Barry's novels gave me faith in true insouciance, plus permission to get hyperbolic with gestures and language.

What're some of your favorite books, and what have you been reading lately?

Kevin Barry's *Night Boat to Tangier* is practically sacred to me. It's a tightly written crime novel with a dialogue-driven frame narrative confined to a ferry terminal and flashback sections that rove from Ireland to Spain to Morocco, distilling entire decades into vivid narrative summary. McCarthy's *All The Pretty Horses* is recklessly laconic, and appeals to that tragic ideal of a protagonist striving for a life that's beyond his actual reach. John Grady Cole was born a century too late, and perhaps too far north. I've been reading a lot of Elmore Leonard lately to study tight plotting and fast pace.

Are you interested in any other mediums? What do they add to your writing?

I can draw you a stick figure and play two chords on bass guitar. Most of my creative thinking outside of writing happens physically; climbing and surfing are both like problem-solving with your body. You've got to imagine how to make your limbs fit where they weren't meant to, if that makes sense. Both practices require a meditative level of mindfulness. They get me out of my head long enough to be restorative, providing a daily reset from writing. I've had the good fortune of leading undergraduate fiction workshops at FSU, and I think that good teaching is also an act of creativity.

Are you interested in writing other forms, say poetry or nonfiction?

I've spent most of the past two years novel-minded, but I'm an occasional writer and frequent reader of short stories. The requirements of short fiction are distinct enough to qualify it as a different form in my thinking. Teaching undergraduate workshop has given me the opportunity to revisit some of my favorite expressions of this genre—Denis Johnson's Fuckhead stories, Barry Hannah's early stuff, and Lee K. Abbott's stories consistently amaze me for their vocal range and potential as empathy machines.

To what extent is there a didactic component in your writing?

To the exact extent that my characters value it. I never write toward a moral, but I try to inhabit people who are moved by their own convictions. The writing that has moved me most portrays rather than explains; that is, it puts me in the mind and life of someone who's being irreversibly changed. Maybe they learn something, but they don't have to—and very often it's a thing too big for them to articulate.

What are you working towards in your writing? Many writers keep to similar themes in their work. If you have one, what, would you say, are yours?

I can't seem to let up off of folks consumed by superstition and compulsion. Fortunately, that provides an almost distressing degree of freedom. Right now, a lot of people without noses are showing up. I'm writing something incorrigibly dystopian, with witches and noise-canceling androids and a floating theocratic city.

Have you ever worked in this genre before? What are you modeling this project after? Of course, there are plenty of great literary sci-fi novels, both classic and contemporary. *Dune* **comes to mind; Marlon James' new trilogy, too.**

I've written some speculative short stories, but this novel is my first effort at anything substantively dystopian or steampunk-y. *Dune* is high-up in my personal canon. Every sci-fi novel that comes after it branches from it, in the same way that the Victorian novel cannot exist without *Madame Bovary*. I love Philip K. Dick for the elaborate scope of his novels, the hardboiled aspect that he brings to the genre, and the sheer syntactic energy. I also spent a lot of time in the *Warhammer 40k* universe in my teens.

What other projects are you working on?

Does a doctorate count as a project? I'm chewing through a 140-novel reading list in preparation for my qualifying exams, which will cover the history of the novel, crime fiction, and some rudimentary theory. I'm also seeking a publisher for a multigenerational mystery series about a collapsing coal mining dynasty.

What are your ambitions as a writer? What would you like to work on in the future?

I want to get that mystery series into print, then round out the aforementioned dystopian trilogy. I've got a novella about a cult of squatters in Peru that deserves returning to, and enough solid stories to get out a collection soon. Beyond that, more and more and more novels. The form is all-consuming. I don't see myself quitting the habit anytime soon.

This book is for Scott, Stephanie, and Jackson Boyles, who loved me enough to put up with my writing before there was any good reason to believe in it. Thank you to Mary Boyles for teaching me to apply the word "unison", and to Bob Boyles for compelling me to read broadly and deeply. Thank you to David and Violet O'Leary for the faith that you placed in my person and pursuits. I am grateful to Michelle Latiolais, Mark Winegardner, and Daniel Wallace for nurturing my reading and writing, and to all of the brilliant writers I crossed paths with at UNC, UC Irvine, and FSU. I am fortunate to have had James McNulty's editorial eye to help hone this writing. Thanks to him and everyone at *Driftwood Press* for their unerring dedication in giving this work a platform.

Photograph courtesy of Jamarcus Crump

Mason Boyles grew up in southeastern North Carolina, where he trained and raced as a nationally competitive junior triathlete until the tired caught up to him. He studied writing at UNC Chapel Hill, earned his MFA from UC Irvine, and is pursuing his PhD at FSU. His fiction has appeared in publications such as *The Masters Review, The Adirondack Review,* and *Driftwood Press Magazine*, and received nominations for the Pushcart Prize. *Bark On* is his first published novel. He watches informative videos about hammerhead sharks, and enjoys mountain biking, surfing, and Jiu-Jitsu.

CPSIA information can be obtained
at www.ICGtesting.com
Printed in the USA
JSHW020444230323
39305JS00002B/10